SPIKED

Randall Donley

RANDALL DENLEY

SPIKED

A Kris Redner Mystery

OTTAWA
PRESS AND
PUBLISHING

OTTAWA PRESS AND PUBLISHING

Ottawa Press and Publishing

Copyright © Randall Denley 2019

ISBN (softcover) 978-1-988437-18-7
ISBN (epub) 978-1-988437-19-4
ISBN (mobi) 978-1-988437-20-0

Cover, design, composition: Magdalene Carson / New Leaf Publication Design

Printed in Canada

Library and Archives Canada Cataloguing in Publication

Title: Spiked / Randall Denley.
Names: Denley, Randall, 1951- author.
Identifiers: Canadiana (print) 20190080477 | Canadiana (ebook) 20190080485 | ISBN 9781988437187
   (softcover) | ISBN 9781988437200 (Kindle) | ISBN 9781988437194 (EPUB)
Classification: LCC PS8607.E637 S65 2019 | DDC C813/.6—dc23

ACKNOWLEDGEMENTS

I would like to thank veteran Ottawa criminal lawyer Michael Edelson and his former law partner, Vince Clifford, for their invaluable assistance with the details of the trial that is central to this story. Michel Juneau-Katsuya, the former CSIS officer and co-author of the book *Nest of Spies*, was one of the first to detail the insidious effects of Chinese espionage. His work was the genesis of *Spiked*. Thanks also to Magdalene Carson for her usual outstanding job on the cover and Deborah Richmond for her detailed edit. Special thanks to my reading group for their support and ideas about how to make this book better. Linda, Cathy, Cynthia, Ray, Susan, Roger, Vern and Emma, you did a great job.

ONE

When I woke up, a dream about Sonny Sandhu was still fresh in my mind. I was interviewing Sandhu, which made sense because I am a newspaper columnist, but why were we drinking white wine at a restaurant beside a lake? The lake looked familiar, but I wasn't sure if it was from real life or other dreams. It was a hot day with a stiff breeze and power boats were bobbing and clunking against the docks of the marina that the restaurant overlooked. Gulls circled overhead.

I didn't remember a word Sandhu had said in the dream, just how he looked. He was a striking man with intense eyes, skin the colour of dark chocolate, perfect white teeth and hair that had been carefully mussed, then gelled in place. Sunglasses were perched atop his head and he wore a white linen shirt. When he reached out and ran his hand slowly along my forearm, I awoke.

I lay in bed, not quite wanting to let the dream go, although I found it disturbing. I was flushed, as if the moment had been real. I had never met Sandhu and now I was having a borderline sex dream about the guy, and this on the day when I was going to be covering his trial.

When I was on a major story, I often felt like the characters invaded me, took over my mind, and lived with me 24 hours a day. Although today was my first official day back at work, I had spent weeks researching Sandhu, reading every word written about him and looking at every picture and video clip. They told a story that was perplexing and totally out of sync with the mess Sandhu found himself in now.

Sonny Sandhu was about as far as one could get from the kind of deadbeats and losers I usually covered in the Ottawa courts. The member of Parliament from Brampton had been a media star and the new face of the Conservative Party. Sandhu was charming, quick with a quote, an entrepreneur and an immigrant. He was a pollster's dream and it didn't hurt that he looked like a Bollywood star. Conservatives saw him as a saviour who could rescue Canada from the charming Liberal prime minister.

And then Sandhu had stepped in shit of a very surprising kind. In Ottawa, when a politician got into trouble, it was usually because he had expensed too many limos or made a drunken pass at a colleague. Sandhu was accused of taking money from a couple of business guys to grease the path to federal grants for a windmill project that sounded like a scam from the get go. The mystery was why he did it, if he did. Sandhu was a rich guy and all of this was over twenty-five grand.

The trial on influence peddling charges promised to offer the kind of entertainment that had been attractive to the public since the days of the guillotine. My job was to make sure that it did. I was guaranteed front-page play in the *Ottawa Citizen* every day, but I hadn't written a word in months and now I would be churning out stories on deadline. Somehow I was supposed to once again become Kris Redner, star crime columnist. Colin, the editor, had told me it would be like riding a bicycle. I wasn't so sure.

I shook my head to clear away the remnants of the Sandhu dream. At least it was a welcome change from my normal dream, the one where men with guns were chasing me through gloomy woods. I always awoke from that one just before they caught me. Too bad it hadn't worked that way in reality.

I rolled out of bed and automatically reached to the night table for my cigarettes, then remembered that I was trying to quit. I had gone six days without a smoke. Not exactly a record, but a small step. For the last eight months, small steps had been the only ones I had taken. After 20 years of covering crime in Toronto and Ottawa, I had thought I was tough, maybe even invincible. Then I went back to my hometown in the Adirondacks in a quest to get some justice for my sister Kathy, who had been murdered when I was still a child. I found that my little town had been taken over by men of overwhelming ambition, men who considered me an irritant to be eliminated. Let's just say that things didn't end well, and I had spent the last eight months figuring out if I could still be me.

I stepped into yesterday's shorts and pulled on a T-shirt, then padded to the living room, the hardwood floors of the apartment cold on my feet. As usual, Ranger was whimpering at the door. The dog had a bladder the size of a thimble. If I didn't jump to it the minute he started to complain, he just let loose on the rug. He was an ugly little runt, too. Ranger combined the rat face and bat ears of a chihuahua with the elongated black and brown body and stubby legs of a dachshund.

Like the apartment, Ranger was a loaner. Both belonged to my friend Caroline Malloy, a CBC reporter who needed someone to house sit in a hurry when she had been posted to Syria. Never having owned a pet, I didn't quite understand that it was like having a child, another choice I had never made. When Caroline had offered me the opportunity to move in, it had seemed like a quick and graceful way to stop living with Colin. Ranger had been the only hitch. At the time, exchanging a troublesome lover for a troublesome pet had seemed a good swap, but I hadn't taken into account Colin's superiority in the area of continence.

The only upside was that, during my worst times, Ranger's regularity had gotten me out of the apartment on days when I knew I wouldn't even have gotten out of bed. I would take him for a walk today before heading to court, but I had to pull myself together first. I walked across the apartment and opened the door to the tiny balcony. Ranger followed, sticking his nose out and sniffing the fresh May air. I figured that if he was really desperate, he could go on the balcony and I could discreetly wash it off later.

I headed to the bathroom to see if I could start to make myself look human, and to assess the damage from last night's bottle of cabernet sauvignon. I knew I should stop drinking, but I had already given up smoking and, apparently, sex. I had to keep at least one vice.

I relieved myself, then stood and looked in the mirror. I saw a 40-year-old woman with garish, dyed-red hair cut short enough so that I could run my fingers through it and be ready to go. It was my new look. I certainly wasn't cute or pretty, but I had sometimes been called handsome. I had never been sure if that was a good thing. I pulled at the little lines that were starting to form around my eyes, hoping that the skin would bounce back. Maybe after a shower.

For now, I would settle for a strong black coffee. I filled the stainless steel kettle and put it on the gas stove top, then measured out the coffee from a bag I had bought at the Bridgehead shop on the ground floor of my building. The coffee was called Bytown Boom and the bag assured me that it was both organic and fairly traded. I didn't care as long as it had caffeine.

Once the water was boiled, I poured it through an old Melitta drip, then tossed the used coffee filter in the sink, where several of its predecessors were composting. I would have preferred the ease of a Keurig, but Caroline was one of those types who thought that the world could be saved one unbleached coffee filter at a time. She bought into the whole save-the-whales world view. It must be comforting to have so much certainty about right and wrong.

I'd met Caroline while covering courts. Not even the parade of crooks, losers and amoral shits that we saw every day had dimmed her sunny view of life. But then, Caroline was 25. Let's see how a couple of decades covering human behaviour would affect her.

Despite the powerful smell of the fresh coffee, I realized that the kitchen had developed a bit of a pong, perhaps due to the rotting bananas on the counter and the two-day old pizza box on the glass kitchen table. Pong. That was one of Colin's words. Sleep with a Brit and you eventually start talking like one. But that was all past tense now. I was pretty sure of that. Colin had a different idea.

I took my coffee out onto the balcony and settled into the single plastic chair. The air was still cool for May and I thought about going back into the apartment to get the fluffy white robe I had boosted from the Royal York, back when Colin and I used to meet there for sex. I would appreciate the warmth, but not the memories. I really should throw the thing out.

I noticed that Ranger had left a wet spot on the corner of the balcony. That was one problem solved. I sipped my coffee and looked at the scene six storeys below me. I found that the world always looked best when I was looking down on it from above, observing it but not really part of it. I saw a placid early spring Ottawa morning, sunny, full of hope, the trees just starting to green. People sat on the Bridgehead patio, sipping coffee and looking at their devices.. A girl in a grey sweatshirt leaned in to kiss her boyfriend, who had long, red hair and was wearing a baseball cap. On Elgin Street, office workers headed purposefully past the bars, restaurants and small shops that lined the street, going downtown to do something they thought was important. Good for them. In an hour or two I would try to pretend I was one of them.

I had just brought the coffee to my mouth when I saw a woman's face right in front of me, followed by flailing arms. For a split-second, she stared straight at me, a look of horror in her eyes, her mouth open in a silent scream. Long black hair streamed behind her. I jumped to my feet, the coffee cup falling from my hand and shattering on the balcony.

By the time I understood that she had fallen from the apartment building's roof just above me, she was gone. Peering over the railing, I could see she had landed on the wrought-iron fence that surrounded the building, grotesquely impaled like meat on a fork. The woman hung limp, a rag doll with an arm and a leg on either side of the fence.

I stood paralyzed with shock. In the little world below, it was as if time stood still while people registered what had happened. Then it turned to chaos. People were crying and screaming. Some were climbing the fence in their rush to get away. Across the street, bystanders were pointing and shooting pictures with their phones.

No one was coming to her assistance. What if she was still alive? I had to do something. I stepped into a pair of sandals, stuck my phone in my back pocket and ran for the apartment door. I glanced at the building's ancient elevator. There was a guy waiting there, looking impatiently at his watch. I quickly noted a square jaw, the usual two days' growth of beard, jeans, ball cap, tan jacket, sunglasses. There was no time to wait. I raced down the claustrophobic stairwell, a gloomy passage with cracked plaster walls painted institutional green, a shabby red carpet and stale cooking smells.

When I reached the front door, an obviously terrified young blond woman in a grey and maroon University of Ottawa sweatshirt was pounding on it, as if she didn't know how to open it. The young lover from the coffee shop, I realized. The woman was crying and screaming like she'd lost her mind. Some of the coffee shop patrons clustered on the sidewalk, looking on in horror. A heavy man in a grey suit used his briefcase like a scythe, clearing his path to safety. Jesus, did he think there was going to be an avalanche of falling bodies?

On the patio, heavy metal tables and chairs lay overturned, one glass table top shattered, the shards glistening in the morning sun. As the crowd cleared, I saw the woman and registered a series of quick images: a red silk blouse, one high-heeled shoe, glossy black hair, Asian features, and several silver bracelets. Blood poured from her upper body and glistened on the metal of the fence.

As I ran toward her, I saw that the vertical spikes had pierced her torso in several places, driven deep by the impact of the fall. Her head was on my side of the fence and was twisted so that she was looking at me. She opened her mouth to speak and blood began to drip from it. Her voice was weak but her words were clear. "Help me," she said. Then her eyes closed.

What could I do? I looked around and saw several people on their cell phones. Surely one of them was calling 911. I felt for a pulse, and thought I detected a faint one. I had to do something. I wasn't sure whether getting her off that fence would help, but it looked like the woman didn't have long to live. I decided that the best thing would be to get her down and put pressure on the worst of the wounds. I couldn't do it by myself, though.

The only other person who hadn't run was an exceptionally tall guy in his early 20s with long bushy, red hair, and a Blue Jays cap. The boyfriend.

"You, get over here," I said. "We've got to get her off that fence." Looking relieved at being told what to do, he rushed to the fence. "Grab her shoulders and lift."

I took the woman's legs. She was surprisingly light. No sweater or coat, even though the morning was cool. Almost certainly a jumper. You didn't worry about staying warm when your priority was suicide.

We laid the woman on the patio stones, but that didn't seem right. "Your coat," I said. "Put it under her."

The guy hesitated for just a second. I could see him registering that his black, North Face jacket was going to be a write-off. "Just do it," I said.

We moved her onto the coat and I quickly assessed her wounds. The worst one was in her abdomen. It pulsed with blood every time her heart beat.

"Your T-shirt," I said to the kid. "Take it off and put pressure on that bleed." This time he didn't hesitate, stripping off his shirt, balling it up, and holding it over the wound. Her breathing was shallow and irregular, then I couldn't detect it at all. Blood had stopped flowing from her wounds. I started chest compressions, pushing down as quickly as I could. I had taken a CPR course at work years ago and vaguely remembered that you were supposed to do 30 compressions, then two breaths. They kept changing the procedures, but I was sure that anything would be better than nothing. The woman was dying in front of me.

Putting my lips against the other woman's was eerie, like kissing the dead. I could taste the cherry flavour of her lipstick and smell her jasmine perfume. This wasn't exactly my first dead body, but I had never had to get intimate with one.

I kept frantically pushing down on the woman's chest, not sure if I was accomplishing anything but not willing to give up.

It seemed like far longer, but I guessed that no more than two minutes had elapsed before an ambulance pulled up out front, lights flashing. A stocky, grey-haired paramedic got quickly out of the vehicle and rushed towards us, followed closely by a dark-haired woman who looked too young and small for the job.

"We've got it from here, ma'am," the male paramedic said, and quickly set to work.

I stepped back and wiped my face on my sleeve. Despite the cool day, I was sweating. I looked down and saw that I had blood on both of my hands.

The older ambulance attendant looked at his partner and shook his head. The urgency went from their movements and the woman headed back to the ambulance, no doubt to get the stretcher.

I wondered if I had ever had a shot at saving the woman, and why I had tried. You don't jump off a six-storey building if you want to live. In my own darkest moments, I had thought about not going on, but I would have gone out painlessly with an overdose of pills and a chaser of Jameson, a Leonard Cohen tune on the stereo. How could someone stand on a roof, six storeys up, teetering on the edge with life behind them and death in front of them and decide to go over? I couldn't do it.

It was time to do my job. I knew I had only minutes before the police took over, with the central station just blocks away. I picked up a bottle of water that had fallen to the ground in the chaos, poured it over my blood-stained hands, then wiped them dry with a handful of napkins from a container on one of the patio tables. It would have to do for now. I tried not to think about blood-borne diseases.

Adrenaline helped push me into the routine of work. I used my iPhone to fire off four quick shots of the woman, then a few more of the scene, showing horrified onlookers across the street. The city desk would want video, too, but there was a limit to how far I would go towards what the new corporate speak called "embracing the digital culture." What they really would have wanted was a picture of the poor girl impaled on the fence, but there was no way I was going to stand by taking pictures while she bled out. In the end, my efforts to save her had been futile, but I had to try.

I called the city desk, to tell them what I had. "Peterson," a gruff voice answered.

Bad luck. I'd hoped to get Barry Peterson's sharp young assistant, Melinda Khoury. Peterson himself was a superannuated warhorse who finally rose to city editor only because there was no one else left to do the job after continuous rounds of buyouts. Peterson, an alcoholic, couldn't afford to stop working.

"Barry, it's Kris. We've got a jumper downtown, right in front of my building."

"Humph, suicide then. Sounds routine. We don't normally cover suicides."

I was all too familiar with the Petersons of the news business. They'd seen it all before. Nothing ever excited them. If flames came out of Peterson's ass and ignited his pants, he'd remain calm and say he'd seen the same thing back in '82.

"She was actually impaled on a spiked fence and there is a crowd of screaming people in the street."

"Gruesome," Peterson said. "Now you're talking. How quick can you give me a web hit?"

"Five minutes. I've got some pictures I can upload right now. I've got the woman, and the crowd reaction."

"All right. Give me all of it. We'll post it and if people complain about the body pictures, we can pull them off the site."

I decided not to tell Peterson about my attempt to save the woman's life. Then he'd want some kind of self-glorifying first-person account.

"You want me to keep on this?" I asked.

"No, she's most likely a jumper. Unless she's someone prominent, it will be a brief by this afternoon. We need you down at the Sandhu trial.

"You say she jumped from your building. I don't suppose you can ID her, can you?"

I thought the woman did look vaguely familiar, once I imagined her standing in the building's creaky old elevator rather than impaled on the fence. I saw a young Asian woman in the morning sometimes. Well dressed, carrying a briefcase. Sometimes she was with a man, but I couldn't visualize him. I wondered if there was a husband or a boyfriend who was going to be in for a shock. I had never spoken to the woman, though. The Prince Albert was a building that housed quite a few government and media types. It was a somewhat uncomfortable mix and people respected each other's privacy.

"Don't know who she is," I said. "And I'm not going to go fishing in her pockets for ID. I'll file in five, then head over to the court."

I sat at one of the empty tables and started to type. I would knock off 200 words and file to Peterson by e-mail.

I wondered who the woman was and what had made her end her life in such a spectacular way. If she was really so desperate to die, the fence had been a blessing. There was no saying the fall would have killed her otherwise. If she'd hit one of the umbrellas on the patio, for example, she might have lived, only to experience years of pain and disability.

The story I e-mailed to Peterson was bare bones, the few paragraphs the web demanded. Not that I knew even the most basic facts, except to say that an Asian woman who appeared to be in her early 20s had fallen to her death from the roof of an apartment building on Elgin Street at 8:10 on a bright and hopeful spring morning. I decided not to call her a jumper, although she almost certainly was. My natural curiosity made me want to know more, but Peterson was probably right. By this time tomorrow, at best, the woman's death would be bumped from the news cycle by some other macabre event.

The Sandhu trial was going to top every front page and newscast today and I had to get moving before I got tangled up with police questioning. I also needed a shower, preferably scalding hot. Despite my attempt to wash them, my hands were stained with blood and I could still taste the dead woman's lipstick on my mouth.

It was a horrifying start to the day, but curiously, it made me feel glad to be alive. There was nothing like someone else's death to give perspective on your own life. Suddenly, my day didn't seem so bad.

I finished the brief story and hit send. I was done, but the images of the woman's death continued to run through my mind like a GIF. I saw the horrified face, the flowing hair, the rapid descent, the terrible impalement, and finally, I heard the last two words she uttered, "Help me."

If only I could.

TWO

As I walked up Elgin toward the courthouse, I tried to clear my mind, but it was a futile attempt. As soon as I pushed out the images of the jumper, they were replaced by my creepy dream about Sonny Sandhu.

I had been looking ahead to my first day back on the job with a combination of fear and anticipation, but I hadn't figured that it would start with me trying to save a life and ultimately witnessing a death. I reached into my purse and pulled out the cigarettes that I shouldn't be keeping there, then put them back. I couldn't start falling apart now.

The courthouse was situated beside City Hall in the heart of institutional Ottawa, just five blocks from Parliament Hill. I could see the crowd around the entrance of the court when I was still a block away. The curved drive that led to the building was swarming with reporters carrying TV cameras and microphones. Everyone wanted a shot of the accused MP as he headed into court. I knew they were all hoping Sandhu would allow himself to be scrummed, but it would be a stupid play on his part.

As I got closer to the courthouse, I felt a familiar depression. Although I spent a large part of my work day there, I hated the building. It was a modern atrocity. I didn't know much about architecture, but even I could see that. It was a windowless concrete mass, its walls punctuated by what looked like boulders erupting. I had never seen anything like it, anywhere. Maybe it was meant to give the accused a feel for what prisons looked like.

I decided to take a chance and pass up the crowd scene out front. I knew the rest of the media gaggle would be gossiping and speculating on how the Sandhu trial would unfold, but I wasn't really in the mood for it. Maybe it had something to do with the jumper, or maybe I just didn't like being part of a pack. When I covered trials now, most of the other reporters acted like pals and were eager to help each other out so that no one missed an angle. What had happened to competition? When one of your rivals missed a story, you were supposed to be happy.

I ducked into the courthouse through the revolving glass doors and went up the steps to the security area. Not too long ago, anyone could walk into the building. Now, it was like an airport for people who weren't going anywhere. Bored security staff went through the motions, eyeing the endless parade of lawyers and losers with only mild interest.

Behind them there was a three-storey atrium that was the only source of natural light in the gloomy building. The courtrooms themselves and offices for the Crowns and judges ringed the atrium. Everything in the building was either concrete or a greyish bland fabric. Despite the constant human drama that took place there, the courthouse was as soulless as a parking garage. Over the years, I had worked in some ornate nineteenth-century courthouses, the ones that sent the message that justice was a grand and important thing. Perhaps that was debatable, but it seemed preferable to a government processing centre.

The courtrooms themselves were like a series of theatres, each presenting a different type of drama. On the lower level, number two was used for trials or pleas. Number three was usually for bail hearings. First appearances were held in six, for accused who were in custody. Number four was where they tried domestic assaults. Sometimes the sexual assault cases that went there could produce a good column. Number eight was the drug court. The provincial courts were on the ground floor and the superior courts on the top floor. Sandhu's trial was in 36, one of the biggest. Whoever had designed the building was literal-minded, with the most important courts and their judges being just a little closer to God.

If you were going to cover the courts, you needed to know what was likely to produce a story, because it was all happening at the same time. My normal routine was to check the dockets at the number two desk to see what sounded promising, but court was like any other beat. You counted on your contacts to point you to the best stuff. That meant having a good relationship with the Crowns and the key defence lawyers.

I figured I was in solid shape with Ben Bernstein, Sandhu's defence lawyer. I had covered a lot of his cases and I had been pretty good to him. It wasn't much of a challenge. Bernstein could always be relied on to present clear arguments and he had a knack for framing media-friendly quotes. In past cases, Bernstein and I had engaged in a little off-the-record briefing. It helped me understand his strategy, but I wasn't naïve. It was his way to try to get his preferred interpretation of the day's events into the paper.

I wasn't so sure about the assistant Crown attorney on the case. Sharon Faulkner was a 35-year-old former Canadian national team hockey player who looked like a peppy soccer mom, but she knew how to battle in the corners. I'd seen her get her elbows up with lots of defence lawyers, and most of them came away bruised. I didn't think it was fair, but Faulkner regarded me as too friendly to the defence. Maybe it was because I had seen the Crown put up too many weak cases.

I headed straight up the concrete stairs to the third floor. I wanted to make sure I got in ahead of the reporters who were still milling around out front waiting for Sandhu. They hadn't unlocked the courtroom yet, but there was already a crowd of people waiting to enter. Trials were free entertainment and there was a regular group of retirees who came to the courts for their daily outing.

I recognized Rose Malone, a woman of about 75 dressed like she was going to a high society party, makeup perfect, hair just done and a red dress that looked like it came from Nordstrom. Not that I shopped at Nordstrom, but I had wandered through on my way to catch a bus. Rose had either been a lawyer or thought she had been. I was never sure which. I knew from previous trials that Rose would try to buttonhole me, to give her critique of the proceedings. It was one of the things I didn't like about a long trial. It felt as if you were trapped with the lawyers, cops and hangers-on. It was like a cruise, but without the booze or the scenery.

At least the old folks were harmless. I wasn't so sure about the three clean-cut young men in dark suits who sat in identical poses, like three crows on a wire. All three were hunched over their iPhones, getting their marching orders for the day. They didn't interact with the others in an unsuccessful attempt to be discreet, but they were obviously political aides from the Hill, there to give their masters a blow-by-blow on the Sandhu trial. I expected one was a Conservative focused on ass covering, one a Liberal watching for references to Sandhu's former boss, the turncoat Luc Champagne, and the third an NDPer looking for moral outrage. His job would be the easiest.

The court security officer swung open the heavy oak door of the courtroom and the crowd began to surge in. People hurried to their favourite spots, but politely. This was Ottawa. My own choice was back row, right-hand side. I liked to see everything unfold in front of me and it let me slip out the back when required.

I had just stood up when the elevator door opened and Sonny Sandhu and his entourage stepped off. Sandhu didn't look much like the man from my dream. His dark suit was expensive and perfectly pressed, but his expression was as flat as his lapels. His movements seemed awkward and forced and he had already put on what would be his courtroom expression, that of a man who had encountered an unexpected problem, but one he could overcome with diligence and attention. His wife, Gail, was at his side, half a step back and looking as if she had just rushed from somewhere. Gail Rakic had a broad Slavic face that could be described as attractive. Her unnaturally blond hair was frozen in the kind of windproof do that TV reporters favoured. She wore a black suit that was neatly tailored, sensible black shoes and a single strand of pearls. It seemed a little too close to what one would wear to a funeral. Rakic's father, Dragan, was big development money from Brampton, just west of Toronto, and a major donor to the Conservative Party. It was one of the little twists that made the Sandhu tale so interesting.

Ben Bernstein was to Sandhu's right. In his black court robes, the lanky lawyer looked like a bird of prey. Trailing the big three were two other lawyers: Paul Pitman, whose black-rimmed glasses made him look sexy in a Clark Kent kind of way, and Aimee Nicholson, a redhead whose main function would be to drag big boxes of evidence on a little cart. Everyone had to start somewhere.

The courtroom's three blocks of seats were quickly filled. Sandhu nodded to his supporters, mostly people from the Indian community and a smattering of teenage girls who should have been in class. Because Sandhu's alleged crime didn't involve anything as crude as violence, there had been no need to sit him in the glass-sided box that was used to contain lesser types of accused. He ushered his wife into the front row, right hand side, then sat beside her in the seat nearest the aisle. He reached for her hand and then held it up, making sure everyone could see him doing it. It was a touching show of support, but I wasn't convinced it was genuine. One of my goals was to get a few minutes alone with Gail Rakic, to gauge what she really thought. Sometimes the best stories took place outside the courtroom and the dynamics between this couple had to be worth writing about.

At the front of the court, Bernstein sat with the other two defence lawyers at the table to the right, flipping through the thick binder that contained the facts of the case, as disclosed by the Crown. On the left, Sharon Faulkner conferred with a middle-aged man who wore a navy suit, well-cut, a white shirt and a red tie with a small polka-dot pattern. His grey hair was gelled and a little bit spiky, his goatee beard close cropped. Probably the lead investigator, although the quality of the suit didn't say cop. Faulkner had her thick dark hair drawn back in a French twist. Combined with her black robes, it gave her the appropriate appearance of seriousness.

Everyone was waiting for The Honourable Roderick Macpherson to enter the courtroom, but they didn't have to wait long. The judge valued punctuality.

"All rise," the court clerk said and everyone got to their feet as ordered. It must be nice to have a job where everyone stands up when you enter the room and bows when they leave your presence. One of the reasons I sat in the back row was because it allowed me to avoid the bowing. I was all for rules, as long as they only applied to other people.

It was difficult for any judge not to look distinguished while wearing the black robes, red sash and the badge of office that looked like an important military decoration, but Macpherson's face could be most charitably described as well-worn. He had a bulbous nose, deep bags under his eyes and a perpetual squint. His hair was full on the sides, sparse on the top and he had a greyish-white goatee that made him look like an unkempt Colonel Sanders.

The judge nodded to the Crown and the defence, then said, "All right then, Ms Faulkner, are you ready to proceed?"

"Yes, your honour. What we have before us today is a case of political corruption at the highest levels of this country. Mr. Sonny Sandhu, a former minister of the Crown, stands accused under Section 121 of the Criminal Code with the offence commonly referred to as influence peddling.

"The Crown will show that Mr. Sandhu and his associates, Mr. Thomas Fung and Mr. Vikram Gill, engaged in a business arrangement whereby Mr. Gill and Mr. Fung were able to use Mr. Sandhu's influence with the government to receive preferential treatment for a proposed green energy project, specifically, a wind farm.

"The Crown will show that, in fact, the supposed power project was nothing more than a sham and that Mr. Sandhu and his associates were fully aware of that when Mr. Sandhu sought, and the government approved, a grant in the amount of $1.5 million. In exchange for arranging that grant, the Crown will show Mr. Sandhu received an illegal cash payment of $25,000. Both Mr. Gill and Mr. Fung will testify to that."

There was the weakness in the Crown's case. If the two crooks had bagged $1.5 million, why was Sandhu's cut so small? And why would a guy who had married into money risk throwing it all away for a relatively tiny sum?

"In addition, your honour, Inspector Terry Carmichael of the RCMP commercial crime branch will testify as to the results of a thorough examination of Mr. Sandhu's finances."

Faulkner gestured toward a stack of banker's boxes piled six feet high to the left of Crown's table. God knew what was in them, but one was supposed to get the impression that there was all sorts of dirty stuff. Faulkner was definitely playing to the media. I could see my colleagues across the back of the courtroom furiously tweeting the details of the Crown's allegations.

Ben Bernstein sat with his arm draped across the back of his chair, half turned so that he could watch Faulkner's performance. Bernstein affected a look of studied indifference, as if Faulkner were referring to a number of jaywalking citations. To his right, Paul Pitman and Aimee Nicholson tried to wear exactly the same expression as their boss. Behind them sat an even larger stack of document boxes. Sandhu himself sat erect on the hard wooden bench, staring straight ahead.

"Further, your honour," Faulkner said, "the Crown will show that Mr. Gill and Mr. Fung had no background or expertise in green energy, a fact that should have been apparent to the accused, Mr. Sandhu. We will also show that a federal grant was approved within two weeks of their meeting with Mr. Sandhu.

"Now, I don't work in the bureaucracy, your honour, but I'm pretty sure that's not business as usual in government," Faulkner said.

"Objection," Bernstein said, waving his right hand as if batting away a fly. "Opposing counsel is giving testimony."

"Sustained," the judge said. Roderick Macpherson was looking particularly flushed this morning. I wondered if he'd taken a wee dram with his morning coffee.

Despite his ruling in Bernstein's favour, it was clear that Faulkner had given the media another good line for Twitter.

'In addition, your honour, the Crown's case rests on the testimony of a number of friends and political supporters of Mr. Sandhu who have intimate knowledge of the matter before us."

Intimate knowledge, interesting turn of phrase. I wondered how intimate their knowledge would prove to be.

Faulkner carried on, detailing other witnesses and experts that the Crown would call, going into some detail about what she hoped they would say. I had covered enough trials to know that a good Crown's opening remarks always created the impression of an airtight case and an accused who was undeniably guilty.

This one was special, though. With the usual losers who paraded through court, there wasn't all that much at stake for the Crown one way or the other. Once the system decided to prosecute a high-profile person like Sonny Sandhu, they were going to get him, whether he was guilty or not. Too many people had told their bosses that this was a solid case. Whether it was or not, the Crown would go for the throat now.

Once the defence had taken a run at it, matters could seem quite different.

In a way, the case looked straightforward. Two shady guys who had engaged in a fraud said that Sandhu had misused his influence. The MP appeared to have received the cash they claimed to have given him. Their deal had gone through, apparently in record time. No doubt Faulkner would soon be telling the court that no windmills were ever built. The Crown would invite the judge to connect the dots. Kris was sure that Bernstein would argue that there might be dots, but they had nothing to do with his client, and everything to do with two crooks that had turned on a bigger target to save themselves.

I rolled those thoughts over in my mind, thinking of an angle for the column. My trademark was filling in the blanks between what was said in court and what was really happening. The other media would report on Faulkner's opening and presumably the testimony of her first witness. All that would make Sandhu sound guilty. I could put it in perspective, remind people who didn't follow the courts that there was plenty more to come, that they were only hearing one side of the story. It wasn't going to win a National Newspaper Award, but once you found an angle, a column would come together. The deadline jitters I had experienced earlier started to dissipate.

It was an approach that might help me connect with Gail Rakic, too. My instinct said that she would know a great deal that wasn't likely to come out in court. Winning her trust would be a challenge, but it would give me some insight and angles that no other journalist would have.

At the front of the courtroom, Sharon Faulkner was wrapping up.

"In conclusion, your honour, the Crown will show, beyond any reasonable doubt, that Mr. Sandhu is guilty of this offence."

"Well, that's certainly the standard," Macpherson said drily. He looked at the clock on the courtroom wall and said, "It's now 11:45. Do you think it feasible, Ms. Faulkner, to deal with your first witness before the lunch break?"

"No, your honour. I will require more time than that."

"In that case . . ."

Bernstein rose to his feet to catch the judge's attention. "Your honour, if I may?"

"Not objecting to the lunch break I hope, Mr. Bernstein?"

"Not at all, your honour. With the leave of the court, I would like to present my opening remarks before Ms. Faulkner begins to call her witnesses. As we can see from the substantial media presence here today, this is a matter that will be tried, not just within these four walls, but in the court of public opinion. I intend to present quite a different version of the events the Crown has described here this morning. I would like the public to hear that version, so that they can weigh those competing stories in a timely manner. Your honour, I don't think this court should let the Crown's inter-pretation of this matter stand unchallenged."

"Well, that's why we have a trial isn't it, Mr. Bernstein? Your request is a bit unusual, but perhaps not unreasonable. Let me pon-der it over the lunch hour. Both of you be ready to begin when we return. One p.m. sharp."

With that, the judge got to his feet and swept out of the court-room, the assembled mass of gawkers and media struggling to their own feet to show respect and relieve the cramps caused by the hard courtroom benches.

THREE

I went into the washroom and soaped my hands under hot water, again and again. Despite the shower I had taken earlier, I imagined that there were still some last vestiges of blood. In the courtroom, I had been totally engrossed in the trial and what I would write about it. As soon as the break started, my thoughts turned again to the jumper. Vivid images of her death flooded my mind. I couldn't shake the sight of the young Asian woman impaled by sharp iron spikes. What a way to die. I was glad that I had at least gotten her off the fence. It hadn't saved her life, but no one should have to be displayed like that for the public to gape at.

In the last minute of her life, the dead woman's eyes had been wide open, staring at me, and yet they revealed none of her secrets. Why had she done it? What had literally tipped her over the edge? When a woman killed herself, it was usually because of a man. Who was the other player?

There was bound to be money involved, too. Despite its somewhat decrepit condition, the Prince Albert was pricey. You didn't get in there unless you had some and the woman looked young, surely in her 20s.

I knew about dark places and how they could make suicide seem like a rational act. Fortunately, rational acts weren't my style. Every blow somehow made me tougher. That's what I told myself on the bad days.

Maybe if the jumper had the same kind of self-protective instincts, she wouldn't have ended up on the fence, or maybe she had experienced things I couldn't even imagine.

All I could do now was tell her story. I felt like I needed to explain her death, to give her a name, at least. The little bit of information I had quickly put together would likely appear under a heading like, "Woman dies in apartment plunge." Anyone deserved more than that.

When the cops contacted me later to take a witness statement, I would see what I could squeeze out of them. Maybe there would be a weekend column in it.

I rushed down to the food court and grabbed a sandwich. It was some kind of slimy ham and what purported to be cheese, although it had been described as "artisan." Like most things in the courthouse, that was more a contention than a fact. I ate half, then chucked it in a metal waste bin and headed back upstairs to the courtroom.

I liked to be a few minutes early, to check out the waiting area to see what I could discreetly overhear. The scuttlebutt from the civilians who had watched the morning's proceedings was that Sandhu was clearly guilty, but people tended to be persuaded by the last thing they had heard. If Bernstein got his chance to open, in a couple of hours these same people would probably be sure the politician was innocent. I certainly hoped the judge was going to let Bernstein have his at bat. It would make it a whole lot easier to write a column criticizing the Crown's case.

People had just settled into their seats when the court clerk said "All rise," and Macpherson reappeared. He didn't waste any time getting started. "Mr. Bernstein, I have considered your request over the break. I am certainly alive to the fact that perception is an element of what's before us here today. I wouldn't count on a lot of other concessions, but I am prepared to let you take your turn now. Please proceed."

Bernstein got to his feet and said, "Thank you, your honour. I will try to keep it brief."

Macpherson smiled at that. The word "brief," at least as it related to time, had no fixed meaning in the legal world.

With a quick glance back at the reporters in media row, Bernstein began. "Your honour, the Crown's case, as just outlined, is a curious mixture of supposition and testimony that I will show the court is unreliable, at best.

"Consider the Crown's two key witnesses, Mr. Gill and Mr. Fung. By their own admissions to the Crown," Bernstein said, tapping the binder in front of him, "these two gentlemen colluded to defraud the government, and yet they face no charges. As the defence will show, Mr. Gill and Mr. Fung have a long history of dubious business practices.

"And yet, the Crown would have the court believe that despite their consistent track records, these two witnesses will tell the truth.

"As the Crown indicated, its case will also rely heavily on an extensive forensic examination of Mr. Sandhu's financial records. Records, I might add, that my client offered voluntarily. Not to spoil the suspense your honour, but the Crown will not be able to identify even ten cents that passed improperly from Mr. Gill and Mr. Fung to my client, Mr. Sandhu."

Glancing back at the reporters again, Bernstein underlined the point. "Not a dime, your honour."

"Please address the court, not the media, Mr. Bernstein," Macpherson said, showing a touch of irritation.

Bernstein ignored the mild rebuke and carried on. "Now, the Crown is going to direct the court down a complex path, a trail of breadcrumbs if you will, that the Crown asserts links Mr. Gill and Mr. Fung's money to Mr. Sandhu.

"And how are they going to do that? Do they have a witness that saw a briefcase of money?

"No your honour, they do not. Instead what they have is a political event that these two witnesses organized for Mr. Sandhu's riding association. The Crown is going to take the commonplace business of political fundraising and portray it as something that benefited Mr. Sandhu personally, when it emphatically did not."

That was new. I could see the excitement of the reporters who were madly thumbing out Twitter updates. Over at the Crown table, Sharon Faulkner was examining her manicure, as if Bernstein's attack was barely worthy of her attention.

"The Crown will take the thin tissue that connects these three men and stretch it beyond the very limits of elasticity, your honour."

Bernstein paused to make sure the media would have time to get that one down. He knew the value of colourful phrases and he wielded them like a stiletto.

"Now, we have to ask ourselves why, then, is Mr. Sandhu here today? What are the motives that underlie this case? The Crown would have the court believe that Mr. Sandhu was willing to risk his good name and a rising political career to put $25,000 in his pocket, even though Mr. Sandhu and his family are quite wealthy.

"The Crown would have the court ignore the fact that Mr. Gill and Mr. Fung clearly have a motive to transfer their guilt to Mr. Sandhu, to save their own skins. The defence will also show that there are others who would benefit from casting the routine work of politics as some kind of shady affair, indeed have benefited from Mr. Sandhu being displaced from his position as a leading figure in the Conservative Party."

This seemed to electrify the three dark-suited political aides in the front row. Two furiously worked their iPhones while the third shot up the aisle, phone in hand. Bernstein's allegations were vague, purposely so, no doubt. The defence lawyer's move was designed to get the media speculating about political names other than those of his client.

"These individuals will be called to testify under oath as to what they know about this matter," Bernstein said.

A wise lawyer had told me long ago that simply being under oath wouldn't compel people to tell the truth. The smart ones always stuck to their story. Still, Bernstein's ploy was certain to be effective. I would almost guarantee that Luc Champagne's name had already been mentioned in social media. Sandhu had been his parliamentary assistant at Industry and later his chief rival for the party leadership.

This was going to play well with the media, but it would take more than supposition to impress Macpherson. What did Bernstein really have up his sleeve?

"Your honour," Bernstein continued, "I said I would be brief, and I don't intend to reveal my entire case here today. I did feel, in the interests of fairness and getting at the truth of this matter, that certain points had to be made at the outset. I thank you for giving me that opportunity."

Bernstein had made a number of reportable points, offered a couple of quotable phrases and hadn't gone on long enough to exceed the attention span of the average reporter. In all, a nice piece of work and so much the better because he had made my job easier. I could already see the shape of my column in my mind.

"Thank you Mr. Bernstein. I will wait with interest to see how you support these points," Macpherson said with the understated scepticism that was his trademark. I had seen him in action before.

He was a dry old coot, but he knew how to cut through the BS.

The judge glanced at the clock and said, "Is the Crown prepared to proceed with its first witness?"

Sharon Faulkner rose and said, "We are your honour. We would like to call Mr. Vikram Gill."

"And how long do you think you will be with this witness?"

"Several hours, your honour."

"Any prospect of finishing with him by the end of the day?"

"Unlikely, I'm afraid."

"Well then, we'll have to run late. Half an hour break, then we resume."

Macpherson was up and gone in a swish of black robes before the clerk could even bring the spectators to their feet.

The break was unexpected, but I decided to take advantage of it.

FOUR

Cutting Gail Rakic loose from the Sandhu herd was going to be a challenge, but I decided to play a hunch. I had noticed the nicotine stains on Gail's hands that morning and she had disappeared in a hurry when the lunch break was called, not joining her husband while he conferred with his lawyers.

I understood the compulsion of smoking addiction better than most. After sitting patiently in court, knowing that the whole room was staring at her, Gail Rakic would be twitching for a smoke.

People spilled out of the courtroom into the hallway. The reporters headed towards the temporary media room to file brief hits on the developments since the last break. Some of the onlookers broke into social groups, others headed for coffee.

Gail Rakic was powering down the stairs, heading for the exit. Definitely smoke time. I hung back and allowed her to get a bit of a lead so that it wasn't too obvious that I was following her. Getting Sandhu's wife to talk was a long shot, but it would be a great exclusive if I could pull it off.

Gail's body language in court suggested that she was seething with anger. Her clenched jaw, overly erect posture and refusal to acknowledge anyone around her except her husband told me that she was furious at the turn her life had taken. And who could blame her? In only a few months she had gone from being a wealthy Conservative power bitch to being Mrs. Felon. She'd blame someone. The most obvious choice was her husband, but Gail was there beside him, even if there was a bit of space between them. Perhaps her anger was directed at whoever had blown the whistle on him. All the Crown and police had said so far was that Sandhu's problem came to light because of an internal report.

Anyway, it didn't matter. The angry wife was a good story, whatever direction the anger was pointed.

As Gail walked out of the courthouse through the revolving doors, a stiff breeze nudged her blond hair, but only a little bit. She reflexively raised her right hand and fussed with it, making sure everything was still in place. Gail wasn't even ten feet from the door when she pulled a cigarette from her purse, then turned her back to the wind to light it. I slowed and pretended to check my phone. I wanted Gail out of sight of any of Sandhu's handlers before trying to start a conversation.

Gail headed to the paved courtyard between the courthouse and City Hall. The old part of City Hall was a former women's teachers college, a Gothic stone pile that looked like a miniature of the Parliament Buildings and was typical of the jumble of old and new that characterized downtown Ottawa. The stone buildings now had a modern office building tacked on, and people with business at City Hall were walking past Gail in both directions, seemingly unaware of her celebrity.

The temperature had risen since I had first entered the courthouse and had reached that point where it felt neither warm nor cold. The sky was a light blue, cloudless. It was a perfect day, unless you happened to be Gail Rakic or that poor woman who had jumped from my building. I was seeing a theme here, men who messed up and women who paid the price. It probably went back to Odysseus, maybe longer.

I put the jumper from my mind and focused on Gail. She was already nearing the end of her first cigarette, drawing greedily on it like the nicotine was as comforting as a mother's breast. Gail examined what was left of the cigarette, then stubbed it out with a shiny, black high-heeled shoe. I was sure they were from some famous designer and so expensive that a mere newspaper writer couldn't even afford to dream of owning them.

I wondered which Sandhu loved more, Gail or her daddy's money and connections? Gail wasn't exactly the kind of wife I had expected a heart-throb like Sonny Sandhu to have. She had the big boobs that men liked, but unfortunately, she had hips to match. She must hate them. I pegged Gail as about 35, but in a few years she would be a matron. You could see the middle-aged spread starting already. They said black was slimming, but Gail's dress had met its match. Even being rich couldn't make you thin.

I had found the secret of staying thin. All it took was a poor diet, high anxiety and lots of cigarettes. My own ass had gotten so skinny that I had a hard time keeping up some of my pants. After my ordeal last summer, I'd tried to change myself completely, become a new person. I'd cut my hair short and dyed it a ridiculous shade of red. For the first time in my life, I made a point of painting my fingernails and toenails, usually black. I'd even gotten a small tattoo inside my left wrist. It was MCMK in a looping script, the initials of my dead family. When people asked me about it, I said it was just a design. From a distance, I probably looked shiny and new. I wondered if I had fooled anyone. Certainly not myself.

Just as Gail began to rummage in her purse for a second cigarette, I approached her, pulled out my own pack of Belmonts and said, "Smoke?"

Gail looked me over cautiously, knowing that I was familiar but not yet remembering who I was, exactly. Then I could see the light of connection in her eyes. "You're that columnist from the *Citizen*, right?"

"Yes. Kris Redner."

"I'm not going to talk about the trial."

"Of course not."

Gail had accepted the cigarette, though, and I lit it for her. Then I lit one, too, telling myself I was only doing it because it would seem odd to offer Gail a cigarette without smoking one myself. I could always quit again tomorrow.

"I hope you're not here to form some sort of girl-to-girl bond," Gail said.

"Well, I can certainly empathize with you."

"Oh please. Don't pretend you care."

"All right. I won't, but your situation interests me."

Gail didn't respond, looking down at her cigarette instead. She had rings on every finger and both thumbs. They were gold, ornate, almost certainly custom designed, and worth more than I earned in a year. The jeweller must have been disappointed when Gail ran out of digits.

"I will be watching to see what you say in your column," Gail said. "You're not a big fan of Ben, are you?"

I quickly weighed which way to play it. It was true, I had been critical of Bernstein at other trials, but he was hardly at the top of my hit list. I was surprised that Gail would know what I had said. It was even more surprising that she was talking about the defence lawyer, not her husband. Maybe not being a fan of Sonny Sandhu was just a given. If Gail wasn't a big fan of Ben either, it could be a connection, but she'd called him Ben, not Bernstein.

'If I were in your husband's situation, he's the guy I'd want to defend me," I said.

'Yes, Ben is very smart, but they've stacked the deck against him."

"In what way?"

"You'll see. There are witnesses coming who are going to say what they've been told to say."

"Really? By whom?"

"I'm not going there. Just watch for it when it happens."

"All right," I said, trying to appear grateful for this vague piece of paranoia. "At some point, I'd like to do a piece on you and what you've been through, maybe after the trial is complete and before the verdict."

"My life is private."

'I'm sorry, but it isn't any more. I can tell you that everyone else will be going after the same angle. This could be a chance to shape your story, tell it the way you want to."

Wooing a source was a delicate task. You usually had to appeal to their egos, show them that there was something in it for them. I saw it as salesmanship, not lying. An exclusive interview *would* give Gail a chance to tell her side, but through my filter.

Gail tossed what was left of her cigarette on the pavement and let it smoulder. "Ben says I'm not to talk to the media at all. I shouldn't even have said what I did."

"Don't worry. I'm not going to use anything you said. We were just chatting, and I doubt you let Ben Bernstein tell you what to do."

Gail smiled. It was the first time I had seen it. It was the sort of smile that reflected a sardonic amusement at life. Maybe we did have something in common.

"You've got that right," she said. "Look, if you want a better story, check out what Luc Champagne has been up to."

Unfortunately, I knew little about the cabinet minister and what he might have been up to, not being part of the little village of politicians and media on Parliament Hill.

"What's the connection?"

"You're the reporter. You figure it out."

Was Champagne the guy behind the Sandhu charges? If so, I had just taken a big step towards getting the real story.

FIVE

I gave my column one last look while ignoring my phone. I knew it would be Peterson from the city desk, bugging me to file. In the digital world of journalism, there were no more deadlines. The desk wanted everything right now, or better yet, five minutes ago. I was sure the world could wait another few minutes to learn what I had to say about today's chapter of the Sonny Sandhu story.

There had been a bit of a twist at the end. When court returned, Sharon Faulkner said her witness, Vikram Gill, wasn't able to testify because of a sudden illness. Pre-lying jitters, I expected. Even veteran liars could find a courtroom intimidating. The judge had suggested that Faulkner bring on her next witness, but he wasn't expected to testify and wasn't even in Ottawa. Presumably this would be the other partner, Fung. The judge gave Faulkner a stern warning about wasting the valuable time of the court, ordered her to be prepared when the trial resumed Monday, then called it a day. He was flying in from Toronto for the trial, and I imagined that he wasn't totally heartbroken about getting out of town early.

I was alone in the tiny, narrow room the courts liked to call a media office. It had the size of a broom closet, but not the ambience. The dominant features were dirty white walls and a litter of documents, old newspapers and discarded pizza boxes. The other reporters were all up on the third floor, enjoying the relative space of the temporary media room provided for the Sandhu trial. I knew they would be chatting and cross-pollinating their ideas. I wasn't into that.

There was a knock at the door, but I ignored it. If it were someone who had a right to enter, he would. If not, he could piss off.

The door swung open and there was Staff Sgt. Mike Reilly. Not the first guy I expected to see. Before Reilly could speak, I held up a finger, then pointed at one of the two empty chairs and said, "Sit. Five minutes."

I could tell by the look on Reilly's face that he didn't appreciate being talked to like it was dog obedience school, but he did sit. One learned to be patient working homicide. Reilly straightened the crease in the pants of his navy suit, then glanced around the little room, his square-jawed Irish face starting to show that he was in his 50s. His brushy moustache and curly black hair seemed to have just a bit more grey every time I saw him. It was his eyes that looked most tired, showing the strain of a long career and a lack of promotion.

I was sure his breakup with my colleague Suzy Morin hadn't done much for his disposition either. The two of them had been together for years. How a police reporter and a homicide investigator worked out their boundaries was beyond me, but somehow they had made it last, until it didn't.

I turned my attention back to my laptop, giving the column one last look. There was a vast gap between Bernstein's version of reality and the Crown's, but I was taking a skeptical view and shading to Bernstein, for now. Maybe the Crown's witnesses would be better than I imagined, but their self-interest was glaring. Of course, that didn't mean they were not telling something close to the truth. Just because they were crooks didn't mean that Sandhu wasn't.

As much as I enjoyed keeping Reilly waiting, I was curious to know why he was here. No doubt it was about the jumper, but I would have expected a constable to handle the interview. What had caught Reilly's attention?

I e-mailed the column to Peterson and said, "So Reilly, what brings you here?"

He scratched the side of his face, then spoke in the distinctive baritone voice that lent authority to everything he had to say. "Maybe you don't remember, but earlier in the day there was a woman who fell to her death from the roof of your building. Landed on the fence in front in kind of a nasty way."

I looked away, the experience of the morning still raw in my mind. I had been surprised by how much emotion the young woman's death had triggered, but I wasn't going to share that with Reilly. Veteran cops and veteran crime writers both used distance and black humour to keep themselves from being swallowed up by the horrors they saw on the job. I liked Reilly and he was a good source, but I didn't expect him to play Dr. Phil.

"She sure did," I said. "Hell of a way to start a day. I'm just surprised that you're spending time on a suicide. Murder business slow?"

"Steady. I'm sure a woman of your experience knows that we treat every suspicious death as a homicide until we have reason to believe otherwise."

"And do you?"

Reilly shrugged. "There are a few complications."

"Such as?"

"Such as things I'm not going to tell you about right now. What I do need to know is what you saw, exactly."

"You should read the *Citizen* online, Mike. Everything I saw was in the story I filed."

Reilly paused, creating an awkward silence to see if I would fill it with information. It was a trick I used too, and I wasn't going to play. Finally, Reilly said, "That must have been rough, seeing a young woman like that die right in front of you. It was a pretty gruesome scene."

Ah, I thought, the empathy tactic. As much as it would be good to unburden with someone, it wasn't going to happen.

"OK, humour me here," he said. "Tell me about it again. You were on the patio, what, looking at your laptop, checking out the surrounding scenery?"

"No, I had just sat down on my balcony to have a cup of coffee when I looked up and saw the body heading straight down. Then I leaned over the railing, and saw that she was on the fence."

"And what did you think then?"

"I thought I was looking at a jumper falling from the roof. That's obvious, right?"

"So the woman comes flying through the air and ends up skewered on the fence. Bad luck or good luck, depending on how you look at it. What did you do next?"

"I raced down to the patio."

"To help?"

"No, because it was a story."

"But you did try to help?"

I hoped that he wouldn't have uncovered that fact, but I should have known better. There were lots of witnesses. "I did. She cried out 'help me.' I couldn't just stand there."

I expected Reilly to give me shit for interfering with a possible crime scene, but he nodded sympathetically and said, "And you had some pictures, too."

"I did. And they're all online."

That wasn't true, but I had no reason to turn all my cards up for Reilly, especially if he wasn't willing to offer information in exchange.

"Really?"

"What did you think, I was going to hang around and do a photo shoot? I took a few quick images, then I headed down to court."

"Right. Anything that shows the street scene, who was around, that kind of thing? Could be useful to our investigation."

"Maybe so, but I can't help you."

"I could get a warrant."

"Go for it. Come on, Reilly. You know it's not my job to collect evidence for you. The stuff online is going to have to do. Besides, you must have lots of other witnesses. The place was packed with people. Dozens would have seen what I saw. Obviously you have been talking to some of them."

"Funny how that goes. The first thing anyone saw was the body on the fence, then most of them screamed and ran like hell. About what you'd expect. The only odd thing they remembered was you getting some young guy to help you get the woman off the fence, then sitting there beside the body, using your phone. Writing your story, I guess."

"I've seen lots of dead bodies. When something like that happens, I have a job to do. Just like you."

"I hear you were pretty cool about it."

I had been far from cool, but I said, "What did you think I was going to do, shriek like a B movie actress?"

Reilly laughed. "Not bloody likely, but I'd have paid admission to see it." Then he turned more serious, leaning forward like he was going to share a confidence. "The thing that surprised me wasn't that you were cool at the scene, but that you got that girl off the fence and tried to save her life."

He had a point. Journalists were professional spectators, always where the action was, never part of it. "Well, it seemed like the human thing to do. Too bad it didn't work out."

"Yeah, it was. I hate suicides, especially someone so young. They don't even know what life's all about yet and they're already pulling the plug."

For just a second, I considered telling him how I really felt. Good cops were good listeners, and Reilly was among the best. I didn't let others into my head easily, though. Instead, I said, "So you're taking quite an interest in this. Do you think it was murder? She didn't jump?"

"Oh, she probably did jump," Reilly said, sounding a little too casual. "We just need to find out why to wrap it up."

"You even know who she is?"

"We're working on that."

"How hard can it be? Surely she must have lived in the building?"

"Seems like she didn't. All the tenants are accounted for."

"So what was she doing on the roof, then?"

"That's the question, isn't it?"

"Are you going to let me know when you get the answer?"

Reilly shrugged, as if it were no big deal. "Sure. I doubt there will be a story in it."

I wasn't so sure, but I said, "You're probably right, but it does make me curious. What sent her flying off the building?"

"You're always curious."

"It's what they pay me for."

I closed my laptop and began to zipper the case, giving Reilly the hint that we were done. Then he surprised me by saying, "You've got a whole new look."

His comment was carefully neutral. I didn't imagine that my short red hair and black fingernails would be exactly Reilly's style. If Suzy Morin was any indication, he favoured women who were more on the babe end of the scale.

"It was time to shake things up," I said. "You reach a certain stage in your life, you know?"

"Right, right," Reilly nodded, seeming to have found something interesting to examine on the floor. Still looking down, he said, "Sometimes those stages sneak up on you. Take me and Suzy for example."

When I didn't speak, he said, "So how is Suzy?"

Now I saw why he had run this information gathering errand personally. Surely Reilly wasn't still hung up on Suzy Morin? The *Citizen* police reporter was as slim and blond as a woman could be, I had to admit, but she wasn't exactly deep. It was easy to see why

Suzy would have been attracted to Reilly. He had a faded Celtic charm and an encyclopedic knowledge of crime in Ottawa. Pretty handy for a police reporter. I hadn't understood the reverse attraction, beyond the obvious, but who was I to second-guess other people's relationships? I had made a mess of all of my own.

"You know I don't see her much," I said. "We do overlap on some stories. You might have guessed this, but I'm not really the type of girl who inspires others to share their woes."

Reilly smiled. "I had guessed," he said. "But how does she seem? Happy?"

I wasn't sure whether the best answer was yes, or no. Either would be bad news for Reilly. Either he'd be encouraged to carry on his obsession or depressed that she had moved on. Besides, I really didn't know. Suzy Morin always had the same vaguely excited and pleased-with-herself expression regardless of what was going on. It was a miracle that the woman hadn't gone into television.

I knew that it wasn't really my job to scoop Suzy on police stories, but I still enjoyed it every time it happened, and it had happened more often since the breakup with Reilly.

Thinking about that, I said, "I think she does miss you in some way."

"Good, that's good," Reilly said, nodding.

The guy actually looked happy at the news. Was it because of the false hope my comment might have created or because he liked the idea of her suffering? Probably the former. When it came to women, most men were about as sophisticated as high school kids, no matter how old they actually were.

"Look," Reilly said. "I'm wrapped up for the day. Do you want to go for a drink? You could fill me in on the Sandhu trial. That's an interesting mess."

A drink with Reilly would mean only one of two things. Either he'd sit around moaning about Suzy and getting more morose with every pint, or he'd hit on me. Either way, I could do without it.

"Maybe another time, Mike. I'm busy tonight."

It was a convenient social lie when the words formed in my mind, but as soon as I said them, I realized it was true. I'd forgotten that Colin was coming over and bringing Indian food. All I really wanted was an evening of peace and quiet, but I couldn't say no to Colin. I owed him too much.

SIX

"Where do you want me to put the takeaway?" Colin said, surveying the mass of confusion that was my kitchen counter. It was covered with old newspapers, withering apples, blackened bananas, two empty tin cans and what was once the carcass of a barbecued chicken, thankfully contained under its plastic dome.

"Anywhere you can find a spot," I said.

He surveyed the mess while holding the white plastic bag that I knew would contain butter chicken, rice, naan and samosas. Colin was predictable in most things.

"Have you got a shovel?" he asked, as Ranger pawed awkwardly at his legs, reminding him that I wasn't the only one who wanted treats.

"Sorry. I don't have time to house clean. The guy I work for drives me like a slave."

I could have afforded a housekeeper but someone else having a key to my place and the freedom to root around made that a non-starter. The apartment was my sanctuary, or so it had seemed until death went flying by the window. The only person granted access was Colin, and even that was somewhat grudging.

Colin's own condo on the edge of the Byward Market was just the opposite of my place. Everything was new and either black or white. It had been a mess, too, when I lived there, but since I moved out, Colin had restored the antiseptic order one found in a high-end hotel room. I had been back only once, to pick up a few things I had forgotten.

My apartment featured Persian rugs on creaky, uneven hardwood floors, old, baggy couches paired with expensive leather chairs, and walls covered in original art. None of it was mine, of course. It had all come with the apartment when I had sublet it. The only personal things were two family photographs arrayed on the white mantelpiece that framed a small gas fireplace meant to look like the original coal model. They showed my mother and father on their wedding day, smiling optimistically, unaware of what the future held. My father had huge sideburns, long dark hair and a checked suit that might have been in style back then. My mother wore a wedding dress that she had made herself, a simple white cotton affair, and she carried a bouquet of yellow roses. The other photograph showed them with my sister Kathy and myself, back when I was about six. We were standing in front of an Adirondack fishing cabin that my grandfather used to own, and Dad was holding up a string of brook trout. In happier times, as newspaper photo captions often said.

As I watched Colin clean up my mess, I reflected on how complicated things were between us after all we had been through in my wrongheaded quest to solve the murder of my sister. You couldn't just break up with a man who had saved your life and nearly lost his own doing it, but I couldn't live with him, either. So now we were in this awkward spot, with me trying to gracefully wind down our relationship and Colin hoping to reignite it.

I had to admit that I was still attracted to him. Colin's smile was his best feature. He had good teeth, for an Englishman, and smiling turned the creases that age had added to his face into a positive. He was tall, a couple of inches over six feet, and even though he'd grown a bit heavier with middle age, he was still an impressive man. His grey hair, which he wore swept back, gave him a look of distinction that was accentuated by his inevitable dark suits, handmade in London. He looked the way a newspaper editor should look, but seldom did.

It wasn't a complete mystery why I had fallen for him back in Toronto, even though I knew an affair with the boss seldom ended well. It was something I hadn't given enough thought to at the time, a typically impetuous decision that had gotten worse when Colin had been appointed editor in Ottawa and had insisted I come along as part of the "package," as he called it. I thought this reduced me to the level of a perk, like a company car, but Colin hadn't seen that, of course.

He cleared space on the counter for the bag of Indian food, then delicately picked up the container that held the chicken remains.

"You really ought to give this a decent burial. I'll bin this stuff for you. Where do you keep your bags?"

I wondered if I still had any. Shopping was another thing that didn't really fit into my agenda. "Try under the counter," I said.

I was relieved when Colin found a whole package of green garbage bags. They might have belonged to Caroline, but at least their presence allowed me to look somewhat less than completely incompetent.

I settled into one of the couches, a down-filled affair with a soft green cover that reminded me of a child's blanket. It was my favourite spot. Ranger soon joined me, rolling over so I would scratch his belly.

"Wine's in the fridge," I said, anticipating Colin's next question. I had a nice Niagara gewurtztraminer that would be good with the Asian food. Wine was the one staple item of which I never ran out. I should be drinking less, but life was short.

"Hell of a thing with that jumper," Colin said, sweeping the debris from the counter top into a garbage bag. "Nice job, by the way. The photos you filed were our top gallery today."

Colin was trying to say something nice, but you didn't compliment a writer by talking about pictures. I decided not to share that observation.

"It was a pretty bizarre way to start the day. That poor woman was like a rag doll someone had spiked onto the fence." I considered telling Colin how affected I had been by her death but decided against it. He worried too much about my mental health as it was.

"A suicide, I presume," he said.

"Police aren't sure yet. Mike Reilly came by the courthouse at the end of the day to ask me some more questions. Apparently the woman doesn't live in the building."

"Rather odd, don't you think?" Colin said, tying up the bag.

"I do think it's odd. And I'm sure that Reilly isn't telling me everything either. He said there were 'a few complications.' I think it's worth looking into."

"Agreed. I'll have Suzy Morin pursue it further."

"I meant worth *my* looking into. This is my story. I'm the one who experienced it. That adds something that Suzy just couldn't duplicate."

"You thinking a first-person piece?"

"God no. I don't want to be part of the story, but there's something off about all of this. I can feel it."

"I agree, but what about the Sandhu trial?"

"Tomorrow's Friday. Court isn't sitting."

"Yes, but aren't we counting on a weekend piece wrapping up the developments so far?"

"Maybe *you* are, but we've only had one day of sitting and they didn't even get to the first witness. I put everything I had into today's column."

"Yes, well, I suppose the thing to do is look ahead, the upcoming witnesses and so forth."

"A perfect assignment for Cunningham," Kris said. Tyler Cunningham was the young court reporter who had been covering the news side. He was still in the eager-to-please phase of his career.

"I guess that would work," Colin said. He was looking in the cupboard for clean plates. "You know Kris, you really ought to get a housekeeper. I can give you the name of mine."

"I don't think so. Maybe I should just stock up on paper plates."

Colin was already using the dishrag and soapy water to clean two of the least dirty plates.

"You could always come to my place from time to time."

I let that one lie.

Colin inspected the two plates, wiped them dry with paper towel and then began serving the food. "You hungry?" he asked.

"Starving. I had a part of a crappy sandwich for lunch."

"You really should take some fruit with you."

Ever since I nearly died last summer, Colin had been mothering me. It was as if he had a whole new personality. If he had been that good to his four former wives, he might still be married to one of them.

"Yes, dear," I said.

Colin looked up, just for a second hoping that the remark wasn't delivered with my usual sarcasm.

"Right then. So tell me, how do you think the Sandhu trial is going to shape up? We've built it up as the political trial of the century."

"That's probably true, but the century is still young. I think the testimony of Sandhu's former business connections will be interesting. And Sandhu himself, of course, if he takes the stand."

"Bernstein tipping his cards there?"

"Not at all. I don't think he'll call Sandhu unless he has to. Too risky. All the Crown would have to do is trap him in a couple of contradictions and his credibility would be shot. Maybe if there had been a jury. Sandhu could probably have charmed them, but I doubt the judge will be so easy to impress."

"If history's a guide," Colin said. "People loathe politicians, even judges."

"I can't imagine why," I said, then paused to sample the butter chicken right out of the container, before it got cold. It was aromatic and subtly flavourful. Indian takeout had been one of our staple dishes when we lived together, along with Colin's other favourites, fish and chips and pot pies. No wonder I had lost weight once I moved.

"There is one other angle I'm working. The wife, Gail Rakic, is an interesting story in herself. Her father, Dragan, is a big developer and Tory bagman in southern Ontario. You can tell she's seething at the way the party has turned on Sandhu, given all that her family has done for the Conservatives. It must be hell sitting there beside her husband, knowing that most people think he's a sleazy crook."

"Do you think she will stick by him?"

"At least for the duration of the trial. I expect Sandhu will face sentencing in the court of Gail regardless of the outcome in the real court. Unless he's innocent, of course."

"Any chance of that?"

"I haven't seen many accused who are truly innocent. It's more a case of how guilty they are, and how much can be proven."

"Any hope the wife will talk to you?"

"She already has, a little bit. I'm trying to gain her confidence, take it slow. Her story would be a great exclusive, if I could get it."

"Well done," said Colin, handing me a plate of food and a glass of wine. He seated himself in an overstuffed armchair with a muted red paisley pattern.

"The wife says I'm supposed to check out what Luc Champagne has been up to."

"That's awfully vague."

"Yes, and I don't pay much attention to those people. I know who Champagne is, of course, and I see his picture on the society page. He must attend every event in town, always with a different woman on his arm. I think he races cars, too."

"You read the society page?" Colin asked, clearly amused.

"Only when it runs opposite the sports scores."

"I've met Champagne a few times. Charming chap, in a Gallic sort of way. Bit of a swordsman, according to what I hear. No harm there, of course. He's a single man. Rather like Pierre Trudeau, I suppose, although not as bright."

I always smiled at how men inflated their credentials with terms like "swordsman." Typically more like a paring knife in my experience.

"It's interesting how the Sandhu mess doesn't seem to be sticking to Champagne," I said. "Gail Rakic certainly implied that he's the one who blew the whistle."

"Ah, the unheralded hero of the piece then. I can see why Champagne would want to keep that up his sleeve. Nothing to be gained by getting tangled up with Sandhu, but if it does get sticky, he can show he has high ethical standards. He's positioned himself rather well."

"The thing I don't get is why the party has been so quick to dump Sandhu. They've been chasing the ethnic vote since they came to power. Then they expelled their most prominent ethnic star from caucus at the first rumour of an investigation."

"Yes, it is odd, unless the party is absolutely convinced he's guilty. One would have expected a brown chappie like Sandhu to be untouchable, unless he did something like bugger a goat. Even then, it wouldn't be a problem unless it was on YouTube."

Sometimes Colin reminded me of Prince Philip, but not in a good way. "He doesn't strike me as the goat buggering type," I said. "The real question is why a smart guy like Sandhu would get involved with some shady scheme, just to get $25,000 under the table. His wife is loaded."

"Greed," Colin said, shrugging. "Chaps who have money usually want more, especially if it's free. Maybe he got tired of having to ask his wife for an allowance."

"An allowance? MPs make a shitload of money, and he was a

parliamentary secretary when this was supposed to have happened. He must have been making 180 grand."

"Not an inconsequential sum, but I'm sure he has quite a lifestyle. From what you tell me, it would be worth digging a little deeper into the connection between Champagne and Sandhu. There has to be more at play there than the fact that one was the other's assistant."

"You're right. I'll look into it."

But not before I spent a little more time on the jumper. The Sandhu trial was expected to run for three to four more weeks. There was plenty of time to explore Gail Rakic's vague comment about Champagne. I planned to squeeze her a little harder before I went on a wild goose chase.

The jumper intrigued me more. There was something there, some connection I couldn't quite make. It was as if I had seen the woman somewhere before, although it seemed unlikely since she didn't even live in the building. Reilly had been uncharacteristically cagey, though. Something was up. I intended to find out what.

"So, an early start in the morning then?" Colin asked.

I knew what he really meant. I'd bet that he had a new toothbrush in his coat pocket on the off chance that I would invite him to stay over. The idea wasn't entirely unattractive, but it would be a mixed message that would just take us in the wrong direction.

"Yes. It's been an exhausting day. I should turn in early."

Colin nodded and said, "Of course. I understand. Let's try to find something short on Netflix, then."

The new Colin was too damned understanding. Maybe he really had changed. He clearly thought that if he were patient, I would come around. For just a moment, I wondered if he was right.

SEVEN

When the call came at 6:30 a.m., I was in that stunned state between sleep and dreams, trying to get away from men with guns who were chasing me through woods that were too open to offer escape or cover. I called it a dream but it was more like a documentary. I reached drowsily across the bed, fumbled for my iPhone on the clutter of the night stand, then looked at the call display. Reilly? He was about the last person I would have expected to hear from at this hour. Or any hour, for that matter. The staff sergeant in charge of major crimes didn't make a habit of phoning reporters, unless he wanted something.

"Hey Reilly, you're off to an early start."

"Yeah well, something has come up about your jumper. Can you meet me at the Corkstown footbridge in about half an hour?"

Jumping out of bed and racing off to meet Mike Reilly wasn't exactly how I had planned to start my day, but I could tell by his abrupt tone that his news was urgent, and surely exclusive at this time of day. How could I resist?

"OK, where exactly?"

"There's a bench overlooking the canal, on the west side."

"Can't we just meet in a coffee shop? I'll be dying for caffeine."

"I'd rather be some place where people can't easily eavesdrop."

"You want me to wear a disguise?"

"Funny. Just meet me in half an hour."

Reilly hung up, and my mind began to race. The jumper was someone significant. That much was obvious. Or she didn't jump. Either way, it was a story.

I rolled out of bed, pulled on jeans and a T-shirt and ran my fingers through my hair. I was sure I looked like shit, but there was ball cap in the hall closet. That would help. Reilly would have to take me the way I was. What could he expect, calling so early? I realized that some people were up and out the door by 6:30 but I was a start late, work late kind of girl.

If I hurried, I'd have time to grab a cup of takeout coffee from the Bridgehead downstairs. I shoved a notebook into my purse, a bulky black canvas bag big enough to carry a small animal and still have room left over for a six pack. I clipped Ranger on to his leash, and we were off.

It was a cool morning for May, and my T-shirt felt a bit inadequate, but the sun felt good and the takeout cup of coffee warmed my hands. Elgin wasn't busy this early and I didn't have to dodge the usual annoying dawdlers who would soon crowd the sidewalk. I cut down Lisgar, going behind City Hall and around the yard of Lisgar High School to the Rideau Canal, a green-banked ribbon of water that wound through the centre of Ottawa. Even this early, the runners were out, thumping along the canal. I ran only when someone was chasing me.

Reilly was on the bench, as promised, wearing another of his dark suits. Or maybe it was the one from the day before. He was leaning forward, forearms on his knees. I tied Ranger to a small tree and slid in quickly beside Reilly.

"You've got a dog," he said.

"It's just a loaner."

"I had a dog. It died."

"That gives me hope."

Reilly looked at me and shook his head. Not everyone got my sense of humour.

"So, you certainly know how to grab my interest. What's up?" I said, snapping the lid off my coffee. Too late, I realized I should have gotten him one, too.

Reilly looked towards me, serious now. "First thing, we never met and you didn't get any of this from me. You OK with that?"

I wasn't keen on off-the-record stuff unless it was likely to lead to a solid, provable story. You could spend a lot of time on things that would never make the paper. On the other hand, you had to be flexible with your sources, and Reilly could be a good one.

"All right. Nothing came from you, but so we're clear, if I can get this, whatever it is, from other sources, I can go with it, right?"

"Yeah," he said, then ran a big hand across his bristly jaw. The usually meticulous detective hadn't shaved since the day before.

"The jumper case has gone south. We've got a homicide, but it's been taken out of my hands."

I could see from Reilly's scowl that he was less than pleased with that development. "How's that even possible?" I asked.

"Big boys stepped in to grab it, then it got worse."

"You're going to have to spell it out for me."

"It didn't take the coroner long to figure out that there was more to this than a suicide. The woman had scrapes on both knees and wounds on her arms and hands. Someone attacked her on the roof, judging by the gravel imbedded in her knees. She might have been thrown off the roof, or she might have jumped to escape her attacker, or attackers. We don't know yet.

"As soon as I reported up the line that we've got a homicide, the RCMP showed up and started talking joint investigation. They sent a superintendent, not the usual corporal, so I knew it was something big, but those boys don't like to share information.

"Somehow they know who she is. Mae Wang. A student at Carleton, they say. I asked why the Mounties were so interested in a Carleton student and all I got was a shrug. This prick superintendent actually said, 'It's above your pay grade.' Can you believe it?

"They've got a story about how the girl's roommate knows some guy at the RCMP, so when she doesn't come home night before last, the roommate phones this unnamed Mountie and reports her missing. For this reason, she's on their radar. And she's a foreign national, so they're saying they ought to be involved."

"Sounds like they're stretching a point. What do you think the real interest is?"

"Don't know, but it gets worse. About nine o'clock, a posse from the Chinese Embassy shows up at the morgue demanding they release the body. They've got a limo, a hearse and two big SUVs. Some bullshit about Chinese burial customs and the need to ship the body home to China quickly. They're waving all kinds of official-looking paperwork. There's one guy still on duty and a bunch of Chinese in suits yelling and shouting. He caves in and releases the body, coroner's investigation not even complete.

"My new Mountie friend says it's 'regrettable' and someone from Global Affairs will write a stern note of protest. Do you believe these bastards?"

"I can see why you'd be pissed off. What's this mean to your case?'

"There is no case. I'm off it, ordered to focus on existing case-load. Not a damned thing I can do. With this joint investigation, they've moved it up to inspector level. Couple of brass hats from our place and the Mounties are going to sit around and play with their joints. That's how these things work. But I'll tell you, no one's going to chase or throw some kid off the top of a building two blocks from the police station and walk away. Not in my town."

I nodded. "So what do you think is behind it?"

"Could be just the usual diplomatic ass kissing. Same stuff we see when a drunken Russian runs someone over. The government makes some noise about it, but most of the time they let it blow over. Looking for the same consideration if there is a drunken Canadian in Moscow, I guess."

"That doesn't make it right."

"It sure as hell doesn't. I took this straight to the chief who gave me a line about the situation being complicated, all part of life in a national capital, that kind of thing. Meanwhile, whoever killed this girl is still walking around out there."

"Or on his way back to China."

"That's possible, too. Lover's quarrel, maybe. Could be a guy from their embassy."

"So what do you think the chances are of anyone talking about any of this on the record?"

"Slim. Our guys will refer everything to the Mounties. You'll probably get a generic statement from A Division, but that's all. You might get a canned quote from Global Affairs as well. I'm thinking that, as a columnist, you've got a little more freedom to say how outrageous this is, even if all the facts aren't available."

I was certainly interested. This was a big story if I could nail it.

Reilly reached into his suit-coat pocket and pulled out a photo of the woman I had last seen on the fence.

"Morgue shot," he said. "It's not bad, though. There was no dam-age to the face. Maybe you can ask a few questions, see what you can find out about this girl. She's more than just some Carleton student, that's for sure."

I took the photo, looked at it for a moment, then put it in my purse. Even in death, the young woman was beautiful in that soft way that Oriental women had. How had she ended up on the roof? And why that building, of all buildings?

No need to tell Reilly that I had already planned to spend the day finding out more about the woman. Now it seemed a lot more worthwhile.

"My day *is* pretty clear," I said. "And you've got me off to an early start."

"Good, good," Reilly said, nodding. Then he turned to me, his dark eyes locking on mine. "Anything I can do to help, let me know. I just can't make an official move. Don't call me before noon, though. Right now, I'm going home to crash."

"You look like you could use it. Thanks for the tip."

I looked again at the photo of Mae Wang. Who are you, I thought? And who killed you?

EIGHT

Mae Wang was a ghost, in every sense of the word. I had spent the morning in the apartment searching for her trail online, but the bread crumbs were few and far between.

When I started in journalism, putting together a person's life story consisted mostly of initial guess work, leads and interviews. It was a slow process, unless you got lucky or the person was prominent. Now, you could usually learn quite a lot about someone in a single day, and the place to start was Facebook, where they would tell you all about themselves, with pictures.

Mae Wang wasn't so forthcoming. I did learn that she was a graduate student at Carleton's School of Linguistics and Language Studies. She was also a teaching assistant and freelance interpreter. She listed her interests as reading, piano and ping pong. What was it with Asians and ping pong?

If Mae was in a relationship, she wasn't saying. She had only three Facebook friends, and two of those were in Vancouver, which Mae identified as her home town. There was a lie. If she was from Vancouver, the Chinese Embassy wouldn't be shipping her body back to China. It was a good back story if Mae Wang was really someone else, though. Vancouver had to be wall to wall with Wongs and Wangs. Who would question the authenticity of Mae's story?

Mae's Facebook page seemed to be mostly a way of advertising her availability as an interpreter. There were few postings and those were mostly cryptic. "Attended Canada-China Friendship Society event," things like that. It was enough to show that she was out there, but Mae Wang didn't feel the usual compulsion to tell the whole world about everything she did. Either her life was dull or she wanted to keep it private.

There were only two photos. In one, a smiling Mae sat on a stone wall in a knee-length white dress with a thin pink sweater over top. It was taken in some kind of garden, with cherry blossoms in the

SPIKED   49

background. It would have been a shot from Vancouver, or China. The look on Mae's face was gentle, and yet somehow knowing. I printed the picture out. No need to use a morgue shot if I didn't have to.

The other showed Mae with her arm around a similar-looking young woman, standing in front of some tulips on Parliament Hill. The other Facebook friend, possibly. It was a typical tourist shot, but it had been taken from too far back to be a selfie. I wondered who the photographer was.

I extended my electronic search farther. Mae had no presence on Instagram or Snapchat. Infomart, the data base that logged every mention of a person in a newspaper, TV or radio newscast and even in a blog, produced an elderly woman in Bismarck, North Dakota, and an American in technology. No surprise. Most ordinary people didn't appear in the news and Mae Wang didn't seem like an attention seeker. All Google offered was a lot of information about a Mae Wang park in Thailand.

For someone with more attachment to society, I could have looked at mortgage records, court records that would show lawsuits or divorces, disciplinary records of professional societies and political donation records. As it was, at the end of my electronic search, I knew what Mae Wang wanted people to know, and it wasn't much. There was no saying any of it was even true.

There were two useful leads. The only Facebook friend Mae had in Ottawa was Lily Liu. Odds were that was her roommate. A quick call to the media relations person at Carleton had revealed that Mae's graduate supervisor was a Professor Ronald Horsley. I decided to start with him.

An hour later, I was in Horsley's crammed little office in Paterson Hall, one of a jumble of Carleton University buildings that would have seemed modern 30 or 40 years ago. They hadn't aged well and now they were punctuated by towers that had all the grace of aging condo buildings.

Horsley's office was a narrow white rectangle with books on battered wooden shelves down one of the long walls and photographs of Horsley all over the other. I glanced at them while Horsley finished a phone call. There was the professor as a young, bearded backpacker with the Great Wall in the background. The picture had to be 40 years old. In another, he was part of what looked like a group of students greeting Mao. There were pictures of him as an older man, too, at various functions with Chinese people that I didn't recognize. In all, there were probably more than 50 photos on his trophy wall.

Horsley himself was no prize. His backpack had become a front-pack, a round potbelly that could have qualified him to play Santa. His beard was as unkempt as it had been 40 years ago, but now grey. Horsley hadn't visited a barber lately either, his wispy hair long and shooting in all directions. I knew the type, students who just kept going back for more degrees and ultimately never did leave the security of the campus and the life they had enjoyed in their 20s.

"Yes, yes, I'll pick it up," Horsley said, sounding somewhat annoyed. Then he put the phone down and rose to greet me. He was close to six feet tall and didn't look quite as rotund standing up. "Ron Horsley," he said, extending a hand. "Tragic story about Mae Wang. How can I help?"

I had had the task of giving Horsley the bad news over the phone when I called to make an appointment. There was a considerable pause when I explained what happened, but he had pulled himself together and agreed to co-operate on what I had told him would be an obituary. It was a truish statement.

I sat on the single hard wooden chair, opened my notebook and said, "I'm really trying to find out everything I can about Mae. Did you know her well?"

Horsley paused slightly before answering, then said, "I knew her in a *collegial* way. It's a smallish department. One gets to know everyone."

Right. He had wanted to get into Mae's pants and felt guilty about it now, or perhaps regretful about his failure. "When did you first meet Mae?" I asked.

"When she was assigned as my graduate student. Very bright girl. Excellent Mandarin skills, but she was looking for the academic qualification to go with it. She had hoped to teach, ultimately."

"A fine ambition," I said, hoping I had managed to keep the sarcasm out of my voice. "I can see that you've certainly had a fascinating career," I said, gesturing toward the wall of photographs. I didn't really want to hear a lot about Ron Horsley's life, but I was certain it would be his favourite topic and buttering up a source a little bit never hurt.

"Well, I have seen some remarkable things. I've been a sinophile since a rather young age. Fascinating people and culture. Canadians know so little about the Chinese, beyond the stereotypes."

"I'm sure you could write a book about it."

"Actually, I have. Three in fact."

I needed to change the topic before Horsley started to tell me all about them. I wondered if anyone had ever read his books, other than students assigned them as course work.

"I'll have to check that out," I lied. "But back to Mae Wang. Can you tell me what kind of person Mae was? Her interests, what mattered to her, that sort of thing?"

Horsley tugged on his beard, considering his answer. "She was rather quiet, in that way that Asian women often are. Somewhat introverted, I would say. Highly intelligent. Well read. I can't say I recall her mentioning any hobbies or activities. Our focus was strictly on her academic work."

"Of course. Did she have many friends here at the school?"

Horsley frowned, making a bit of a show of concentrating. Then he said, "I don't think so. The only one I really saw Mae with was one of our former students, Lily Liu. In fact, I believe they are roommates."

"That's useful," I said, although all it did was confirm something I had already assumed. "How about politics? Was she for or against the regime in the old country?"

"I have no idea," Horsley said quickly. "She certainly wasn't Falun Gong or anything like that. They're a cult, you know."

"Really?" I didn't know much about Falun Gong, but I did know that the Chinese government hated them and seemed determined to stamp them out, anywhere in the world. I wondered if there was some kind of political reason why the embassy had been so quick to seize Mae Wang's body. She had to be more than just a quiet student at Carleton.

"Oh yes," Horsley replied. "A quasi-religion with an agenda to destabilize the Chinese state. I've researched it thoroughly. Not that the leadership in China is without its faults."

I was no expert on world politics, but I knew that the government in China was one of the most repressive in the world. Not without its faults didn't quite capture it. There was no point getting into a political debate with Horsley, but I could see that he was one of those Canadians who loved everything about China and were willing to overlook little things like torturing dissidents and locking people up for saying what they thought. Apparently meeting Mao made up for a lot.

"Mae was from Vancouver, was she?" I asked.

"I believe so. Rather an Asian city, Vancouver."

"How about her family? I'll need to contact them."

"I don't believe she ever talked about them, now that you mention it. Nothing that sticks in my mind, in any case."

Horsley gave an incongruous grin. I suspected he was enjoying being no help at all. The question was why.

"I see that Mae did freelance translation. Any idea who she might have worked for?"

"That wouldn't have been directly relevant to her work here, but I do believe that she mentioned working for the Chinese Embassy from time to time." Horsley nodded his head, as if confirming his recollection. "Yes, I definitely remember that. The embassy has a rather large contingent here in Ottawa. Regrettably, relatively few of them speak English well. There are a lot of social events on the diplomatic circuit. I believe Mae would sometimes accompany their diplomats to act as an interpreter."

Now we were getting somewhere. Mae Wang was young and attractive. Maybe one of the diplomats wanted something more than interpretation. Or perhaps she had fallen in love with one of them. I had covered a lot of murders where women were the victims, and most of them had to do with sex or love, or some confusion over the two.

"I don't suppose you would know who she was interpreting for?"

"I do move in those circles myself," Horsley said, just so I would be clear on his status. "Unfortunately, I can't recollect being at any diplomatic event where Mae was working."

Interesting choice of words. Horsley wasn't saying that he didn't attend any events where Mae was present, just that he didn't recollect. It was a phrase recommended by lawyers when they suspected their client was lying and there was a chance the other side could prove it. It left the door open for improving one's recollection later on.

"And if Mae had been present, surely you would have remembered, her being a student of yours and all."

Horsley reddened a bit. He clearly knew what I was implying by the words "and all." I still didn't think he'd gotten anywhere with Mae Wang. Young women weren't attracted to men of Horsley's age and looks unless they had a lot of money, fame or power. Horsley couldn't possibly have enough of any of those to overcome his other deficiencies.

"Yes, I suppose I would have remembered. Mae was a memorable woman."

I made a point of writing that in my notebook.

"I'd rather you didn't quote me on that."

So he was married. That made his crush just a little bit more pathetic.

"One last thing. Do you happen to have an address for Mae Wang? I should talk to the roommate."

"I think I just might," Horsley said, making a show of riffling through a Rolodex on his desk. Like he hadn't memorized it and maybe even spent afternoons lurking around outside Mae's place like a lovelorn teenager.

'Yes, here it is," Horsley said, plucking a card from the file and passing it over. I noted the address, an apartment on Metcalfe in the 300 block, pretty much downtown. Mae's cell phone number was there, too. I scribbled that down as well, but didn't say anything about it.

"You've been a real help professor," I said.

Horsley smiled, seemingly confused by my generous assessment of the interview.

"When will your article run?" he asked.

"Soon. It looks as if there really isn't much of a story to tell."

Horsley nodded vigorously, finding that a little more reassuring than the idea that he had been a big help. I wasn't sure what Horsley's angle was yet, but I was pretty certain he had one. The thing I didn't know was whether this dumpy, China-loving Carleton University professor was connected to Mae Wang's death. I decided to try my luck with Lily Liu. Maybe she could connect the dots and explain what was happening between Horsley and Mae Wang.

NINE

Reilly rolled out of bed and looked at his watch. Two o'clock. Shit. He'd slept through half of the day. The sun was forcing its way through the thin curtains. How had he slept so late? And not so much as a drink the night before. He couldn't pull all-nighters like he used to.

He turned on his phone and listened to the assortment of dings and dongs it made as it downloaded texts, e-mails and voice messages. When you were the staff sergeant in Major Crimes, the world never slowed down and let you take a day off. The stabbings, shootings and homicides in the city were up, but the chief and the mayor kept on telling people how safe it was while squeezing the police budget so that they were short staffed everywhere.

Reilly often wondered why that was still his problem. He was 55 with 35 years in, well past the time when he could retire, collect his pension and spend his time fishing. He knew that would please the brass, too. There was always a long list of protégés and relatives looking for promotion. Knowing that his very presence pissed off the eager climbers and their mentors was worth something, but it wasn't always enough.

In a good week, he could still help take some shitbag off the street, maybe even put him behind bars if the system didn't commit some technical violation of his rights along the way. That used to be satisfying, but after so many years on the job he knew it usually just meant that another guy the same would step up. Rinse and repeat.

It wasn't the criminals that bothered him the most, though. What could you expect from them? They broke laws for a living. It was Reilly's own colleagues that he found hardest to take. It was as irritating as jock itch to watch people who were incompetent and full of themselves push their way to the top, taking jobs that he always imagined would be his. That was the curse of being the son and grandson of former chiefs. Early on, he assumed that he would have a similar career path, but so did other people. He had become the guy they had to stop to get to the top. He had to admit that his tendency to tell so-called superiors exactly what he thought probably hadn't helped.

Still, more than three decades of service and not even an inspector. It was embarrassing, something his father Seamus never failed to mention. Nasty old fart living in a mobile home outside Fort Myers, playing 36 holes of golf most days and still knocking back enough Scotch to pickle a hog. His old man had come up in the days when knowing how to swing your fists and your baton was grounds for promotion. Now, it would get you flayed alive on social media. It seemed like every time someone in uniform got a little too enthusiastic there were 20 people filming it.

Not that Reilly condoned that sort of shit, but it was tough living in a world where people demanded action on crime, and then expected you to treat the criminals like they were visiting royalty.

He pulled on a blue robe that he had owned for decades and walked the few steps into the apartment's little white kitchen. He started the coffee maker and surveyed his surroundings. The kitchen was IKEA, cheap and glossy like the rest of the apartment. Reilly didn't care. He was seldom home and the place on Cooper was an easy walk to the central station on Elgin. So what if the building looked like a parking garage. He was renting.

His old house on Grove in Ottawa South had been home, but it seemed pointless to stay there after Jenny had left him. Almost seven years ago now. It was hard to believe. He would have had to buy out her half of the house in the divorce settlement. It just didn't make sense financially and there were too many memories of his failed marriage.

Now he had done it again. The apartment had been his place with Suzy, and she was gone, too. He opened the cupboard to get his favourite black mug and saw hers still sitting there, white with a bold red S on it. The mug hadn't been worth hanging on to, just like him.

His relationship with Suzy seemed almost surreal now. Maybe it had been wrong from the start. Suzy had been dating his son, Sean, and she showed up at Reilly's place one night, pissed at Sean and demanding to know where he was. Feeling that he owed her after shamelessly misleading her to help solve a case, Reilly had invited her in. After a few whiskies, one thing had led to another and she ended up staying for five years. And now she was gone and he didn't even know why.

The thing with Suzy had cost him his relationship with Sean. He hadn't thought his son was serious about her, but Suzy knew how to put a hook into a man. Sean was an inspector now, out in East Division. They hadn't spoken in more than two years, and then only because of a case.

Reilly poured his coffee and tried to push all of that to the back of his mind. There wasn't a day he didn't think about Suzy, but that wasn't going to bring her back. He had work to do and he had to get focused. Maybe the deep thinkers weren't going to bother themselves about the dead Chinese girl, but that didn't mean he wasn't. In the world Reilly lived in, there weren't special sets of circumstances that meant some homicides weren't worth exploring. He didn't care whether the victim was an MP or a street hooker. He went after the perp just as hard.

His gambit this morning with Kris Redner might pay dividends, but he needed a few other lines working, too. There wasn't much doubt that someone at the RCMP knew what was going on. Probably CSIS, too. Something like this had to be on the spy agency's radar because of the Chinese Embassy's involvement. Whisking bodies away in the middle of the night smelled a lot like Ministry of State Security work. Reilly had done a few joint ops with RCMP and CSIS guys. They figured at least half the embassy personnel in Ottawa were MSS agents.

There was one guy he had hit it off with, one who didn't take well to the internal bullshit. Farrell, that was his name. Had started out as a Mountie, then switched over to CSIS. Reilly had heard that Farrell was some kind of a private contractor now. That could mean anything in his line of work. Maybe he was still plugged in. If so, he seemed like the type who would give it to Reilly straight. He decided to make a few calls, see if he could track Farrell down.

Reilly wondered if Kris Redner would make any progress, and if she did, whether she would share it with him. Right now, he didn't have a lot to trade in exchange for information. He liked Redner. She called it the way she saw it. The *Citizen* writer was smart and seemed tough, but he knew she was just showing him her outer shell. You had to have a thick one to spend your life dealing with crime and criminals, whether you were a cop or a reporter.

Reilly hoped that he hadn't made a mistake in enlisting her help. If the Mae Wang case played out the way he thought it would, they were going to be up against some pretty serious people, ones who didn't really care about the rules.

He had always thought Kris Redner would be up for that, but she'd changed somehow in the last few months. She'd been away for a while, then when she came back, she was off for months on medical leave. His instinct was that she'd gotten her nose into something serious, maybe illegal. Now he was pointing her at more trouble.

Reilly vowed to keep close tabs on Kris. He'd made the mistake of drawing Suzy into a dangerous story once, back before they were together, and it had put her life in danger. He couldn't do that to another woman. He had already made more mistakes in life than his conscience could bear.

TEN

I powered down the windows of my old Honda Accord to let in some air. The temperature had shot up to 25 degrees Celsius, typical of May's unpredictability in Ottawa. The sun was beating down in a cloudless sky, but I had found a maple to park under across the street from Lily and Mae's building. The parking spot wasn't legal, but it wouldn't matter as long as I was in the car. If I did get a ticket, I'd just throw it in the glove compartment with all the rest.

The car was a 15-year-old beater, but it was good enough for my rare trips out to the *Citizen* offices on Baxter Road, and the occasional stake out. The thing would probably collapse into a heap of rust before I put enough miles on it to change the oil.

I was going to have to get lucky to connect with Lily Liu. I didn't have a cell number for her and no one under the age of 30 was in the telephone book. Most people came home around dinner time, though, and I was prepared to be patient.

Metcalfe must have been a grand street once, way before my time. Most of the homes were red brick Victorians, the showy ones built by people who had money and wanted everyone to know it. Lily's apartment building was the exception, a six-storey brown brick rectangle, circa 1960. It was a rundown joint much like those that ruined just about every major downtown street in Ottawa. The late afternoon sun at least gave some kind of life to the drab apartment block.

I could see why Mae Wang would have chosen it, besides relatively cheap rent. It wasn't terribly close to the university, but it was more or less equidistant between there and the Chinese Embassy on St. Patrick in the ByWard Market. The two poles of my life were the cop shop and the courthouse. For Mae, it was the university and the embassy.

It was 5:30. I wished I had thought to take a pee break, but if I left now, it would be the moment Lily Liu showed up.

I wondered if I would be able to discover what was really behind Mae Wang's death. There was obviously a story there, but perhaps no one had the whole picture. It would be up to me to try to piece it together, but so far, the shape of the pieces wasn't very clear.

I did have the horrible and graphic image of Mae being spiked on a fence right in front of me. It was an unbeatable way to start a column, but then things got fuzzy. It was a homicide, Reilly said, but the police weren't confirming anything. I had already checked that. The RCMP was even less co-operative. Wait for a press release, their useless flack said. Not likely. Then there was the angle about the Chinese spiriting the body away in the dead of the night. I didn't expect either the Chinese or the RCMP to confirm that. Too embarrassing all around. My portrait of Mae herself was still sketchy. What Horsley had told me was only a percentage of the truth, and a small one at that.

I could always go with the old intriguing mystery, series of question marks approach, but I knew I would never be satisfied with that. Even though I had never met Mae Wang, the outline of her story pushed a button with me. It felt like a case where a woman had been used by a powerful man or men, then eliminated when she became a complication. The same thing had nearly happened to me. My own situation had been different than Mae Wang's, and I had been luckier in the end, but the apparent injustice of Mae's death had reminded me why I did this job in the first place. I had to admit it felt good after months of hanging around the apartment brooding, burning up my sick time.

In the passenger side mirror, I saw a young Asian woman walking down Metcalfe, coming from downtown. She wore a bright yellow sleeveless dress and cork wedge sandals. What looked like the strap of a backpack was slung over her shoulder. Even in the mirror, I could see that this woman was beautiful, with delicate features and long, glossy black hair. There was no saying it was Lily Liu, but she looked a lot like the girl in the picture that Mae had posted on Facebook.

Once the woman was about 15 feet behind my car, she looked both ways, then darted across Metcalfe toward the apartment building. It was time to move. If this woman wasn't Lily, it would just be a mildly awkward mistake.

I got out of the car and hurried across the road, just in time to evade a speeding Blue Line cab. As the woman I hoped was Lily reached the door of the building, she put down her black backpack and pulled out a door security card.

"Excuse me," I said. "Are you Lily Liu?"

It was apparent from the look of surprise on her face that she was, but Lily hesitated a moment before answering. Then she said, "Are you some kind of bill collector?"

"No, not at all." I had my media credentials on a lanyard around my neck and quickly showed Lily my identification card. It was meaningless in a situation like this, but I had found that if I brandished it confidently, some people were more likely to co-operate.

"A journalist?" Lily said. It was clear from the look on her face that she'd have preferred the bill collector.

"Yes. I'm with the *Ottawa Citizen*. I'm working on an obituary on Mae Wang. Mind if I ask you a few questions?"

Lily looked left, then right, as if she was concerned that someone might be watching her. Then she quickly swiped her card through the security device on the building's main door. "Hurry up," she said.

I stepped quickly behind her into the building's small main lobby. It was landlord green and smelled like someone was cooking onions. There was an outdated bank of brass mailboxes on the right side, most of them with no name in the little slot that was supposed to identify the tenant. There was a single elevator to the left and a flight of stairs straight ahead.

"Follow me," Lily said. "I'm on the second floor."

I trailed behind in a cloud of Lily's perfume. It was some kind of jasmine scent, much like Mae's. The image of a dying Mae flashed in my mind, but I pushed it aside.

Lily's apartment was the first on the right. When she got to the door, she set down her backpack and reached into her purse for her keys. Then she turned and said, "You'd better tell me a bit more about this. I don't want my name in the newspaper."

"No need for that. I'm just trying to get a fuller picture of who Mae was. When a person dies so publicly, we normally do an obituary. It's a way of honouring her life."

I couldn't count how many times I had given some version of that pitch to relatives and friends of people who had died violently. It was always true, as long as you defined obituary broadly.

Lily tilted her head to one side, as if weighing whether this was something she wanted to be involved with. She had very large dark eyes set in a girlish face. Her skin looked like it belonged to a child, it was so smooth. What would it be like to be so effortlessly beautiful?

Finally, Lily nodded twice, then opened the door. The kitchen and living area was really all one room, but Lily and Mae had divided it with a folding screen depicting cherry blossom trees on a red background. There was a bamboo mat in the middle of the room and the furniture was black and low to the ground. Down a hallway, I could see two bedroom doors and a bathroom at the end of the hall. Even with the afternoon sun, the room was gloomy, the sunlight filtered by a big maple in front of the building.

"You want some green tea?" Lily asked.

"Love some," I said, although I really would have preferred a coffee or a shot of Glenfiddich. "Do you mind if I use your washroom?"

"No, go ahead. It's at the end of the hall."

I quickly headed down the short hall and closed the washroom door. I really did have to pee, but a person's washroom could tell you something about them. I saw the chaos one would expect from two young women living together. The ledge around the bathtub was cluttered with shampoos and body washes in brightly-coloured bottles. There was still a faint tinge of body wash in the air. The beige formica countertop around the single sink was overloaded with cosmetics and a hair dryer rested precariously on one corner. Two pairs of actual stockings hung drying on the shower rack. Interesting. Most women in the modern world only wore stockings during sex. No doubt Mae and Lily were getting plenty of that. I needed to find out who Mae was having it with. Judging by the mess, they weren't having it here. I knew from personal experience that men were turned off by a mess of girly stuff in a washroom, even if most of them were slobs in their own way.

I carefully opened the door of the medicine cabinet. There was the usual acetaminophen and ibuprofen, more lipsticks, tweezers, various perfumes and a box of ribbed condoms. No prescription medications of any sort. That certainly supported Reilly's information that this was a homicide. Most people would resort to mood-improving medications before jumping off a building.

Other than that, my quick survey of the washroom had told me only that Lily and Mae were young, sexually active and not very tidy.

I relieved myself, hovering over the toilet seat, and then went back into the main room. I heard the sound of a teapot clanking, then the whoosh of a kettle coming to the boil.

"Have a seat," Lily said. "It will just be a minute."

I lowered myself into one of the black chairs. It was like a regular chair, but without legs. I hoped my back didn't seize up completely.

Lily handed me a mug of tea, then descended gracefully into a chair just like the one I was struggling to adjust to. I didn't think I had ever been that flexible.

On the street, Lily had seemed nervous, almost jumpy. In her own apartment, she was starting to relax. I pulled a reporter's thin notebook from my purse, to remind Lily that this was business.

"So, Mae Wang, what can I tell you?" she said. "I think I'm still in shock about her death. It's just hard to believe that she's gone. And the way she died? It was horrible. I just can't believe that Mae would kill herself. I didn't see it coming at all."

"You can't blame yourself for that." Remembering what Reilly had said about Lily knowing some guy in the RCMP, I said, "So you reported her missing, I heard?"

"Me? No. The first I heard about Mae was when the police came here."

"OK, I must have gotten that wrong," I said, knowing I hadn't. "What kind of police were they?"

"RCMP. They said something about it being because Mae worked at the embassy."

"Right, right," I said, nodding as if that made some kind of sense. Maybe it did, but it wasn't what the RCMP superintendent had told Reilly. I'd have to raise it with him.

"Now I have to do something with her stuff. I don't even know where to send it. Mae was from Vancouver, but she never really said anything about her family. I don't even know who they are."

Probably because they don't exist, at least not in Vancouver. Did Lily really know so little of Mae's life? I had told her I was writing an obituary. The smart move would have been to tell me a few harmless things and send me on my way.

At least the cup of tea created a politeness window that would give me time for a few questions. I decided to take it slow. "How did you and Mae meet?" I asked.

"I'm a interpreter. I do work for business and government. There are a lot of Chinese business people coming here to discuss commercial interests. I actually met Mae at a gig at the Chinese Embassy, though. She did quite a bit of work for them, especially at social events."

A person working at those kinds of events would hear a lot of things. I wondered if Mae had heard something she shouldn't have.

"I see. I take it the two of you must have hit if off, since you became roommates."

Lily shrugged. "We had a lot in common. Mae was new in town, looking for a place to live. I needed a roommate. As crappy as this little apartment is, the rent is expensive for one person."

"Right," I said, nodding sympathetically. "How long have you two lived together?"

"Almost a year now."

"So you must have gotten to know Mae pretty well."

Lily sipped her tea, then said, "Not really. Mae was always busy with school or work, you know? It seemed like she was hardly ever here."

"Not much of a social life?"

"She wasn't a party type of person or anything like that," Lily said. Then she hesitated, about to add something, but stopped herself.

"But?" I prompted.

"She always went out Tuesday and Thursday nights. And she didn't come back until the next morning. I assume she had a boyfriend, maybe a married guy? I never met him, anyway. You won't use that in your article, right?"

"No, of course not." Interesting, though. Where did Mae Wang sleep those other two nights of the week? Not wanting to seem too interested in the mysterious boyfriend, I said, "So, did Mae have any hobbies or interests? Sports, maybe?"

"No, she really wasn't that type of girl. More of a bookworm, really."

"How about politics? I understand there are a lot of strong feelings among expatriates about the situation in China."

"Well, she worked for the embassy. I guess that tells you something. I never heard her talk about any of that stuff from home, though."

"Home. That reminds me. Maybe you can clarify something. Was Mae born here or in China? It's one of those basic biographical facts we like to include in a piece like this."

"She always said she was from Vancouver. To tell you the truth, I never asked."

"How about you?"

"Me? I was born in Scarborough. Not very exotic."

"Better than Mississauga," I said, smiling. "Now what about school? I know Mae was a graduate student in the language school at Carleton, but she was already fluent in Mandarin. Why was she at Carleton?"

"She wanted to teach. She talked about that quite a bit. Did you talk to Horsley?"

"I did. This afternoon in fact. Do you know him?"

"I've seen him at embassy events. Horny Horsley, Mae called him. He was always coming on to her. It was gross."

"I'll say. The guy must not own a mirror. Mae would have had to be crazy to hook up with him."

Lily laughed, the first time she had done so. She was beginning to trust me. It was time for one more request. "Do you think I could see her room? It can help a writer get a bit of a feel for the person."

"Sure," Lily said, rising from the low chair just as gracefully as she had descended. As I got up, I felt a twinge of the feared back pain. I really should get that looked at.

Lily led me down the short hall and opened the door to Mae's room. Unlike the shared bathroom, it was neat, almost monastic. The bed had a white cover, perfectly smooth, with two fluffy pillows in shams. There was a single dark wood dresser, but not a personal picture or memento on its glass-covered top. A book case stood by the closet, loaded with books, mostly Chinese. The closet door itself was closed. I would have liked to see inside, but that would be asking too much. In all, it was as impersonal as a hotel room.

"Not much to see," Lily said. "She was the neat one. I'm the slob."

"I'm just the same. Who's got time for housecleaning?"

Back in the living room, I put away my notebook and said, "What about you Lily? You said at the start that this was very hard on you. I can only imagine."

Actually, having lost almost every member of my family to violent death, I could more than imagine, but it wasn't the time or the place to talk about that.

When Lily shrugged again, I said, "When I met you at the door, you seemed afraid."

"Well, it did kind of spook me. It's just hard to believe that Mae would kill herself, especially in such an awful way. I can't imagine jumping off a building. At least she didn't do it here."

'Thank God for that."

"You've talked to the police, right?"

"Yes, I have."

"Is there any chance this is something other than a suicide? I mean, Mae seemed unhappy sometimes, maybe more than sometimes, but I don't see her killing herself. She had a lot going for her. It just doesn't make sense."

Lily's intuition was almost certainly correct, but there was no use worrying her any more than she already was. Whatever trouble had found Mae, Lily didn't seem to be part of it.

"No, it doesn't make sense, but it usually doesn't when someone kills themselves. We all have an inner life that other people don't know about. Sometimes, that life is worse than anyone imagines. It doesn't sound like Mae was the sort who was eager to share her problems. I've covered a lot of these kinds of situations. You can't always make sense of them."

"All right," Lily said. "Talking to you has made me feel a little bit better. Do you have a card in case I remember anything else important?"

"Of course," I said, handing her one. "If there is anything at all you think I should know about, or if you just want to talk, give me a call."

Lily put the card on a little black table by the door, nodding her thanks.

As I went back down the steps toward my car, I hoped I was right in my assumption that Lily wasn't part of whatever was going on and wasn't in any danger. For just a minute, I second-guessed my decision not to level with Lily about how Mae had really died, but the knowledge would probably just worry the poor girl for nothing. She already had enough to handle after losing her roommate. All young people thought they were invincible. I knew only too well that they were not.

ELEVEN

Back in the car, I called Reilly's cell. It rang five times before he picked up. "You back among the living?" I asked.

"Barely. You making progress?"

"Some. Up for a beer?"

"Always."

"Meet me at the Black Thorn on Clarence. You know it?"

"I've made a thorough study of every pub in town. Get a table on the patio, if you can."

The Black Thorn was my go-to pub in the ByWard Market. It had an easy-going, lived-in look, the kind that didn't immediately say interior decorator. The two-storey Victorian that housed it sat just below the fortress-like American embassy, which formed the western edge of the market. The Parliament Buildings loomed above it, casting the patio in early evening shadows by the time I arrived.

The area behind the Black Thorn was framed by even older stone buildings on Sussex, creating a private courtyard in the midst of the noise and chaos of the market, Ottawa's main area for nightlife, such as it was. Fifty years ago, people had come here to buy cucumbers. Now, they came to get pickled.

Reilly entered through the patio's back entrance, wearing jeans and a navy golf shirt hanging outside his pants. He probably imagined he was blending in with the crowd, but he might as well have had the police logo on his shirt. You could make Reilly as a cop the minute he entered a room and I was sure that the tails-out shirt was meant to disguise the fact that he had a holster clipped to his belt. At least he looked a little better than the last time I had seen him, now freshly-shaven and his grey hair dark and still wet from the shower.

Reilly sat heavily on the chair across from me, caught the server's eye and pointed at the pint I had been sipping, raising his finger to indicate another.

"So, how's your investigation going?" he asked.

"I think that's supposed to be my line."

"I've only got one thing. You go first."

"OK. I've found out a bit more about Mae Wang."

I detailed the basic stuff I had learned from Horsley and Lily Liu, then said, "There are two things I think are important. First, the roommate tells me that she learned about Mae's death when the RCMP came to her door. She didn't report Mae missing and she said nothing about any contact in the RCMP. I didn't push her on it, but there's no reason for her to lie about that, and the other things she told me rang true."

Reilly shook his head. "Lying pricks. It doesn't surprise me. I was pretty certain this superintendent I was dealing with was bullshitting me from the get go. Good thing he's a cop because he'd never have made it as a criminal. Lousy liar."

"So that means the RCMP knew who Mae Wang was and decided to get into this on their own. Any theories?"

"Could have come from a lot of directions," Reilly said. "CSIS, CSEC, maybe their own intel people. They all pay a lot of attention to the Chinese Embassy and the people associated with it."

"I know what CSIS is, but what's CSEC?"

"Communications Security Establishment Canada. They're out in the east end. These guys eavesdrop on electronic communications, hack into computers, Christ knows what. They monitor everything that comes in or goes out of the embassy. They're not spies like the guys at CSIS, but it's the same line. The CSIS guys themselves watch the people who work there or visit the embassy. The RCMP boys who provide 'security' outside the embassy gates note everybody coming and going, too. Mae Wang must have been on their radar."

"Yeah, but that doesn't explain why they were so quick to know about her murder."

"Had to be under surveillance."

"Because of her work as an interpreter?" I asked, not hiding my scepticism.

"If that's what she was."

"You know different?"

"Not yet, but I had a buddy with the Vancouver police check into the idea that Mae had family in that city. This guy has a pretty good feel for the Chinese community there, but he came up empty. Mae Wang, Carleton student and embassy interpreter, doesn't exist. Not by that name. Mae, or whoever she really was, simply made up her background. There are people in China who make a damned good living creating fake identities for people who want to come here. Usually, they're rich gangsters who want to launder their money."

What Reilly was saying confirmed my own thinking, but that didn't make it helpful. "As much as I like the woman of mystery angle, I'd like it a lot better if we could prove that her identity was fake."

"There are people who probably can. If the Mounties or their spook friends were paying attention to Mae Wang, there's a decent chance they know her real identity. She was either a Chinese spy, or they suspected she was."

"Seriously?"

"Sure. The embassy here is full of spies. Really, that's the only reason they bother to have one. They keep an eye on the local Chinese community, but the real work is stealing military and industrial secrets."

"But Mae didn't have any diplomatic status. She was just an interpreter."

"There has to be more to it than that," Reilly said.

"You think the Chinese killed Mae?"

"No. If they had, they wouldn't have had to pull that stunt at the morgue to get her body back. She'd just have disappeared and no one would be any the wiser."

"It's a great story, if true, but even in a column, I need something more than speculation. If the Mounties aren't telling you what's going on, they aren't going to tell me."

"Doesn't mean we can't find out. It pisses me off when a fellow cop lies to my face. I'm sure it's the usual national security bullshit, but they use that to cover up a multitude of sins. I'd like to find out who Mae was, even if it's just to twist their noses."

"I'm for that, but how are you going to do it?"

"I know some people. Let me see what I can find out.

"You said there were two interesting things. What else have you got?"

"The roommate tells me that Mae Wang slept somewhere else two nights a week, Tuesday and Thursday."

Reilly smiled. "I'll bet she wasn't doing much sleeping. Could she have been working for an escort service? That could take this in a whole different direction."

I hadn't considered that. "No, I don't think so. I'm not basing that on anything but gut instinct, but Mae seemed pretty busy with school and her work. Would she have been working as an interpreter if she could have made easier money doing something else? I don't think the roommate would have told me about Mae's two-night-a-week thing, either, if she was in the life."

"Probably not," Reilly conceded, nodding. "Tuesday and Thursday suggests someone who is maybe here during the week for business or has a wife and family he needs to spend the weekends with. I'm thinking the boinking must have taken place at your building. We've got a pretty heavy surveillance camera presence on Elgin. Let me see what I can find out."

I took a long pull on my Keith's White and said, "You thinking the boyfriend was worried she would blow the whistle on him?"

"Maybe. If so, he's a boyfriend with a lot to lose. Of course, our investigation was at a very preliminary stage when the plug got pulled. All we had determined was that Mae Wang didn't rent an apartment in the building. She could have been visiting anyone there."

The idea that there could be a killer in my building was creepy, even creepier if he found out that I was asking questions about Mae Wang's death.

"I can give you one lead on the boyfriend. I interviewed a guy called Ron Horsley, Carleton professor. The guy clearly had the hots for Mae, something that was confirmed by the roommate. He's got to be 60, though. I can't see the two of them together."

Reilly laughed. "Yeah, who'd want to screw an old bugger like that?"

"You haven't seen Horsley."

"I'll check it out."

"So what's next?" I asked.

"Normally, I'd get some uniforms, canvass the building, show Mae Wang's photo, see if anyone recognized her. I've got no resources on this, though. Maybe this joint task force will get around to doing the basics, eventually. More likely, they will sit on their hands because no one is going to speak up for this girl. No family, no one who gives a shit."

"Well, don't look at me. I'm not going to knock on my neighbors' doors asking if any of them committed murder lately."

"Leave it with me." Reilly drained his pint and said, "I've got to get going. I do have actual cases I'm responsible for. Let's stay in touch on this, shall we? Someone is trying to get away with murder here, but the coverup from guys who are supposed to be on our side is almost as bad. When you get into this diplomatic shit, none of the normal rules apply. I have a hard time with that."

"Me too," I said. The Mae Wang story was proving to be more layered and complex than I had at first imagined, and I was still skimming along the surface. If Reilly was right, what lay beneath was dynamite, but it was frustratingly difficult to establish anything as a fact.

"Look, Kris, be careful with this," Reilly said. "Whoever is behind this killing is obviously dangerous and you might have already put yourself on their radar by asking around."

I nodded. I had been interviewing hardened criminals and gang members for years, and I used to think I was invincible. I had found out the hard way how easy it was for powerful people to take someone like me off the board.

I thanked Reilly for his help and watched him make his way through the maze of tables on the patio and back into the pub itself. He hadn't asked me a single question about Suzy Morin. Either he had accepted that I really had no information or he was finally starting to move on. Hopefully not in my direction.

TWELVE

"Tea?" Colin asked.

I would really have preferred coffee. Saturday morning at 9:30 was time for a caffeine jolt, not for fiddling with tea. Colin was already fussing with the teapot and his beloved Earl Grey, though.

"Sure, tea would be great."

When I had called earlier in the morning to update him on the Mae Wang developments, I had been thinking that it was something that could be done on the phone, but Colin had insisted I come around to his apartment. Given our history, I was wary of that. When a man is in love with you, and you're not sure if you are in love with him, managing expectations is important.

I glanced around the condo, searching hopefully for evidence of recent female habitation; a lipstick-stained glass, a lingering whiff of perfume, maybe even a discarded thong. Any of those would be a welcome sign that I had been replaced.

I searched in vain. The place was pristine as usual, the white leather furniture and black granite kitchen countertop setting the simple theme chosen by the developer's designer. I was a bit surprised to see that Colin had started to personalize things since I had moved out. When we were together the place was basically a hotel room, but Colin had added a bank of four televisions to the living room wall, tuned to the news networks of CBC, CTV, CNN and Fox. He had acquired a massive oak desk, shoved up against the main window to take advantage of the fifteenth floor view. The desk top was neat and I suspected he didn't do much actual work there. Arrayed across the desk was part of Colin's collection of celebrity pictures, showing him with Tony Blair, Jean Chretien, Stephen Harper and Benjamin Netanyahu. In a slightly larger frame and placed in front of the rest was a shot of a much younger Colin wearing a flak jacket and helmet during his war correspondent days. I knew that he had always been miles from the action, but his time in the Falklands was the high point of Colin's career, in his own view. He never tired of talking about it, unaware that others tired of listening.

I was sure the rest of Colin's vast collection of trophy pictures was still in the bedroom. I'd always found that a bit creepy. Who wanted to have sex in front of a picture of her boyfriend with the Queen?

It was definitely a male lair, without a trace of a woman's presence. Before me, Colin was noted for consuming women the way other men consumed potato chips. I wasn't sure whether our relationship had saved him or ruined him.

He finished with his tea preparation. Pot pre-heated, tea steeped exactly five minutes, just a touch of milk.

"Black for me," I said.

"Yes, I recall," he said, smiling.

On the weekend, he didn't wear his usual dark-suit editor uniform, looking much more relaxed in a denim shirt, khaki pants and some sort of reddish loafers with tassels. Those could be improved upon, I thought, but overall, I preferred weekend Colin.

"Right then, tell me about your jumper."

Clearly, he was humouring me. "*My* jumper?" I asked.

"Well, you have rather taken her on. What's her name again?"

"Mae Wang. At least, that was the name she went by. There is no record of such a person actually existing."

"Not entirely unusual. With the Chinese one-child policy, a lot of children never officially exist, especially girls."

"This is something more than that. The story has moved quite a bit since we spoke about it Thursday night. For starters, this is definitely a homicide. I have that from the Ottawa police."

"Ah, not a jumper then. Interesting."

"That's just the start. It looks like there was a struggle on the roof of my building and that she was pushed off. And get this, a big posse of people from the Chinese Embassy showed up at the morgue and basically bullied the guy on night duty into giving them the body. Some bullshit about Chinese burial customs. The body's long gone now."

Colin sipped his tea and leaned forward in his leather armchair.

"Now this is starting to sound like a story."

"There is one other intriguing angle. The Mounties bigfooted the Ottawa Police and turned this into a joint investigation, with them in the lead. National security. They gave my police contact a line of bull about how they were the first to know the girl was killed. From what I hear, she might be some kind of Chinese spy and the Mounties had her under surveillance."

"Hmm, I can see the headline: Chinese Spy Murdered In Ottawa Love Nest," Colin said.

I wasn't sure whether he was serious or having me on. "Fleet Street flashback?" I asked.

"They do know how to present a story. Tell me, what inquiries have you made so far?"

"I have spoken to Mae Wang's graduate student adviser at Carleton and to her room-mate. I'm working with an Ottawa police source, as well. Even though he's off the case, he's still digging into it."

"Reilly?"

"Yes," I said, annoyed that Colin would know my source's identity.

"We're certainly not at a publishable stage yet," he said. "We could go with something on the death being a homicide, but all that would do is attract the jackals from the other news organizations. No one else is on to this yet, I trust?"

"No, I'm quite sure of that."

"You and Reilly, do you have a special relationship?"

"Jesus Colin, are you asking if I'm screwing him? Last time I looked that was Suzy Morin's beat."

"Well, quite, but I hear that's not on any longer."

"You hear correctly, but I'm certainly not lining up to take her place."

"So there is a line then?" he asked, smiling. No doubt happy that I wasn't in it.

"Only the same one that every middle-aged guy imagines."

"Ah, touché."

"Here's my problem. I'm going to be stuck in court day after day covering this Sandhu trial. Interesting situation, interesting back story, but a lot of the trial itself will be as dull as mud. The star witnesses will be interesting, and Sandhu himself, if they bring him on. The usual arm wrestling between the lawyers and the judge will be deadly stuff, though."

"I'm sure. Still, those who care about such things tell me your coverage of the trial is getting more hits online than anything else we're offering."

"Well, that's something, I guess. Must be the celebrity gossip angle. It's still going to make it tough for me to dig into the Mae Wang story. That could be huge, and exclusive. We can't just let it go."

"Agreed," Colin said, placing his teacup on the black coffee table that filled the space between us. "My inclination is to ask you to work with Suzy Morin on this. She *is* the police reporter. She and Reilly, are they able to work together?"

"I think he's still madly in love with her. Christ knows why. The woman's an airhead. What she thinks, or if she thinks, I have no idea."

Colin sat back in his chair, as if to escape the range of my claws.

"I guess this is your way of saying you and Suzy wouldn't make a natural pairing."

"You got it."

"Perhaps I should ask her to undertake the entire thing, then."

"Oh, don't be an asshole. This is my story."

"There's something else," he said, frowning and sweeping back his longish grey hair. I had seen this gesture before, and it had never been the prelude to anything good.

"It worries me that this girl was thrown from your building. Why that building, and why just at the time that you habitually leave for work? And then there is the Chinese angle. The Chinese are very serious people, Kris. Embassy employees aren't here to attend the Dragon Boat Festival and thrill us with the details of their bloody culture. They're looking for the weak links in the human chain, to collect as much military, business and political information as they can. Despite their vigorous efforts, not everything can be learned by hacking into our computers."

"I get that, but I've spent my whole career dealing with scumbags and criminals."

"Just so, but these people act unfailingly in their own interest and there is really no limit to what they are capable of. They can commit murder and get nothing more than a slap on the wrist from our government and a ticket back home. That stunt you described at the morgue was just an opening act. I hear things on the diplomatic circuit, you know. I don't go to all these tedious dinners just for hors d'oeuvres."

"So what do we do, give them a free pass because they're bad guys? I'm not afraid of these pricks."

"Well, maybe you should be. The last time you took on ruthless authority figures, things didn't turn out terribly well."

"Yes, I'm aware that several people ended up dead, that it was mostly my fault, and that you and I were lucky to escape with our lives. Does that mean that I have to spend the rest of my life in the fetal position?"

Only a few days ago, I had been wondering whether I still gave a damn about anything. The Mae Wang story and all the arrogant string-pulling had shifted my attitude.

"First of all, what happened down there was not your fault. Those who helped you volunteered, and those who received rough justice got what they had coming to them."

It was a message Colin had given me many times in my recovery period. Maybe I would eventually come to believe it.

"Now, I understand that you're a lone wolf, Kris, but I want you to get Suzy to do some legwork for you. She has good contacts in the RCMP and in the intelligence agencies. I think that's where this story lies. What you've uncovered so far is intriguing, but it's a story full of questions with very few answers. There is a lot more work to be done.

"It will still be your story, top byline and nothing in the paper until we are all satisfied. Let her gather some information and then we can assess where we are at. There are extremely serious implications in what you've told me today. We need to make sure it's locked down tight."

"What, and you think I can't do that?"

"Of course not, but I need you to cover that trial. It's going to be page one for weeks. The approach you proposed with the wife is intriguing. I also want to know what Luc Champagne's angle is. You can be sure he's got one. Chaps like that always do. The wife is already pointing us in that direction."

"All right," I said, knowing I really didn't have a choice and that there wasn't one other person in the newsroom who would have had the chance to debate this with Colin at his place on a Saturday morning. His normal style was command and control.

The idea of sharing a story with Suzy Morin was repugnant, but there would probably be a way to get Suzy to do the grunt work and still grab the story back later.

"So it's back at the courthouse Monday morning, and no more poking into the Chinese business for now," Colin said

"Sure." I was certain that I would deliver on at least one of those demands.

"Excellent. And you'll meet with Suzy, bring her up to speed?"

"Yes. You might want to give her a head's up, just so she doesn't think I'm sticking her with some piece of crap that I don't want."

"Done." Then, switching personas in that disconcerting way he had, Colin said, "It's a lovely morning. Fancy a walk down to the market? We could grab a croissant."

My first inclination was to say no. I had worked hard to keep Colin at bay. On the other hand, I had probably loved him once, I still liked him now, and he had saved my life. All of that ought to be worth an hour of my time.

"Sure, why not?" I said, trying not to think of the obvious answers to my question.

THIRTEEN

Justice Roderick Macpherson settled into his position and said, "All right people, it's Monday morning and I intend to make up some ground this week. My aim is to resolve this matter within the allotted sitting days.

"Ms Faulkner, I hope you are going to tell me that Vikram Gill is present and ready to testify."

Faulkner rose and with an apologetic shrug said, "I'm afraid Mr. Gill is ill again today, your honour. I'm told he suffers from migraine headaches."

I felt my day slowly starting to circle the drain. Testimony of one of the two accusers would make an easy column, leaving me mental energy to think about what to do next on the Mae Wang story. I was eager, too, to see just how wobbly Gill would be.

Macpherson shook his head, clearly frustrated. "All right then," he said, his tone suggesting that this latest delay was anything but all right. "Who do you have for us, Ms Faulkner?"

"The Crown would like to call Inspector Terry Carmichael."

Macpherson looked up in surprise. "Not Thomas Fung?" he said, shuffling through papers on his desk with visible annoyance.

"We would like to keep those witnesses in sequence, your honour. Inspector Carmichael will lead us through the genesis of the case."

"Genesis, always a good story to start with," the judge said.

I shot a glance at the rest of the media crowd. The older ones were smiling at Macpherson's remark, the younger ones didn't seem to get it. Had any journalist under the age of 30 ever opened the Bible? Not that I had spent a lot of time with the book myself, just enough to know that I favoured the Old Testament rules.

On the surface, it looked as if Faulkner's case was in a bit of disarray. Lawyers carefully planned the order of their witnesses to help build the story they wanted to tell. I had expected that Faulkner would use her two star witnesses, Fung and Gill, to establish the case against Sandhu, then lead the investigator through questions designed to shore up any weaknesses Bernstein uncovered in his cross-examination.

At the defence table, Bernstein and his two colleagues were scrambling through documents and binders, bringing to hand the materials the Crown would have released about Carmichael's investigation, and the questions the defence planned to ask him.

Bernstein and his second, Pittman, were conferring in low voices, so as not to help the big ears in the media. Pittman was trying to make a point, but Bernstein dismissed it with a curt shake of the head. I guessed that Pittman was arguing for a protest over shaking up the witness list, but Bernstein wouldn't bite.

"Bring him on then, Ms Faulkner," the judge said.

Carmichael took the stand, was sworn and settled in like he was at home in his favourite chair. I remembered that I had seen Carmichael in action once before. He was a strong witness and tough to shake off his version of the truth.

Faulkner opened the large binder in front of her and flipped to the appropriate tab. "Now, Inspector Carmichael, for the benefit of the record, could you describe your position and experience with the RCMP?"

"Yes. I am the lead investigator with the commercial crime branch in the National Capital Region, which investigates matters such as fraud and political corruption. Myself, I have been with the RCMP for 27 years, 10 of those with commercial crime."

Nice work to mention political corruption right in the opener. Maybe I wasn't going to miss Vikram Gill after all. Carmichael's testimony would still be the first time the Crown had really gotten into the details.

"All right, inspector, I think that establishes your credentials. Now let's turn to the matters that brought us here today. Can you tell the court how you first became aware of these allegations against Mr. Sandhu?"

"We were contacted by an official in the federal government, a person with oversight of the program that Mr. Fung and Mr. Gill had applied to, seeking a federal grant for their wind power project.

The person alleged that the project was bogus and the grant was improperly obtained."

"And the allegation seemed credible to you?"

"The source seemed credible. I had no view on the validity of the allegation at that time."

It was important to show the investigator to be completely impartial, but I had read the documentation Carmichael had put together to obtain search warrants. It was typical of the dark picture the police painted to persuade a judge or justice of the peace to grant the warrant. The media routinely reported on the "information to obtain" in an important case as if it were all factual. Faulkner would pick and choose now.

"And your initial focus, inspector, that was on Mr. Gill and Mr. Fung?"

"That's correct."

"And how did Mr. Sandhu come to be involved in your investigation?"

Smart move. Don't dwell on Gill and Fung and what a pair of crooks they likely were. No doubt Bernstein wouldn't be as kind.

"We investigated the normal procedures for the Renewable Power For A Strong Canada program, as they call it. The typical paperwork and due diligence that was done, the amount of time it took to get an approval. That sort of thing."

"And generally, what did you find?"

"It was a slow process. Federal bureaucracy, lots of paperwork and delays. Some grants were given out."

"And how long did the process take, typically?"

"Eighteen to 24 months."

Faulkner paused to let that one sink in.

"So up to two years to get an approval through. Inspector, remind us how long the Gill-Fung project took."

"Just two months."

"Did that strike you as unusual?"

"Objection," Bernstein said. "Inspector Carmichael is a police officer, not an expert on federal project approval."

It was a weak objection, but Macpherson sustained it. "Please rephrase Ms Faulkner."

"Inspector, in your direct research on this particular grant program, did the Gill-Fung project stand out in terms of how quickly it was approved?"

"Yes, it did. This was the fastest approval given. The next fastest was one year."

"And given the anomalous nature of this project, did that lend credibility to the original information you received?" Faulkner said.

"It did. It seemed that there was something unusual about this particular project."

"And in what direction did your investigation go next?"

Carmichael shifted in his chair, and adjusted his tie. I imagined that he spent a fair amount of time in front of the mirror on the average day. Typical middle-aged guy who thought he still had it.

"We dug deeper into the particular approval process for this project."

"And what did you discover?"

"The standard application form was filled out, but the usual bureaucratic evaluation was missing. We inquired with departmental staff and were told that the project had been flagged from the political side."

"Flagged from the political side? Can you explain that for the court?"

"Of course. The assistant deputy minister in charge of the program had received a call from the industry minister's parliamentary secretary, suggesting that the minister would be very pleased if this particular application were quickly approved."

"The minister?" Faulkner said, adopting an expression of fake surprise.

"The minister of industry, yes."

"And who was the minister at that time?"

"That was Luc Champagne."

My media colleagues started to tweet furiously, thinking they were going to get a Luc Champagne angle out of this. Maybe this was what Gail Rakic had been referring to when she talked about what Champagne was up to. Champagne and Sandhu had been seen as the two leading contenders for the future Conservative leadership at the time that Champagne had deep-sixed his deputy. The political motivation was obvious.

"And you spoke to Mr. Champagne about this, I assume?"

"I did not," Carmichael said "but my colleagues did. I can tell you that their inquiries established that Minister Champagne had no familiarity with this project whatsoever and that he had not spoken to his parliamentary secretary about it."

Bernstein was up again. "Objection. This is a critical point. I am going to want to cross-examine the officer who gathered that information."

"Agreed," the judge said. "Ms Faulkner, I expect you will present this information direct from that particular horseman's mouth at some point."

The lawyers gave the obligatory laugh at the judge's witticism. One of the many great things about being a judge was that at least some of the people in the room were going to appreciate your jokes.

"I will, your honour."

"Let's hold this line of questioning until then. Please focus on matters of which Inspector Carmichael has direct knowledge."

"Of course. So, inspector, returning to your investigation, you determined that the accused, Mr. Sandhu, was the parliamentary secretary involved?"

"I did."

"Very good. Now, I'd like to lead you through your forensic investigation of the financial affairs of Mr. Gill and Mr. Fung."

Christ, this was going to be tedious. I wasn't really a numbers person. I hoped Faulkner wouldn't take too long to get to the part where dirty money from the two crooks had shown up in Sandhu's bank account. If she could prove that, Bernstein was going to have a problem. Faulkner had already opened the door with the testimony about Sandhu's call to the bureaucrat. Would he deny it?

As Faulkner continued to outline her case, I thought back to my conversation with Gail, and her vague comments about Luc Champagne. Did she mean anything more than that Champagne had dimed Sandhu to cover his own ass and kneecap a rival? That would be practically standard operating procedure.

I needed to talk to Gail again. If I was going to be stuck in court for weeks, I wanted to find out what was really going on, not just the competing exaggerations that the lawyers would spoon feed to the judge and the media. It was going to be a challenge with Bernstein's legal team keeping a protective eye on their client and his wife. The smoking thing would get old in a hurry, too. I needed a new gambit.

I saw my chance about 15 minutes later. The Crown was nearing the conclusion of Carmichael's testimony and a break would be coming up, but Gail was going to beat the rush. She walked up the aisle of the courtroom without acknowledging the curious spectators who were gawking at her from both sides. I gave her a short head start, then ducked out of the back of the room myself, just in time to see Gail heading into the washroom.

I followed, but by the time I entered, Gail was already in a stall. I washed my hands and reviewed my rudimentary attempt at makeup, then ran wet fingers through my short hair. My new look had the virtue of low maintenance.

I was rooting in my purse, watching the mirror for action behind me, when Gail emerged from the stall, rolled her eyes up and said, "You again. Are you stalking me?"

"Powdering my nose. I hope you aren't put off by the Crown's bluster. They try to make everyone sound like a mass murderer."

"Yes, I'm aware. What do you want?"

I glanced around to make sure we were alone in the washroom, then said, "OK, let's cut right to it. Last week, you implied that Luc Champagne was behind your husband's troubles. Something more than what we heard this morning. It wouldn't surprise me a bit. I've looked into the guy enough to know he's a snake. You want to nail Champagne, I'm the one to do it. I'm going to need a little more than vague insinuation though. You going to help me out or not?"

Gail smiled, showing perfect teeth, and plenty of them. I imagined that they were sharp.

"Interesting offer. I'm not so sure about the timing. We've got a lot to deal with right now."

"Of course. No need for the story to appear until after the trial. I'm sure it will take me a while to get to the bottom of all this. It could be a real PR counterattack for you, though, if it pans out."

"It will pan out."

"So what do you think, can we get together to get into the specifics?"

Gail washed her hands, her bright red fingernails shining under the flow of the water. She gave her hands a shake, made sure the

nail job was intact, then inserted her hands in the Dyson dryer. I
wondered if I was being literally blown off.

Once her hands were dry, Gail snapped open her black leather
Prada bag and fished out a business card. It identified her as senior
vice-president of Rakic Construction and included cell and office
numbers. "Call me on my cell," she said. "I might pick up."

With that, Gail visibly composed herself, squared her shoulders
and went back out to face her public ordeal.

FOURTEEN

The courtroom lunch break didn't come a minute too soon. It was the key to sanity when covering a long trial, a much needed chance to stop being constantly attentive to the droning of lawyers. The idea of occupying that little bit of time talking to Suzy Morin was extremely unappealing, but Colin had dispatched her to the courthouse for the turnover on the Mae Wang story. Saying no wasn't really an option.

I could see her now, weaving her way through the tables of the little lower-level cafeteria that served the courthouse. Suzy Morin was a newspaper reporter with TV looks. Her blond hair was shoulder length and probably natural, if the blue eyes were a guide. Her nose was a little bit big, but other than that, Suzy's face was flawless. She had to be about 35, but you'd never know it in her form-fitting black dress.

Suzy and I probably wouldn't have been BFFs at the best of times, but it didn't help that we did different versions of the same job. Until I showed up, Suzy had owned the police beat. Now, I got to dip in and scoop up the juiciest stories for my column. Maybe Suzy getting a piece of the Mae Wang story was some kind of karmic payback.

When Suzy had texted me earlier, she had uncharacteristically offered to pay for lunch. She must be expensing it. Suzy seated herself at the Formica-topped table in a swish of perfume and handed me a sandwich overflowing with breaded chicken, cheese and mayonnaise, then delicately unfolded her own, cucumbers and lettuce on a petite whole wheat bun.

Suzy crossed her panty-hosed legs, gave me her insincere smile and said, "So, what can you tell me about this Chinese spy thing?"

"We don't even know if she is one. That's what we're trying to find out."

"OK, so let's start at the beginning."

What a logical idea. Would all of her interview questions be this astute?

"I'm really too busy with the Sandhu trial to take this on myself. Colin said you could do some of the leg work, get things rolling."

Suzy sniffed in distaste at this, but settled for a noncommittal "Oh yes."

"Here's the thing. I think there is a hell of a story in this, but we're only seeing the tip of the iceberg." I immediately wished I could edit out the cliché, but I didn't expect that it would bother Suzy.

Glancing at my watch, I said, "She called herself Mae Wang, but I think the name and identity are probably phoney. Whoever she was, we know she was young, attractive and an interpreter who often worked for the Chinese Embassy. We also suspect that she was seeing someone mysterious on a regular basis, Tuesday and Thursday nights. We believe she was thrown off the roof of my apartment building. We also know that people from the Chinese Embassy bullied their way into the morgue and made off with the body. As far as we can tell, the RCMP was aware of Mae and what-ever she was up to.

"The interesting part is that now they want to cover it up. They are supposedly leading a joint investigation into the homicide, but there doesn't appear to be any investigating going on. I think they have put this one on their national security shelf, filed somewhere between So What and Who Cares?"

Suzy nodded and said, "So, we find out who Mae Wang was screwing and I think we've got our story."

"That would take us a long way towards it. Colin tells me you've got some pretty good contacts with the Mounties and in the intel-ligence agencies."

Suzy shrugged her slim shoulders. "Some," she said. I imagined that Suzy's "some" was the equivalent of a poker player with a full-house saying he had "some" cards. Reporters with real con-tacts kept the names close to the vest. The ones who bragged about everyone they knew didn't know much at all.

"Just so we're straight up from the start," Suzy said. "We work on this together, pool our resources, joint byline. Are we on the same page?"

"Sure." I could afford to be generous, having held back the

roommate, the Carleton professor and Reilly's involvement. I wasn't sure if Reilly was a no-go zone for Suzy, but I hoped so.

She took a small bite of her sandwich and then ran a manicured fingernail across her glossy red lips, looking for possible crumbs. "Look Kris, I know we are basically rivals and this is all a bit odd, working together. Let's try to make it work out, OK? This sounds like a really good story. This Mae Wang, or whoever she was, deserves some justice."

I struggled to keep my eyes from rolling up. Maybe Suzy still believed in justice, even after all her years on the police beat, but I would bet she would take a scoop over justice any day of the week.

"Yes, well, that would be something wouldn't it?" I said. "Look, I've got to get back. The trial will be starting again in a few minutes."

"Of course. I've got to run myself."

Suzy wrapped up the half of her sandwich that she hadn't consumed and tossed it in a waste receptacle. She got quickly to her feet, straightened her dress, flashed me a quick smile and headed back towards the main courthouse doors.

How did other women learn to roll their hips like that? I didn't even understand the mechanics of it. Not that it would matter if I did. I had no ass at all.

Watching Suzy slide elegantly through the crowd, I had to admit that I was a little jealous of her. She couldn't have sunk the hook so deeply into Reilly unless she had more than I gave her credit for. Suzy and Reilly had made it work for quite a while, too. I had never been able to sustain a long relationship with a man.

Maybe the problem was just that we were natural rivals, doing two different versions of the same job. When I had a competitor, I wanted to beat her. "Plays well with others" wasn't a comment that teachers had ever marked on my report card.

Perhaps Colin had been smart to put the two of us together. We would both work furiously to get the bigger slice of the Mae Wang story. That didn't mean I had to like it.

* * *

Suzy pushed open the heavy glass doors of the courthouse and stepped into the fresh spring air. What a relief to get away from that grotty food court and its greasy smells. She hoped it hadn't stunk up her dress.

And Kris Redner. What a bitch. Suzy hoped that neither Kris nor her lovelorn admirer the editor seriously thought Suzy was going to do "leg work" and let Kris get all the glory. Suzy had owned the police beat for years before Kris came swanning in from Toronto with the new editor and had suddenly become the crime columnist, a job the paper had never even had before. If they needed a crime columnist, Suzy knew she was the best and most obvious choice. She just hadn't had the foresight to screw the editor. Apparently that relationship had hit the rocks, but Kris was still treated like a queen. Who could forget that ridiculous puff piece *Maclean's* wrote about her when she was still back in Toronto? Canada's queen of crime. As if.

Still, the Mae Wang story was intriguing and a welcome relief from writing about drug gang shitheads who always seemed to be shooting at each other, but never connecting. That was really getting old.

If this Chinese girl was actually a spy of some sort, the story would go national, probably international. She could definitely look forward to a number of TV appearances. Suzy had great connections with all the key network producers. They knew she was always good for a clip or a whole interview. Kris might get top byline in the *Citizen*, but Suzy was sure she could still make the story her own. Why would anyone on television want to interview that gloomy string bean? Suzy had to admit that Kris looked a bit better now that she had finally done something with her hair, even if it was a garish red dye job. Suzy was proud of her own natural blond hair. So what if she did colour it slightly?

Suzy had kept her plan vague when talking to Kris, but she knew just who she was going to talk to first. Pierre Lacroix was her main guy at A Division. The Mountie had recently been promoted to assistant commissioner and always seemed to know everything that was happening over there. Pierre was 50 years old and married, but he was also a real hound. She could guarantee that he'd be up for drinks tonight. They'd exchange information for flirtation. It seemed like a good deal all around, especially because Pierre had never had the nerve to try to take it to the next level.

Then Suzy had an idea that was even better. What about Vanessa, her workout buddy from the gym? Vanessa was one of those cute, earnest, smart young women who flocked to the Hill to serve the great men who worked there. In Vanessa's case, that meant being EA to someone in the PMO who Vanessa always said "knew everything about everybody."

Suzy and Vanessa had met in pilates class and kind of hit it off, although Vanessa did like to go on and on about the world of politics, like it was the biggest thing in the universe. She loved to gossip, though. Who knew what she might be able to find out about something as juicy as a Chinese spy story? If there was really something to it, her boss would know. Suzy was pretty sure Vanessa was doing the guy, too, so her access would be even better.

Suzy smiled to herself. She felt confident that she could outdo the great Kris Redner on her own story and do it quick, too. This was going to be fun.

FIFTEEN

Sometimes it seemed like a trial would poke along forever, but things could change in a hurry. Faulkner had finished with the police inspector and Bernstein had been unexpectedly brief in his cross-examination. I expected he was saving his ammunition for the less credible witnesses, Gill and Fung.

Faulkner said, "Your honour, Mr. Gill has received some medical treatment and is here in the building and prepared to testify. I will call him as my next witness."

"All right, Ms. Faulkner. Glad to hear that. Let's hear what Mr. Gill has to say," the judge said.

I wondered again if the whole Gill out, Gill in thing had been nothing more than a way to screw with Bernstein. As a columnist, I could suggest it, but it wouldn't win me any points with the Crown. Maybe it was a little early in the trial for scorched earth. The bad news was, the column I had already worked out in my head was likely headed for the mental wastebasket. Whatever Gill had to say would almost certainly top the day's news now.

The doors at the back of the court opened and I turned to watch Vikram Gill shuffle his way up the aisle toward the witness box. In contrast to the GQ approach taken by the RCMP inspector, Gill had chosen a gold-coloured polyester jacket that looked too large for him, as if he had been ill and lost weight. Maybe it had been on sale at Moore's and 46 tall was the only size left. Gill's brown pants were rumpled and his green tie was askew. He was dark skinned but it didn't offer the sense of vitality projected by Sandhu. Gill's eyes were baggy and his features slack. I made him as mid-50s. As he passed by my seat, I could smell some kind of hair oil that was meant to enhance Gill's suspiciously dark comb-forward fringe.

One thing for sure, he didn't look like the kind of guy to whom anyone would give $1.5 mil. Good thing they didn't ask for a photo with those grant applications.

Gill took the stand and was sworn in. He had a thick, guttural accent that made his words difficult to understand. I began to wonder why the Crown was in such a hurry to get this joker on the stand. Or maybe Faulkner was just in a hurry to get him off.

"So, Mr. Gill," she said, "let's start by filling the court in on who you are. You have a background in engineering, correct?"

"Oh yes. Delhi Technological University."

Bernstein was furiously scribbling notes. I guessed we would later discover that there was a difference between a background in engineering and actually being an engineer.

"And how do you earn your living, Mr. Gill?"

Defrauding the government would be the correct answer, I thought, but Gill said, "I am a property developer in the Brampton area."

"And how long have you been in that business, sir."

"Twenty years. Ever since I came from India."

"So it would be fair to say that you are quite well-established, then?"

"Oh yes, very much so. I am a pillar of the Indo-Canadian community."

It took some balls to say that, given the circumstances.

"Now, tell us about the particular development proposal that led you to make an application for the federal wind energy program."

"I have, for many years, owned a fine piece of property on the edge of Brampton. Farm land today, but a wonderful subdivision tomorrow. In Ontario, with provincial rules, it is very, very difficult to get approvals for new housing. I had made a proposal to Brampton city council, asking for a focus on Indo-Canadian community. This is my target market."

"And what happened with that proposal, sir?" Faulkner asked.

"They turned it down flat. That's when Mr. Fung and I, we put our heads together, and came up with a new idea."

"And that was the sustainable, wind-powered subdivision?" Faulkner asked, leading him along.

"Oh yes. A very clever idea. I hear from friends in the Conservative Party that there is a fine wind program to help make Canada greener. I see the opportunity to do something for the environment, while helping council to discover a good new reason for our project to go ahead."

"So you looked into the program, and applied for it in the usual way?" Faulkner said.

"Yes, we did that. We even used consultant to help us fill in the paperwork. Very, very complex paperwork."

"And what happened next?"

"Nothing. A month went by, we heard nothing."

"A month, but that wasn't really very long for a government grant approval was it?"

"Well, time is money in development. We had gone back to city council to talk about our new wind subdivision, see if they liked it. Another consultant, more money. Councillors are liking the idea but they say it will only be credible if we can get federal grant. If our project is not ready to go, they will approve one from competitor instead. For us, that would mean the window is closed."

"So you needed a quick answer from the federal government?"

"We did, but you know government. Nothing quick." Gill laughed at this remark and got a titter of laughter from the audience as well. Everyone in Ottawa knew the pace at which the feds worked.

"So what did you do next, Mr. Gill?"

"We turned to our MP, Mr. Sandhu."

"And did you know Mr. Sandhu before seeking his assistance with the wind project?"

"Everyone in Brampton knows Sonny Sandhu. I myself met him on more than one occasion at Conservative Party events, and one time he came and spoke to us at the Indo-Canadian Chamber of Commerce."

Gill paused to take a drink from the water glass in front of him, then took a somewhat grimy-looking handkerchief from his pants pocket and wiped his brow.

"So you were acquainted with Mr. Sandhu. Did you consider him a friend?"

Gill shrugged. "A politician is everyone's friend."

"So did you approach Mr. Sandhu personally, or deal with someone from his office?"

"I went to his office, but asked to speak to him directly. As I said, we had met before."

"Mr. Sandhu must be a busy man. Was he able to accommodate you?"

"Oh yes, he was very gracious. He saw Mr. Fung and myself right away."

"And where did this meeting take place?" Faulkner asked.

"It was at his constituency office."

"His private office?"

"Yes, he has his own space at the back."

"So you outlined for Mr. Sandhu your experience with the wind power program and your requirement for a quick approval?"

"Objection," Bernstein said. "Counsel is testifying."

"Let Mr. Gill tell the story in his own words, please," the judge said.

"Of course. So what did you say to Mr. Sandhu?"

"We talked about the very fine program, but the really large problem of how long it might take to get approval for our good project."

"Was Mr. Sandhu sympathetic?"

"Very much so. He has always been a great supporter of the environment and of business people in Brampton."

"And did he offer to help you with your application?"

"He did."

"Could you be more specific, Mr. Gill?"

"He said he would make some calls on our behalf, try to hurry things up."

"And did Mr. Sandhu suggest that there was anything you could do for him?"

"Yes. He mentioned that his riding association was always raising funds for his next campaign, and that he could use our support."

That caused a murmur in the courtroom. Faulkner was heading toward the crux of it, what Sandhu got out of the deal.

"Let's be specific Mr. Gill. Was Mr. Sandhu's suggestion a general request for campaign support or something in particular?"

"Mr Sandhu suggested that Mr. Fung and I should organize a fund-raiser for him, reaching out to our contacts in the Indo-Canadian community and also selling tickets to our fellow developers."

"And how did this strike you?"

"Well, that he wanted money."

"Money in exchange for helping you, you mean?"

"Yes, clearly. He had never asked me for money before, and I had never asked him for help."

"How did this request strike you, Mr. Gill?"

"Well," Gill said, shrugging and holding his hands out in a "what can you do?" gesture.

"I'm going to have to ask you to expand on that," Faulkner said.

"As I said earlier, I come from India. In that country, the culture of business is different. The wheel only turns when it gets an application of oil. Mr. Sandhu is from the same background. I understood that he wanted us to oil his wheel."

I tapped that one into my laptop for later use. No doubt it would be all over Twitter within seconds.

"So you saw nothing wrong with Mr. Sandhu's offer to help in exchange for some help for his campaign?

"I did not. It was not as if we were handing him a suitcase full of cash. This money would all go to his riding association. Proper receipts would be issued and tax papers given."

"So it didn't feel like you were putting money in his pocket?" Faulkner said.

"Not directly, no."

"So, in your view Mr. Gill, you and Mr. Sandhu had reached a business arrangement?"

"That's what it was to me, yes. I will itch his back, he will itch mine."

Politicians had been trading access for fundraising dollars forever, but they always claimed it didn't influence their decisions. To me, it still seemed like the Crown was in the grey area. If Sandhu didn't have a direct personal benefit, where was the crime?

"I see," Faulkner said. "And what happened after your meeting?"

"Mr. Fung and I set a date for the fundraising event and began to send out invitations to many hundreds of contacts. About a month later, we got good news. Our federal grant had been approved."

"And had you held the fund-raiser by that time?" Faulkner asked.

"No, but it came a few weeks later. The event was a great success. We raised $25,000 for Mr. Sandhu's upcoming campaign."

"Was this his leadership campaign or the general election?"

"I am not aware of that detail. He referred only to his campaign."

"And did you hear from Mr. Sandhu, either about the approval or fund-raiser?"

"Yes, both. He phoned me personally to say he had made some calls and he was confident that our project would be approved. Then, later, he called me again to thank me for my good work on the fundraising event."

Bernstein had been taking notes throughout Gill's testimony, the occasional wolf-like grin appearing on his face. I expected the cross-examination to be more entertaining than the Crown's examination in chief.

"Your honour, I have a few more questions for Mr. Gill, but I am cognizant of the time," Faulkner said. "I think I can wrap up with him this afternoon."

Faulkner was managing the day's proceedings like a football team running down the clock before kicking the winning field goal. By the end of the day, she would have put up two damaging witnesses and Bernstein wouldn't have had a chance to grill either one. Sure, Gill's testimony took the line that Bernstein predicted last week, but that wouldn't matter to the media. If something was said today, it was new. If the plan was to make Sandhu seem guilty in the public's eyes, it was moving along nicely. I wasn't yet sure that Faulkner was getting it over the bar for the judge, but she no doubt had a few more cards to play.

My phone pinged and I saw that a text had come in. I expected it to be from the city desk, pressing me for my angle, but it was from Reilly. I would have thought him too old to be texting. The message was simple. "News. Tonight 7. The bridge."

SIXTEEN

"I saw the PM this morning," Vanessa said. "You know, he's even more handsome than people think. I know he's like in his 40s but he's so fit. And he's tall, too. Did you know he's taller than Obama? You wouldn't think it, with Obama being so skinny, but when they met when Obama was still president, there was the PM, taller."

Suzy sipped her mango smoothie and nodded as if Vanessa's crush on the PM was really interesting to her. She had known that Vanessa would be at the gym on Queen Street, just two blocks from the Hill, by 5 p.m. It had been a perfect opportunity to hook up and see if she knew anything about this Mae Wang thing, without forcing it. What could be more natural than two girls sharing a healthy drink after a workout?

Suzy had already heard about which of Vanessa's girlfriends had moved to new and better jobs with ministers, none of whose names rang a bell. All Vanessa's friends seemed to be named either Brittany or Kelsie. Suzy figured they were about 25, like Vanessa, which made them seasoned veterans on the way up in the strange culture of Parliament Hill. Odds were they all looked like Vanessa, too; cute, dark-haired, nice figure, full of energy, not yet seasoned by life's realities.

By the time they were 30, they would be working for some consulting company, making more money than Suzy did. She could understand the career path if they were cynically using the system to get ahead, but Vanessa actually acted like a true believer who thought the PM was a rock star. She was right about his looks, though.

"Look at me, I'm just talking about work all the time," Vanessa said. "When you've got a job like mine, it's almost all you think about. In fact, I have to go back and do a bit more work tonight."

Suzy wondered if the work would be vertical or horizontal.

Vanessa had never quite come out and said that she was hooking up with her boss, but it wasn't hard to read between the lines. Suzy had seen Derek Hall only in pictures, but he was actually kind of hot for a politico. Thick, dark hair, always a couple of day's growth of beard, sharp suits, and chief of staff to the PM, as well. Power made almost any man look more attractive.

"But what's up with you?" Vanessa asked. "You working on anything interesting?"

"Homicide investigation."

"Wow. That must be exciting. I'd love to have a job like yours."

"Nothing like as important as what you do, but this one is kind of mysterious."

"Really? I love a good mystery."

Suzy wondered if Vanessa read actual books or just watched those reality TV re-enactments. "This one involves that girl who was thrown off the building on Elgin a few days ago," she said.

"I read about that. What a terrible story. She was a beautiful girl. I thought I heard that was a suicide."

Suzy leaned towards Vanessa and lowered her voice. "I shouldn't really be talking about this yet, but the police say she was murdered. And there's more, too."

"Come on, tell me the good part," Vanessa said. "I can keep a secret. I work in the PMO."

Suzy feigned reluctance, then said, "All right. It's not confirmed, but what I hear is that the police think she was a Chinese spy."

"Right here in Ottawa? A real Chinese spy?"

"Sure. What better place to be one? This is where most of the secrets are."

"Well, that's true," Vanessa said.

"I'll bet you know a lot of them yourself," Suzy said.

"Some, for sure."

"Here's the odd thing about this one. The RCMP have taken over the case, although they're calling it a joint investigation with Ottawa police. From what I hear, absolutely nothing is happening. And it gets weirder. A bunch of people from the Chinese Embassy showed up at the morgue and made off with the girl's body. Something is really wrong here. I've never seen anything like it."

"Maybe the Chinese killed her. Would that make sense?"

"It might. Who knows?"

"I hope the office has been briefed on this," Vanessa said. "It's the kind of thing that could generate a lot of news coverage and embarrassing questions in the House. People don't like to think that there are spies here and nothing is being done."

"Exactly. I wonder if your boss knows about this? Seems like he should."

"There isn't much that Derek doesn't know about," Vanessa said, proudly.

"I'm sure, with a job like his. I bet he'd appreciate it, though, if you mentioned this to him. You never know with the Mounties. They keep their information pretty tight."

"You know, you're right. I should tell him. Thanks, Suzy. Good advice."

"I'm working my police contacts and I'm likely to find out more. What do you say we collaborate on this? I'll keep you informed of what I find out, you tell me what you're hearing on your end?"

"I'm not sure that would work," Vanessa said. "Everything I do has to be completely confidential."

Even her pout was pretty. Must come from practice, Suzy thought. "Of course, I understand that completely. Anything you give me would be absolutely off the record. That's how it normally works. You'd be amazed how many important people I work with on that basis."

"So you wouldn't use it in your story, but just to help point you in the right direction?"

"Yes, like that."

"Maybe I could do something then. Let me talk to Derek. I might even be running into him later."

Good, Suzy thought. If things were as she suspected between Derek and Vanessa, it could be just the right time to share a confidence. Men were at their most vulnerable with their pants down.

"Great," Suzy said. "Let me give you my cell number. If you find out anything, call me, even if it's late. I'll do the same for you. These stories can move pretty fast."

"Perfect," Vanessa said.

Suzy looked at her watch. There would be just time to grab something light for dinner before she had to meet Pierre Lacroix at 7. Fortunately, it was just around the corner at D'Arcy McGee's on Sparks.

She couldn't say she was looking forward to spending a couple of hours hearing Pierre brag about his police exploits while she fended off his hands, which had a habit of landing on her knee or her shoulder. The thing with Pierre was to get the maximum information while sustaining the illusion that there could be something between them, without actually having to deliver.

The Mae Wang thing sounded like a hell of a story, but screwing Pierre Lacroix to get it would be beyond the call of duty. She'd had enough of a hard time from other reporters when she was hooked up with Mike Reilly, but that had been different. With Reilly, it had been real.

SEVENTEEN

I waited for my moment, then sprinted through the steady stream of cyclists coming west off the Corkstown Footbridge and turning on to the Queen Elizabeth Driveway. Ranger struggled to keep up, his pathetic little legs churning. What was it with cyclists? They were always whining about the treatment they got from drivers, but they refused to slow down, much less stop, for a pedestrian.

Reilly was sitting on the same bench as before, just as he'd promised. The bench itself was situated in a little clearing on the wooded bank of the Rideau Canal. In a way, it was conspicuous, but to the cyclists, walkers and joggers cruising by, Reilly and I would look just like a middle-aged couple out walking the dog on an unseasonably warm May evening. I wondered what it would be like to be part of an actual middle-aged couple, then quickly dismissed the thought. My experience with coupledom hadn't been entirely rewarding.

Reilly had removed his navy suit coat and loosened his red tie. Seeing me coming, he moved the coat to make room. I sat down, keeping to my end of the bench, and said, "You going to wear a suit all summer?"

"It's not summer yet, and it sure beats a uniform." He pointed at my dog and said, "What do you call that sorry little thing?"

"Ranger, believe it or not. Thought I might as well take him for a walk. So, news. What have you got?"

"Not much for small talk, are you?"

"I figure you didn't text me to make small talk. Nice evening to sit by the canal, though. That cover it for you?"

Reilly smiled. "God you're a hardass, Redner."

"Some have said that."

Reilly snapped open a beat-up black leather briefcase and removed a file folder. "I ran the footage of the surveillance cameras around your building. We've got quite a few."

He opened the folder. I could see a good-sized pile of enlarged black and white screen captures inside.

"There are a couple of interesting things here. I followed up on your information about Mae Wang seeing someone Tuesday and Thursday nights. She's killed at your building, makes sense that whatever else was going on took place there, too, right?"

"Sure," I said, nodding. I wondered if I had ever passed her in the hall.

"I looked at the surveillance tapes for those two nights, going back a month. Every Thursday evening, about 7 o'clock, we see this joker show up. It's the only time he's there, so he's not likely a resident."

He passed me a picture of a heavyset man in a dark overcoat, the face blurry. The only remarkable thing about him was his bomber hat, an oversized thing with ear flaps. It looked as if it was made of some kind of fur and the guy had it tied tight under his chin. It was the kind of hat that someone not from Canada would wear because they thought southern Ontario was just a short snowmobile ride from the Arctic.

"If he was there for sex, he had to have been paying for it," I said. "No other way he could get laid, showing up in that kind of hat."

"I've got a hat like that," Reilly said.

"Seriously?"

"Well, I don't wear it in town."

"I hope not."

"Then we see him leaving again, always around midnight."

"More staying power than the body type would suggest. Maybe he takes a nap."

"Could be. Let's call him Mr. Thursday. At this point, he could be anyone. He arrives on foot, which could mean that he works nearby, or that he's smart enough not to leave an easy trail.

"Now, it gets a bit more interesting. When I looked at the Tuesday tapes, I also see a regular, but this guy shows up much later, around 9 o'clock. He stays all night, usually leaving around 7 the next morning."

Reilly handed me a photograph that showed a tall man in a well-cut overcoat, scarf knotted loosely around his neck in a European style, dark hair swept back, striding through the little courtyard in front of my building like he was really someone. The face was unclear but somehow familiar.

"Know him?" Reilly asked.

"No, should I?"

"Take a look at this one. The light is better in the morning."

The second picture showed a closer, clearer view of the guy's face. "Shit, that's Luc Champagne."

"It sure is."

"When was this taken?"

"The week before Mae Wang was killed, and every week I looked at before that."

"What about the week she died?"

"A no show."

"Wow, so Luc Champagne is Mr. Tuesday. That explains why your RCMP friends have grabbed the wheel."

"Yeah, maybe they grabbed the wheel, but they haven't stepped on the gas. They should have looked at this CCTV footage, or had us do it. Hasn't happened."

"So we know Champagne was a regular visitor at the building, but that's all, right?"

"Yeah. He could have been seeing someone else in the building. Lot of political types there, right?"

"There are. And media, too."

"There's no evidence that Champagne was in the building when Mae was killed and we're a long way from connecting him to what happened to her, but it's pretty interesting, when you put it with what you got from the roommate.

"Now, if Champagne were some normal guy, I'd be knocking on his door, but the way things stand, that's just not going to happen. Anything you can do there?"

"Maybe," I said, thinking of Gail Rakic and her veiled comments about Champagne. It was another avenue to pursue with her, although what Gail had to say might have nothing to do with this.

"So what's happening on your end?" Reilly asked.

"They've brought Suzy in on the story. She's supposed to be pursuing RCMP and national security angles."

"If Suzy is pursuing them, she will probably get them. You've got to hate that."

I shrugged. Of course I hated it, but I wasn't certain I could share a confidence with Reilly where Suzy was concerned.

"Suzy going to feed that stuff back to you?"

"That's what she says."

Reilly smiled. "So it probably means she will keep anything good for herself. You, of course, will do the same. What are they thinking, putting you both on the same story?"

"It's a complicated situation."

Reilly nodded and said, "There is one other thing." He reached back into his photo file. "This is probably nothing, but it's just setting off that feeling I get when something's not quite right. You know what I mean?"

"Sure."

"Now this guy shows up at the building at about 9 o'clock on the morning Mae goes flying off the roof. We see him again leaving the building just after she lands on the fence. The weird part is that, while everyone is going ape shit, except you, this guy just strolls out of the building and walks calmly away like nothing is going on."

He passed me the picture. It showed a good-looking, well-built man with a short beard, jeans, a ball cap, tan jacket and sunglasses. He seemed vaguely familiar, and then I remembered.

"Holy crap. He was waiting for the elevator the morning she was killed. If I hadn't been in such a rush, I might have ridden down with him. You think this is the killer?"

I shivered at the thought.

"Person of interest," Reilly said. "He doesn't show up in any other CCTV footage. Just that morning."

"But he could be anyone."

"Could be, but I think you'd better keep your head up."

He put the pictures back in his briefcase, then reconsidered and gave me a copy of the man from the elevator. "Just in case you see him again," he said.

"I think I'd recognize him, but I hope I don't run into him."

"If you do, just back off and call me, all right? I know it's not like you, but it would be the smart thing to do."

Reilly rubbed Ranger's ears, then stood and said, "I've got to get back. Still some paperwork to be done on another case. I'll call you if I hear more."

I watched as Reilly headed down the Queen Elizabeth Driveway, walking back to the police station. I had felt safe when he was there, despite the information he had given me about the guy in the elevator. Now, with him gone, I looked around, trying to see if anyone was watching me. When I thought about it, the elevator guy had pretty much been wearing a disguise. The sunglasses and beard were a common look, but only one step down from a mask. Who knew what he looked like normally?

When I had decided to dive into the Mae Wang story, I hadn't thought much about my own safety, but that was the way I had always been. If some bastard tries to take you down, give it back to him twice as hard. That was what my Uncle Martin had taught me in the brief moments when he contributed to my upbringing. I decided not to dwell on how the advice had worked for him.

Should I warn Suzy, or would Reilly do that? I should have asked. Whoever was behind Mae Wang's murder wasn't going to take kindly to nosy journalists snooping around. Suzy would have to keep her head up, too.

I wasn't sure what to do with the Luc Champagne angle. Presumably he was getting a weekly piece from Mae. That didn't exactly make him a murder suspect, unless he thought she was going to blow the whistle on him. Had it been blackmail? If Mae really was working for the Chinese, surely they would have wanted to play the long game, given Champagne's political position. Imagine having that kind of leverage over a senior cabinet minister.

So if the guy in the elevator was working for someone, who was it? Maybe Champagne, but it was hard to see a Canadian cabinet minister ordering a murder. But then, I had hardly been able to believe it when the people I dealt with in the Adirondacks last summer were willing to kill for political gain. No doubt it was much easier if you could outsource the work.

And who was Mr. Thursday? It was plausible that the relationship between Mae and Champagne was some kind of romance, or something that would seem like romance to a person in Mae's position. But the schlump in the fur -hat? That was something else, for sure.

Maybe Gail would be willing to make sense of all of this. I opened my purse and took out her business card. She had said to call, although she hadn't made any promise to pick up.

Gail answered after one ring, her voice low. "Who is this?" she said.

"Kris."

"Do you think we're on a first-name basis?"

"You said to call."

"Sure, but I didn't say I would tell you anything."

"I've found out some things about Luc Champagne. Interesting things."

"I'll bet you have. Luc Champagne is an interesting guy. Lot going on there."

"It's his personal life that's especially interesting."

"Isn't it, though?"

Was this one of those parallel conversations, where both parties were talking about different things?

"Should we be more specific?" I asked.

"Not on the phone."

"Should we meet?"

"It's not convenient."

"I'm going to go out on a limb here and say Luc Champagne had your husband set up because he was a political rival."

"If you can prove that, you've got a good story, but Luc Champagne doesn't leave fingerprints."

"When we spoke earlier, you implied that maybe you could connect some dots for me."

"Maybe I can, but I'm going to have to think about it. Sonny is my priority right now."

I considered telling Gail about the connection between Champagne and Mae Wang, but we didn't have anything like that level of trust yet. Besides, I didn't want to give up something that good without getting something better in return.

"So Champagne falls under phase two, revenge?"

Gail gave a tight laugh. "That's always the best part, don't you think?"

That depended on what the act of revenge turned you into, I thought, but I said, "Absolutely. And always glad to help."

"Let's leave it at that, for now."

"OK, see you in court tomorrow."

It was a start. I had at least planted the idea that I could be a tool in Gail Rakic's planned revenge. Maybe Champagne had better keep his head up, too.

EIGHTEEN

With all that was buzzing in my head about Mae Wang and her killer, the Sandhu trial felt like a distraction, but at least this morning's session promised to be entertaining. Unless Faulkner had some other trick in her bag, this would be Ben Bernstein's first attempt to undermine her case. I was anticipating a lively cross-examination of Vikram Gill. It was one thing to be led gently through Gill's version of the truth by the Crown, quite another to have every word that was already uttered sliced and diced by a tough defence lawyer.

I was betting that Gill would look as ragged as the cheap suit I had seen him wearing in the waiting area outside the courtroom. Today's effort was grey with a blue tie and blue shirt. Better colour sense, but there was something black on Gill's right sleeve. Maybe he had been oiling someone's wheel.

I was anticipating a column that would do quite a job on Gill, with Bernstein providing all the heavy lifting. It would be lively and readable and, as a bonus, Gail Rakic would like it quite a bit.

I felt like I was making some progress with Gail, but it was also clear she was a woman who was used to being in charge. She would do what she thought would benefit her and her husband, at the time she thought most appropriate. I would need to draw her slowly in my direction, not push her.

Gill was called and again shuffled towards the stand, as if something was wrong with him. Maybe it was more migraines or just the stress of trying to keep his dodgy story straight. You'd think that would be a basic skill for a con man, but even I wouldn't have looked forward to being cross-examined by Ben Bernstein.

"So, Mr. Gill. Let's dive right in, shall we?" Bernstein said. "Yesterday, you told the court that you have a background in engineering and mentioned the Delhi Technological University. Are you in fact a graduate of that institution?"

"I attended there, yes."

"That's not what I am asking, Mr. Gill. Did you graduate?"

"I did not complete all of my course work, no."

"So, in fact, you are not an engineer are you?"

"Not technically, no."

"You either are or you aren't, Mr. Gill. Which is it?"

"No, I am not an engineer."

"And do you have any experience in wind energy at all?"

"I have read much online, but this was my first wind project."

"I see. You read about it online. Now, when you met Mr. Sandhu to discuss this project, did you hold out to him that you were an engineer and an expert on wind energy?"

This was what I had expected from Bernstein. He liked to work quickly and pace was important. It kept the witness from having a lot of time to think about his answers or to deduce where Bernstein was headed.

Gill looked toward Faulkner, as if seeking help. He was having a hard time with Bernstein's aggressive approach and they were just getting started. Faulkner made a point of not looking up from her notes.

"Don't look at her Mr. Gill. My question is for you. Did you tell Mr. Sandhu that you were an engineer and wind power expert?"

As if finally remembering his lines, Gill said, "I don't recollect that at this time."

"Come on now, Mr. Gill. You are here as one of the two principal witnesses against my client. I'm sure you have made your accusations repeatedly to the police and the Crown. Are you telling the court now that you have memory issues?"

Faulkner had heard enough. "Objection, your honour. Mr. Gill's academic achievements are not what's at issue here."

"No, but his credibility is," Bernstein shot back.

"Continue Mr. Bernstein, but remember that there is no jury here," the judge said.

"Let's try again Mr. Gill. Do you remember telling Mr. Sandhu that you were an engineer and wind power expert?"

"I probably did," Gill admitted. "Not all knowledge is acquired in school."

"All right, let's move on. You told the court yesterday that Mr. Sandhu had never asked you for any money until you approached him about the wind project, correct?"

"That's right."

Bernstein walked over to the defence table and picked up a few pieces of paper. Turning and walking back toward Gill, he said, "Now, Mr. Gill, I'm going to ask you to look at these three pieces of correspondence. Do you recognize them?"

Gill removed a pair of eyeglasses from the inside pocket of his suit, put them on and examined the papers.

"Do these look familiar Mr. Gill?"

"They are addressed to me, yes, but I receive a great many pieces of correspondence."

"Did you received these three particular pieces, Mr. Gill?"

Gill rubbed his chin and made a show of concentrating. Buying time while he decided whether he could get away with a lie or whether Bernstein was setting a trap, I would bet.

"These are letters from Mr. Sandhu seeking campaign contributions in each of the three years prior to your meeting with him, correct?"

"That is what they say."

"Once again, Mr. Gill, did you receive them?"

"They look familiar now. I must have, yes."

"Thank you Mr. Gill. Now we're getting somewhere. Your honour, we have copies for the court and we would like to enter them as the first exhibit for the defence." Bernstein passed the copies to the clerk, who passed them to the judge.

"So wouldn't that make you reconsider your earlier statement, that Mr. Sandhu had never sought your financial help before? In fact, wasn't seeking that help a routine thing, not some kind of special deal?"

"I am not expert on political fundraising, but these letters look like the kind I receive from all parties."

"You mentioned that you receive such letters from all parties, Mr. Gill, but you are a card-carrying member of the Conservative Party, are you not?"

"Yes, very proudly so, and for many years."

"So there would be nothing unusual about Mr. Sandhu reaching out to you for a donation, would there? I'm sure your name is on a list."

"I suppose it must be."

"In your earlier testimony, you said that you and Mr. Sandhu had agreed to 'itch each other's backs,' as you put it. Now, were those words ever said, Mr. Gill, or was that just a thought in your mind?"

"Not said in so many words, but it was clear that was the arrangement."

"And you assumed that because Mr. Sandhu is Indo-Canadian, like yourself?"

"It is a perhaps regrettable part of our culture."

"But you are aware that Mr. Sandhu was born and educated in Canada."

"I was not, but cultural values run deep."

"Indeed," Bernstein said. "Now let me take you back to your thinking when you first chose to contact Mr. Sandhu about this wind energy grant. Were you reaching out to him because you thought he was an Indo-Canadian backscratcher, or simply because he was your MP?"

"Well, yes, he was my MP. So, a person I should talk to."

"Just something business people and community leaders do in every riding of the country, wouldn't you say?"

"Objection," Faulkner said. "Mr. Gill is not an expert on every riding in the country."

"Withdrawn. Mr. Gill, you said in your earlier testimony that the wheels of government turn slowly. No dispute there. Wouldn't you say that part of an MP's job is to make those wheels go a little faster, when he has been persuaded that a project is in the public interest?"

"I suppose so, yes."

"Very good, Mr. Gill," Bernstein said, as if finally approving of Gill's performance. "Now, let's move on to the wind project itself. Did it go ahead?"

Gill gave the world-weary shrug that was becoming his signature gesture. "Alas, there proved to be many, many complications. Provincial rules, setback regulations, noise issues."

"I see, so the proposed wind turbines were not erected, then?"

"Regrettably not."

"And what of the subdivision proposal itself? Did it proceed?"

"Oh yes. Competing developer had pulled out by the time the unfortunate decision about the wind power had to be made. Council was very pleased to approve my backup plan."

Bernstein nodded, as if in understanding, then said, "Mr. Gill, are you familiar with the term bait and switch?"

"Does it have to do with fishing?"

"In a way, yes. Now, this is the last thing I wanted to ask you about Mr. Gill. We're almost there. What about the federal program grant, the $1.5 million?"

"Well, we did not receive that, as the project did not go ahead."

"So in the end, you didn't get any federal money at all, right?"

"That's correct."

"Excellent. Nothing further for this witness."

Not a bad job. Bernstein was obviously going to be working hard to establish the idea that Sandhu had done no more than any good MP would to help out a constituent and speed up those famous wheels of bureaucracy. Surely the Crown had a bomb or two to drop, though. I figured it would have to do with where the $25,000 had gone.

Faulkner was back on her feet, trying to look unruffled by the working over one of her two star witnesses had just experienced.

"Your honour, at this point I would like to request a short break, then return to re-examine Mr. Gill."

"Very well. Thirty-minute recess."

As Gail Rakic walked up the aisle, a couple of steps in front of her husband, she shot me a quick look. It was difficult to read. I thought Gail might have afforded at least a small smile. Her side was having a good day.

I decided to get to work on my column while monitoring the rest of the day's proceedings from the media room. Faulkner would try to undermine Bernstein's cross-examination of Vikram Gill, but I thought she was unlikely to succeed, and Bernstein had given me plenty of ammunition for my column. Gill's testimony certainly left the impression that he had never even wanted the green energy grant, that the whole thing was a gimmick to get his subdivision approved. The question was, did Sandhu know the project was a scam, or was he a dupe?

NINETEEN

Suzy scrolled through the police budget again, trying to make sense of the impenetrable jargon and the massive columns of numbers. If a police reporter couldn't understand this thing, how did they expect the public to? But then, that was probably the point.

At least there weren't any distractions. The newsroom was a morgue since the latest round of layoffs and buyouts.

The thing Suzy didn't get was why she had to waste her time on a budget story. She certainly understood that people were pissed off with the idea that a constable was being paid $100K to drive around in a cruiser, but this would inevitably be a story full of numbers and university professors who had never even been on a ride along trying to pass themselves off as experts. No real cop was likely to discuss it, and she couldn't blame them.

"Excuse me officer, do you think you're way overpaid?" Jesus.

It was the kind of story on which she just hated to put her byline. Really, if someone wasn't dead, or at least bleeding seriously, why should the public even care?

First, Colin had put her on this so-called spy story and expected her to work with Kris Redner, which was annoying enough. Now, the assistant city editor, Melinda Khoury, was telling her to plow through the police budget while she was at it. She wondered if Colin even wanted her on the Mae Wang story, or if it had just been a hollow gesture to make her feel better when Kris swooped down, yet again, to sink her talons into a prime crime story. If it was one. Suzy had her doubts. She had wasted two hours with Pierre Lacroix, who had seemed far less interested in this supposed national security issue than he had been in the length of her skirt, which admittedly was short. He had given her the company line. Chinese national, looked like a tragic suicide, etc. Yes, it was true that someone from the embassy had shown up and made a fuss at the morgue. He understood Global Affairs would be following up. When she told him that she knew for sure there was a homicide investigation and the RCMP were involved, he had said, "Well then, you should talk to Ottawa police about that. I've heard nothing at all on our end. Can't imagine it would get much attention from us. Probably just a chance to show how we can co-operate with the locals."

Suzy could usually tell when Pierre was lying. He had a habit of licking his lips nervously. Wasn't happening last night. Just because he didn't know what was going on didn't mean that there wasn't anything, but he was her best contact.

She had heard nothing yet from Vanessa. That wasn't good, either. If there was something juicy to tell, Vanessa would be sharing pretty quickly. Then Suzy's cell rang, and she saw it was Vanessa. Maybe things were about to pick up. "Hey," she said, "anything new?"

"Yes. Derek Hall is an asshole."

That was probably news only to Vanessa, Suzy thought. The young political assistant sounded like she was somewhere between rage and tears. Badly timed lovers' quarrel?

"Sorry to hear that," Suzy said, trying to muster some sympathy. "I've worked for a few of those myself."

"So I ask him about that thing we were talking about, thinking I am doing him a favour by bringing him something more important than his goddamned coffee. And he goes, 'I know all about that, and there's nothing there. It's a suicide. The Chinese were acting crazy like they do. The police are investigating just to keep the Chinese happy.'

"I might have known. Big Derek Hall. There is nothing in the whole freaking world that he doesn't know before anyone else does. He blows me off like I am some kind of idiot, then it gets worse. He starts to give me shit for talking about it with someone outside the office.

"So I tell him, the information *came* from outside the office. How am I supposed to know about it if I don't talk to someone from outside the office? Then he gets all squirrelly about where I got the information from."

"Did you tell him?"

"No. Fuck him. Let him figure it out for himself."

Hall wouldn't exactly have to be Sherlock Holmes to deduce that the information came from the media. The witch hunt was probably already under way. Maybe they would zero in on Kris. That would be sweet.

"OK, good. Thanks for keeping me out of it. I appreciate it when someone sticks to a deal. Derek does sound like a bit of a prick."

"You're telling me. I thought he was a really nice guy. And now I have to keep working for him. It's a big deal being in the PMO, you know. If that doesn't work out, I'll end up back in the Department of Agriculture or some other cobwebby, godforsaken place."

"Look, I appreciate you trying. Don't worry about Derek. Guys like that are all bluster. It will blow over. If it doesn't, just mention sexual harassment. That scares the shit out of them every time."

"Well, there hasn't been anything like that," Vanessa said, maybe a little too quickly.

"There has been if you say there was. All it takes is an accusation. I wouldn't play that card unless you have to, though."

"No, I don't see myself doing that. No one would hire me again."

Good point, Suzy thought. From what she heard, a lot of the big guys on the Hill thought sexual harassment was just part of the job description for their female assistants. They were typically young, attractive, available and unlikely to complain. For a politician a long way from home, it was the magic formula.

"Plus, I am supporting my mom, who has cancer. I don't suppose you want to hear about that."

Suzy really, really didn't, but she said, "Oh, I'm sorry to hear that. That's terrible."

"Yes it is. She's only 50, but she has brain tumours. Without me working, and living with her, there wouldn't be anyone to look after her. My Dad has already passed."

Suzy glanced at her watch. She really had never been that interested in other people's woes, unless there was a story in it. She wondered if it was a character defect.

Suzy was almost relieved when Vanessa said, "Did you find out anything more about the Chinese girl?"

Suzy felt a little alarm bell go off. What if Vanessa's slagging of her boss was just a diversion and her real mission was to find out what else Suzy knew? Better to play it safe.

"No, nothing. I think what Derek told you is probably right. The Chinese were just making a fuss to try to score diplomatic points. They've got me working on something about the police budget now."

"Too bad. It was kind of fun to think about a Chinese spy here in Ottawa. It's like something out of a movie."

"Right, well I'm sure there are Chinese spies, but it doesn't look like she was one of them."

"Well, OK then. Got to go. See you at the gym soon," Vanessa said, and hung up.

It sounded as if Vanessa had returned to her usual cheerful self again. Pretty quick transformation.

It didn't matter whether Derek Hall really had flipped out or whether he had just asked Vanessa to see what she could get out of Suzy. Either way, it meant that there was something there he didn't want a reporter to know about.

Suzy closed the police budget file on her screen. That could wait. She really should update Kris, but that could wait, too. There was one more source she could try.

TWENTY

I had just snapped open a Corona when I heard the knock on my door. That just never happened. Was it Colin? It wasn't his usual habit to just show up without calling, but maybe he had brought dinner. I hoped so. Almost anything would be an upgrade on the aging pizza I had in the fridge.

The knock came again, harder. Definitely not Colin. His style was a quiet double rap, polite and patient. I debated whether to answer. It had better not be a bloody Jehovah's Witness.

Then I thought about the guy from the elevator, and Reilly's advice to keep my head up. Truthfully, I had been thinking about him ever since Reilly implied the bearded man might be the killer. The building did have front door security, but there was always some idiot who would buzz anyone in.

I put the beer down and pulled my largest butcher knife from the block on the counter. I was probably just being paranoid, but it wasn't like people hadn't tried to kill me in the past, and pretty recently, too. I wished I had installed one of those little peepholes, even if it meant messing with Caroline's door.

Belatedly realizing that he had a role to play, Ranger started barking aggressively. He didn't sound like a dog that could do anything more than nip an ankle, but the person on the other side of the door couldn't know for sure.

"Who is it?" I asked.

"Police. Open up."

Fucking Reilly. I swung open the door, pissed that he had rattled me.

"Whoa, guess you're not glad to see me."

I looked down at the knife in my hand. "A guy I know said I needed to watch out."

"Glad to see you've taken the advice."

"I was just going to have a beer. Want one?"

"Still sort of on duty," he said, reaching down to pay attention to Ranger, who had rolled over on his back and was looking to get his belly scratched. Some watchdog.

"I think it's time I had an informal chat with your super. Want to tag along?"

I had only ever had one encounter with the building manager, as he liked to call himself, and that was about the clogged drain in the kitchen sink. Mr. Mo hailed from one of the sandier countries where women were supposed to walk 10 feet behind the men and wear veils. I wasn't sure which one, but they were only different by degree. Mr. Mo himself favoured black track suits and gold chains, although he was certainly no athlete. When he'd gotten under the sink with his wrench, I'd seen a lot more of his hairy belly than I wanted. The worst part was the way he had stared at my chest, not that there was much to look at. I had been tempted to ask him if he wanted a magnifying glass. After that, I had paid for my own repairs.

"The guy's a dick. You think he knows something?"

"Only one way to find out. The least we can do is spoil his day."

"I'm down with that."

As they rode the elevator down to Mr. Mo's basement apartment, Reilly said, "This is kind of on the down low, given the circumstances, so I'm not going to get any more official than I have to. You OK with that?"

"Sure am." I was familiar with the technique of inferring that you had knowledge or authority and letting the subject fill in the blanks.

The basement was a dump. You'd have thought the owners could afford a real office for the super, with the rent people were paying in the Prince Albert. Upstairs, the building's age gave it a quaint charm, but in the basement it was just old and creepy. Exposed heating pipes ran along the ceiling in the corridor and the landlord-green paint was flaking off the walls. I could smell something spicy cooking and there was high-pitched, wailing music leaking out into the hall.

"Looks like our boy is home," Reilly said. The door to Mr. Mo's apartment had the words Building Manager stuck on it in those gold letters you could get at a dollar store, except that the M had fallen off manager. It did little to reduce the overall effect.

Reilly knocked on the door and said "Police," in his authoritative baritone, the same one he had used to screw with me upstairs.

First the music was shut off, and then there was a loud round of shushing, presumably Mr. Mo bringing some order to Mrs. Mo and whatever little Mo's he had stashed in the apartment.

When the door swung open, Mr. Mo looked nervous, running a hand through his oily black hair and zipping up his black track suit in a vain attempt to contain his forest of chest hair. He was probably only about 40, but he looked shop worn. I imagined that police knocking on the door was pretty bad news where he came from.

The building manager looked at me and sniffed, then focused on Reilly, stuck out his hand and said, "I am Mr. Mo, manager of this building. How can I be of assistance?"

Reilly didn't take the man's hand, but quickly flashed his ID and said "Homicide. We need to ask you a few questions."

Mr. Mo was looking at me with that "where have I seen her before?" look. I hoped he wouldn't figure it out. An officious super had infinite ways to make a tenant's life miserable.

"Well, my family is here and we were about to start the evening meal. Can we find a more convenient time?"

"This time works fine for me," Reilly said. "Just close the door."

Mr. Mo obeyed and stepped out into the hall. "This must be about that poor girl who killed herself."

"That's right. Know her?"

"I am not knowing her at all," he said quickly.

"Not a tenant, then?"

"Certainly not. We vet our tenants very carefully."

"I'll bet. I'm going to need a list of those tenants."

"Well, I think there must be very many issues of privacy there. I will need to consult with building ownership."

"And who is building ownership?"

"A numbered company."

"Of course it is. Look, here's how it's going to work. This is a homicide investigation. I will need your complete co-operation. I can only share this with you because of your position, but it looks as if that girl might not have killed herself. I imagine that building

ownership would not be pleased if it turned out that a homicide
had been committed here. Imagine what that would do for the
building's reputation, ownership's ability to rent units, and your
own position."

"Still, I must consult with building ownership."

"Maybe I should consult with them myself. I would like to get
ownership's point of view on how this girl, and her killer, got onto
the roof of the building. You have a key to gain access to the roof,
right?"

"Well, yes. I have such a key. I am the building manager, but I
have nothing whatsoever to do with this unfortunate incident."

"I hope that's true, I really do. But tell me, who else has a key to
get to the roof?"

"Only building ownership."

"So should I tell them that you refused to co-operate and suggested that ownership might be involved with this crime? Or maybe
you negligently left the door to the roof unlocked."

"No, certainly not. Contacting ownership will not be necessary. I
will be happy to provide you with a list of all tenants."

"Excellent," Reilly said, clapping Mr. Mo on the shoulder like
they were pals. "I knew I could count on your good judgment. Now,
one other thing."

Reilly reached into the breast pocket of his suit coat and withdrew a picture of the guy who had been waiting for the elevator
and walked so calmly through the crime scene. "I'd like to know a
bit more about this person. Is he a tenant here?"

Mr. Mo took the picture and extended it at arm's length to study
it.

"Feel free to get your glasses, if that would help," Reilly said.

"My vision is excellent. I do not know this gentleman. He is certainly not a tenant and I have not seen him in the building."

Mr. Mo sounded pretty sure of himself. He was probably telling
the truth. If he could have pointed the police away from his door
and toward someone else's, he would have.

"Is this man the suspect?" he asked.

"Person of interest," Reilly said. "Now what about that list?"

"I will have to photocopy it."

"Great. Let's do that now."

"I have in the office. Please wait here," Mr. Mo said.

While they waited, Reilly said, "That was pretty easy. Didn't even have to give him my name."

"The way you look, if you flash a shield and say you are police, no one's going to question it," I said.

It didn't take Mr. Mo long to reappear with the photocopied list. Reilly folded it and put it in the inside pocket of his suit. When Mr. Mo scuttled back into his office/apartment, Reilly said, "That offer of a beer still on?"

TWENTY-ONE

Derek Hall settled in at his usual table at Leo's. Just a couple of blocks from Parliament Hill, the steak-house was still the top spot for people in his business and he was there so often that the leather armchair had practically shaped itself to his butt. It wasn't an entirely private location, but the table was up against a red brick wall and the heavy wooden blinds provided an acceptable level of gloom. Generous tips at the taxpayers' expense guaranteed that the tables next to his were never occupied when he came in for his regular lunch. His glass of Aberlour was already on the table, two ice cubes as usual.

Derek pulled out his work BlackBerry and quickly scanned his email, news sites and Twitter, hoping that nothing had burst into flames in the time it had taken him to walk down from the Hill. He needed to be on top of everything before Question Period at 2:15. The PM wouldn't be in attendance, so that reduced Derek's personal worry level just a bit. On the other hand, his boss's latest parliamentary secretary was an idiot, so anything could happen. The Opposition was in full roar about the party's fundraising practices.

Done with work for the moment, Derek pulled out his personal iPhone to see if Vanessa had sent him another selfie. She was an intern, sweet girl with a real sense of how to get ahead. Nothing new from her, so he scanned through her most recent shots. The one where she sat on his desk wearing considerably less than she had come to work in was his favourite.

Derek shut his phone down, much as he would have liked to linger. Plenty of time for the real thing this weekend, as long as she wasn't still pissed off at him. She had been pretty wound up yesterday. He looked forward to helping her relax.

Derek shot his monogrammed cuffs and adjusted his club tie. It was a tie for some club, he was sure, but not one he belonged to.

He thought it suited his young professional look, and if anyone thought it was too stodgy, he could say he was wearing it ironically. His navy wool suit was tailored to his measurements, but ordered online. He always liked to look like the best-dressed man in the room, but that didn't mean he wanted to spend accordingly. Job security was notoriously tenuous for a prime minister's chief of staff. Still, he'd survived 13 years on the Hill, starting out as a gofer in the PMO back at the end of the last Liberal era and working his way relentlessly to the top of the heap by what he liked to think of as a combination of hard work, intelligence and the kind of ruthlessness that politicians prized in their underlings.

Ah, there was Sharpe now, heading across the crowded restaurant. Part of the reason people came to Leo's was to see whom they could see, but there was only the slightest chance that Sharpe would be recognized. He had the kind of bland anonymity that was so helpful to people in his trade.

Sharpe was past middle age, verging on old, average height, grey hair in a business cut, black suit, white shirt, blue and black striped tie, horn-rimmed eyeglasses that were trendy now, but had been Sharpe's style for decades. He could easily pass for an accountant or mid-level bureaucrat. Certainly nothing in Sharpe's appearance suggested that he had once been one of the most important men in government.

Sharpe was a dinosaur, a spymaster who had served both Liberal and Conservative governments, but who now did a lot of work for international consulting companies of the greyer sort. A useful guy to know, Derek thought, but not exactly the type you'd like to invite to a party.

Sharpe slipped into his seat opposite Derek Hall with a nod, no handshake. Young Hall was famous for his bone-crushing handshakes. It was a juvenile way to intimidate others, and Sharpe wasn't interested in games. The waiter caught his eye, and Sharpe gave a small gesture with his hand, declining the option of a drink. He was abstemious in all things, always had been. Drink was a weakness, and weaknesses were little cracks that others would eventually prise open and use against you.

Sharpe had seen a legion of Derek Halls come and go in his time in service. They always thought they knew every secret there was to know, just because they knew which MP was a drunk, who was getting some on the side, and the devious moves necessary to keep them all in line.

The kid knew a lot of things, but not as much as he imagined. There were whole layers of secrets that never came through a political office, even the top one in the country. When it came to the big stuff, the things that could really rock nations and change the course of events, the Derek Halls knew very little at all. Like the prime minister himself, they had to be managed so that the work that kept the country safe could be conducted as it had to be, without worrying about polls and the short-term political future.

"How can I help you, Derek?" Sharpe said.

"We might have a situation with the Chinese. I hear one of their nationals might have been murdered in town earlier this week and from what I gather, she was working in your line."

"I'm retired, as you know. Perhaps you should ask the minister over at Global Affairs, or the current national security adviser."

The minister was Luc Champagne, who thought the Chinese were his friends and the new security adviser was a recent diversity hire who had told him there was nothing to it, just an accidental death. Derek had been quite willing to take another problem off his plate until Vanessa had come rushing to him with new details. The idea of an intern knowing something he did not almost made Derek's head explode. Surely it couldn't be true, but it was going to be a shit storm of colossal proportions if it were. His job was to make sure the PM knew what forest fires were coming and to squelch them whenever possible.

"I have raised it with them, but they seem completely unconcerned. Then another source brought me additional information."

"What source would that be?" Sharpe said.

"One of my assistants."

"Is she reliable?"

"Primarily as a collector of gossip. I need this looked into a little further by someone who knows the ropes."

"I take it you are not offering to retain me?"

"I'm sure we can both agree that this is best kept off the books. We can find a way to make it up down the line."

Sharpe considered the situation. A marker with the PMO was

always handy to have, even if he loathed the current PM. "Tell me about this girl."

"She worked as an interpreter at their embassy. Jumped off a roof on Elgin Street, or so it seemed. Then the Chinese made a big fuss and spirited her body away. Full war party from the embassy. It seems to have aroused some media interest."

When it came to acting ruthlessly in their own interests, there was virtually nothing that the Chinese government and their gang of Ministry of State Security agents in the Ottawa embassy would not do, Sharpe knew. Their weakness was the predictability of their self-interest. This, however, was uncharacteristic. If there was a reliability issue with one of their agents, she would simply have disappeared. The bare facts that Hall described suggested that something had gone awry. He found himself mildly intrigued.

"I could make some inquiries," he said. He already had a few names in mind.

"That would be much appreciated, by myself and the PM."

"Have you apprised him of the situation?"

"Not yet. I need to know more. If this proves to be something where Champagne has to field questions, careful ground work will have to be done."

"You don't trust him?"

"He's a Conservative turncoat, although a very useful one. Clearly a man who puts himself ahead of the team. The PM has asked me to keep a close eye."

"Wise advice." Sharpe had long experience of working with politicians, and as a group he found them narcissistic, unreliable and unable to put the big picture ahead of their own electoral prospects. Certainly not people one would want to trust with any knowledge that could damage the country.

Sharpe looked at his watch, a modest Timex. "I've got a meeting," he said, rising and departing without so much as a farewell.

Derek had grown somewhat accustomed to Sharpe's peculiarities. The man certainly lacked even the most basic social skills. Or maybe he just didn't need to bother with them, in his line of work. Derek wished he knew a little more about what Sharpe did these days, then realized that it was probably better that he didn't.

If there was anything to Vanessa's story, Sharpe would get to the bottom of it. With reasonable luck, this would prove to be another of those problems that dropped to the bottom of the list as the attention of what was left of the Press Gallery drifted elsewhere. That would be vastly preferable to a story that might run under a headline like "Chinese Spy Murdered While Government Sleeps." Avoiding those kinds of problems was both the best and worst part of Derek's job. He sometimes thought of it as like walking on a tightrope over a pit of fire. If someone was going to burn, political staffers were first on the list.

Derek wondered who Vanessa had been talking to. It would be useful to know. He was pretty confident that a couple of drinks and some make-up sex would reveal the secret. His job wasn't all bad.

TWENTY-TWO

Were it not for the changing of witnesses, one day in court could seem remarkably like another. The lawyers and the judge, of course, were always in their robes. The spectators sat in the same seats, wearing their best court outfits. The room was windowless, so even the passage of time was not visible. Despite that, I thought and hoped that Wednesday would be different from Tuesday. If Sharon Faulkner's next witness wasn't better than Vikram Gill, she had a problem.

The morning had been taken up with Faulkner bringing Gill back to the stand to try to reduce the damage Bernstein had done to his testimony. I hadn't rated it a particularly successful effort. Her day would depend on the testimony of Thomas Fung. He was the other barrel of Faulkner's shotgun. If he didn't fire any better than the first, this case was going down.

I had been looking forward to Fung's testimony and it quickly became apparent that I wasn't going to be disappointed. Most witnesses came down the aisle to the stand sombre, serious and worried about whether some smart lawyer was going to trip them up. Not Fung. He was grinning and waving to people in the audience like he was about to receive an award.

Fung wore one of those super-slim suits in a luminous blue material and a thin black tie, white shirt. It was a look that not many could pull off, but somehow it worked for Fung. The guy was as thin as a pool cue and didn't look a day over 25. With his carefully cut black hair and bold, red-framed glasses, he looked more like a fashion designer than a businessman.

The first words out of his mouth to the Crown attorney were, "Call me Tommy," like they were meeting for drinks. Clearly, Tommy was the charmer, the deal-maker, while his partner Vikram Gill provided the development and political connections.

Ignoring the offer to call him Tommy, Faulkner said, "I would like to quickly establish your background, Mr. Fung, before we get to the heart of your testimony. Could you briefly tell the court about your line of work?"

"Entrepreneur," Fung said, smiling like that was something special.

"Perhaps not quite that brief, Mr. Fung. What kind of businesses are you engaged in?"

"My specialty is cutting-edge green technologies. I am what you could call a middle-man, connecting investors with opportunities in wind, solar and other renewable technologies."

"So your specialty is just the kind of deal that brings us here today," Faulkner said, underlining it.

"Yes, exactly."

"And you have an engineering degree from the Harbin Institute of Technology, is that correct?"

"Yes, and an MBA from Wharton."

Faulkner had gotten hung up on Gill's fudged credentials. She wasn't going to make the same mistake twice. I hoped she didn't expect people to believe that Fung couldn't be a crook because he had been to prestigious universities.

"How many renewable energy deals have you done, Mr. Fung?"

Fung gave a look of concentration, as if he was doing a big calculation, then said, "Twenty-three."

Like he didn't know the exact number as well as his own name.

"So you have considerable experience in the field. Tell us how this particular deal with Mr. Gill and Mr. Sandhu got started."

"Objection," Bernstein said. "The Crown hasn't shown that my client was part of any deal."

"Sustained," Justice Macpherson said. "Let's stick to the established facts, shall we Ms. Faulkner?"

"Of course, your honour. Now Mr. Fung, tell us how your deal with Mr. Gill got started."

"I research land ownership records online to find owners of significant parcels, businessmen who might be willing to use their land for an energy project. In fact, there had been some media coverage of Mr. Gill's attempt to develop his land near Brampton. I called him up and told him that I might be able to get him a better deal."

"Better in what sense?"

"Once the wind turbines are up, you just watch the blades go round and the money come in. And the environment benefits, of course. I envisioned a turnkey operation where Mr. Gill would be paid a substantial annual fee for the use of his land. I would put the deal together with a wind power company and take a percentage of the profits as my commission."

"That all sounds pretty easy. Was there a holdup?"

"Well, as you might imagine, there are a lot of others trying to do the same thing. Some of them far larger players than me, companies with deep pockets. For this deal, a federal green energy grant was a big sweetener, a sign to potential investors that the deal was sound and would go ahead."

"So you had the land and the plan, but you needed someone to back it up. What was your strategy?"

"This is where I got a bit lucky," Fung said. "It turned out that Vikram, Mr. Gill, was well connected with the Conservative Party and he knew Mr. Sandhu as part of his cultural community. I was happy with that because Mr. Sandhu was parliamentary secretary to the industry minister. He seemed like a man who could move things along."

"And how about you, Mr. Fung. Did you have any connection with Mr. Sandhu?"

"I did. I knew him personally."

There was a murmur of excitement in the courtroom and the media started to light up Twitter. This was something new and potentially troubling for Sandhu. Bernstein flipped through his binders, getting ready for the counter-attack.

"And how did you come to know Mr. Sandhu?"

"I knew him socially, but not well. Some of the lobbyists I deal with in Ottawa had a Friday night poker game. Mr. Sandhu would sit in occasionally."

"How was his luck?"

"Not very good I am afraid," Fung smiled. "He lost every time I saw him play."

"What kind of amounts are we talking about?"

"I saw him drop two or three thousand most nights."

Faulkner shook her head, feigning surprise. "All right, but Mr. Sandhu is a man of considerable financial means. Did he ever indicate to you that those losses were a problem?"

"We went out and had a couple of scotches one night after the game. I think Mr. Sandhu had a few others at the table. Anyway, it was like he was looking for someone to confide in. He told me that he could handle the losses at our game. He had a pretty good salary. But there was another game, dodgier players, and his luck wasn't any better. He told me he was down $25,000 to one of the guys from the game. To clear it, he would have to get money from his wife and own up about his gambling situation."

It was starting to become clear why Sonny Sandhu was in court. Motive had been the weak part of Faulkner's case. Maybe not so much now. Sure, $25K wasn't a lot of money to a guy like Sandhu, but it was if he had to go crawling to his wife and explain that he was a problem gambler. Gail Rakic didn't strike me as the kind who would just give him a hug and write a cheque.

Bernstein remained studiously unconcerned. Lawyers were paid not to look worried. Of course he would have known this was coming, but it was a body blow all the same.

"And did Mr. Sandhu seek your financial assistance?" Faulkner asked.

"He did ask if I could help him out, like a favour, just between the two of us. He said he'd owe me. I said that I couldn't."

"And what did you take the words 'he'd owe me,' to mean?"

"That he'd do something for me."

As if anticipating Bernstein's line in cross-examination, Faulkner said, "But isn't that what you wanted, Mr. Fung?"

"Not like that. I keep a clean set of books. Look, I'm from China. I know how it works over there, but I didn't expect this in Canada."

"How did Mr. Sandhu take your refusal?"

"He said, 'What if there was another way, a legal way?'"

"And did he propose one?"

"He suggested that Mr. Gill could organize a fund-raiser. He and I could ensure a good turnout at top dollar. Mr. Sandhu said the money would go to his riding association, but he would take care of it from there."

This time there was an actual gasp in the courtroom. I looked at Sandhu and Gail Rakic. They both sat ramrod straight, eyes forward. This was the bad day they knew was coming. That didn't make it any easier when it happened.

"And what did you take that to mean, Mr. Fung?"

Bernstein was on his feet. "Your honour, this calls for the witness to speculate on matters of which he has no direct knowledge."

"I take it you will bring a witness to describe that next step, Ms. Faulkner," the judge said.

"I will, your honour."

"Then let's move on."

"One last point, your honour. Mr. Fung, did you help organize a fund-raiser for Mr. Sandhu?"

"I did."

"And after that, Mr. Fung, how did the deal proceed?"

"Well, we got confirmation of the federal grant very quickly, but then Mr. Gill ran into all kinds of problems getting approvals for the project. The community was opposed and in the end, Mr. Gill decided to proceed with housing instead."

"And did you have any financial interest in that project, or make any kind of commission on it?"

"I did not. Once the wind deal fell through, I was out. I'm not into property development. In the end, I got nothing out of this deal."

And there was an important point, if you believed it. One could choose to think that Fung had been duped by a crooked politician and a shady business partner. It was a bit of a stretch, but Faulkner had been smart to put Gill on first. He was such an obvious liar that Fung looked like Mother Teresa in comparison.

Faulkner had made major progress if Fung's testimony held up in cross-examination. She hadn't shown yet that the money had ended up in Sandhu's hands, but she had shown motive and intent.

Faulkner looked at her watch and said, "Nothing further for this witness, your honour."

"I sense that you will want a bit of time with this witness, Mr. Bernstein," the judge said. "Do you want to have at him now or start fresh in the morning?"

Bernstein quickly conferred with his second, Pitman. The choice was between trying to quickly undo some of the damage Fung had done or own the media coverage with a day of cross-examination tomorrow.

"I think we will wait, your honour," Bernstein said. "I intend to examine Mr. Fung's testimony with a highly skeptical eye and that will take some time."

It was the smart move. Bernstein had lost the battle today, but the outcome of the war was far from certain.

It had been a tough day for Sonny Sandhu, but I was happy. My column would practically write itself and I was pretty sure that the odds of Gail Rakic opening up about Luc Champagne's involvement had just gone up substantially.

The big picture was starting to become a little bit clearer. I didn't believe in coincidences. I believed in connecting dots. Luc Champagne had played some kind of role in Sandhu's downfall. The guy who had triggered the Sandhu deal was Chinese. So was Mae Wang. Champagne had been seen entering my apartment building, the one where Mae had died, just a week before her death. I didn't know how all those dots connected, yet, but my experience said they did. I just had to figure out how.

TWENTY-THREE

Tony Yam came out of the kitchen of his Chinatown restaurant, spotted Suzy and rushed through the crowded chaos of tables to give her a big hug, greeting her like a long-lost daughter. He was a small man in his early 60s, but he was surprisingly strong.

"Suzy, so good to see you. I hope that it is not bad news that brings you here today."

"Not compared to what you went through, Tony. I just have a few questions about a girl who died, a member of the community."

Suzy had gotten to know Tony pretty well when she covered his son's murder, a drive by right on Somerset in the heart of Chinatown. The killing was a case of mistaken identity. The killers thought Philip Yam, an engineer who lived in Kanata, was part of a gang. Suzy's legwork had helped reveal the identity of the killers, who now had a minimum of 25 years to reflect on their stupidity.

If there was one thing that she had learned covering that murder five years before, it was that the Chinese community in Ottawa was small and tight. Chinese people knew who was who, and nobody knew more than Tony. If anyone could fill her in on Mae Wang, it would be him.

She had chosen to drop by his restaurant at 3 p.m., hoping to catch him between the noon-time and dinner rush hours. The Golden Dragon was an Ottawa institution and Tony was proud that celebrities and politicians often came in when they were in town. The front lobby of the restaurant was full of pictures of Tony and the famous, although the restaurant itself looked as if it had been decorated with garage sale castoffs. The tables and chairs didn't match and the place hadn't been painted in years. The air was heavy with the smell of spice, oil and an undercurrent of fish.

"You are so thin, Suzy. Let me get you something to eat."

"No, that's OK Tony. I don't want to put you to any trouble."

"Eggrolls, then. No trouble." Tony shouted something in Mandarin to one of his staff, who scurried back into the kitchen.

"Thanks Tony. They're the best. Now, the thing I wanted to talk to you about involves a young woman from the community who died a few days ago. You might have seen a little bit on the news. This is the one who fell to her death over on Elgin Street."

"I did see that. Was it not a suicide?"

"Doesn't look like it, according to what I hear. And here's the strange part. It's not even clear what her real name is."

"Maybe not so strange," Tony said. "Lots of people come here to get away from something back in China. Best way is to change your name, become a new person."

Suzy took the picture of the dead girl from her purse and placed it on the table in front of Tony. "She went by the name Mae Wang. Said she was from Vancouver. She was a student and worked as an interpreter at the embassy. That much we know for sure."

Tony lifted the picture gently with his stubby fingers and turned it toward the light coming from the Somerset Street windows. "She has been here a few times," he said. "Always by herself. Unfortunately, I don't know her."

Suzy realized that she had been hoping for too much. Even Tony Yam didn't know every Chinese person in Ottawa.

"Maybe someone here does," he said, then called out loudly in Mandarin again. "Xi," was the only word she understood.

On hearing his boss's order, a man appeared from the kitchen, wiping his hands on a soiled apron. He didn't look much like a cook, more like an accountant, a serious looking guy in his mid-30s with intelligent eyes. Suzy always noticed eyes.

Tony handed the picture of Mae Wang to Xi. "You know this girl?"

Xi gave the picture a quick glance, then shook his head. "No, never seen her."

His English was flawless, without accent. Why was this guy working as a cook? Despite his quick denial, Suzy thought she saw a flash of recognition. She handed him a business card and said, "Well, if you have any further thoughts, give me a call."

Xi disappeared quickly back into the kitchen and Suzy said, "So what's the story on him?"

"Recent immigrant. You know how hard it is for people to get credentials recognized in this country."

"What was he back home?"

"Lawyer, now he makes great Szechwan dishes."

"I don't imagine he's too happy with that."

"It's a job. Plenty of lawyers in the world."

"Why did you think he'd know something about this girl?"

"Xi helps a lot of newcomers. Understanding immigration rules, things like that."

"He seems pretty wary."

"You have to be. There are three types of Chinese people here. Three generation people like me. New people coming here to escape the regime, then new people coming as eyes of the regime. Those ones are very tricky. You can't trust them, but the question is who's who?"

From what little she knew, Suzy thought Mae might fall into the latter category. It might even be reason enough to get her killed. "So, these eye of the regime, what are they up to?"

"Keeping tabs on all other Chinese. The government in Beijing thinks that a Chinese is a Chinese, no matter how long they live in another country. They expect us all to act in the interests of China?"

"Even you?"

Tony laughed. "No, I am an old man who runs a restaurant. I have little value to them, but I keep my own eyes on what is going on. Some of these new people, they are dangerous. When Philip was alive, he told me that some of the people in technology are here to gather up secrets for the home country."

"What makes them want to do that? Shouldn't they just be glad to have gotten away?"

"Some are forced to come. I'm sure you have read how many people the regime has imprisoned. Threats to family are common. Some are just true believers."

Suzy felt the Mae Wang situation getting murkier, not clearer. The question wasn't just who Mae Wang really was, but how she fit into the big picture. Suzy wondered if Kris knew all this stuff and if she was getting any closer to cracking the mystery of Mae's identity. Part of her hoped not. Suzy wasn't sure yet what Mae Wang's story was, but it felt like something big.

Xi appeared from the kitchen again, carrying a plate of eggrolls. He set them in front of Suzy, briefly touching her hand. Was it meaningful? She really didn't want to take in a bunch of excess calories, but she couldn't refuse Tony's hospitality. He was a good guy, and one who might still come in useful.

"Wow. These look great Tony," she said, digging in. Maybe she could skip dinner.

Tony smiled, pleased at her compliment, then his expression became serious. "One piece of advice Suzy. Stay away from the embassy. It's a nest of spies. People there don't play by the rules we have here and if they get caught, the only consequence for them is to be sent home. These are dangerous people."

Suzy was sure that was excellent advice, but she wasn't going to further her career by staying away from trouble.

TWENTY-FOUR

Even though I had been dangling bait in front of Gail Rakic for days, I was still surprised when she called and suggested we get together for a drink. Of course I agreed and suggested we meet in the Red Dart, the pub on the ground floor of my building. If Gail just wanted to feed me useless tidbits, at least I wouldn't have wasted much time.

More likely, though, she would be angling for some kind of favourable coverage to help offset the miserable day her husband had in court.

The Red Dart was one of those faux British pubs with wainscoting on the walls, fake timber on the ceiling and a pervasive odour of fish and chips that sometimes found its way up into the rest of the building. Not really my favourite spot, but I wasn't going to suggest the kind of snooty downtown cocktail bar I imagined that Gail would normally frequent. Let her slum it.

Right on time, Gail slid onto the bar stool beside me and signalled the waiter. "Vodka martini," she said, then looked across at me. "You?"

"No thanks, I've already ordered a beer." I had never been one for fancy drinks. If you couldn't drink it straight out of a bottle or can, it wasn't my style.

It was the first time I had seen Gail in casual clothes instead of the suits or pantsuits she wore to court. Her jeans were designer, of course, and the thin red sweater that clung to her ample upper body had a designer logo on it. I vaguely remembered seeing the same one on the discount rack at Winners, although I'm sure that's not where Gail picked it up.

"Hell of a day in court," I said.

"Jesus, tell me about it. That Tommy Fung is a lying prick. You spend all day listening to his bullshit, then the evening is all about rehashing it. To be honest, I just had to get out of that hotel room. That's why I gave you a call."

In my experience, when people said "to be honest," it meant that they weren't going to be, but what she said was plausible, up to a point. I decided to encourage her. "If so, he's good at it," I said.

"Just wait until Ben takes a run at him."

"I'm looking forward to it."

"I read your column online. I thought it was fair."

I wasn't sure whether she meant fair to middling, or even-handed. I had expressed some scepticism about Fung, so I was going to go with the latter.

"Thanks. I learned a long time ago that maybe half of what the average witness says is true. Fung is clearly not the average witness."

"No, he's a hustler."

The waiter set Gail's martini and my Beau's Lugtread on the bar. As he walked away, I decided to push a bit, to see if this was the night when she would finally give me some real information or if it was just another small step on the road to becoming her bestie.

"So what's his angle? He said he didn't get anything out of the deal."

"He didn't get anything from that deal, but he got something from someone, you can be sure of that."

It was another one of those oblique answers that seemed to be her specialty. "You're going to have to be a little more specific," I said.

"You think a guy like Fung walks away with nothing while his half-wit partner Gill makes millions on a land deal? I don't think so."

"OK, that makes sense," I said, although I wasn't yet convinced that it did. Maybe Fung had just struck out. It happened in business all the time.

I decided to take it in another direction. "What about the gambling debt angle? I've got to be honest. That seemed like a big score for the Crown. It was the first time they established a motive for why your husband would want to pocket $25,000."

"Sonny didn't pocket a cent," Gail said, eyes flashing with anger. "You want a scoop, here it is. There was no gambling debt. They're just making it up. It's all part of the deal those two clowns made to get themselves out of jeopardy for trying to bribe Sonny."

I could see that. If you were going to roll over and point to a bigger fish, you had to have something to hook him with. "If that's so, why do you think the Crown bought it?"

"Politics and ambition. Nail a couple of grifters for trying to bribe a politician, who cares? Nail a cabinet minister, now you've done something."

"Sure, but the Crown is still going to have to prove that the debt was real."

"I'm sure that they've already got some patsy lined up. That's Fung's real world, you know, gambling. That's where he gets a lot of the cash for his so-called entrepreneurialism. Sonny did meet him at a card game, that much is true. He likes a good game of poker."

"And you knew about his gambling?"

"Of course I did. I know Sonny inside out. It's the competitive challenge for him, not the money. Sometimes he wins, sometimes he loses. It's never enough to matter to us."

"All right. What about the fund-raiser?"

"Sure, Gill helped organize a fund-raiser. So what? It happens all the time."

"What happened to the money?"

"It went to the riding association, like it always does."

"I have a feeling that the Crown has someone to say it didn't."

"I'm sure they will. This is a put-up job, but it's a thorough one."

"It seems like you're telling me your husband is the victim of a conspiracy."

"I guess it comes down to that."

I had met a lot of people who talked about conspiracies over the years, but I hadn't seen many. Truth was, most people weren't smart enough to organize one and if they tried, some weak link would always do it in. I decided that observation wouldn't do anything to advance my relationship with Gail. I switched gears.

"You haven't said anything about Luc Champagne tonight. I assume you think he's the guy behind it all."

"Who else? When this broke, Sonny was the leading contender to replace the PM. Champagne wanted the job, until he cut a different deal and defected to the other side. That ought to tell you something about him."

"Yeah, that he's a politician. No offense to your husband."

"There's a difference. Sonny's Conservative to the bone. That's based on his values. Champagne is an opportunist, lining up with whoever he thinks can win or will give him the best job."

It was a fair point, although it didn't make Champagne guilty of anything. "All this seems like a lot to do to knock off a leadership rival. Champagne's pretty popular. Who's to say that he couldn't have beaten Sonny without dirty tricks?"

"There's something else," she said. "Sonny was ready to take some action of his own, something that would have finished Champagne. And no, I'm not going to tell you what it was."

Of course she wasn't. I decided to take a chance. Reaching into my purse, I took out the picture of Mae Wang and passed it to Gail. "Does it have something to do with her?"

Gail took the photo delicately between her manicured fingers and tilted it so that she could see better in the bar's dim light. "Who is this?" she asked.

"It's the girl who took a swan dive off the roof of this building," I said.

"Really. And you think she's connected to Luc Champagne?"

I wasn't about to tell her why I thought that. It was my hole card. "I was hoping you could tell me."

"Well, I can't, but I might know someone who could."

Gail took out her phone and snapped a shot of the Mae Wang picture. "Let me see what I can find out."

"Good. We might have a mutual interest here."

"It's possible."

Just then, I saw two guys who had been sitting just a little farther down the bar get up and head our way. Both wore grey suits and blue shirts, no ties, like they'd gone shopping together. One was heavy-set, bordering on fat with a pink shiny face and an old-school blond brush cut. The other guy was taller, square jaw, dark hair, couple of days' growth of beard. He looked like an actor, but not a leading player. They both appeared to be in their mid-30s.

"We're about to get hit on," I said to Gail.

"Happens all the time. It comes with big tits. Do you want to tell them to fuck off or should I?"

I didn't like that she assumed the two were drawn by her, although she was probably right. As if to underline the point, the heavier of the two charmers split right toward me while the good-looking one zeroed in on Gail. Seeing an opportunity to establish sisterhood, I said, "Let's see what they have to say. This could be fun."

The big guy stuck out a meaty hand, which I declined to shake, and said, "Hey, I'm Chip Leggett and this is my buddy Don Platt. We're in town for that plumbing supply convention out at the EY Centre, but we're looking for a little fun. Can't stand around talking plumbing parts all day and all night, too."

Great. Salesmen, and from the mid-west, too judging by Chip's flat vowels.

"I suppose not," I said. "About two minutes of that would do me. Where are you boys from?"

"Iowa," Chip said. "Go Hawkeyes."

It looked like Chip's conversation was limited to plumbing supplies and football, while Don might well be mute. I knew that I was skinny-assed and getting older, but it was depressing to think that guys like this might be the only ones who still considered me worth chatting up.

Just to see if Don could speak, I said, "So Don, what role do you play in the big world of plumbing supplies?"

"Sales rep. My specialty is pipe."

I was trying to decide whether Don was attempting what he might have thought would be a clever double entendre when Gail surprised me. "Let's cut to the chase. I take it you guys want to get your rocks off?"

Don held up his hands in a slow-down gesture. "Well, we thought we might buy you a drink first, but I like the direction you're going in."

"Great. Glad we could clear that up." Then she reached into her purse and withdrew two tissues, handing one to each. "Washroom is right down that hall, boys. Go have yourselves a party."

Chip's salesman's grin immediately turned nasty. "Very funny," he said. "Now that I see you up close, you're a little outside our age range anyway. Let's go Don."

As they turned to leave, Don said, "See, I told you that's what these Canadian women were like. Weather up here's so cold they freeze up and never thaw out. We need to find us a couple of the local French girls, that's what we need to do."

Once they were out of earshot, I said, "Nicely played. The only way those guys are going to get laid is if they pay for it."

The phrase tickled at something in the back of my mind. When had I used it recently? And Chip, he had looked somehow familiar, but out of context. Had I seen him somewhere before? The two of them had been sitting close enough at the bar to overhear the conversation I was having with Gail. Maybe her paranoia was contagious. And then I wondered why two guys coming from a trade show out by the airport had ended up in a bar on Elgin Street instead of some place downtown in the Market, where the real action was.

TWENTY-FIVE

Thursday had been a frustrating day so far on the Mae Wang front. Neither Suzy nor Mike had reported in with anything new and I heard nothing more about Gail Rakic's offer to check into Mae. Despite our newfound sisterhood, Gail had not given me so much as a glance in court or in the waiting area outside. Smart move. There was nothing in it for her to be openly friendly with the media. That would just attract the rest of the pack. I just hoped she hadn't been leading me on.

The challenge now was to bear down, pay attention to the trial and get my job done. The first hour of court time had been consumed by the procedural and scheduling fussing that lawyers loved, but Bernstein was just about to begin his cross-examination of Tommy Fung. I hoped it was all Gail expected it to be. Bernstein had to undermine Fung's testimony about gambling debt as a motive. No doubt he would try to demolish whatever credibility Fung had.

"Now Mr. Fung," Bernstein began, "the Crown has established a little bit about your background, but I'd like to give the court a fuller picture." Bernstein smiled, as if this would be another opportunity for Fung to demonstrate how clever, green and well-educated he was.

Fung smiled back, like he expected the same thing. He wore a black suit today, white shirt, grey tie. The only flash of colour came from the brilliant purple frames of today's eyeglasses. I wondered if he had a pair for every outfit.

"Mr. Fung, my office has looked into your business history in considerable detail and we uncovered some interesting things I would like to get your take on today."

It was smart for a lawyer in a heavily publicized trial to underline for the media that something interesting was coming up. It wouldn't do to have your best shots slide by unnoticed.

"Tell the court, if you can, about your business relationship with Fung Holdings, based in Shanghai."

Faulkner began to rise but the judge anticipated her objection. "The Crown has had ample time with this witness Ms. Faulkner. Let Mr. Bernstein get started."

"It's a family corporation. My father owns it."

"I see. And what sort of business is your father in?"

"He has many, many interests, primarily in shipping and manufacturing."

"And some political interests as well."

"Yes, he is involved in that."

"In fact, your father is Fung Chunlan, a member of the politburo, is that not correct?"

"It is."

"So, a very important man in China. And large sums of Chinese money are passing through you for investment in Canadian projects, is that correct?"

"I am the North American representative."

Bernstein paused and flipped through a binder, pretending to look for something. "Mr. Fung, have you had any discussions with any Canadian police or security agency about possible money-laundering concerns?"

"I really have to object," Faulkner said, clearly exasperated. "Mr. Fung is not on trial here, and neither is his father."

"That's true," Justice Macpherson said, "but this goes to witness credibility. I'm interested in the answer. Mr. Fung?"

"No, your honour. Of course not," Fung said.

Bernstein scribbled a note, then said, "All right, Mr. Fung. We have that on the record then."

It felt a lot like Fung had just walked into a trap and Bernstein wanted him to know the jaws would snap shut later. At a minimum, he had made Fung look like a money launderer without having to prove it. The media would like that, but it would take something a lot more solid to persuade the judge.

"Let's turn to your own personal income, Mr. Fung. I understand that you're quite a successful gambler."

Fung nodded enthusiastically, as if this were a compliment. "Yes.

It's all about numbers. I have a good head for numbers."

"I'm sure you do. In your earlier testimony, you referred to a poker game that you say Mr. Sandhu participated in, one with 'dodgier players,' as you called them. Can you tell the court who runs this game."

"I'm afraid I don't recollect. I play in a lot of games."

"I see. Can you identify any of the players at this game where you say my client lost $25,000?"

"Not at this time."

"Really? Here you are in court, Mr. Fung, testifying against my client, but you can't remember basic facts about your key allegation. Would you have the court believe that you were gambling tens of thousands of dollars, but you didn't know who the other players were?"

"Well, it wasn't like these were friends of mine."

Bernstein made another note. "All right, Mr. Fung. Perhaps we will return to that later, see if your memory has improved."

I could see why Fung wouldn't want to name in court anyone who played in a dodgy card game, but I wondered if the game had ever existed. Of course, I had already been pointed in that direction by Gail, but I thought Bernstein had achieved his goal.

"Let's move on to the fund-raising event. Did you attend it?"

"I did not, although I bought a full table, 10 tickets."

"I see. And did you make any connection with any officials from Mr. Sandhu's riding association?"

"No. I got the tickets through Mr. Gill."

"So you weren't very involved, but you told the court earlier that, after the money went to the riding association, Mr. Sandhu 'would take care of it from there.' What did you take that to mean?"

Faulkner said, "Your honour, my friend objected to this very question on the grounds that the witness had no direct knowledge of what happened next."

"I did," Bernstein said, "but now I'd like to explore Mr. Fung's thinking a little further."

The judge waved away Faulkner's objection. "Very well, Mr. Bernstein, but you made a good point the first time."

"Let me repeat that for you, Mr. Fung. When Mr. Sandhu said he would take it from there, what did you take that to mean?"

"That he'd find a way to get that money to settle his gambling debt."

"Ah, and how did you deduce that, sir?"

"Well, he didn't say it in so many words, but I thought that was the whole point of the exercise."

"You thought that. Is that what you're telling the court? This isn't something Mr. Sandhu told you specifically?"

"Not specifically, no."

Tommy, as he called himself, didn't look like he was enjoying his second day of testimony quite as much as he had the first. His face was flushed and his smile looked artificial.

"But it was what you would have done yourself, right?"

"I wasn't the one with a gambling debt."

"No? Mr. Fung, I have a document here that I'd like you to take a look at." Bernstein handed several pages of paper to Fung, then said, "Can you verify that this is a summary of your corporate bank account for the last six months?"

Fung quickly leafed through the document, then nodded.

"A yes or no for the court, please Mr. Fung."

"Yes, this is the corporate account."

"Excellent. Now Mr. Fung, you will notice the highlighted withdrawals, and very helpfully they were cheques. You will see that the amounts range from $10,000 to $30,000, all made out to individuals. Are these corporate payments?"

"They must be," Fung said. "This is my corporate account."

"So I would have expected, but then I researched these individuals a little further. Do the names Paul Abrams, Larry Tsu or Pierre Groulx mean anything to you?"

Fung shook his head. "No, not that I can recollect."

"My investigator tells me that these are all gentlemen who make their livings primarily from playing poker in private games. Ringing any bells now?"

"Still not coming to me."

"Let me ask you this, then. Mr. Fung, were you clearing personal gambling debts using corporate funds?"

"Certainly not. Our books are carefully audited."

"I'm sure. Let's move on."

I thought Bernstein was going after this with just the right touch.

He didn't need to prove that Fung had done anything wrong, just plant the idea that he was the kind of guy who would.

"Mr. Fung, you were initially interviewed about this matter by the RCMP, is that correct?"

"It is. I offered to co-operate fully."

"That's grand. Did your offer come before or after the Crown offered you immunity in exchange for your testimony."

"I don't remember exactly."

"Let me help you out. According to the transcript of your original interview, you denied any knowledge of what was behind this supposed deal with Mr. Sandhu and you never mentioned a gambling debt. That didn't come until weeks later."

"If you say so."

I flicked on Twitter on my phone. Judging by the running commentary from my colleagues, Fung was going to get eaten alive.

"It isn't me saying so, Mr. Fung. It's the RCMP. Surely you must have seen the transcript. Do you dispute their account?"

Fung shot a glance at Faulkner.

"Don't look at her, Mr. Fung, look at me. I'm sure the Crown has reviewed the RCMP's statement with you. Did you find it accurate?"

It didn't seem like the biggest point on which to hang Fung out to dry, but I expected that the real point was to rattle him in preparation for the next question. It was working because Call Me Tommy was looking flustered.

"Sure, all right. It was accurate."

"Very good, Mr. Fung. One last question. Isn't it true, sir, that you and your partner, Mr. Gill, concocted this story about the gambling debt to escape your own responsibility for attempting to bribe a government official?"

"Not at all. That's completely false."

"Completely false? All right then, that's your testimony."

Bernstein leaned over the defence table to scribble another note on his yellow legal pad. "That's all I have for you, Mr. Fung."

Faulkner rose to redirect. It would be her shot to try to mitigate the damage done to her witness by Bernstein. I didn't feel optimistic about her chances. It was time to head back to the media room and bang out my column.

TWENTY-SIX

One of the good things about Ottawa is that, no matter which direction you drive out of the city, you hit the boonies pretty fast. Having spent my childhood in the Adirondacks and my teenage years up the Ottawa Valley, the middle of nowhere was my kind of place.

With court not sitting on Friday, I was free to chase the Mae Wang story. When Reilly called first thing and suggested a drive in the country to meet a source, I thought why not?

We were deep in the Lanark Highlands, northwest of the city. Out the window, I saw swampy wetlands, jagged granite outcrops and heavy maple forest. It was the kind of country that had way more deer than people.

For a miled-out cop car, Reilly's personal Crown Vic was surprisingly quiet, and so was he. The only annoying sound was Ranger's snoring in the back seat. I had brought him along with the thought that a run in the country would do him good. A snooze seemed to be a higher priority for him.

I felt comfortable driving in silence with Reilly. I had never been one of those people who felt compelled to open my mouth just for the sake of making sound. Reilly was the same way. I wondered what he was thinking about. He was putting his ass on the line helping me with the Mae Wang story when the brass hats had explicitly told him to drop it. Maybe he had reached the age where he just didn't give a shit what the bosses thought any more. Me, I had hit that point back in my 20s.

Reilly's only piece of news had been delivered just after I got into the car. He was still digging into the apartment tenancy records so helpfully supplied by Mr. Mo, but he had discovered that a unit on the top floor was rented to the China-Canada Trading Company, a shell corporation with a fake address and no named directors. It was intriguing, but I knew better than to assume that Point A and

Point B were connected just because it would help a story. It was still a tangible link between the Chinese and the building where Mae had died.

We hadn't seen a house for 25 kilometres when we finally approached a small hamlet of half a dozen worn-out, unpainted wooden homes. A road sign, equally tired, told me that it was Mee-cham's Corners. The rusted-out cars up on blocks reminded me of the upstate New York town where I had grown up.

"This it?" I asked.

"No, no. This guy lives deep in the bush."

"If we get any deeper, we're going to come out the other side."

"He values his privacy."

"Plenty of that around here. How do you know him anyway?"

"We worked a case together once. Thing with a Russian diplomat who was smuggling drugs. Guilty as hell, but of course they just shipped him home. That was years ago, but we were close at the time. Then he transferred over to CSIS. He's out now, but he's still the best shot I've got to find out what's going on with Mae Wang."

"You tell him that I was coming?"

"I did. He's not exactly the kind who normally talks to the media. Wants to meet you before he'll say anything. Even then, this is all going to be deep background."

"I'm OK with that. You think he's reliable?"

"Who knows? When I worked with him, we both had the same view of the system, you know what I mean?"

"Yeah, I think I do."

Reilly slowed the car and said, "OK, this is it."

A reflective green sign said 3472. It was one of those that town-ships put up so that the volunteer firefighters know where to come to hose the ashes after your home burns down. Other than that, I wouldn't have guessed that the narrow, rutted lane led to a house.

Reilly nosed the Crown Vic into the lane and said, "The house is about two kilometres back."

"Great. I'm thinking he doesn't get many door-to-door salesmen. What's his name again?"

"Farrell."

"Seems appropriate."

As we got farther back, the lane narrowed even more and

branches whacked against the side of the car, their fresh green leaves tearing and sticking to the windshield.

"I'm glad I drive a beater," Reilly said.

After he navigated around a half dozen flooded potholes and rocky humps in the road, we finally came to a clearing. I could see a squat stone house, the kind they built a lot of around Eastern Ontario back in the 1850s. I could smell the thin plume of smoke that came from one of the two chimneys and drifted up among the branches of a massive maple that was probably as old as the house. In the side yard, there was an open-fronted shed of weathered wood that was partly filled with split firewood. In front of the shed stood a shirtless man wearing jeans and beat-up construction boots. He raised an axe over his head and brought it down with great force, splitting a heavy piece of firewood like it had exploded. The guy was built like Thor and had the heavy beard and long hair to match. It was either white or blond. It was hard to tell from a distance.

"How old is this Farrell?" I asked.

"Somewhere in his 40s."

"I guess splitting wood is a good fitness program."

Farrell put another chunk of firewood on the stump he used for splitting and whacked it into three pieces. I was sure he had known we were on the property the minute we came up the lane, but for the moment, he was ignoring us.

We got out of the car. I heard nothing but birds and the wind in the trees. Somehow, I felt like I was home again.

"Hey, Farrell," Reilly shouted. "You've got company."

Farrell sunk the axe into the chopping block, then picked up a blue denim shirt and wiped his face with it before putting it on. He walked across the yard towards us. If his face had an expression, it was masked by his thick beard. I learned more from his intense blue eyes, which were surveying me up and down, trying to determine whether I was likely to be friend or foe.

He held out his hand to Reilly and said, "Been a long time, buddy. You good?"

"The best," Reilly said. "I'd like you to meet my friend Kris Redner, the writer from the *Citizen*."

Interesting that Reilly would call me that. Did he really think of me as a friend or was he just trying to ease Farrell's co-operation?

Farrell offered me his meaty hand. It was calloused and strong. "Thanks for agreeing to meet with us," I said.

"I haven't agreed to anything yet," he said. "People in my type of work don't spend a lot of time talking to reporters."

"Columnist," I corrected. "And what is your type of work?"

"Security consultant, mostly in places that are hot, sandy and have no income tax."

I wondered what "security consultant" meant, exactly. Mercenary, soldier of fortune, assassin? Maybe it didn't matter as long as Reilly trusted the guy and he could help us. I had to admit I found him intriguing. He had something an old boss of mine at the *Star* liked to call command presence.

"Come on in," Farrell said and turned toward the house.

"I brought my dog. OK if I let him out for a run?"

"Sure," Farrell said, then smiled when he saw Ranger. "I hope he doesn't get terrified by a squirrel."

I unleashed Ranger, deciding that coming to his defence was pointless. Reilly and I followed Farrell into the house. Inside, you'd never know it was a warm spring day. The old stone walls still held winter's chill, somewhat offset by a black cast iron woodstove that smouldered with the remains of last night's fire. When it came to home furnishings, Farrell was clearly a minimalist. His kitchen held a pine harvest table, well used, and four mismatched wooden chairs. Other than a Keurig machine on the counter, that was it. The cabinets were rickety and covered with layers of paint, the top one whitish. They looked original. The only really notable feature was a glass-fronted gun case with a half-dozen long guns on display. There were pump and double-barrelled shotguns, an old Winchester deer rifle like the one my Uncle Martin used to have and three dark, evil-looking assault rifles. I wasn't an expert on guns, but I knew he wasn't using these to hunt groundhogs.

Gesturing toward the gun case, I said, "You expecting a war?"

"There are plenty of wars. You never know when one might come here."

"Seems like a pretty quiet, out-of-the-way place."

"That's the idea." He pointed to the table and said, "Have a seat. Coffee?"

I said yes just to see him use the Keurig. He seemed more like the kind of guy who would have chosen one of those old-fashioned pots with the speckled metal finish.

"When does a cop ever say no to coffee?" Reilly said.

"Never." Farrell pulled three Keurig pods from one of his ancient cabinets without asking what we wanted. "So, Reilly, you said you had a case involving Chinese diplomats and you were hoping I could help. What crimes did they commit now?"

"We're not sure if they committed any, but there's some strange shit going on."

I drank my coffee black, there apparently being no milk or cream. Maybe his cow died. I was content to let Reilly outline the facts, or what we thought were the facts, about Mae Wang's death. As he told the story up to now, I watched Farrell's reaction. He had that focus that all good cops and interviewers have. His eyes never left Reilly's face.

After hearing it all, Farrell stroked his beard and seemed lost in thought. Finally, he said, "So if I am going to help you, there have to be some ground rules. We never met, I didn't help you and if anyone asks, I don't even exist. No quotes, no off the record, no deep background. I might be able to act as a guide, point you in the right direction. After that, you're on your own."

"This is all under the radar on my end anyway," Reilly said. "Kris, those rules work for you?"

"Sure." What did I have to lose? A shady mercenary wasn't exactly a top on-the-record source anyway.

"The last couple of years I was with CSIS, I worked mainly on Chinese files. I understand how those fuckers think. They play the long game. They hack into any business or government computer they can, looking for technology and intel. What they can't steal, they buy or get through pressure. Canada is prime money-laundering territory for the gangsters who run the country. Take some shady dollars, offshore them and invest in a nice Canadian company, preferably in natural resources. All the while, they are sucking up to gullible political leaders, acting like their best friends. Think of a snake wearing a puppy dog costume.

"So let's break it down. The girl is a Chinese national, true name unknown. She's an interpreter at the embassy, which means either they trust her or they control her. She dies on the roof of an apartment building after a struggle. Maybe she was thrown off or maybe it was just a desperate jump. Either way, there is a question mark. If the Chinese wanted to get rid of her, why make such a mess of the killing, then create an incident to get the body back? They had her in their power. If they wanted her gone, she'd simply have disappeared."

"Right," Reilly said. "The Chinese are woven in here somewhere. One of the units in the building where Mae died is rented by a Chinese shell corporation, by the way. Still, I doubt they killed her."

"More like someone sending a message to the Chinese," Farrell said.

I decided to sit back and let the two of them go at it, without taking notes. Farrell would be more comfortable with Reilly.

"Or to someone the girl was associated with," Reilly said

"This joker Champagne, maybe."

"Maybe, but all we've got to tie her to him is video of him going into her building. He could have been going there to see anyone."

"From what I know of Champagne, he's a skirt chaser. What if the Chinese were using Mae Wang to get a hold on him? The honey trap is the oldest gambit in the espionage game."

"That seems farfetched, but let's say it's true. Who benefits by getting rid of her?" Reilly said.

"The guy is the foreign affairs minister. If he was hooking up with someone working for the Chinese, that's a huge problem for the government. The RCMP clearly knew something about this and I'm sure my old buddies at CSIS did, too.

"If they got wind of it, our allies would worry about what secrets might have been getting out. That brings in any country that's part of the Five Eyes. Certainly the Americans. Maybe the Brits."

"Excuse me guys," I said. "That's a hell of a story if true, but I don't live in spy world. What's Five Eyes?"

"It's a co-operative intel arrangement between the Brits, the Americans, the Kiwis, the Aussies and us," Farrell said. "We share what we learn. So they say anyway. It's a big back door into American intelligence efforts. Some countries see Canada as an easy point of entry, especially the Chinese. Those Chinese files I mentioned? That's what I was working on."

"What made you quit?" I asked.

"Too much bureaucracy and bullshit. I reached the point where I was only sticking around to boost my pension. It was time to get out. No offence, Reilly."

"None taken. My pension is maxed out. I just stick around to piss them off."

"Good a reason as any," Farrell said.

Farrell seemed like he knew what he was talking about, but if he was right, the scope of this story was a lot broader than I had imagined. Mae Wang's killer could be any one of a number of murky bad guys who would be hard to bring to justice. Assuming we were even on the right track.

"So what next?" I asked.

"I'm going to make some calls to people who are still in, see what I can find out."

"Won't that put a flag on our investigation?"

Farrell smiled for the first time. "Give me some credit. These are people I talk to regularly. I'll just tell them I'm working for a client. There is a network of people who get the Chinese problem and want to act. I do them some favours, they do some for me."

"How long do you think this will take?"

"Probably not long," Farrell said, putting his chipped white coffee mug back on the pine table. "Now, security measures. Reilly, your phone is probably secure. Kris, yours is not. All this stuff you've been reading about Quebec police tapping in to journalists' phones is not a one-off. You need to assume that someone could be monitoring every key stroke on your computer, every text and e-mail you send, and every call you make. They can use the GPS in your phone to track your every move. That's why I asked that you bring no electronics here."

When Reilly had told me that the guy we were seeing would only meet us if we had no phones or computers, I took him to be a bit paranoid. Now, I wasn't so sure. I certainly wasn't naïve enough to think that government and its many agencies were the good guys.

Farrell got up, pulled open a balky kitchen drawer, and took out two experienced-looking cell phones. "These are burners I got cheap on Kijiji. When I find out something, I will contact you that way."

I wondered what Reilly thought about all of this. Like me, he was a skeptic by nature, but he said, "All right. Thanks. Best to assume we're dealing with serious people here."

"We know the Chinese are in play," Farrell said, "so yeah, about as serious as they get."

I began to worry just a little bit more about what I had gotten myself into. I was used to bad, even dangerous, people but most of them were after sex, money or drugs, not me. The people Farrell was talking about were in a whole different league, and I felt like I had painted a target on myself.

TWENTY-SEVEN

It was just after 1 p.m. by the time Reilly got back to the Major Crimes squad room at police headquarters on Elgin Street. The room was empty, except for the usual stacked up cardboard boxes and squeezed-in desks. His squad had too few people to do the job, but too many to fit into the space. Right now, the other detectives were out working cases, or maybe just at lunch. Not everyone was as work obsessed as Reilly.

He had said that he was taking the morning to pursue a lead, without specifying the case. He was glad there was no one there to quiz him about it. With his workload, there was no way to justify his personal Mae Wang crusade, but hopefully he wouldn't have to.

When you were the staff sergeant in charge, you had quite a bit of latitude, but his inspector still expected results. Larry Ferguson was a decent guy, but he was one of the many Ottawa officers with acting-rank status. Ferguson had to make his mark if he wanted permanent promotion and it had made him obsessed with stats. Right now, the squad's stats weren't good. Ottawa already had eight homicides for the year and five were unsolved. Reilly was carrying three personally, all Somalis, all involved with the drug trade and in every case, no one was willing to come forward with information. That was understandable. Ratting out a drug gang member who had already committed homicide could be a life-shortening experience. It made his job difficult, though. Most days, he felt like he was pushing three big rocks up a very steep hill.

Reilly settled in behind his desk and fired up his computer. His inbox was jammed. He seemed to spend half his life sending case updates in all directions to create the illusion of progress. Sometimes that seemed harder than progress itself.

At least the drive out to see Farrell had not been the wild good chase that Reilly had feared. Farrell sounded like he was still well plugged in. Reilly wondered exactly what kind of hairy shit Farrell did for a living these days. Judging by the armaments he had on display, it didn't just involve putting on a suit and advising corporations about computer security. Reilly was sure that what he could see in the gun case was just a fraction of Farrell's personal armoury. The really good stuff would be kept well out of sight, although probably not far out of reach.

He hoped that Farrell would produce some results, because the case wasn't getting much traction despite Kris's efforts. It was frustrating not to know who Mae Wang actually was and how she fit into the big picture. For that matter, what was the big picture?

The case kept coming back to Luc Champagne. The fact that Champagne was showing up at the building on Tuesday nights and Mae Wang almost certainly stayed in that same building Tuesday nights was extremely unlikely to be a coincidence. What was Mae's connection to Champagne? The idea that she was some kind of Chinese spy trying to woo secrets from Champagne was plausible, but he couldn't support it yet with any hard evidence. He'd love to sit Champagne down for a chat, but that would never happen until he had something ironclad, something solid and incriminating enough to get it past his own bosses.

There was still the problem of Mr. Thursday. Who the hell was the hefty guy in the oddball winter hat? He had been showing up regularly, too, and his timetable overlapped with Mae's just as well as Champagne's did. Maybe the guy was just some schlump paying for sex but that theory would fly only if Mae was a hooker, and there was no evidence of that.

No, Mr. Thursday had to be part of the puzzle, but Reilly literally did not have clue one about who the guy was beyond the fact that he was Caucasian, at least six feet tall and owned a bad hat with earflaps. There were probably at least 10,000 guys like that in Ottawa.

Reilly had thrown out his own similar hat after Kris's comment about a guy wearing a hat like that never getting laid. Not that it had changed his luck in that regard. The problem was more serious than his hat choice.

Reilly thought about Suzy, as he did several times most days. He had stopped asking Kris about her because she was either unsympathetic or on Suzy's side, but that didn't mean he was any less thirsty for information about his former lover. He did know that she was working some angles of the Mae Wang story, and that worried him. If Farrell thought there was danger in this case, then there was danger, and Suzy hadn't been warned. Whoever was behind Mae's death obviously considered homicide a solution when facing a problem. Were her computer and phone being monitored?

Suzy had always been irritated about the way Reilly worried when she was putting herself in risky situations. Sure, that was her job, but she just didn't see the dangers the way he did.

Work was what broke them up. When they had started up, they had talked about ground rules and Reilly had thought a police reporter would understand a cop's job nearly as well as a fellow cop. She knew that he couldn't lay out all the details of his cases for her, but she got pissed when he held back on her.

She had a driving ambition to become a big media star, someone who appeared on the national news every night. Reilly had ambition himself, back when he was her age, but you either got your break or you didn't. Blowing up your life over work just didn't pay off.

As they went on, things got worse. It all came to a head when he caught her trolling through his work phone. He felt he had to draw a line, but she stepped right over it and out the door.

When it was good between them, though, it was the best connection Reilly had ever had with a woman, even better than with his former wife, Jenny. Suzy had a formidable ability to focus and on those occasions when all of her attention was on him, Reilly had felt like the centre of the world.

Then there was the whole younger woman thing. At first, it had been exciting, non-stop sex of the kind that he hadn't had in years. Maybe it was a generational thing, but Suzy had no inhibitions and treated sex like a particularly enjoyable sport. When Reilly had been young, women like that didn't seem to exist.

Then the novelty wore off, as it always did. Being 20 years older, Reilly could never admit to so much as an ache or pain for fear of looking like an old man. Every morning, the first thing he did was to see if his jaw line had gotten softer or his hair greyer. He worried about the time when he would really be old and Suzy would still be middle-aged.

Well, not his problem now.

Maybe it had all been wrong from the start. What kind of man steals his son's girlfriend? Reilly used to justify it to himself with some kind of "it was just meant to be" crap, but that didn't wash any more. Karma could be a bitch.

If there was a bright side, it was that he had spared Sean from a relationship that wouldn't have worked out. Suzy just wasn't a long-term girl. Or maybe Sean *would* have made it work. Already an inspector and well-regarded in the senior ranks, he had played his cards better than Reilly had. It made Reilly proud. Too bad he never had the chance to tell him.

Kris Redner reminded Reilly of Suzy in some ways, but she seemed to have mellowed out a bit. She never talked about whatever it was that had happened to her last year, but she seemed less cocky and overconfident than she used to.

Reilly sometimes wondered if he had a chance there. Kris wasn't bad looking, if you didn't mind them bony, and they seemed to have found a natural rhythm working on the Mae Wang story. He'd see how it went once the story was over. That would be the test of whether he was someone she had a connection with or just a handy guy to know.

Reilly's train of thought was interrupted by the arrival of Pete Dombrowski, an old-school detective who used to be Reilly's partner. Pete looked like a basset hound in a fedora, a hat style so out of date that it had become retro. Despite his unlikely appearance, Pete was a damned good cop.

"Hey Reilly, you getting anywhere with your dead skinnies?"

Reilly winced. Pete had a derogatory term for every racial group there was. He could zero in on the way people looked, like the slim Somalis, or their colour or their race. In fairness, he called himself a Polack. Reilly was just glad that Pete didn't understand how to use social media. Reilly had enough problems as it was. The last thing he needed was to get caught up in some kind of racial sensitivity issue.

TWENTY-EIGHT

I sank into the baggy couch in my borrowed apartment, put my feet up on the glass coffee table and scratched behind Ranger's ears while managing a piece of pepperoni pizza with my left hand. The local CTV news recounted the day's tally of shootings and car crashes, but I didn't find it engaging. Normally, I always had my antenna up looking for column angles, but between the Sandhu trial and the Mae Wang story, I had my hands full.

Ranger rolled over on his side so I could scratch his belly. It had taken time, but we had developed quite a rapport. I would probably miss him when I handed him and the apartment back to the real owner. He lifted his chin up and I gave him a little rub there, too. I tried not to dwell on the fact that I was a single woman on the brink of middle age who was spending Friday night at home alone with her pet. It was probably a warning sign that I was moving toward crazy cat lady status. Maybe I'd check online later and see.

I reached for the bottle of beer that was propped between my legs and then had one of those thought sequences that comes out of nowhere. First, I thought it had been a long time since I had had anything between my legs, then I thought of Farrell. Dr. Freud would have had fun with that.

My first impression of the semi-retired spook was that he was yet another hairy woodsman, a type I knew well from my youth. It didn't take long to figure out that he was a smart guy with strong opinions who had been in some tough spots and walked out alive. There was something else, though. Charisma wasn't the right word, exactly. It was some blend of confidence, calmness and strength. He was the kind of man you found yourself thinking about hours after you had met him, like he was still present in the room. In that way, he reminded me of a mature version of L.T., the young cop I had gotten tangled up with last summer in the Adirondacks.

I hoped that I wouldn't bring Farrell the kind of luck that I had brought L.T.

Or maybe I just liked the look of him with his shirt off. It was a reminder that I needed to get laid, but I seemed to have gotten myself into a spot where that was impossible. Colin was available, of course, but I couldn't get back into bed with him without setting off a whole chain of emotional complexity that I just couldn't handle right now. For just a moment, I considered going down to the Red Dart to see if I could get lucky, but then I remembered those two dickwad American salesmen. Some things were worse than celibacy. I just hoped I didn't shrivel up before the problem resolved itself.

Farrell had given me a feeling of reasonable confidence that Reilly and I were going in the right direction on the Mae Wang story, but what he said scared me, too. When Reilly dropped me off at my place, I had immediately started digging into stories about the Chinese regime. Farrell might be paranoid, but he was spot on about the Chinese. They were ruthless when it came to furthering their national interests and the laws of other countries didn't slow them down at all. The news was full of stories about people detained and tortured, or dragged in front of a "justice" system that had a 99.5-per-cent conviction rate.

I still didn't see them as the ones behind Mae Wang's death. It appeared that she was working for them, willingly or otherwise. Her messy demise didn't appear to further their interests. If not them, then who?

I wiped my greasy fingers on my jeans and picked up my cell phone. It had been two days since I had heard a thing from Suzy. Either she was striking out completely or she was holding back whatever she found. I knew which option I would put my money on. I brought up her number in my contacts and tapped it. The phone rang four times, then went to voice mail. Had she seen that it was me calling? "Hey, it's Kris," I said. "I've found out a few things. Wondering what you've got. We should get together, compare notes. Call me."

I wouldn't be holding my breath waiting for the return call. It would probably take a direct order from Colin to get her to give up anything, but I wasn't ready to drop that bomb yet. I would give the nice route a try and if that didn't work, I'd drop the hammer tomorrow.

Then I had an idea. Reilly had told me that unit 603 was rented by that dubious Chinese holding company, but he couldn't get a warrant to check it out because, officially, he wasn't on the case. Maybe the place had already been cleaned out and scoured, and maybe it hadn't. There was only one way to find out.

When I knocked on Mr. Mo's door, the superintendent was even less glad to see me than he had been the last time. He was wearing his usual black track suit and a worried expression.

"The police lady," he said. "What do you want now?"

If he thought I was a police lady, who was I to contradict him? "Our review of the records shows an issue with Apartment 603. I will need the key to conduct a search"

"Ah, and do you have a warrant for this search?"

"I could get one, but then I'd probably want to look at several other apartments as well. I'm very thorough. I'm afraid it would cause quite a disruption. That's why I am focusing only on this one apartment, to make things easier for you."

Mr. Mo clearly wasn't buying it, but I could see him doing the mental calculation. What if what I was saying was true? And 603 had no regular tenant. If I got in and out quickly, perhaps no one would know.

"All right, but this is a very kind act on my part. I will get the key."

He went back inside his own apartment and quickly reappeared with a brass key. "Please, do this as quickly as possible," he said. "Management would frown on such activity."

"Don't worry. Management will never hear about it from me."

I took the elevator back up to the sixth floor. As I had hoped, there was no one in the hallway. Number 603 was to the right of the elevator, at the end of the hall. My shoes made no sound on the stained red carpet of the hallway. I could smell someone frying fish and could hear the sound of television in 602. To be safe, I tapped lightly on the door. There was no answer. I turned the key in the lock, opened the door just a crack, then waited to see if I could hear any sound inside. Nothing.

I swung the door open wide, then stepped quickly into the

apartment. In the weak light of the evening sun, I saw an impersonal space with two grey, cloth-covered couches facing each other, separated by a glass coffee table. The walls themselves were a dark grey. There was no mess, no disarray, no personal photos. A cheap print of a generic sunset hung on one wall. I took my shoes off and walked quietly into the kitchen, careful not to alert the tenants below. The room had been updated with white IKEA cupboards and stainless steel appliances. I opened the fridge. It was empty except for half a dozen cans of Bud, a container of orange juice and a part loaf of rye bread that was growing some interesting looking green mould. The cupboards contained a set of white dishes, neatly stacked.

The bedroom held a king-sized bed with a headboard of faux black leather. The bed was so neatly made that I half expected to see a chocolate on the pillow. There was a single dresser. The drawers were empty. I pulled open the night table drawer, wondering if I would find Gideon's Bible. Instead, I saw an array of sex toys, one of them black and quite impressive. The love nest theory was starting to shape up, although the sex toys didn't say much for the stamina of Mae's lovers, if that's what this place had been all about.

The bathroom was tiny, just like my own. It held a walk-in shower the size of a phone booth, a pedestal sink, a toilet and a medicine cabinet. In the perfect world, there would have been a pill bottle with Mae's name on it, but instead there was only Aspirin and a half-used bottle of Astroglide. Everything a woman really required.

I pulled back the covers from the carefully made bed and sniffed the two pillow cases. One smelled of coarse male cologne. Brut, I thought. I had once inadvisably gone on a date with a guy who wore it. The other held the lingering odour of a perfume. I thought it was one that I had smelled at Mae's apartment, but there was no way to know for sure.

I checked the closet next. Empty of course, except for a bunch of hangers. Nothing on the upper shelf. I got down on my knees and lifted the red comforter that hung nearly to the floor. Peering under the bed, I saw a nice collection of dust bunnies on the hardwood floor. Then something shiny caught my eye.

I reached under the bed and fished out a thin silver necklace. It was broken at the clasp, but a Chinese symbol pendant still hung from the chain. I had no idea what the symbol meant, but it certainly upped the chances that Mae had been in this room.

I sat on the bed and ran my fingers along the necklace, feeling the pendant, then rubbing it with my thumb. I closed my eyes and imagined the necklace on Mae. Had there been a struggle in this room or had the necklace simply broken?

The last rays of the sunset came through the bedroom window and I could see dust motes floating in the air. The apartment had that particular quiet that occurs when the occupants are absent. The air seemed stale, almost heavy, and yet somehow disturbed. Mae hadn't died here. That chain of events happened on the roof, but I would bet that it had started here.

I considered what to do with the necklace. It was evidence, maybe, but at best it would prove that Mae had been in the apartment. We already knew that she had been in the building. I slipped it into my pocket. Maybe the piece of jewelry would spark something with Mae's roommate.

It was time to go, but first I took out my phone and took a few shots of the bedroom. If this story ever landed, the desk would want art.

That task complete, I stepped quietly toward the door, my feet cool on the wooden floors. Just as I reached the door, my phone started to ring. Shit. I pulled it from my jeans. It was Colin. "Can't talk now," I said, conscious that I was whispering. "I'll call you back."

"What's up? Why are you whispering?" he said in his usual booming voice. I hung up. Maybe Farrell's caution about phones was just paranoia, but maybe not.

TWENTY-NINE

Suzy Morin parked her BMW in front of the Poplar Street address she had been given by Xi, the lawyer/cook from the Golden Dragon. Poplar was a short street of modest, mostly flat-roofed houses in the area on the borderline between Chinatown and Little Italy. Night had just fallen, but there was still a faint pink glow in the west. The streetlights had come on, and that was a relief. The street looked a bit sketchy to Suzy. She hoped her car would still be there when she was done talking to Xi.

She would have loved to get this interview done earlier, but Xi had to finish his shift. Nearly two days had passed since Suzy met him at the restaurant and she had almost given up on him when he phoned and offered to meet. She was pleased that her intuition about him had been proven right. He had been cryptic and sounded a bit paranoid. Maybe it was because he had been at work. She had heard kitchen sounds in the background.

Still, it was a lead.

Suzy walked up onto the verandah of the little house, which had dingy white siding and some kind of fake stone across the lower part of the front. As instructed, she took the door on the left and climbed a steep and narrow flight of stairs until she reached a red door with a shiny new lock on it.

She knocked and Xi opened the door but didn't release the security chain. "Ah, it is you," he said.

"As promised. You going to let me in?"

"Of course," he said, swinging the door open.

Suzy was surprised by the apartment. It was tidy and modern, the walls white, the furniture black leather or an imitation of it. A red and white rug in a geometric pattern filled most of the living space. A desk stood in one corner of the main room. The computer was shut down, but she saw stacks of books on the left side of the workspace. Law books, by the look of them.

Xi was neatly dressed in black pants and a white shirt. His hair was still wet as if he had just gotten out of the shower. Getting rid of the cooking smells, she thought. He waved her to the couch and said, "Tea?"

"Do you have green?"

"Of course."

Xi went down the hall to the kitchen to put the kettle on. Suzy took the opportunity to give the room a closer look. There was only one personal touch. On a little table between the couch and the chairs was a framed photograph of a slightly younger Xi with a Chinese woman who was holding a child of perhaps two. His family, she presumed. What had happened to them?

Xi returned quickly with the green tea. It wasn't her favourite, but if she went with Earl Grey at this hour the caffeine would keep her up all night.

Suzy reached into her purse and took out a notebook and her phone, which she used to record interviews. Xi immediately held up his hands in a "stop" gesture and said, "I am willing to give you some help, but I can't have my name in the paper. My situation here is complex."

Suzy put her phone back in her bag but kept the notebook out. "Actually, I don't even have your full name," she said. "I won't need to quote you or name you, but I do need to take some notes, for accuracy. So, let's start with you name."

"You can just call me Xi."

"No first name?"

"What's the point? You are not going to use it. My last name might not even be Xi."

Suzy smiled, reminding herself to be patient. One thing she had learned investigating Philip Yam's murder was that Chinese people never went in a straight line if they could reach the same destination by going in a circle.

"All right. Xi it is then. Tell me a little bit about yourself. I know you were a lawyer back in China. How did you end up here?"

"In a cargo container on a ship, but that's a different story."

"Trouble back home?"

"You could say that. Lawyers who defend opponents of the

regime are branded opponents themselves. I was lucky to get out."

Suzy gestured toward the photograph of Xi with the woman and child. "What about your family?"

"They are alive and safe. Someday, I hope to bring them here."

"I'm guessing you are here illegally."

"I prefer the term 'undocumented'," Xi said, allowing himself a small smile.

"You do sound like a lawyer."

"An occupational hazard. I am not a lawyer here. Seeking that status would put a spotlight on me that I cannot risk."

"I understand. Tony said that you do some work helping new immigrants, though."

"Yes. I try to help others. I actually enjoy cooking, but working for Tony does not occupy my mind."

Suzy could see that Xi wasn't going to be particularly forthcoming about himself, and it didn't really matter. While it was important to break the ice with a source, it was what he knew about Mae Wang that really counted.

"Let's switch gears," she said. "Mae Wang. She was murdered. I am trying to find out who did it, but the first problem I have is that I know next to nothing about Mae. She was an interpreter at the embassy and a student at Carleton. Those things are true. She said she was from Vancouver, but that's pretty murky. I suspect you are going to tell me that Mae was someone else altogether."

Xi sipped his tea and looked closely at Suzy, as if he were making one last effort to read her intentions. Then he said, "That's exactly what I am going to tell you. The woman you call Mae Wang is actually Zhao Mei. I knew her family in China. I was shocked when I saw her in the restaurant. I had no idea that she had gotten out."

"And you knew her family how?"

"Her father, Zhao Yang, was a great defence lawyer, a champion of those who criticize the state. To punish him for this, they sentenced him to 10 years in prison. That was more than two years ago. I was a junior associate at his firm. I got out before they could lock me up, too."

"So what was she doing working for the embassy?"

"I don't know exactly how that came to pass, but consider the leverage the regime had over her, with her father in jail. They might well have sent her here to be among their eyes in the capital. Many important world players come here and attend events at the embassy. Mei was an attractive woman. I don't know the details."

"So her job was to charm information from people who were guests at embassy events?"

"Charm is perhaps too delicate a word."

Now Suzy could see it. First they lock up Mae's father, then they basically whore her out while threatening to do him harm. What a bunch of bastards.

"She tell you all of this?"

"Not exactly. I am offering some surmise, but she is not the first one to be used like this."

"Did you try to help her?"

"She didn't want my help and she didn't want anyone to know who she really was. We only met one time after I ran into her in the restaurant. She was afraid that she would be seen talking to me. With my reputation with the regime, that would have been very bad for both of us."

"Of course, I understand. What you've told me really makes me want to get these guys."

Xi smiled in a way that was closer to enigmatic than friendly. "That is a very noble ambition, but I assure you, these people are well beyond the reach of a journalist."

We will see about that, Suzy thought. "So Xi, what's your theory on why she was killed? Apparently she was pretty useful to the people here and I'm sure having her in their power gave them even greater control over her father. Why kill her?"

"A perplexing question. It would not seem to be in China's interests to do so, although their agents would not hesitate to act if it was. There is something more there."

"Maybe she was going to go to the authorities here with her story."

"No, I don't think so. That would have led to her father dying in prison. Accidentally, of course."

Suzy picked up her now-cooling green tea and tried to think what more she could get from Xi. Who knew if he'd ever meet with her again? Finding out Mae Wang's real identity was huge, but there was still so much she didn't know.

"Is there anything else you know about Mae? Anything that would help? I really do want to bring to justice whoever did this to her."

"Ah justice. I have researched you, Suzy Morin. You have covered the so-called justice system for a long time. Do you really think there could be justice for Mei?"

"I'll admit that it's not going to be easy. The police don't seem motivated. Politics and diplomatic considerations will come into it. That's not going to slow me down, though. Letting the world know what these guys did is worth something."

"Just so," Xi said. "I wish you well in your quest. I have told you everything I know, and I expect that we will not meet again. If asked, I will deny ever meeting you."

Suzy still hoped to sweet talk him into being a source later on. Her success rate there was pretty high, but Xi wasn't the typical cop or crook. And really, the name and family connection were the only facts he had. Or the only ones he was going to give her.

"I should go," she said. "You have been very helpful and I appreciate that you are doing this. It's the right thing. Should I keep you up to date on developments?"

That was her best technique for drawing a source into the story and making him feel like it was a joint project.

"I will read the newspaper and see what happens," he said.

Suzy stood up and shook his cool hand. Xi didn't seem like the kind of guy you'd hug. Her next task would be to head back to the newsroom and start scouring the web for anything she could find on Zhao Mei and Zhao Yang. She really should tell Kris the news, but it was getting late. Maybe tomorrow.

Suzy let herself out, then paused on the verandah to look at the starry night. She had done a good day's work. And there was her BMW, still parked across the street with all four wheels intact. She started the car and pulled quickly away from the curb, eager to get back to her apartment for a cold drink and a hot bath. She didn't notice the black SUV several car lengths behind her.

THIRTY

The old spymaster contemplated the peace and calm of his Rock-cliffe study. It had long been Sharpe's one oasis in the turbulent and secret world in which he worked. Walnut shelves lined two walls of the study, heavy with volumes from his rare book collection. History of the British Empire was his specialty. The books gave the room a faintly musty smell that he rather enjoyed. Persian carpets, passed down through generations of Sharpes, covered the creaky wooden floor boards. A three-paned, leaded window looked out on his back garden, just coming into fresh leaf. That had been Janet's domain and it had grown rather wild since she died two years ago. Somehow, he couldn't quite bring himself to replace her with a gardener. With his wife gone, all he really had left was his work. Maybe that was all he had ever had.

Sharpe drew his heavy grey cardigan tighter. It was cool in the study. Perhaps he would lay a fire later. For the moment, he needed to think about the phone call he had just received. It confirmed what he had been hearing from other sources, and it was from a person with first-hand knowledge. One that was entirely reliable. A situation that seemed mildly intriguing when he had been talking to young Derek Hall earlier was proving to be a much more complex problem with multiple dimensions, significant implications and, he was sure, opportunities to advance his own interests.

The challenge was determining how best to play it. He had immediately ruled out taking his information to Hall. Intel of this value wasn't something one would simply give away to a lackey who would then take all the credit. He had briefly considered approaching the PM directly, but the truth was, he couldn't tolerate the man. After all of his years of serving the country, under both Liberal and Conservative rule, the new administration had summarily dismissed him in favour of Hakeem Agbaje, an academic who knew little or nothing about the real world of intelligence, but who reflected the PM's enthusiasm for diversity.

Sharpe knew that he had put a foot wrong when he warned the new PM about the threat from China. It was not just the hacking directly into government computers, but the organized attempt to take over resource industries and infiltrate defence corporations. The PM would hear none of it. He was a great fan of the Chinese. Loved their culture. Closer ties were required. Nothing could be said or done that might cause offence to prickly Chinese billionaires or their despotic government. Not incidentally, those Chinese billionaires who were here to enrich themselves and their cronies back home were among some of the Liberal Party's more generous donors.

Sharpe knew better than most that the world was filled with governments that were cruel, corrupt and despotic. One still had to do business with some of them, but surely with eyes wide open. In his view, Canada's new attitude to the Chinese was simply foolish.

Speaking of fools, only one would believe the tale his replacement had offered the PMO. The Chinese themselves were responsible for the young woman's death, so the story went, and this was a Chinese matter best left alone. Not bloody likely. Not when Mae Wang was really Zhao Mei and her father was the famous dissident lawyer, Zhao Yang.

How Mei had come to work at the embassy in Ottawa was still a matter of some speculation, but it was a pattern with which Sharpe was familiar. Young women were used as pawns to ensnare powerful Westerners, to get their secrets in the bedroom or through blackmail. The regime could have found a loyal comrade for the work, but so much the better to choose the daughter of a dissident, increasing their leverage with him in the process. No doubt Zhao Yang still held many secrets that his government wanted to know.

Sharpe opened the drawer of the small walnut table beside his favourite leather wing chair and withdrew his pipe. Smoking his brier had been a habit he had been forced to give up while Janet was alive, but now that she was gone he could do as he pleased. He took a pinch of G.L. Pease Maltese Falcon and tamped it in the bowl. He lit the pipe with a wooden match, then charred the tobacco on top while puffing until it was evenly lit. He watched with satisfaction as a cloud of smoke drifted toward the room's 12-foot ceiling. Sharpe always felt that he thought most clearly when in a haze of tobacco smoke. It was irrational, he knew, uncharacteristically so. Back in his government days, he had enjoyed lighting up at inter- departmental meetings to see who had the balls to complain. Few did.

Sharpe contemplated his options. It really was an expansive buffet.

The simplest course of action would be a well-placed call to one of the handful of influential journalists still employed on Par- liament Hill. Were all that he had learned ever to become public, the prime minister would be forced to resign and the government would collapse. Even in this age of low expectations for political leaders, some errors were intolerable. The whole chain of events would be delightful.

Of course, he needn't be so dramatic. Even a quiet word to one of his connections would set off an internal storm that would put the PM under great pressure.

Knowing what he now did, Sharpe could offer to save the day in exchange for getting his old position back, but then he'd have to work for the pack of idiots that purported to run the country. While the vindication would be sweet, it would be a poor way to spend his remaining years.

The problem with any of these approaches was, that once the story was out, his leverage and control were gone. Perhaps the best thing was to sit back for now, savour what lay ahead for those he loathed, and wait for the pot to come to a boil.

Poor Derek Hall. He seemed a decent enough fellow. Miles out of his depth, of course. Sharpe hoped the lad kept a fire extinguisher in his office. He was going to need it.

THIRTY-ONE

An Uber pulled up in front of my building at 7 p.m. sharp, just as Colin had promised. Before I had even reached the shiny black Toyota Camry, he had leaped out to hold the door open for me. He even took my hand as I slid into the grey leather seat. Colin could be charming when he wanted to be. I had to give him that. He looked pretty good in what I recognized as his best black suit, with a white shirt and a red and grey tie in a subtle pattern. His grey hair, although still longish, had been freshly cut and judging by the pink glow on his cheeks he had had either a professional shave or a stiff shot of scotch. He had a look of pleasure that I tried hard to match.

As Colin settled himself on the seat beside me, he said, "Great dress. I've never seen that one before."

"I'm afraid it's a loaner. One of Caroline's."

"Ah, I see."

When Colin had invited me to a "dressy function," I had panicked. I had scanned my jammed closet, hoping that if I stared long enough something appropriate would present itself. Fat chance. Dressy and function were two words I worked hard to avoid and my limited wardrobe reflected it.

Fortunately, my friend Caroline was a glamorous CBC TV type who probably attended galas and soirées all the time. She had left her fancy clothes in the closet of the second bedroom and we were about the same size, although that was like saying that a new car and a 15-year-old version of the same model were about the same.

Caroline had a bright green thing that had caught my eye, if only because it would look so garish with my red hair. Unfortunately, it had a plunging neckline and when you plunged below my neck, there was really nothing to see. She actually had six of what I think real women call "little black dresses." The third one fit like it didn't belong to someone else. The neck came up to my collarbone and the skirt to my knees. It would do.

The small, girlie part of my brain liked that Colin approved of the dress. I had even shaved my legs and put on a pair of stay-up stockings that I hoped would live up to their name. I drew the line at pantyhose. I noticed Colin's gaze drifting to my legs. I knew he would be speculating on whether those were stockings. He shared the English fascination with hosiery and if I told him what they were I knew it would drive him mad with lust.

Nothing could be farther from my intention. When I had phoned Colin on Friday night on the burner phone, he had surprised me with a social invitation that I really couldn't refuse. I hadn't thought there was such a thing.

He had been invited to an evening in honour of the Chinese ambassador at Global Affairs headquarters on Sussex. The host was none other than the intriguing Luc Champagne. As Colin had suggested, it would be a great opportunity for us to scope the man out, maybe even ask a rude question or two. The presence of the Chinese ambassador was a bonus, although I didn't expect that I would be able to get within 20 feet of him, imagining him to be constantly surrounded by burly men with dark suits and earpieces.

As the Uber worked its way up Elgin toward Sussex, Colin said, "I'm confident that we can get a few minutes with Champagne. He enjoys using the media as a mirror to reflect his glory."

"Gee, I guess I should have bought sunglasses. Good idea, though. Maybe we can separate him from his handlers and talking points. It will be interesting to get a feel for this guy, after all I keep hearing about him from others."

"I thought you'd be pleased," Colin said, brushing his fingers lightly across the back of my hand.

I knew that in his mind, this was some kind of date, an opportunity to use his legendary charm to draw me back into his orbit. It wasn't the time to burst his bubble.

"What about the ambassador?" I said. "Any chance of a chat with him?"

"Perhaps. I hear he's a very friendly chap. One simply has to put to one side that he's a mouthpiece for a cruel and corrupt regime."

"Maybe I'll ask him out for a drink."

Colin regarded me with a look of shock, then realized I was joking.

"Right, very droll. Seriously though, I wouldn't say anything to raise a red flag with him, given the nature of your investigation."

"You know me, Colin. I'm the soul of discretion."

"I do know you. That's why I am urging caution. Perhaps in a quieter moment, you can bring me up to date on developments."

"Of course. And you can fill me on what Suzy has learned. She won't return my calls."

"Nor mine. Curious."

Now I was worried. If Suzy had gone off the radar it almost certainly meant that she had found something big and I wouldn't hear from her again until she had it all neatly tied up. I knew working with her had been a mistake. Not that I had any choice.

The car moved slowly around the National War Memorial, then passed the stately Chateau Laurier before turning left on Sussex. The street was lined with Victorian buildings that housed stores struggling to pay high rents imposed by their government landlord. They weren't the kind of places where I could afford to shop. The incongruous U.S. Embassy, a modern fortress in the heart of downtown, loomed over the street. Its mass of glass and concrete was a blot on the historic ByWard Market neighbourhood but, when it came to Canada, Americans usually got what they wanted. Although I was born in the United States, I had long passed the point where the sight of the Stars and Stripes made me want to salute.

"How long do you think this thing is likely to go on?" I asked Colin.

"Why, do you have plans for afterward?"

"No," I said, then quickly realized that he would think I was suggesting that we make some. "Just things to catch up on."

"Well, let's see how long it holds our attention, then."

The Uber pulled up in front of the Lester B. Pearson Building, an artifact from the 1970s that looked like a layer cake composed of brown concrete and glass. The driveway in front of the building was jammed with black limousines with red diplomatic plates. Bored chauffeurs in dark uniforms lounged beside their cars, smoking cigarettes.

As we entered the lobby, a security man with close-cropped hair and the build of a weightlifter checked our names and ID against the guest list. It seemed a minimal precaution for a social event that no doubt involved a flock of ambassadors. A uniformed RCMP officer and a young woman from Global Affairs escorted us to the elevator that would take us to the reception.

Colin leaned into me and said, "Time to paste on your smile."

I did as instructed, but it was annoying to be told to smile. People had been doing that all my life. I had never quite understood the value of grinning like an idiot, but apparently it was socially-expected behaviour.

We rode up to the ninth floor, then the elevator door opened on to a large room with expansive views out across the Ottawa River to the Gatineau Hills and back across the city itself. Ottawa was a remarkably flat place, so even a modest building had great vistas.

"Right, here we go then," Colin said.

Little knots of people clustered together, drinks in hand, just like every other boring social event to which I had ever been dragged. The difference here was that some had chosen colourful national costumes, especially the diplomats from Africa, who had turned out in force. Eager to curry favour with the Chinese, I was sure. I was no expert on international affairs, but from what I had read, the Chinese were in the process of colonizing Africa. I hoped it went better for them than it had for the Europeans.

Colin glided effortlessly from group to group, shaking hands and introducing me to people with complex names that I forgot instantly. I had never known much about this part of his life, having refused to attend these kinds of affairs when we were together.

As we drifted away from a cluster of Africans and headed towards a flock of Scandinavians, I said, "You actually like this sort of thing, don't you?"

"Well, like might be a strong term, but I'm accustomed to it. In my foreign correspondent days, parties like this were prime places to make connections and pick up useful gossip."

I hoped that he wasn't going to start repeating his foreign correspondent stories. He had been to several war zones, but I had heard all of his tales. Besides, I knew he had often used the stories of his hairy-chested past to get the pants off young reporters. That wasn't going to work with me.

"Do you see Champagne?" I asked.

"I spotted him earlier over near the bar, in the far corner. Surrounded by sycophants at the moment, I'm afraid."

"I guess we will have to wait for the crowd to thin. Speaking of the bar, any chance you might be able to fetch me a drink?"

"Of course. Scotch, rocks?"

"Yes. Better make it a double."

I watched Colin elbow his way to the bar, wondering if ambassadors ever thought about the undernourished people at home as they scarfed down hors d'oeuvres and free drinks. I was pretty sure I knew the answer.

I noticed a long balcony that offered not only a great view, but a chance to get away from the bulk of the diplomatic crowd. I headed for it before I could be cornered by some lonely diplomatic representative who would expect me to make small talk. I was confident that Colin would find me easily enough.

The sun was just setting, creating a silver glint on the Ottawa River and leaving the Gatineau Hills in a purple gloom. Streetlights emitted their artificial glow in a grid spreading out to the horizon. I had just leaned forward on the metal railing, hoping for a few minutes of silence, when I detected a presence at my left elbow and a male voice said, "Fantastic view, isn't it?"

I turned and was surprised to see Li Jintao, the Chinese ambassador to Canada. No flunkies, no security guards, just a middle-aged guy with a touch of grey in his hair and a black suit, white shirt, no tie.

"Ambassador Li," I said, hoping that was the correct form of address. "I thought you would be in the main room, surrounded by admirers."

Li laughed, then surprised me again by picking up my sarcastic tone. "Oh yes, China has many admirers. Everyone wants something."

He must have assumed that I was some diplomat's wife. Who was I to contradict him? What I really wanted to do was ask him what he knew about Mae Wang. Maybe even ask if he had ordered her murder, but that wouldn't be very strategic. Instead, I said, "Lots of politics in diplomacy." It seemed a safe guess.

"Yes. That is certainly true. I came out here to get a short break from it. You?"

"The same."

"Fantastic weather we are having. Very similar to Beijing at this time of year. I got in my first round of golf today."

"Oh yes. Where did you play?"

I couldn't imagine spending even 10 minutes whacking at a little ball with sticks and couldn't have named a single local golf course, but I did know that it took only a few encouraging words or phrases to get men to describe their various triumphs.

"Royal Ottawa. I am a member there. I finished eight over par. A little off my regular score, but not bad for a first game."

I had no idea if eight over par was good, but the ambassador seemed to think so, so I agreed. "Oh, well done. I'm glad you are enjoying your time here."

"It is a fine posting. Canada is an important friend of China."

More like a witless vassal state according to my research, but I supposed it was all a matter of perspective. I settled for a non-committal nod and said, "Glad to hear that Ambassador Li."

"Please, call me Jin. And you are?"

"Kris Redner." I felt I was safe in assuming that he didn't follow crime in the *Ottawa Citizen*.

Jin leaned in a little closer and said, "I am having a few people back to the embassy for drinks after the party. Perhaps you would like to join me?"

"What a thoughtful offer. I'm afraid my date and I have other plans, though," I said. Where the hell was Colin anyway? The ambassador was hitting on me and I needed rescuing before I said something undiplomatic.

"Ah, that is unfortunate. Perhaps another time?"

Before I could answer, Colin appeared carrying two scotches.

"I see you have met Ambassador Li. How are you this evening ambassador?"

"Ah, you are with this young lady then, Colin. Very fortunate for you."

I took my drink, then snuggled up against Colin to show him what a pair of lovebirds we were.

The ambassador shook Colin's hand, then said, "I really must get back. It is a party for me, after all."

The ambassador gave me a slight bow, then presented me with his card. It was a heavily embossed thing in red and gold that read Li Jintao Ambassador Extraordinary and Plenipotentiary of the People's Republic of China to Canada. It was quite a mouthful. I wondered what kinds of titles they gave the people who were really important.

As the ambassador walked back into the party, Colin said, "That was a surprise."

"No kidding. First he talked about the weather and his golf game, then he invited me back to the embassy for drinks after the party."

"Really? So much for the perception that the Chinese always take the oblique approach."

"Oh bugger off, and don't sound so surprised."

"I'm not surprised at all. Well, perhaps surprised that I have the same taste in women as the Chinese ambassador.

"You didn't mention Mae Wang, I hope."

"No, I'm not that stupid." No point in telling him the thought had crossed my mind.

I began to steer Colin back into the main room. His taste in women wasn't a topic I had any interest in discussing. "Let's get back to the party. See if we can find Champagne,"

"All right," he said, sounding reluctant. "It is rather pleasant out here."

"True, but we're on a mission, remember?"

"Of course. Let's go brace our man."

Meeting Luc Champagne proved easier than I would have imagined. As soon as we were back in the main room, I spotted him shaking hands with a tall African couple, then sneaking a quick glance at his watch as they walked away. He was no more than 15 feet away. If I were quick, I could nab him before someone else did.

"Let me do this," I said to Colin. "You hang back."

"But surely . . ."

"I know men."

Colin merged into the crowd and I walked up to Champagne with a big smile and a look that said he should be glad to meet me. I hoped the little black dress would do its job again.

Once he saw me zeroing in on him, Champagne returned my

smile with one of his own. It was a dazzler, and it wasn't just the
perfect white teeth. I knew a smile was an essential part of any politician's mask, but Champagne's actually looked genuine. It didn't
stop at his mouth, but extended right to his eyes, which were the
kind of blue that never looked quite real. He looked as if I were a
particularly welcome sight.

To say that Luc Champagne was handsome didn't quite capture
it. His face was long, his cheekbones high, his nose a bit too big and
twisted slightly to the right, as if he'd taken a punch somewhere
along the line, perhaps from an angry husband. His hair was dark
and swept across his high forehead. His suit was navy, expensive,
his shirt a fine blue pinstripe with a red tie. I knew him to be 45,
but he could easily pass for a decade younger. He had the obses-
sively lean look of a long-distance runner.

Once I was within range, Champagne reached out a long arm
and grasped my hand in his own. It was warm and surprisingly
soft.

"Luc Champagne. Good to see you," he said, as if he really meant
it. His words implied that we had met, but I knew it was just a politician's trick to avoid saying "good to meet you" to a person whose
hand they had shaken before.

"Kris Redner. I saw you looking at your watch. Party starting to
drag?"

"Only in the predictable way. I admire your directness Ms. Redner. It is what I have come to expect in your columns," Champagne
said in flawless English.

Another politician's trick. Some flunkie had probably briefed
him on the guest list so he could appear to take an interest in the
people he met. Flattery was disarming, for most people. I hoped he
would pretend to know something about my family, so I could tell
him that they were all dead.

"Really? I'm surprised to know that you are a reader."

"Not all the time, I will admit. You seldom write about
politicians."

"Only when they get caught, minister."

Champagne smiled again. "Please, call me Luc. I have been following your coverage of the Sandhu trial. Very insightful. Really
a shame to see Sonny in that situation. He was an exceptionally

promising man."

And there was my opening. "Quite a fall from grace. You must have known him well, since he was your parliamentary assistant."

"Should I assume that we are talking casually at a party, not on the record?"

"You should assume that," I said, not to say that I would necessarily share the assumption.

"Sonny was exceptionally ambitious. Perhaps he just reached too far."

"It's a curious case, though. What was his motive? Why would a guy with so much money ruin his career over $25,000?"

"I understand that the money in the family was his wife's. That can be uncomfortable for some types of men. But who knows? Perhaps the trial will explain that. I can only assume so. Of course, I shouldn't say too much. It *is* before the courts."

"Sure, but we're just chatting at a party. I hear that you might be called to testify. Anything to that?"

"Well, we will see what the future brings. I doubt I can add much to the case for either side. But this is a party. Let's not spend our time talking shop. You see, I am motivated to keep engaging you in conversation. The minute you walk away, I will be besieged by yet another diplomatic representative with a special need he hopes Canada can fill. As soon as we stop talking, that boy over there in the cheap suit will tap someone on the shoulder and send them my way."

"Must be tough work, spending taxpayers' dollars that way."

Champagne sipped his drink, a white wine. "I gather you are not a huge fan of government, Ms. Redner."

"Since we are apparently on a first-name basis, call me Kris. And you're right. I think that government does a lot of harm under the guise of doing good and mostly benefits the people at the top. Do you disagree?"

"Ah, a firebrand. I was one myself, once upon a time. And no, I don't disagree. One does one's best, but it's always better to be the guy in the limo than the guy paying the bill."

I found myself getting sucked in by his apparent frankness. In my mind, I had cast Champagne as the villain, a lecher who had imposed himself on Mae Wang and certainly knew something about her death, even if he didn't do the job himself. But then, life was seldom that black and white. I wondered if Champagne was just reflecting back the attitude that I was showing him, if he had so successfully mastered the politician's skills that they seemed natural. I decided to try a different tack.

"Actually, I've been looking into you," I said. "You've had a fascinating career. Started out with the PQ, those being your firebrand days, I presume. Then the Conservative cabinet, now the Liberal cabinet. You're quite a flexible guy."

"I am a Quebecer, Kris. I do what's best for the people of my province, in the moment. As for the Parti Quebecois, anyone with a soul believed in that cause once."

"Not anymore?"

"Clearly separatism is no longer in play. The party now is nothing more than an opportunity for a few people to strike poses. Myself, I live in the world of practicality.

"I am curious as to why you are researching me. Do you think I am about to commit a crime?"

"I don't know. Maybe you already have."

"Is this my opportunity to confess, throw myself on the mercy of the media?"

I laughed at that. "That would be like throwing yourself on a bed of nails." Then I thought of Mae Wang and her version of the bed of nails. "No, I was thinking of doing a profile of you. Can I tell you a secret?"

"Please do."

"I have written a crime column for a long time. Maybe I have had enough of the criminals, the lawyers and the so-called justice system. The same people and the same problems are cycling around again and again. Writing about federal politics is the big game in this town and a lot of the old men who cover it are retiring. There is an opportunity there. If I were to become a columnist on the Hill, it would mean more money, more exposure and more opportunity. I could go with whatever media organization gave me the best deal. So, a substantial profile of you, the real story of your climb to the top, would be a big boost to my career."

"So you are also a pragmatist."

"I think we have both outgrown idealism, don't you?"

"I try to retain just a soupcon of it, but I take your point. What do you need from me?"

"Exclusive access. All the time required to explore your story in depth. Contact info for the people who know you best."

"So, you want me to bare my soul."

If he had one. From the look on Champagne's face, I could see caution and vanity were engaged in a struggle. He finished his wine, set the glass down on a round-topped table and said, "All right. Let's do it. Let's start right now."

That took me by surprise, but I always carried a notebook in my purse. "What about all your eager supplicants?" I asked.

"They will still be eager next week. Come on up to the tenth floor. I will show you my office. Very few journalists have ever been there. I will be happy to answer any questions I think appropriate."

I suspected my list might be longer than his, but Champagne's offer was irresistible. One way or another, he held the keys that would unlock both the Sandhu story and the Mae Wang story. I didn't expect him to spell it out for me, but I also knew there were two types of men. Some valued discretion and would take secrets to their graves. Others couldn't resist sharing their inside knowledge, to show that they had it. I was prepared to bet that Champagne was one of the latter.

"All right. That sounds good. Just let me text the guy I came with."

"Colin Wendover?"

"Yes, my boss. I was the plus one. Wouldn't want him to think that I had gotten lost."

I texted "Going to C office. tenth floor. If not out in 30, come in shooting."

THIRTY-TWO

Mike Reilly eased his Crown Vic into a tight parking spot on River Lane. Unlike the fancifully named lanes of the suburbs, River Lane really was a lane, a road a single car's width that ran through the gentrified neighbourhood of New Edinburgh, just three blocks from the governor-general's grand residence, Rideau Hall. It wasn't the most subtle place for a stakeout but the lane gave a view of Suzy's house on Queen Victoria, about 100 feet away. The house was a small red brick Victorian with a green verandah running across the front. It cost far more than a *Citizen* reporter could afford, but Suzy's family had money. Reilly imagined her old man must have jumped for joy when she rid herself of her aging cop lover.

The view of the house was partly obscured by a line of lilacs just coming out in flower, but Reilly could see there were no lights on. It wasn't the first time that he had sat in this spot looking at Suzy's place, but it was the first time in months. When they broke up, he would sit there hoping for a glimpse of her and, to be honest, keeping an eye out for any new men. He knew it was creepy at some level, but that's how obsessed he had been. He thought he was better now, somewhat, and he had a good reason for being there tonight. He hadn't been able to reach Suzy for two days and he had news to share. Farrell had come through.

Reilly had phoned Kris Redner earlier, to tell her to call him on the burner, but she hadn't responded to his call or a subsequent text. That wasn't really a worry for him, but the lack of communication with Suzy was. He had been trying to reach her since Friday. Suzy needed to know what Farrell had told him about what they might be up against and the likelihood that their phones and computers were being monitored.

Even though they weren't together any more, she was normally good about returning his calls. Reilly wasn't sure whether to attribute that to residual feelings, politeness or the possibility that he was calling with something work-related. If he had to make a bet, it would be the latter.

For all he knew, Suzy could be out of town or shacked up with someone. It wasn't like her to ignore her phone, though. It was like a part of her body. That phrase sent his mind in the wrong direction. Reilly remembered every square inch of her body, but it wasn't just the sex he missed. It was having a woman who actually understood him in a way that his first wife Jenny never had. It was almost scary at times, like Suzy could get right inside his head. He had never had quite the same ability where she was concerned.

Reilly was sure that she would be excited by Farrell's news. He had been able to access the entire CSIS file on Mae Wang, or Zhao Mei as she actually was. Reilly didn't ask how Farrell had achieved that, but he was going to owe him big time. It was easy to see why the RCMP and the spy boys wanted to put a blanket over Mae's death. According to the file, she was working for the Ministry of State Security. In other words, she was a spy. That wasn't unusual, but it was the why that was interesting. Her father was a big-shot defence lawyer who had been imprisoned for doing his job. It didn't take much imagination to see the leverage that the Chinese spy agency would have had over Mae. All that had changed a month ago, when her father died in prison. It seemed likely that the Chinese had decided to shut her up, once they could no longer control her. Something still didn't add up, though. Why stage a public death, then go to so much trouble to get the body back and spirit it out of the country? Unless the goal was to make it look like it was someone else who killed her. Once you started peeling down through layers of deviousness, it was always hard to know when you had gotten to the core.

The RCMP and CSIS had been sharing surveillance on Mae, but there had been some interagency fuckup the day before her death. They had lost track of her on a shift change, then no one had picked her up the next day.

The exact nature of Mae's mission remained a mystery. The identity of her target or targets was beyond the security clearance of Farrell's source. Either Luc Champagne or Mr. Thursday, Reilly was sure, whoever the hell Mr. Thursday was.

It was clear that the primary line of investigation had to be the apparent connection between Champagne and Mae. The foreign affairs minister and Mae showing up regularly in the same building on the same night couldn't be a coincidence. Champagne was a big fish, though, not the type you could reel in without something that would set the hook deep. Right now, he didn't have that. If either Suzy or Kris would bother to tell him what they had found out, maybe he would be making more progress.

Reilly shook his head. After 35 years on the job, he shouldn't be depending on the media to do his legwork for him. He told himself it was a unique situation, with the way the force had put the clamp on the case. He wondered if the brass had any idea what was really going on, or if they were just playing along with the standard national security line to keep the feds sweet for the next time the Ottawa force went looking for extra federal money. If he had been chief, he'd have told the Mounties to fuck themselves and gone after the killer full out.

Reilly knew he could sit for hours, maybe days before Suzy showed up. It wasn't the most productive use of his time. He considered going in to her house for a look. Her locks were easy to bypass. Then he rejected the idea. She'd be pissed if she ever found out.

Reilly had just started his engine when his cell phone rang. He picked it up and saw it was Suzy. Relief flooded through him. He connected the call, but what he heard next turned his blood cold.

Suzy's voice was high-pitched, hysterical. "Mike, Mike. You've got to help me! He took me Mike. He did things to me! I'm naked. I've been hurt. I ran. I'm in the woods. I don't know where. Oh God Mike, come quick!"

Reilly felt a blast of adrenalin and anger unlike any he had experienced in his life. He was squeezing the cell phone hard enough to crush it, but he knew he needed to sound calm. "OK Suzy, I've got it. Are you badly hurt? Are you bleeding?"

"A little. I don't know. He beat me, Mike. I'm just, I can't think."

"Stay where you are Suzy. Leave your phone on. We'll triangulate it. Keep very still. Don't let him hear you. I'll find you. I'll send an ambulance and every fucking car that's on the road."

"No, Mike. This can't come out. You have to come alone! Just hurry, please hurry."

THIRTY-THREE

As Luc Champagne swung open the door to his office, it was clear from the look on his face that I was being offered a very special treat. I expect he had the same expression when he took his pants off, a treat I certainly intended to avoid. My response, naturally, was to appear completely unimpressed by his inner sanctum and it wouldn't have mattered if his office had been an exact replica of the Sistine Chapel.

In fact, it was a lot closer to a rec room, circa 1975. The office was not overly large, about 20 by 20, but the walls were panelled in an oppressive teak that hadn't been in since the last time people thought Denmark was hot. At least the abundance of art on the walls helped cover the panelling,

"So this is it, where I help guide the affairs of the world," he said. His grin told me the remark was tongue-in-cheek.

"Rather a small office for such an important task."

"Ah yes. All the grand offices are in the Centre Block, but the lonely foreign affairs minister is relegated to Fort Pearson. I think the room reflects all the charm of the '70s, not that I remember that decade so well."

"You were born in the 1970s though, right?"

"Yes, in a little town in the Eastern Townships, but I expect you know that."

"I think I read it somewhere."

Champagne opened a cabinet built into the wall and said, "Do you want a drink? I have my own bar."

"Sure. White wine." I'd have preferred a single malt, but I couldn't afford to dull my wits any more than I already had.

"I have a nice Sauvignon Blanc."

"That will be fine." I pretended to take an interest in one of the pictures on the wall. As near as I could tell, it depicted an explosion in a paint factory.

"Are you an admirer of modern art?" he asked.

"Hardly. You?"

"Not in the slightest. These are on loan from the Canada Council's art bank. I don't even select them."

"At least you aren't blaming the choices on the previous government, but of course, you were a member of that government."

"Yes, that does offer a degree of complexity when I answer questions in the House. I have never been one to blame my predecessors, though. The media covers that rather well. I will say that I have made one change in the decor. There was a rather large portrait of the Queen. I have sent that out for restoration. Could take years, I am told."

"Colin would be shocked. You know him well?"

"Not really. We meet at diplomatic affairs from time to time. I view him as a voice of reason."

"Me too."

Champagne handed me a glass of wine and said, "It seems that Colin and I have similar taste in women."

Here we go, I thought, and said, "Really? I must be the flavour of the month. You are the second man to hit on me tonight."

"What? Who was the first?"

"The Chinese ambassador. Very friendly fellow. He invited me back to the embassy for a drink after the party."

"Ambassador Li's wife is back in Beijing. I understand he gets lonely on a regular basis."

I saw an opportunity to start my interview in the forthright manner that Luc Champagne said he admired so much. I settled into one of the two red leather armchairs in front of his desk and he took the one beside me, no doubt to make sure I continued to feel the power of his aura.

Taking my notebook from my purse, I said, "So let's start the interview then, Luc, and I'd like to pick up on what you just mentioned. What about your own loneliness? You're single, you work a job that is stressful and demanding, the hours are long. Who do you rely on for support?"

His smile didn't reach his eyes. He took a sip of wine, then said, "That is an unusual question."

"Not really. When I write a profile, I am interested not just in the biographical facts, but what makes a person tick. I want to get to know the real you."

"That is something that very few people have accomplished."

"All the better then."

Luc, as I was starting to think of him, got up, took off his jacket and draped it across the back of his desk chair. Then he sat back in the leather chair and leaned forward, as if to share a confidence. "I can only tell you this. A person's real identity is a subjective matter, a question of perspective."

"It's your perspective I am after."

"I am not going to bare my soul during our first interview, Kris. Let me get to know you, develop some trust."

It wasn't an unreasonable suggestion. Normally, a profile like the one I was pretending to write would involve a series of interviews over several weeks, but I was impatient for progress on the Mae Wang story. Maybe Champagne was the kind of guy who preferred a courtship, but I would have been surprised. He was too busy, too handsome and had too much self-regard. I took him more for the kind who would offer a quick drink, then try to stick it in. I decided to do the same.

"Let me try something more straightforward then. Is there a love in your life? I'm sure you know that you have quite a reputation as a man who likes the ladies."

"Ah," he said, nodding. "So you *do* think I have brought you up here to seduce you."

"I hope not, because then we'd both be wasting our time."

"Touché. To answer your question, no. There is no one special."

"More of a play-the-field type, then, as your reputation suggests?"

"No, just a man who continues to search for his soul mate."

I wondered how many times he had said that, and if he was looking for someone who liked romantic dinners and long walks on the beach.

"You know about my late wife, I presume?"

"Only that you had one."

"Yes, well this is a story I do not tell too often, but I don't want you to think that I am some kind of Lothario."

I nodded and tried to look as if that was not exactly what I was thinking. "Please, I'd love to know more."

"Carole was the love of my life. We met while we were both undergraduates at McGill. I was studying economics, she, abnormal psychology. At first, I wasn't sure whether she wanted to study me or date me. She was a beautiful woman. Long, thick dark hair, magnificent legs, brown eyes that were gentle, yet probing, but it was her mind that attracted me most. She was the most brilliant and most kind woman I have ever met. We had 12 years together before she died at 32. Brain cancer. I thought my life was over, but, one goes on."

I was scribbling down everything he said, with the idea of checking later to see how much, if any of it, was true. It was a touching story and would have been even more so if I didn't think he had been banging Mae Wang as regular as clockwork.

"That's terribly sad," I said. "And since then?"

"Well, I have had relationships, of course. A man has appetites, but I have never found another Carole. I do not think there is one, not for me."

The look of sincerity and sadness on his face would have brought a tear to the eye of a woman less cold-hearted than me. I wondered if this was a story he told to seduce women, the Luc Champagne equivalent of Colin's heroic war stories. It was tempting to use this spot in our interview to ask him about Mae Wang, but I knew it would bring our discussion to a quick end. The foreign affairs minister was hardly going to admit to having an affair with an interpreter at the Chinese Embassy, especially one who had come to such an unfortunate end. He clearly wasn't going to tell me about his love life, but then, what man would? I switched to something easier, to keep him talking.

"Question I'm sure you have been asked many times, but why did you switch parties? That really threw people for a loop, especially the Conservatives. I'm not a Hill insider, but even I knew you were favoured to take the party leadership. Help me to understand, and please, don't tell me you did it for the people of Quebec."

"But it *was* that, partly. It was clear the party was going to lose power. I could do little for the people of my province in opposition, even as leader. Some say I would have won that race, but it's hard to know.

"Of course there was more. One does not make a life changing move simply for the sake of others. I reached an understanding with the Liberal leader, about what my role would be if we were to win. But it was a gamble, the party was in third place when I joined it."

"That was a bold move. Would you say that was your style?"

Champagne shrugged. "I think that is for others to judge, not me."

I decided to circle back and get a little closer to my real target. "You mentioned the Chinese ambassador earlier. Do you know him well?"

"I wouldn't say well. The relationship between our countries is of great importance, both economically and culturally. We stay in frequent touch. He seems a reasonable man, despite the public's image of China."

"The PM seems to be a great friend of China."

"He is. No secret there. It's such a huge and powerful country, being a great friend is better than being an enemy, wouldn't you say?"

"Certainly. No one wants powerful enemies, although I'm sure that is an occupational hazard in your line of work."

"It can be, but for me, if I believe that I am doing the right thing, then I am content. If others disagree, that is their prerogative.

"Now, let me ask you a few questions, Kris. I am prepared to tell you more about myself, over time, but I need to know more about you, your job, what motivates you."

I decided to answer the part of the question that suited me best. I felt like I was learning from Champagne already. "What motivates me? That's easy. Finding out the truth and sharing it with the public."

"Ah, the truth. Do you find it easy to discover?"

"Generally not. In the world that I cover, telling the truth is not the first option for most people. I expect it is the same in your world."

Champagne smiled and nodded in agreement. He had a warm smile. That could take you a long way in life, I had observed. "Most in my world rely on talking points. I think of them as baloney with just a light seasoning of truth."

"So you, you are a truth teller yourself?"

"Yes. I find it can be quite disarming."

It was true that nothing was more convincing than a clever lie wrapped in sincerity. I weighed whether to put his contention to the test. If national security agencies were really monitoring our phones and computers, as Farrell thought, then there was no way that Champagne didn't know I was pursuing the Mae Wang story.

Of all the people in cabinet, the foreign affairs minister had the closest ties to national security. I decided to go for it.

"That's good to know. Maybe you can give me some insight into a story I am working on."

"Glad to help if I can. I assume this has to do with the Sandhu mess?"

"Actually, it doesn't. I am sure you must have heard about that Chinese interpreter who fell to her death from the roof of the building where I live."

"Of course. It was brought to my attention. I have read the media coverage." His expression was neutral and I saw nothing in his eyes that suggested either fear or wariness.

'I'm hearing that she didn't jump, that she was pushed."

"Really. I have not heard that. If so, it should be thoroughly investigated. I'm surprised that the ambassador has not raised the issue. I will ask my chief of staff to follow up."

"That's very helpful. Perhaps you can have someone keep me informed of what he finds out."

"I will do it myself, happily."

I glanced at my watch. I was five minutes past the 30 that I told Colin I would take. The demand that he come in shooting was an inside joke that went back to our adventures in the Adirondacks, but I knew he would be anxious. It also seemed like a natural place to end the interview, with the promise of more to come.

"Why don't we leave it at that for now, then. Perhaps we can continue our talk in the next few days."

As I stood to go, he said, "I will look forward to that. I will be in touch."

Champagne rose from his chair, then stepped toward me and ran his finger lightly over the tattoo on my left wrist. I felt goose bumps as he said, "That's a beautiful design. Does it hold special meaning for you?"

In fact, the initials of my dead family held enormous meaning, but I wasn't going to share that with Luc Champagne. Stepping back, I pulled a business card from my purse and offered it to him, but Champagne said, "Oh don't worry. I know where to find you."

As I went back down the stairs to retrieve Colin, Champagne's words rolled over in my mind. Was it a casual phrase or was he telling me something more?

THIRTY-FOUR

Mike Reilly blew through a series of red lights on the Vanier Parkway as he pushed the old Crown Vic to its limits. Drivers on intersecting streets were slamming on their brakes and pounding their horns. Fuck them. He had his dash flasher on. This was a police emergency.

Reilly saw everything in front of him through a red haze, the one he usually experienced before he did something he would regret. When he caught the bastard who did this to Suzy, there would be no regrets. Not for him, anyway. He'd feed him his balls for breakfast, and that was just for starters.

It hadn't taken Pete Dombrowski long to triangulate Suzy's phone. She was near a parking lot along Timm Drive, a rural road that ran through the federal Greenbelt between the western suburbs of Nepean and Kanata. Reilly remembered the road from his days on patrol. It was dark, lonely and heavily wooded. It was a bad place to be lost.

Was this guy who had taken her pursuing her through the woods? If so, every second counted. Reilly tried to reassure himself with the thought that the attacker would have been smart enough to take off once she ran. If he wanted to kill her, he would have done so already, but he couldn't convince himself. He had no idea who Suzy was up against.

It was his fault. He should have warned her as soon as he talked to Farrell.

Reilly whipped the car onto the exit for the Queensway and pushed it to 140 km/h when he hit the main highway. He figured Timm Drive was 20 minutes from his original location. He wanted to make it in less than 15.

Reilly realized that his own heart was pounding and he had broken into a sweat. Don't have a heart attack now, you old bastard, he thought.

He took a few deep breaths and tried to think rationally. Up until now, his pursuit of Mae Wang's killer had seemed like a chess game played against an opponent who was always a few moves ahead. Kidnapping Suzy amounted to turning the board upside down. Who the hell was behind it, the Chinese? The move had their style. Those bastards didn't give a crap about Canadian laws and always acted like they were on their own turf.

Was this a warning or were they really trying to eliminate Suzy? Maybe they thought it would scare him off, shut him and Kris down. For just a second, Reilly wondered if it was a trap, whether someone was using Suzy to draw him out into the country, then deal with them both. His hand brushed the Glock he wore in a holster on his belt. He considered calling for backup, but that would mean that the story about the police reporter found naked in the woods would spread through the force in minutes, expanding the humiliation exponentially. Many of his fellow cops gave Suzy a hard time just because she was a woman. That would make it impossible for her to do her job. Besides, by the time a proper search was organized, it could be too late.

Whatever was out there, he'd have to deal with it alone. He just hoped that decision wasn't another mistake. What if the guy *was* in the woods, looking for her?

Reilly weaved the car from lane to lane, looking for openings in the traffic. He was up to 150 now and moving out of the city core. He missed some asshole plodding along in a beige Corolla by inches. The guy had the nerve to lay on the horn.

Reilly saw the Moodie Drive exit just ahead. Timm was less than a kilometre away. He slowed the car, but kept the flashers on. Turning right at a fruit stand not yet open for the season, he hit the high beams and slowed further. The road was several kilometres long, but Pete had pinpointed her phone near a parking lot that led to a nature trail, but where was Suzy now? What if she had made it out to the road?

If Suzy was in the ditch, it wouldn't be easy to see her. The road was dark as hell. He'd have to hope she saw the flashers. What if she had passed out? He had no idea how seriously she was hurt and she had sounded nearly hysterical when she called him.

He powered down the windows, hoping to hear her call for help. The lights of his car seemed dulled by the thick mass of underbrush at the edge of the road. Reilly struggled to see. The ditch looked steep and dark. He saw a deer's eyes reflected in the lights, then the animal darted out onto the road. He braked and let it pass. The night air flowing in through his open windows smelled of cedar and swampy decay.

Finally, a kilometre down the road, Reilly reached the parking lot where the signal from Suzy's phone had been picked up. He pulled off to the shoulder, but left the dash flasher on. Maybe it would scare off the kidnapper, if he hadn't already left.

Reilly picked up his phone and called Dombrowski.

"Pete, any fresh location on that phone?"

"No, it hasn't moved. Boss, what the hell's going on?"

"Personal matter, Pete. Don't worry."

Reilly hung up and eased the car slowly down the narrow track that led to the parking lot. He remembered it as a lover's lane, a secluded spot where young couples could enjoy a few drinks and each other. Pity there hadn't been any there tonight.

The only vehicle in the lot was a black Chev Suburban. The rear plate was covered with mud, but Reilly could see a dull red through the dirt. Diplomatic plates. Shit, it was the Chinese, then. That was bad, really bad.

Reilly parked his vehicle across the rear of the SUV, to block its escape. It was locked up. No one in sight. That meant the guy in the woods, looking for Suzy.

Reilly got out of the car and drew the Glock. He hadn't fired his gun in the line of duty in years and didn't spend a lot of time at the range. He hoped he could hit something if he had to.

The moon was half full, but it did little to reduce the gloom of the surrounding forest. Reilly liked the woods, in the daytime. At night, it was a different world. He had a Maglite under the passenger seat, but using it would just make him an easy target. He tucked it into his belt anyway, in case he found Suzy.

He studied the perimeter of the parking lot. Most of it was surrounded by low, thorny growth. No one would take that route. When Suzy had run, she would have headed straight for the trail that led back into the woods. It was the logical place to start.

Reilly edged down the trail just far enough to make himself hard to see, then stopped, listening for any sign of other humans. All he heard was the wind blowing through the trees. He moved cautiously down the trail, treading silently on the wood chips that made up its surface. The night was cool and he was wearing only a suit coat, but he could feel sweat trickling down his sides.

Suzy must be freezing. She had said she was naked. Had this bastard raped her?

Reilly made his way stealthily down the path, listening intently, looking for any kind of unusual shape in the forest around him. Part of him knew finding her was a long shot. The forest was dense with cedars. He could be standing practically right beside Suzy and not see her.

Another hundred yards down the trail, Reilly stopped and admitted the obvious. This wasn't working. The Chinese guy had to have found her. Her phone was off. He'd told her to leave it on. He'd played this wrong. By going deeper into the forest, he'd given the kidnapper the chance to circle around behind him.

It was time for a new tactic. He had to let Suzy know he was here, try to flush the other guy out. Reilly ran back to the parking lot, stumbling over a tree root, but not going down. The SUV was still there, dark and silent. He turned on the dash flasher in his car and the Maglite and shouted, "Police. It's all over. Lay down your weapon and come to the parking lot."

His demand was met with silence. Reilly pointed the Glock in the air and let off a round, then shouted, "Police, surrender now."

His ears were ringing from the sound of the gun. By the time he heard the footsteps behind him, it was too late.

THIRTY-FIVE

I reluctantly closed the door of the Uber Colin and I had taken back from the party. I knew I should really invite him up for a drink, but he was pissed, or "not best pleased" as he liked to put it. I tapped a farewell on the car's window, then turned and headed towards my building.

In Colin's opinion, I had spent a worrisomely long time "sequestered with Champagne in his private office." I took his reaction to be some combination of jealousy and the mother-hen approach he had taken with me ever since my brush with death last year. I wished he had been able to see what a smooth character Champagne actually was. I started to describe it, but that just made things worse.

I had learned some things about Champagne, principally that he was slippery and multi-layered. I certainly wasn't willing to take anything he said at face value. At the same time, we seemed to have some sort of connection. Maybe I would do better in the follow-up interview, if there was one.

I decided to take the stairs instead of the elevator. I took off my heels, hoping that they hadn't permanently crippled me. The stairs were no doubt none too clean, but the carpet still felt good on my feet.

By the time I had gone up three floors, I was beginning to think the elevator would have been a better bet, but I persisted. When I got to the door of my apartment, I fumbled around in my purse, looking for my keys. I had downed only a couple of drinks, but I hadn't eaten any dinner and the few puff pastries and bits of elk on a cracker that I had consumed didn't do much to dilute the alcohol.

Finally, I got the door open. As soon as I stepped into the apartment, I got the feeling that someone was there, or had been. A tingle ran up and down my spine. Then the smell hit me. It was meaty, sour and raw, like hamburger had been left out on the counter and spoiled. I immediately ruled that out. I had no hamburger and wasn't organized enough to take food out in advance.

Then I detected an undercurrent of shit. The first thought that hit me was Mr. Mo. Had he played some vile prank to get back at me for bullying him? I flicked on the living room light. Nothing looked disturbed. I walked to the fireplace and picked up a heavy poker. Although the fireplace was fake, the poker was real, with a brass handle and a long, round steel shaft.

I advanced cautiously to the kitchen, then I saw it. Ranger was hanging upside down from the three-light fixture over the island. He had been neatly gutted and his entrails hung into the sink. Blood obscured his little face. The foul, rotten stench was overwhelming.

I jumped back, weak at the knees. The poker fell to the floor, then I quickly picked it up again. Whoever had done this could still be in the apartment. I retreated to the living room, pulled my phone from my purse and called Colin.

"Come back, quick," I said. "I need you."

"Well!" Colin said with an enthusiasm that told me he had misunderstood my intent in a predictable way.

"Someone has been in my apartment. They've killed the dog and hanged it from the light fixture."

"Get out of the apartment now, Kris," he said, his voice forceful and urgent. Then I heard him say to the Uber driver "Turn this bloody thing around."

"Call 911 and go down to the lobby. Better yet, get right out of the building."

"Sure, all right. I'll meet you in the lobby." I hung up. I wasn't going to bring the police into this. That would be the start of a long, complicated conversation about why someone would break into my apartment and kill my dog. Poor Ranger. Ugly as he was, I had really grown fond of him.

The kind of gutless person who thought killing a dog was the way to send me a message wouldn't be brave enough to stick around and underline his point in person, I hoped. Brandishing the poker, I checked out the bathroom and the two remaining bedrooms, half hoping there was someone to whom I could give a stunning blow to the head, but there was nothing.

Slipping into a pair of black flats, I closed the door and locked the apartment, then took the elevator down to the lobby to meet Colin. Now that I was out of the apartment, I was shaking. Despite the fact that Mae Wang had died in front of my building, I somehow retained the idea that I was safe in my own apartment. I could now see that was naïve.

The black Camry pulled up in front of the building and Colin leaped out, running towards the building. His expression was a mix of anger and concern. Wrenching open the door, he said, "Kris, are you sure you are OK?"

"Yes, I'm fine. Just a little shaken up."

"Did you call the police?"

"No. We don't want them getting tangled up in this now. It's not going to help."

Colin considered that, then said, "All right, but at least phone Mike Reilly."

"OK, but let's not stand here in the lobby discussing our business. Come on up."

"Really? It sounded a bit grisly up there."

"It is, but we have to clean up the mess and figure out what to do next."

This time we took the elevator. With Colin in his black suit and me in my borrowed fancy dress, we looked like a normal couple returning from a night out. It was a fleeting illusion.

At the door to the apartment, Colin said, "Let me go in first."

"It's quite safe. I've checked it out." Then I touched his arm to stop him from entering, remembering Farrell's caution about electronic eavesdropping. If he thought whoever was behind this was tracking my phone and computer, it wouldn't be at all surprising if there were bugs or cameras in the apartment.

"Something I should have told you. Reilly and I met with a security consultant. He thinks there is a good chance that I am under electronic surveillance. We talked about phone and computer, but now I think my apartment could be bugged, too. If it wasn't before, it is now, with whoever did this having been in there."

"Jesus Kris. You should have told me. I would have arranged protection. What are we up against here?"

"Some kind of security agency, I expect. The question is, whose?"

"The Chinese surely, from what you've told me."

"Maybe. Look, I think we need to watch what we say while we deal with the dog, then head to a hotel room."

"What about my place?"

"Probably safe, but I think a hotel would be better. We can't afford to be predictable."

"All right. Let's clean this up then."

Colin entered the apartment, then said, "What an unholy smell."

He led the way into the kitchen, took off his suit jacket and tie, then took a green plastic garbage bag from under the sink. "I'll cut him down, bag him and clean this up," he said. "You shouldn't have to deal with it. You didn't have feelings for the dog, did you?"

"I had gotten used to him, but where I grew up, when a dog got old, you got out your .22 and took him out behind the barn. I'll be fine." In fact, I had found Ranger's grisly demise more disturbing than I would have expected, perhaps because it illustrated the casual cruelty of the people involved. I didn't want to look weak to Colin, though, or to whoever might be watching or listening.

Colin pulled on a pair of rubber gloves, took a knife from the drawer, then cut the thin rope that held Ranger's rear legs to the light fixture, letting him down into the sink. "Good to know. I couldn't stand the animal myself. Any idea of what we can do with the body?"

"I'm afraid we are going to have to drop him down the garbage chute. Double bag him. I will tell Caroline that he broke free from his leash and was hit by a car.

"If you have got that handled, I'm going to change," I said, then immediately wondered if there was some kind of spy camera in the bedroom.

"Yes, do that. I don't want you to spend the night here. Let's go back to my place."

"Great idea," I said, for the benefit of whomever we might be eavesdropping.

In the bedroom, I left the lights off while I changed into a pair of jeans and a lightweight red sweater. I threw a few clothes into a carry-on bag. There was no telling when I would return.

When I got back to the kitchen, Ranger was gone from view and Colin was scouring the sink and countertop with cleanser. "You seem to be an old hand at this," I said.

"Cleaned lots of game back in Suffolk. And sheep, of course. Amazing amount of entrails there."

"Spare me the details."

"Right, sorry."

We left the apartment and I locked the door, although it seemed pointless. Then we deposited poor Ranger in the garbage chute. I tried to think of it as the urban equivalent of burial at sea.

Back in front of the building, we sat on the outdoor metal chairs of the Bridgehead, now closed for the night. The evening was deceptively benign, with happy strollers on Elgin heading out for a night at the bars. Life as usual, but it was almost the exact spot where Mae had died. So much had happened in just over a week.

I called Reilly's burner with mine, to let him know what had happened, that things had escalated. His phone rang five times before he picked up. He sounded breathless, stressed.

"Mike. It's Kris. You OK?"

"Yes, but Suzy's not. She was abducted and beaten. I've gotten her back and she's seeing a doctor right now."

Suddenly, Ranger's death seemed like pretty small news. "Suzy," I said to Colin, then, "Is she badly hurt Mike?"

"I don't think so, but she's a mess. A concussion for sure. Kris, she was taken by a guy driving a vehicle with diplomatic plates. He roughed her up and stripped her out in the woods in Nepean. She only escaped because a second guy showed up and there was an argument. She took the opportunity to make a run for it."

My first response was anger; my second, fear that I would be next. What would have happened if I had been home tonight?

"Who did it, does she know?"

"No, he was wearing a mask."

"Police involved?"

"Just me. Suzy didn't want that."

I could understand her reaction. What she had been through would be humiliating and getting people she worked with involved would make it worse. Most cops were good people, but some were cruel bastards. She'd have been the butt of jokes for years to come.

"She at the hospital?"

"No, doctor friend of hers. Why were you calling?"

"It's nothing compared to your news, but someone was in my apartment. He killed my dog, gutted it and hanged it from a light fixture."

"Jesus Christ. You're not still there, are you?"

"Out front, waiting for an Uber. Colin is with me."

"All right. We need to meet, regroup. I need to take Suzy someplace. Her own house won't be safe. Where are you headed?"

"Where are we going?" I asked Colin.

"Chateau. I know a chap there. Very discreet. He'll keep it off the books."

"Chateau Laurier," I told Reilly. "Call me when you get there and I will tell you what room."

"All right. Good. Be careful and call me if anything changes."

After she hung up, Reilly gingerly touched the bump on the back of his head. There was no need to tell Kris how badly he had been outplayed. He was cut and bruised from going down head first onto the gravel parking lot. How the hell had that guy gotten up behind him? He knew he was getting old and out of shape, but he didn't think he had lost it that badly. Maybe it was time to hang it up, but not now, when people's lives depended on him.

When he had gotten groggily to his feet, he had seen Suzy, peeking out from the edge of the forest. He looked around and saw that the big SUV was gone, having smashed through some undergrowth to get around his car. Reilly had stumbled to Suzy and draped his muddy suit coat over her shoulders. They had clung to each other, survivors of something neither fully comprehended.

Reilly didn't understand what was going on, but he knew one thing: This had become deeply personal and if these fuckers thought they were going to hurt Suzy, they'd have to go through him to do it. He would be her shadow until this was all over.

It was time to escalate. He called Farrell. "Hey bud, it's Reilly. Remember that problem we were talking about the other day."

"Sure."

"It's gotten worse. I could use your particular type of help."

"I think I know what you mean. Happy to lend a hand."

"Great. Meet me at the Chateau Laurier as soon as you can. Call me when you get there. Come prepared for action."

"I always do."

THIRTY-SIX

Colin and I made a mismatched pair when we entered the lobby of the Chateau Laurier. He was still in his dark suit and I looked like I was dressed for a picnic. I felt out of place, too. The Chateau is one of those grand railway hotels, its walls covered in rich wooden panelling, its lobby soaring, its carpet thick and its furniture tastefully understated. Men and women in suits powered through the lobby, important people with somewhere to go. It was the kind of place that my family could only have gotten into if they were serving drinks. At least my single battered suitcase made it look as if we weren't just checking in for a quickie.

Colin strode to the reservation desk with me in tow. I was sure that his self-confident manner and posh accent would smooth over any awkwardness. Colin had a way of implying that he was upper crust, perhaps an earl, certainly nothing less than a knight.

The first reservation clerk free was an earnest-looking young guy with hair severely short on the sides but long on the top in the absurd fashion of the moment. It didn't exactly work with his grey suit and thin black tie.

"How may we assist, sir?"

"Jean-Luc." Colin said curtly.

"I will see if he is available."

"He will be. Tell him it's Wendover."

The clerk scuttled into a back room and Colin looked impatiently at his watch. In less than a minute, Jean-Luc appeared. He was about 35, with a long, angular face, thick, dark hair and facial hair that was somewhere between unshaven and a beard. His smiled looked genuine when he said, "Ah, Colin. So good to see you again."

The two men shook hands, then Colin leaned in close to Jean-Luc and said, "My colleague Ms. Redner and I are working on an investigative piece. Very confidential. We are meeting some sources here shortly. I will need a suite and an adjoining room. Others have taken a competitive interest in the same story, so I will need you to keep our presence out of the hotel computer system. I trust I can rely on your absolute discretion."

"But of course," Jean-Luc said with a shrug that meant yes. "I am in the discretion business. Have I ever failed you before?"

"Never. That's why we are here," Colin said.

I hadn't really thought about it, but Colin had lived at the Chateau for two months when he was first brought to Ottawa as editor. Naturally, he would know the people who could get things done.

As we rode up on the elevator, I found it difficult not to think of the many times we had gotten together in Toronto hotel rooms, back when I thought our complex relationship was nothing more than good recreational sex. The Royal York had been our spot, and it was much like the Chateau. If my mind was going there, I could guarantee that Colin's was.

As if sensing my thoughts, he reached out and lightly touched my hand, but then he said, "It will be fine. We'll get them, whoever they are."

I wasn't quite so sure, but I said, "I know. We're getting close. What they did today shows they're desperate."

The room was as expected with creamy yellow walls, creamier wood trim everywhere, parquet floors and comfortable furniture that was broken in but quietly expensive. In the main room of the suite, a couch and two chairs faced each other. I could see the bedroom through a door to our right. For just a moment, I considered proposing a brief, no-commitment tension release, but then Colin broke the mood by saying, "This thing with Suzy is really concerning. In all my years in the business, I have only had one reporter physically assaulted and that was in a bar fight. Reilly seems to think she is OK?"

"Shaken up. We'll soon see."

"Right," he said. Then, putting his concern to one side, he said, "This will be our base of operations for now. I will have Jean-Luc locate a couple of laptops and send them up."

So it was to be business, then. "Great. I've got all my notes and files on a memory stick."

My burner phone rang, sooner than I had expected. "We're in the lobby," Reilly said. I gave him the room number and told Colin that Reilly and Suzy were on their way up.

Although my conversation with Reilly had prepared me for the idea that Suzy was in bad shape, I was still shocked by what I saw when she came through the door. Shaky on her feet, Suzy was leaning on Reilly, who looked more haggard than normal, his face scratched and bruised. Usually so carefully dressed, Suzy wore a pair of baggy black sweatpants and a too-large pink T-shirt. Both of her eyes were black and her lip had been split open. Her whole face looked as red as if she had spent a day in the sun. Her arms had cuts and bruises as well. I didn't even want to think about what I couldn't see.

If it had been me, I would have wanted to be treated normally, not like a victim, so I did the same for her. "Hey Suzy. Looks like I got the easy interviews."

She slumped into one of the two beige leather chairs and attempted a smile. "I found out who she really is," she said. "Mae Wang."

"That's fantastic.'

"Zhao Mei. A Chinese spy. Her father . . . " Suzy trailed off, then looked at Reilly. "My head isn't working right. You tell it, Mike."

Reilly shook Colin's hand. I was so used to Reilly that I hadn't thought to introduce him. As Reilly filled Colin and me in, I tried not to be pissed about not having been the one to unearth the biggest development in the story so far. Suzy had a scoop, but she'd paid a hell of a price for it.

After Reilly finished, Colin leaned in toward Suzy and took her hand. "You've been through a lot," he said. "Tremendous job. Now, tell us what happened to you?"

"She hasn't even really told me the details yet," Reilly said. "Suzy, you OK to talk about it?"

"Yes, I think so. I had been to see Xi, the Chinese guy from the restaurant. The one who knew Mae. I drove back to my place. I had just gotten out of the car when a man came up behind me and hit me in the head with something heavy, maybe a pipe or a short bat. He put his hand over my mouth, then lifted me up and tossed me into a black SUV.

"He taped my mouth, then taped my wrist and ankles." She paused, then said, "Mike, can you get me some water?"

When he left to get water from the washroom, she said, "This is bad, what happened to me. I am OK with Mike knowing, because we were, you know. But you two have to swear that you will never tell this story."

"Of course," Colin said, quickly.

"I can keep a secret," I added.

"He took me somewhere. It took quite a bit of time to get there, it seemed like that anyway. It was a parking lot. It was in the woods. Dark. I heard crickets and frogs, lots of frogs.

"He wanted to know what I knew about Mae. He called her by her real name. He wanted to know what you knew, too, Kris."

Reilly came back with the water. "Describe the man to us Suzy."

"He had on a ski mask, dark clothing. He was burly. Probably six feet or taller."

Reilly nodded, encouraging her. He and I both knew that her description wasn't going to help us find the guy.

"Any accents?" he asked. "Was he Chinese?"

"I don't think so. He sounded a bit different, but I can't place it."

"OK, no problem," Reilly said. "What happened next?"

"I told him I didn't know anything about her, but he knew I was lying. Then he started slapping me around. First it was just my face, then he started punching me everywhere. In the stomach, and lower.

"He was hitting me hard, but I knew he wasn't trying to kill me, just scare me. Then he stopped. A second guy had arrived. I could hear them arguing, but not what they said. Then one of them got back in the SUV and I felt him run a knife down my arm. Then he cut the tape off my arms and legs and cut my clothes off. He kept asking me the same questions and every time I didn't answer, his hands would just, they would just go wherever he wanted.

"I tried to think. Who was I protecting? Not Mae. They had to know already about Xi. But I wasn't going to give them the satisfaction. They weren't going to scare me into telling them. Fuck them.

"After a while, the guy went outside the van again and he talked some more to the other guy. I looked out and saw that they weren't looking my way. I got out of the SUV and ran like hell into the woods. That's when I called Mike."

"And what about the second guy, did you get a good look at him?" Colin asked.

"No, it was too dark. He was bigger than the first guy. That's all I know."

"These bastards are going to pay for what they did," Colin said. "Mike, shouldn't we be bringing in the police?"

"No!" Suzy shouted. "I'm not sharing this with the world."

"Besides that, there is the issue of keeping this information close," Reilly said. "I would love to arrest and charge these guys, and I will if I can, but I want to keep my options open for an informal resolution."

"Meaning?" I said.

"Whatever it takes to tee these fuckers up, whether it's by the books or not."

There was a knock on the door and three of us looked towards it, surprised. The exception was Reilly, who went to answer it.

At first, I didn't recognize the man who came through the door. He was clean-shaven with short blond hair and he was big, seeming to fill up the entire door frame. The guy wore jeans and a blue T-shirt that looked like it had been sprayed on to his impressive upper body. He carried a bulky black duffel bag that must have been heavy, but it looked light in his hands.

"Hi Kris," he said. Then I realized it was Farrell.

"I hardly recognized you. Which is the real you, this one or the woodsman?"

"Both. I'm working with a new client. Corporate. The back-to-the-land look doesn't work with them."

Colin stood and shook Farrell's hand. Although Colin was a big man, he didn't look it when stacked up against Farrell. "I take it you are an associate of Mike's?"

"Something like that." Farrell set the duffel bag on the floor with a heavy clank. It sounded like he had brought some of his armoury with him.

"Farrell and I met on a project a long time ago. He was good enough to give us some background advice on the Chinese and the technology and methods they use."

"Excellent," Colin said. "Who were you with?"

"Federal agencies."

Colin nodded, getting the drift that Farrell wasn't there to talk about himself. "OK. We were just about to talk about how we are going to proceed. Please join us. Anyone want a drink before we start?"

Without waiting for an answer, Colin went to an ornate cabinet and withdrew a bottle of scotch and five glasses, then set them on the coffee table.

"Help yourselves," he said, settling beside me on the couch. "Why don't I start? I think we can agree that this story is proving to be something larger and more dangerous than any of us anticipated. We know now that we are dealing with a murdered Chinese spy with a likely connection to our foreign minister. This is a story that will go international. It is our job to lay out just what has happened and who is involved. Kris, I want you on this full-time. The Sandhu trial is small beer in comparison. We will leave that to news to cover. Suzy, you have done tremendous work, but for now I want you to restrict yourself to filling Kris in on what you've got. Our main priority has to be letting you get well."

Suzy began to protest, but Colin held up his hand to stop her.

"There is still a lot we don't know and we obviously don't have much time to find out. The other side is moving quickly and we aren't even sure who they are. From my perspective, the legal angles here are murky and, if foreign diplomatic personnel are involved, the odds are that they will never be brought to justice. We can't help that, but we can put this whole matter into the court of public opinion. Thoughts?"

"I think I can take it from here," I said. "I made a good connection with Champagne tonight. The door is open for a second interview. The guy is in the middle of this somehow. My first priority is to find out how."

"Agreed," Colin said. "Mike, do you or Farrell have anything to contribute on Champagne?"

"He's dirty," Reilly said. "I can smell it."

"He would have been thoroughly vetted before entering cabinet," Farrell said. "Let me see what I can find out."

"Excellent. We know he was regularly visiting the building where Mae Wang died. We can use that as a lever. If it comes to it, we can simply include that as a fact in the story and let readers draw their own conclusions," Colin said.

"Mike, where do we stand on the police side?"

Reilly rubbed a rough hand across his unshaven jaw. "We haven't got much. There is this bogus joint task force with the RCMP, but I think that's just a cover for doing nothing. I am not even on the case, officially. With the abduction and beating, we do have something solid to pursue, but only if Suzy is willing, and I don't think she is."

All four of us looked at Suzy, who simply shook her head. "Not now, maybe not ever. There has to be some other way to get these guys."

"That's where I come in," Farrell said. "They have got to be with a security agency, maybe even one of ours. That's my world, and I don't worry about colouring outside the lines. We've got murder, abduction, a beating. They are covering up something pretty big. This stuff is never held as tightly as they'd like. If it can be cracked, I'll crack it.

"I work alone, though. Mike, I've left you a few things that might come in handy in that duffel bag. If we do come up against these people, you're going to want more than a sidearm. For the rest of you, I would suggest arming yourselves, although I'm sure you won't take my advice."

Farrell looked at his watch, a heavy, military-looking thing. "I've got to get moving. I think our time is short. The other side has to decide whether to step up the action or bug out. We need to get on top of this before they do either one." Farrell stood and said, "I'll report back when I learn more, using the burner phone. Who's my point of contact?"

"Me," I said. "I need to know every detail if we are going to pull this story together."

"Done."

As Farrell made to leave, Reilly said, "I'll walk you out."

I was pretty certain that I wasn't going to be the only person to whom Farrell reported. Reilly's comment about "teeing the fuckers up," stuck in my mind. I was all for it, but not until I got the story.

THIRTY-SEVEN

At first, I wasn't sure where I was. A thin shaft of light came through the bedroom drapes, but nothing looked familiar. I looked at my watch. It was 8:30. Then I rolled over and saw Colin. Now it was all starting to come back to me. We had a couple more scotches after Mike and Suzy had retreated to the other room. Then one thing had led to another.

I couldn't say sex hadn't been on my mind, and it was always on his. Still, it was confusing. I had spent months trying to keep Colin at bay. Now, I wondered why. Maybe I was just overthinking things, as I usually did. He was a patient and attentive lover and clearly devoted to me. He was good-looking, if a bit older, and we shared many of the same passions. What was I looking for? That was a question that I had spent a lifetime trying to answer and too often came up with "whatever comes along next."

Sometimes I liked to blame what had happened to us in the Adirondacks for blowing up our relationship. Knowing that he had saved my life put just too much obligation on me. But I knew the problem had started before that. Our life together had started to become domestic, routine. If I had surrendered to that, at my age, there was a good chance that I would never know the thrill of new love again. Then I found it when L.T. came along. The young cop who had been my lover in the Adirondacks had been fresh and new in every way. We both knew it wouldn't last, but that was part of the attraction. Then he was killed and I just couldn't think of love, or sex, again. Until now.

I watched Colin sleep, his grey hair in uncharacteristic disarray. He was snoring lightly. I ran my fingers down his arm. He was a good man who deserved more than I would ever be able to give him.

My touch awakened him and he snuggled close to me. It was

quickly apparent that either he had to piss or he was ready for a second round.

"Amazing to see you here," he said. "Thank you."

"It wasn't like I was doing you a favour. We both needed that."

"Indeed." He was running his hand along my back. I knew I would quickly have to decide what to do. It was one thing to fall into bed together after a few drinks and a tense day. Sunday morning sex would be more of a deliberate choice.

Then I heard my phone ringing in my purse. I could tell by the ring it wasn't the burner. Damn, I had left my own phone on. Farrell wouldn't be happy with that.

I rolled out of bed, self-conscious at my nakedness and walked across to the bureau to get the phone. I was surprised to see the call was from Gail Rakic, no doubt hoping that I would be at the trial Monday to write something positive about her husband. I was going to have to disappoint her.

"Who is it?" Colin asked.

"Gail Rakic, Sandhu's wife."

"What the hell does she want?" he asked, clearly annoyed that the call was disrupting his plans.

"I'll try to get rid of her," I said, then took the call.

"Hey, it's Gail."

"I know. What's up?"

"There is something I need you to know before the trial starts again tomorrow. You have time for coffee?"

"Kind of a bad day, Gail. I'm working on something else. In fact, I won't be at the trial this week."

"Really?"

Her disappointment was clear. I knew that the trial was the biggest event in her life, but it was no longer the biggest in mine.

"I think you are going to want to hear what I have to say. Remember I told you I knew something more about Champagne? I think the time has come to share it."

"I could be interested in that."

"Good. We're staying at the Lord Elgin. Can you meet there in half an hour?"

"Better give me an hour. I need to freshen up."

"All right. See you in an hour."

I hung up and Colin said, "You're off the Sandhu story, remember? I know it's an intriguing trial, but we just don't have the time for it."

"I know that. She wants to tell me something about Champagne. I don't know if it's relevant to the Mae Wang story, but it could be. At a minimum, it might give us more leverage with Champagne. Gail plays hard ball. I need to know what she's got. It will be worth an hour of my time."

"All right. Makes sense. You have an hour?"

"Yes, an hour to shower, get dressed and get over there." I leaned over and kissed him, gently. "Maybe we don't have to be in a rush."

He smiled at that. "I hope not, but I think you like it that way."

"Sure, gives me less time to think."

I pulled some fresh underwear out of my overnight bag and headed to the bathroom. I knew Colin's next move would be to call room service and ponder the hidden meaning of what I had said.

The Lord Elgin was just around the corner from the Chateau Laurier. It was another old-fashioned hotel, a plainer cousin of the Chateau. I wondered why a person as rich as Gail wasn't staying someplace swankier. Perhaps the attraction was that it was directly across from the courthouse, minimizing the length of the daily perp walk her husband had to endure.

It wasn't hard to spot Gail in the hotel's ground floor restaurant. Her brassy hairdo stood out like a beacon. She was wearing designer jeans and a pink sweater, a change from her usual power suit. I took a chair opposite her, watching as she finished off a croissant. I hoped I didn't have that hungover and just-fucked look.

"You want the buffet?" she asked.

"No, thanks. I've already eaten."

A waiter appeared at my side and filled my cup with coffee. I could never get too much of that.

"I'm surprised that you won't be covering the trial. I thought you were doing a good job."

I ignored the possibly insincere compliment and said, "I had hoped to stick with it, but priorities can change quickly in my business. Does Bernstein start his defence Monday?"

"He does. The reason I wanted to talk to you, there is more to it than he is going to be able to present in court."

"I guess that's not going to help your husband then, is it?"

"Not in court, but we both know it's not just the verdict. It's what the public thinks that will determine Sonny's future. I am confident that he won't be convicted, but we can't afford to have people think he's guilty all the same."

"So you want to present a plausible alternative explanation for how he got into the soup, but Bernstein can't back it up in court. That sound about right?"

"It does. I'm going to give you a file, and I'm giving it to you exclusively."

Unless I didn't use it, then she would give it to someone else exclusively. I didn't like the idea that Gail had chosen me as a mouthpiece for unprovable defence strategies, but if what she had would let me pin down Champagne, I was all for it. I didn't want to sound too eager. "Tell me about it and I'll tell you if I can use it."

Gail pulled her large, soft black leather purse off the chair beside her and set it on the table. It was Coach, I wasn't surprised to see. She removed a manila file folder that was intriguingly thick and held together with a heavy rubber band.

"When the police started to question Sonny, we were suspicious about what was behind the allegations. His relations with Champagne had been cordial, once, but that was before they were the two leading rivals for the leadership. In politics, you have no real friends. Have you met Champagne?"

She seemed surprised when I said I had.

"Well, I guess it's a small town. So you have some idea of what he's like; a charmer on the outside, a snake on the inside."

Even allowing for her bitterness, I didn't think her estimation was far off.

"Preparing to go up against Champagne for the leadership, we had some opposition research done. Standard stuff, looking for embarrassing things he had said or done, policy contradictions, financial issues, old girlfriends with colourful tales to tell, that kind of thing."

"And?"

"Less than we had hoped, except for one thing. That girl you asked me to find out more about, the one who fell off the roof of your building? She was Champagne's girlfriend."

I had pretty much concluded that, but showed grateful surprise all the same. "Really? That's intriguing."

"There's more. She worked for the Chinese Embassy. A cabinet minister screwing an employee of a foreign embassy? You people would have a field day with that."

"So why don't you use it?"

"We were going to leak this out, drop the hammer on Champagne back when he was still in the Conservative race. He beat us to it with this bogus story about Sonny taking a bribe. Then, when Sonny was charged, we came up with another plan."

Gail was telling me that she and her husband weren't any better than Luc Champagne, just slower off the mark. "I assume you have proof?"

"I do, right here in this file. We hired a PI to tail the girl. Champagne showed up at her apartment every Tuesday night, didn't leave until morning. We bugged the apartment. There's no doubt as to the nature of their relationship."

"And this continued when he became foreign affairs minister?"

"It did. There is no evidence here that he was giving away national secrets. He had other things on his mind. But this," she said, tapping the file, "is enough to finish him."

"You're right about that, but how is it going to help you?"

"Ben had a two-part strategy. First, we'd subpoena the girl and put her on the stand. Even if she wouldn't answer a single question, it would give us a chance to suggest her relationship with Champagne, destroying his credibility. Then, he was going to subpoena Champagne and grill him directly on these phoney charges and his role in setting the whole thing up."

"Champagne is a cabinet minister. Would he have to appear?"

"Ben says there are some technicalities about when the House is sitting, but he was confident we could get him. He'd look pretty bad if he didn't show."

Trust Bernstein to come up with the bold play. "All right. Interesting strategy, but now you don't have the girl."

"Exactly. Ben even sent someone to meet with her, try to get a statement, but she refused to co-operate. Now she's dead and he can't find a way to get this in front of the judge. It was going to take some latitude to get her on the stand anyway, but he can't question an empty chair."

"So I destroy Champagne's credibility, then Bernstein subpoenas him."

"That's it."

I pointed at the folder and said "May I?"

Gail shoved it across the table. I opened the file and saw that it consisted of time-stamped pictures of Champagne entering and leaving my building, along with some murky shots of two people who could be Champagne and Mae, in her bedroom. The best picture was one of Champagne and Mae in a daring moment, sharing a coffee on the Bridgehead patio where she later died. It could be passed off as innocent, were it not for the rest of it. There were detailed logs of the surveillance and the PI's observations.

"When did the surveillance end?"

"A couple of months before she died. We had everything we needed."

"So nothing close to the time of her death, then?"

"No, unfortunately. You think Champagne was involved in that?"

"I have no idea."

"Are you going to be able to use this?"

I thought for a moment. I was certainly going to use it, but not in exactly the way that Gail wanted. This was my leverage to pressure Champagne and find out what had really happened to Mae. At this point, I didn't care too much about the fate of slippery Sonny Sandhu and his charming wife.

"Absolutely," I said.

"That's great. How soon? Ben has some other witnesses he can call, but he will want to bring on Champagne this week."

"All right. I can work with that. It will take a couple of days. A story like this will have to be lawyered."

"You see a problem with getting this in the paper?"

"No. I think that everyone will agree that it's a pressing matter of national interest. I'll have to talk to my editor, see how he wants to approach it."

"I was hoping you could just run with what you have in your column. You get to write whatever you want, don't you?"

"Usually, but it won't be quite that simple here. This PI willing to talk?"

"I will make sure that he is. His contact info is in the file."

I considered warning Gail about the attack on Suzy and the fact that there were players in this story beyond Luc Champagne. Serious players. The problem was, I didn't trust her. I had gotten what I could from her without having to give up anything in return. I was satisfied with that deal.

Gail Rakic was a big girl. She was going to have to take care of herself. I needed to tell Colin about the Champagne development and arrange to see my new friend the minister. He wasn't going to enjoy our next interview quite as much as he had the first.

THIRTY-EIGHT

I was working from the hotel room Monday morning, starting to outline what I knew about the Mae Wang story so far. I was wearing my best out-of-office outfit, a pair of fuzzy red and black plaid fleece pants and a washed-out black Oxford T-shirt that used to belong to Colin. I had a full pot of coffee from room service and I was trying to focus on the story, not think about what had happened yesterday with Colin. And then again, last night. I had a gift for making my life complex. Now that I was both living and working out of the Chateau Laurier, it was as if we were married and running a home business. Fortunately, he had gone into the office for the day. That would give me time to think, or not think, whichever was best.

Then my work cell rang. I had left it on in case Gail Rakic called back. I saw that it was the U.S. Embassy. For an expatriate American, a call from the embassy is unlikely to be something good. My first thought was IRS hounding me for tax paperwork. Then, I thought about the Adirondacks. Months had gone by and I had heard nothing official about the somewhat murky end of events down there. I wasn't guilty of anything, probably, but that didn't mean I wanted to be grilled by U.S. officialdom.

I was tempted to let it go to voice mail, but if it was anything serious they wouldn't be put off that easily.

A smooth voice, hint of a New York accent, said, "Hello Ms. Redner. This is Don Platt. I'm the cultural attaché here at the U.S. Embassy."

The guy's name sounded vaguely familiar, but I didn't know any embassy people and I hoped to keep it that way.

"We've got some big events coming here at the embassy this summer and I'm reaching out to prominent Ottawa journalists to raise awareness, maybe get some coverage."

"Not sure who gave you my name, Mr. Platt, but you'd be better off calling the arts editor. I write a crime column." I thought it was a good way to get rid of him, considering that the arts editor had taken a buyout in the last round of staff reductions.

"Yeah, I'm aware of that, but I've got a problem. Maybe you can help me out. The ambassador's wife is a real nut about culture, which is great, of course, but she wants to see that I've talked to a wide range of journalists here in Ottawa. In fact, she reads your stuff and asked that I call you specifically."

That was almost certainly a lie, but now I was growing more interested in what Don Platt really wanted. I decided to play hard to get. "Well, isn't that nice? I wish I could help, but I'm awfully busy."

"I can imagine. Here's the thing. One event in particular I think might interest you. It's a Chinese event, actually."

Now he had my attention. "Chinese? Isn't that a little outside your scope?"

"My job here at the embassy requires me to keep a close eye on the whole cultural scene, ma'am."

I was certain at this point that Don Platt's real job had nothing to do with culture, assuming his real name was even Don Platt. I remembered what Farrell had said about a security agency being involved in the Mae Wang affair. I thought maybe I was about to find out which one.

"As it turns out, I do have an interest in Chinese culture," I said.

"I thought you might. You have time to get a coffee this morning, maybe some place down in the Market, close to the embassy?"

"I could do that. Time and place?"

"How about Planet Coffee, say 10:30?"

I looked at my watch. It was 9:15. That would give me plenty of time to make myself presentable and get to the coffee shop, which was only a couple of blocks away.

"OK. I'll see you then. How will I recognize you?"

"Don't worry. I'll recognize you."

Platt hung up and left me wondering. Would he recognize me because he had seen my picture on my column or simply Googled me? It was the most likely explanation, but then I wondered if he and whichever agency he really represented had bugged my apartment, my computer or my phone. Maybe I would ask him, see what he had to say.

For just a minute, I wondered about the wisdom of going alone after what had happened to Suzy, but I was sure Don Platt wasn't going to abduct me from a Byward Market coffee shop. I settled for sending Colin a text.

I got to the coffee shop a few minutes early to scope it out, see if there were any suspicious-looking men wearing earpieces and pretending to read the newspaper. If there were, I didn't spot them. The coffee shop was one of those places that favoured a modern industrial look with plenty of exposed pipes on the ceiling. I got a large, dark coffee and took a table in front of a wall mural of a whale.

When Don Platt came through the door, the pieces began to fall into place. I knew his name was familiar. Platt was one of the two assholes who had tried to hit on Gail Rakic and me in the bar the other night. He was the tall, handsome one who looked like a slightly aging underwear model. If I had any doubt at all, it was dispelled by the appearance of his sidekick, Chip something or other. Guy was all shiny and pink with a military-style blond brush cut. Definitely the guy from the bar, but I had the idea I had seen him before that, too. Both wore dark suits and red ties, but Chip's looked like a 46 stout while Platt's was a well-draped 42.

Pretending to look at my phone, I snapped a couple of quick shots of them. No doubt they were the kind of people who wouldn't be real keen to get their pictures in the paper.

The two spies, if that's what they were, noticed me over by the whale and Platt waved like we were old friends. I didn't think he would have that misapprehension for long.

I stood when they approached, but didn't offer to shake Platt's outstretched hand. I checked his knuckles for cuts and bruises, to see if he had maybe beaten a woman lately. Nothing, but the other man kept his hands in his pants pockets, as if he was being casual.

"Ms. Redner?" Platt said. "Good of you to see us on such short notice. This is my colleague, Chip Leggett."

"How could I forget? The two lonesome, horny guys who were in town for some kind of plumbing convention, right?"

Leggett reddened a bit but Platt just shrugged. "Yeah, sorry about that."

"So how long have you been following me around?

"Let's not get the wrong idea here," Platt said. He reached into his suit jacket and withdrew a slim black leather case and presented me with a business card that claimed he was, in fact, Don Platt and that he was a cultural attaché with the U.S. Embassy. Leggett handed me a similar card claiming that he was a trade attaché. Naturally, I wasn't buying any of it.

Leggett and Platt sat and I did the same.

"We're here on official business," Platt said.

"That's a pleasant change. Why don't we get right to it? What can you tell me about this interesting Chinese event?"

Platt looked at Leggett, then Leggett nodded and began to speak. Maybe Leggett was the boss after all and Platt was just the door opener.

"Here's the thing, Kris. I hope you don't mind if I call you Kris."

"Not at all, Chip. What's that short for anyway? Chester?"

"No, Charles," he said, scarcely missing a beat. "Now, part of our duty as consular officers is to look out for the interests of Americans here in Canada. That's the context we're acting in today."

"Really? You want to look out for *me*?"

"We do. It has come to our attention that you have been making inquiries about the death of a Chinese Embassy employee called Mae Wang."

"And how is that of concern to you, Chip?"

"Well, naturally we and our colleagues pay a lot of attention to the other embassies, especially countries like China. Between us, this Mae Wang story is dangerous. One person has already died, of course. I can't tell you today that the Chinese are definitely responsible, but I'm sure you can draw your own conclusions. I'm thinking of your personal safety here."

"That's very sweet of you Chip, but I'm sure I will be fine." In fact, I wasn't so sure, not after what happened to Suzy, but Chip seemed more like a threat than a saviour.

"There are other considerations as well, and I'm going to appeal to your sense of patriotism here. This is a complex and convoluted situation. It's the kind of thing where inaccurate or premature journalistic coverage could give a false impression and harm American interests."

"Well, we wouldn't want that."

"Glad to hear you say so."

"Of course, I don't intend to write a story that is inaccurate or premature. In fact, I think coverage of her death is long overdue."

"Perhaps," Leggett said, "but let me bring in another factor. When we were doing a little background research on you, we came across some really interesting events that took place last fall in the Adirondacks. I'm sure you are familiar with the death of Senator Lowell Osborne?"

"Yes, tragic. I understand he was a great American."

"Possibly so, but it's your own involvement in his death that interests us."

I had been waiting months for the other shoe to drop. I wasn't responsible for Osborne's death, but it wouldn't be difficult to make it look as if I was. I shrugged as if this was all of no consequence to me. "That's interesting, but I wasn't involved in his death. Now, tell me boys, what agency do you really work for?"

"Does it matter? Let's be clear. We have the ability to make your life very difficult."

At that, Platt leaned forward with a menacing look. "We're doing you a favour here, Kris. Stay away from the Mae Wang story before you step in a deep, dark hole full of shit."

"So is that what you were trying to say when you killed my dog?"

Leggett and Platt exchanged a look of surprise.

"Sorry to hear about your dog," Leggett said, "but whatever happened had nothing to do with us."

"If you say so." I noticed that Leggett had kept his hands below the table. "Tell me Chip, how are your hands?"

"My hands aren't your problem," Leggett said. "We're here to give you some friendly advice. If you don't want to take it, that's on you."

Then another piece of the puzzle fell into place. I knew Leggett's face was familiar, but not just because I had seen him in the bar. I was looking at Mr. Thursday, the fat guy in the bad winter hat with the big earflaps.

"Say Chip, changing the subject slightly. It gets brutally cold here in the winter. Did you, by any chance, happen to get one of those warm hats with the earflaps?"

Now I had thrown Chip off his game. "What the hell are you

talking about?" he said. "I have a warm hat. So what? What's that got to do with any of this?"

"It's not the hat so much as the fact that you were seen entering Mae Wang's apartment building every Thursday night for weeks, wearing that goofy hat. It really is unforgettable."

"Who the hell are you working with?" he asked, incredulous.

"Doesn't matter, but I have a feeling you're going to find out soon."

"We're done here," Leggett said. "When it hits the fan, don't say we didn't warn you.'

I felt like I had just gotten a lot closer to the truth about Mae Wang, but the picture still wasn't clear. There was a burning American interest in her death, but what the hell was it?

THIRTY-NINE

As I walked back to the Chateau, I sent texts to Mike Reilly, Colin and Farrell. The message to each was the same. Developments, hotel, ASAP.

The morning was sunny and fresh in that way that only May can be. In the Market, vendors were arranging their displays of flowers and vegetables, chatting in French, getting ready for the day. In the midst of the cheery normalcy, I had my own personal storm cloud. Every time I found out more about the Mae Wang story, it became more confusing, the truth more opaque. Clearly there was a U.S. government involvement. Had Leggett and Platt killed her, or did they only want to prevent me from finding out who had? The Chinese were inevitably part of the story. Luc Champagne was no innocent bystander and the way the Mounties were smothering the investigation suggested that someone in government knew the truth. Then there was Gail Rakic. The things she was telling me were true, but only the fragments of the truth she wanted me to see.

When I got back to the room, Mike and Suzy were already there. Suzy still looked as if she had been hit by a truck, but her hair was washed and dried in some semblance of her normal look. Mike must have done that. She wore jeans and a baggy Carleton University sweatshirt. Reilly's suit coat was draped across the back of the desk chair, looking as rumpled as he was. Reilly looked like he had been up all night and the bruise on his face had grown darker. I hadn't really bought his story about tripping over a tree root, but it wasn't my business.

"So, developments," Mike said. "What's up?"

"Let's wait a few minutes for the others. Suzy, how are you feeling?"

"Like my head was put in a blender. Tell me we're getting closer to the guys who did this."

"I think so."

I ordered more coffee from room service and by the time it arrived, so had Farrell. Unlike Reilly, Farrell looked fresh and fired up. To my surprise, he wore a suit which was dark, expensive and well cut. He appeared to be a man with an interesting number of layers. Maybe some time I would get to find out what they were.

Colin was just five minutes behind. As soon as he stepped into the room, he took charge. It had been a long time since I had seen him so energized.

"Right then. Kris, why don't you bring us up to date, then we will hear what the others have to add."

"I got a surprise call this morning from a guy with the U.S. Embassy. Don Platt. Wanted to meet, tell me something important about what he called a Chinese cultural event."

"Those pricks always speak in code," Farrell said. "What did Platt say he did at the embassy?"

"Cultural attaché."

"Right, so he will be CIA. Anyone with him?"

"A guy who called himself Chip Leggett. Said he was a trade attaché."

"Almost inevitably the CIA station chief. That's their usual official job title. Did Leggett do most of the talking?"

"Yes. Their initial pitch was that they were concerned for my safety, worried that I might be stumbling into a dangerous situation with the Mae Wang story."

"No shit," Suzy said.

"That didn't work, so then they appealed to my patriotism. I don't have any, so then they went with threats. Mike, Farrell, without getting into it too deeply, there was a bit of a situation in the Adirondacks last fall that they could use to make my life difficult. Colin knows all about it."

"Should we be worried about that?" Farrell asked.

"I'm not."

"Good. How did you leave it with them?"

"I gave them a bit of their own back. I noticed that Leggett was keeping his hands in his pockets. I asked him what was up with that, but he wouldn't answer. He looked nervous, though. I think he's the guy who attacked Suzy."

"Where do I find these guys?" Reilly said.

"Not yet, Mike. I haven't gotten to the best part. Everyone

remember Mr. Thursday? It's Chip Leggett. He all but confirmed it. And get this, these same two guys braced me in the Red Feather when I was there with Gail Rakic. I think they've had me under surveillance."

"No doubt about that," Farrell said.

"Leggett wasn't too pleased when I told him I recognized him from surveillance of our own."

"Did he ask who was involved?"

"He did. I told him that he'd likely be meeting them soon."

"You're fucking right," Reilly said.

"Very good," Colin said. "I feel like we are really starting to get somewhere. The other side is reacting, feeling the pressure. Reilly, Farrell, what do you have to add?"

"I got my hands on the security vetting for Champagne," Farrell said. "Squeaky clean. Nothing about China whatsoever, although I know CSIS has been keeping a watchful eye on politicians whose ties to enemy countries are a little too close. Champagne's not on the list."

"If his connection with Mae started after he was already foreign minister, would anyone have known?" I asked.

"You would hope so," Farrell said, "but once they've passed the test, they're in and you've got to trust your foreign affairs minister. He's the main link between cabinet and the security agencies."

"So they aren't going to be looking into their boss, and if they are, they aren't going to write a report about it," Reilly said.

Colin had been pacing the room while he took all of this in. Then he said, "I see a two-part strategy here. Farrell, are you willing to meet with Leggett and Platt, see what more you can find out?"

"These guys are diplomats. We can't charge them with anything. Where's our leverage?" Reilly asked.

"That's why I am suggesting that we do this unofficially," Colin said. "Farrell, I take it that you are comfortable in the grey zone."

"Absolutely. Maybe I will take them for a little ride, show them the countryside, get to know them better. Mike, you in?"

Reilly hesitated for just a second. It was one thing for a guy like Farrell to play outside the rules, but I knew it could be a career-ending move for Reilly. Then he said, "Wouldn't miss that party."

"Good," Colin said. "Try to get on that as quickly as you can. Let us know what you find out and the less we know about how you did it, the better.

"Now, on the journalistic side, I think it's time we tried a burning arrow approach," Colin said. Mike, Suzy and Farrell looked at Colin as if he'd just started speaking Greek. Unlike me, they didn't know that Colin had a passion for Hollywood westerns. He had quite an impressive collection. I thought I knew what he meant, but said "You'd better spell that out."

"Right, sorry. I am being a bit oblique. Anyone here watch Westerns?"

Both Reilly and Farrell nodded.

"Think of a situation where the ranch house is surrounded by hostiles, but those inside are well-armed and their cover seemingly impregnable. What happens next?"

"The Indians fire a burning arrow into the roof, set the place on fire, see who comes scrambling out the doors and windows," Farrell said.

Suzy appeared confused, no doubt some combination of the concussion and not having sat through hours of cowboy movies with Colin. "Wait a minute," she said. "We are the hostiles?"

"You're damn right we are," Reilly said, "and these assholes are about to find out just how hostile we can get."

"What I'm thinking," Colin said, "is that we use a story as our burning arrow. Kris, I think it's about time we got a piece in the paper on Mae Wang's death. Tell the public who she really was, what the Chinese did to her father, her connection to the embassy and the fact that the homicide investigation has produced no tangible results, or even any real action. For now, we leave out any mention of Champagne and the U.S. angle, but we put out enough to make them all squirm. Let's see who tries to cover their own ass at the expense of the others."

"I like that," I said. "I can have something together by the end of the day."

"Good. Joint byline with Suzy."

The story would actually be all my work, but we were a team now. And what an odd team we were: three journalists, a cop and a guy from the murky underworld of espionage whose motives were unclear. The hostiles. It was a good name for our little group. The other guys had controlled the play. Now we were coming for them. It felt good.

FORTY

Among the many fixed points in Derek Hall's day was his 11 p.m. perusal of every news source online, bracketed by his next look at 6 a.m. Not to say that his world couldn't go to hell between 11 and 6, but he had to sleep some time.

He rolled out of bed at 6, eager to take a piss, switching his phone on as he stumbled to the bathroom. He scanned the *Toronto Star*, *The Globe and Mail* and the CBC. All quiet, except for the premiers continuing to whine about not getting enough additional health-care dollars. Some of them were even refusing to accept what they had been offered. As a negotiating tactic, it was the equivalent of taking yourself hostage. Nothing he couldn't handle there.

Derek set the phone down on the countertop, then took a long, satisfying piss. Then he turned to the *Citizen*'s web site. There hadn't been a lot to worry him there since the financially challenged newspaper company had cut its staff on the Hill to the bare minimum, but you never knew.

The top story on the web page hit him like a recurring nightmare. Chinese Spy Dies Mysteriously In Centretown Love Nest, the headline ran. Jesus Christ. Everyone had told him there was nothing to worry about. Everyone except Vanessa. He should have listened.

Derek quickly scanned the story. What a mess. The PM could expect a flood of national security questions in Question Period. The Conservatives loved nothing more than to rail on about national security.

Derek flicked on the bathroom light and glanced at his watch. It was 6:10. If he was on schedule, the PM would be enjoying his morning run. Derek had maybe a half hour to get on top of this before the first angry phone call. He rushed to his closet and started to get dressed. He chose a navy blue suit. He'd need to project an image of competence.

He'd have to call the RCMP commissioner and Hakeem Agbaje, the useless tool of a national security adviser who had obviously been asleep at the switch. He should call Luc Champagne, too, see what he knew and if he sounded spooked. Derek had no trouble whatsoever believing the rumours that Champagne had been banging some girl from the Chinese Embassy. Please God, let it not be this one. Every news organization in the country would be chasing the story, pushing for more. Hell, not just the country. This would go international.

Derek went to his contacts and tapped the number for Elise Joly, the press secretary. Elise had spent five years on the Hill for CTV, then joined the PM's staff back when he became party leader. At 30, she was starting to get old in Hill years. In a couple more years, she would leave to join some big consulting firm downtown for three times the money. That is, if she didn't replace him first.

Elise picked up on the second ring. "Hey, what's up? I just stepped out of the shower."

Derek tried to erase that image from his mind. Elise was fit, dark-haired and was at least a 9, maybe a borderline 10. He'd certainly given her some thought, but it would have been just too complicated.

"You see the *Citizen* yet?" he said.

"The *Citizen*? No, have they got something?"

"Here's the headline: Chinese Spy Dies Mysteriously In Centretown Love Nest."

"Fuck. Anything pointing our way?"

"Not yet, but he's going to have to be ready for questions in the Commons. We should probably do a media avail."

"You want the National Press Theatre or maybe better to do a scrum?"

"Probably scrum unless we have something solid."

"What's our line?"

"I haven't worked it out yet. Some kind of informed ignorance, I expect. We need to steer clear of this one."

"How come we haven't heard word one about this until now?"

"This was the young Chinese woman who supposedly jumped off a building on Elgin. Remember that?"

"Vaguely. I thought it was a suicide."

"My sources flagged this one at the time so I checked it out. I was assured that there was nothing to it, a simple suicide of a low-level embassy employee."

"Yeah, well. I guess your sources weren't so hot. Why didn't you bring me into the loop?"

"It seemed to be nothing at the time."

His sources, Derek thought. In other words, Vanessa. That hadn't ended well. He could call her now, see if she had heard anything more, but it would be awkward.

"Who's the reporter?" Elise asked.

"Kris Redner and Suzy Morin."

"That's bad. They're crime writers. Those people are hard to bullshit and they don't owe us any favours."

"Look, I've got to get moving. I will have to brief the PM shortly. Can you get to work on some generic talking points about Canada not getting involved in foreign embassy matters? I think we're probably going to have to go with something about being unable to substantiate the story at this time. All of that."

"Sure. I'm looking forward to trying to keep the media mob at bay with that. Try to get me something solid. Are they saying this woman was spying on us?"

"It doesn't spell that out, but presumably. It happens all the time. Not that we want to say that. Look, I will touch base with you as soon as I can."

Maybe either the commissioner or the national security adviser could contribute to some kind of bland statement. Any sort of quote would give the impression that the government was on top of things.

He could look after that from the office. The one important call, though, he had to make right away. Sharpe. That cagey old bastard would know something. Obviously, he should have pressed Sharpe sooner. No doubt he'd want to extract some favour or reward in exchange for his information. Whatever it was, Derek was prepared to pay the price because his house was about to be set on fire.

Sharpe was in the kitchen making himself his morning toast and tea when the phone rang. Call display told him that it was young Derek Hall. He'd obviously read the morning paper. Sharpe had been expecting his call.

"Derek, no surprise to hear from you."

"I guess you know why I am calling."

"No doubt. I am going to text you a number for a secure line. Call me back on that."

Sharpe hung up, then texted the number. He had a decision to make.

* * *

Chip Leggett looked out at the Chateau Laurier, which dominated the view from the window of his office in the U.S. Embassy. The morning sun was reflecting off the old railway hotel's copper roof, but Leggett was in no mood to appreciate the architecture.

"Bitch is holed up right across the street," he said to Don Platt. "She's too stupid to turn off her cell phone. You'd think she'd know we can track those things."

"Anything interesting on the intercept?" Platt asked.

"No, and she must be using some other computer. We're getting nothing there either."

"Maybe she just stashed the phone in a potted plant to throw us off," Platt said.

"Jesus, Don. Sometimes the simplest explanation is the right one. We know she's not in her apartment and she's not in her boyfriend's apartment. A big hotel offers them safety. It makes sense.

"Our problem right now is her story in the local rag. Washington has already been all over my ass for a sitrep. Thank God the ambassador is golfing this morning, but when he comes in, he's going to start raising holy hell."

"It's about the only thing he's good at," Platt said.

Ambassador George Pickwick had been CEO of a dodgy oil company until he was rewarded for writing big cheques in the last presidential election. In Platt's opinion, he knew nothing about diplomacy and less than nothing about their line of work, but that didn't keep him from shouting and demanding results. Asshole. Platt was glad it was Leggett's job to deal with him.

"Copy that, but we've got to spike this before it goes any farther," Leggett replied.

"That's going to be a challenge. That reporter is out for our balls and she knows way more than she should."

"Maybe, but I think she was fishing."

"That a chance you want to take, Chip?"

"No. We've taken too many chances already. I never should have let you talk me into trying to turn that Chinese girl. She was a low-value asset, not worth the risk."

"So this is my fault now?" Platt said. "You're the one who was running her. If she was so low-value, why did you keep going back? Were you getting a piece on the side?"

"No, but I wish I had been. At least I would have gotten something out of this mess."

"You think they've really got pictures showing you going into that building?"

"Probably. There's CCTV all over the place downtown. That's why I wore that fucking hat."

"Maybe that's why you never got a piece."

Chip Leggett glowered at Platt. His number two was a smart ass and he'd never liked a smart ass. Just what you'd expect from a guy from New York City. Platt was probably already working out his odds of getting Chip's job if this all went south. What a mess that would be. It was his first field assignment after five years at Langley, and he knew he only got it because his father was a major donor to the Republican Party. Ottawa was supposed to be a nice safe niche that would give him the field experience he needed to climb the ranks.

"I might have been running her," Chip said, "but you're neck deep in this one, too. If this blows up, we'll both be posted to some hot, sweaty country where bombs are going off. And that's the best-case scenario."

Platt nodded. "So what's our move?"

"I'm working on that." In truth, Chip wasn't sure what to do next. Why had this Kris Redner held back so much information from that story? Had she been bullshitting them about what she knew, or was she just playing it out to get even more headlines? The only good news was that there had been nothing in their conversation or in her article to suggest that she knew anything about the real story. Compared to that, Mae Wang was small potatoes. If their whole operation was revealed, he'd be lucky to get a job as a security guard at Walmart.

"I hope you're not considering tuning up this one, too," Platt said. "That really backfired. I see Suzy Morin's name is on this story, too, and what you did to her has got her pal Redner all fired up. I told you that would never work."

Chip looked down at his bruised knuckles and remembered how he had gotten them. That Suzy Morin was a sweet-looking woman. It had been a shame to have to mess her up. Tough, too. He figured a little rough stuff would be enough to get her to give up whatever she knew. Wrong again.

"Yeah, you did." Chip said. "I'm beginning to think that is your only real value, Don, to second-guess me after it hits the fan. What do *you* think we should do next?"

"Seems to me we have to find out what else Redner knows, so we can plan the containment. Maybe it's time to use our source."

"Fuck, that's risky. We don't want her to make that connection."

"Sure, but maybe the source has got some ideas on how to handle this. It's his ass on the line here, too."

"Let me think about that," Chip said, not wanting to look too eager to accept Platt's idea. It was risky, but he wasn't seeing a lot of escape hatches. One thing for sure, he couldn't sit on his ass and do nothing.

How had this gotten so turned around? The Chinese were the bad guys here and he was just doing his job, trying to protect his country's interests. Now he was being tied in knots by a couple of women working for a newspaper. He just couldn't allow that to happen.

FORTY-ONE

I called Luc Champagne at 8 a.m. at the cell-phone number he had helpfully scribbled on the back of his business card. The minister had sounded so relaxed and friendly that I assumed he hadn't read the paper yet.

I assumed wrong. He handed me a line about being glad the story would increase the likelihood of someone being held responsible for the poor girl's death. He assured me that he could give me some exclusive insight into the "Chinese situation."

It smelled like bullshit to me, but if he was prepared to open his door, I was prepared to enter. In fact, I was in a cab on my way there now. Champagne had suggested coffee at 9 in his office.

The problem with Colin's "burning arrow" approach, as he liked to call it, was that the resulting fire attracted quite a crowd of onlookers. Every other media organization was aiming to match my story and get out ahead of it if they could. I had even had a call from Trish Porter, who I used to work with at the *Star*, hoping that maybe I could give her a few contacts, just as a sisterhood kind of thing. She really didn't know me very well.

Having started the fire, the pressure was now on us to produce a fresh second-day angle to stay ahead of the pack. By on us, I meant me. Suzy was in no condition to contribute, although she would continue to share a byline.

Colin and I had agreed that it was time to bring in the Champagne angle. Luc Champagne was going to be tomorrow's story, one way or another.

The atmosphere at Fort Pearson was considerably less festive than it had been the last time I visited. The colourfully dressed diplomats had been replaced by an army of grey-suited men and women with serious looks on their faces. The security guy at the main desk gave me a suspicious look, which I guess was his job. His ID badge said he was Allard and his square jaw, trim moustache and heavy build said he was ex-military.

Allard had a brief conversation in French with another minder on a higher floor, then said, "You're cleared to go up. You know the way?"

"I do. Thanks."

Up in the minister's outer office, security was a little less impressive, consisting of a young male assistant who was perhaps 25. He had lovely dark hair and, I was sure, a splendid education. Before he could speak, Luc Champagne himself came out of his inner office. His suit jacket was off and his red tie askew. The only thing missing from the classic politician's look was the rolled-up sleeves. Maybe he was saving that for later.

He welcomed me like a long-lost friend, giving me his A-level smile and opening his arms to offer a hug. Perhaps it was a cultural thing. I declined.

"Kris, so good to see you," he said, settling for a handshake that was reassuringly warm and firm. I didn't expect his pleasure to last long.

"Let's go into my office," he said, ushering me in ahead of him.

The reception boy followed close behind with a tray containing two black coffee mugs, a silver pot and a bowl of creamers. I assumed I wasn't getting the best diplomatic china.

"Please, take a seat," Champagne said, motioning me towards the red leather chairs in front of his desk. I took one and he took the other, sitting, then leaning forward as if he was about to give me his most rapt attention. Maybe he was, considering.

"So, the situation with the Chinese girl," he began. "Very tragic. I did have my chief of staff look into it, as I promised. I am afraid that she came up with nothing that would support the rather colourful headline in today's paper. Although, to be fair, the woman might well have been a Chinese spy. Many embassy employees are."

I opened my biggest black leather purse and took out my notebook, then switched on the record function of my phone. I needed the big purse to carry the PI's file on Champagne, but it was too soon to play that card. "I assume we are on the record," I said.

"If you wish. You can certainly quote me on what I just told you. I could perhaps give you some additional insight if we were speaking more informally."

I paused as if giving his offer careful consideration. My goal was to back him into a corner, not get a bland quote for the next day's paper. I closed my notebook and made sure he could see that I had stopped recording. The second phone, in my purse, was still recording, of course.

"All right, let's be informal," I said.

Champagne poured us each a cup of coffee. He took his black. I went with two creams.

"Perhaps I can start by asking you a question," he said. "What is your ultimate goal here? I know you are a thorough journalist and you have been working on this Mae Wang story for some time. And yet, your article in the paper today establishes only the most basic facts."

"True, but it's more than has come out so far."

"Clearly you think that I have more knowledge of this matter than I have led you to believe."

"That would be an accurate perception."

"Mind if I ask why?"

I didn't like the fact that he was trying to turn the tables and interview me, but if it was a way of drawing him out, I was prepared to accept it.

"I think we both know the answer to that."

"Do we?"

I decided it was time to lay some trump cards on the table. I didn't want to play verbal ping pong with Champagne. I reached into my purse and took out the PI file, then set it on the coffee table between us as if it contained the most important documents in the world. I opened it just enough to show him that its contents were substantial and withdrew a picture I had placed on the top of the file. I passed it to him. He glanced at it quickly and shrugged.

"I think you will recognize yourself in that picture. It is a part of a series showing you entering Mae's apartment building every Tuesday night for several months. I have another set that shows you leaving Wednesday morning."

"And what does that prove? Many people live in that building, including you. I could have been visiting anyone."

"True, but you weren't. You were 'visiting' Mae Wang."

"And how could you possibly determine that?"

"Audio tapes. Does the phrase 'Harder, Luc, harder,' sound familiar at all?"

Champagne leaned back in his chair and exhaled loudly. The interview clearly wasn't going quite as he had hoped. Not that I had gleaned one useful piece of information from him, but I felt like I had him on the ropes.

Champagne looked at me with probing blue eyes, as if weighing a decision. Then he said, "Yes, there is obviously more to the story, as you know, but it's not what you think."

"So what, you and Mae Wang were doing crossword puzzles and she was urging you to concentrate harder?"

"This is not a matter for levity," he snapped, with the first flash of anger I had seen. That was a good sign. I was rattling him.

"No, it isn't. That's why I don't appreciate you trying to sell me a bullshit story."

The way I figured it, Champagne now had two choices. He could throw me out or give me a more plausible story than what he had come up with so far.

It didn't take the man of action long to decide. "All right, come with me," he said. "Leave the notebook, the phone and the purse here."

"I don't think so," I said. I was sure Champagne's nosy assistant would be poking through my stuff the minute I left the office.

"Your choice," he said, "but there can be no written or recorded version of what I am about to tell you."

Now I had to make the choice. I locked my phone. Fortunately I had brought a fresh notebook, not the one with important notes in it. I put them both in the purse, surreptitiously shutting off the second phone as I did so.

"Lead on," I said.

We went down a short corridor to a room with a heavy carved oak door. Champagne entered first. No gentlemanly ushering in this time. I saw a small, non-descript meeting room, its walls lined with grey fabric. A scarred wooden table was surrounded by 10 leather office chairs. Some weak morning sun did little to add cheer to the gloomy little room.

As Champagne shut the door behind us, I said, "What's so special about this place?"

"This is the room where I receive all my security briefings from the national agencies. It's lead-lined. No communications get in or out."

"OK, but I left all my stuff back in your office. You think I'm wearing a wire or something?"

"No, I don't, but in my world, one always has to assume someone is listening. This is for your ears only."

Too bad for him that he wasn't as sharp when he was visiting Mae Wang. I could see where he wouldn't have anticipated a PI bugging the apartment, but surely he should have assumed the Chinese would have done so.

Settling himself in one of the chairs, he said, "Consider what I am about to tell you as an appeal to your journalistic integrity. I find myself in an exceptionally difficult position. If I say nothing, I expect your next story will be something to the effect of Minister Shared Love Nest With Chinese Spy. If I tell you what is really going on, you will see that the truth is something quite different. Should you publish it, of course I will deny every detail, but my hope is that you will use your judgment. Canada's interests are at stake here."

It was the second time in two days that someone had appealed to my patriotism. I suppose it was the downside of dual citizenship. I had some strong views on official manipulators wrapping themselves in the flag, but it didn't seem the time to share them. Instead, I nodded encouragingly.

"I met Mae Wang a little over a year ago on my first official visit to Beijing. It was at an event for Chinese business leaders. Mostly gangsters, I'm sure, but my job was to listen politely all the same. Mae had been assigned to me as a liaison by the Chinese government.

"I remember the evening vividly. The meeting took place in a large hall, draped with Chinese flags. Imagine more than 100 business types in dark suits, all pushing forward, eager to present their business cards and make the case for why they ought to be allowed to buy up whatever parts of Canada they liked. I had an interpreter from the embassy on my right side, an eager young chap who was able to convey my bland assurances with just the right level of enthusiasm. To my left was Mae. Her function was to quickly inform me of who the next businessman was, and what he wanted. She wore a red dress that really set off her skin and dark hair. She was the only woman in the room, you understand, but she would have stood out in any crowd.

"I had expected some kind of stiff, official biographies, but she kept me amused with little asides about the men I was meeting and anecdotes about who they had stabbed in the back to get to the top. I found her intriguing. She suggested we have a drink after the event was over and naturally, I agreed."

I silently applauded his commendable eagerness to learn even more about the backgrounds of Chinese business leaders.

"Before I had left, CSIS had thoroughly briefed me on what to expect. I was to assume that I would be under constant observation and that the only safe place to speak my mind was in the embassy itself. They also warned me that I might be approached by a woman working for the Ministry of State Security. It is standard operating procedure. The honey trap, they call it. The Chinese have long employed it to put foreign diplomats or businessmen in compromising positions to gain leverage on them."

"And apparently it works."

Champagne held up his finger to stop my interruption and fixed me with that persuasive blue-eyed gaze. "But not with me. I was fully prepared and assumed from the outset that Mae had a role beyond liaison for a business group."

"But you went for a drink with her anyway. Maybe that was a mistake."

"Perhaps, looking back, but not at the time. We shared a rather nice Chateau Margaux and, after a couple of glasses, she dropped the pretence of her official cover. She told me about her imprisoned father and how the security agency had coerced her into her role. I assume you are aware of that?"

"Of Zhao Yang, yes I am."

"Good. I assumed you would have figured that out. Mae asked for my help in getting her father freed. I explained that there was really nothing I could do, since Zhao was a Chinese citizen, but she was tearful and insistent. I promised to look into his case once I got back to Ottawa."

"And did you?"

"I did have staff gather the details of his case, but it didn't seem an area where we wanted to expend any of our good will."

"All right, so how did Mae end up in Ottawa?"

"She led her ministry handlers to believe that she had made a fruitful connection with me over the bottle of wine. She told them that I was susceptible and sympathetic, perhaps a person who could be brought under her influence. I knew nothing of this until later, of course.

"The next time I saw her was at a Chinese Embassy reception here, three months later. She was acting as an interpreter. I remembered her immediately and took the opportunity to speak to her alone near the end of the event, to find out the status of her father. Nothing had changed and she was afraid that his health was failing. He had not even had a day in court and she doubted he would ever get one.

"She was desperate and explained that I was her last hope." With an embarrassed shrug, he said, "I'm afraid that I have a weakness for women who want me to be their white knight. In fact, trade talks with China had progressed since I met Mae last. They wanted quite a lot from us, but the problem was the Chinese human rights record. That makes it difficult for the PM with certain elements in the party. I knew it would be advantageous if the Chinese could make a goodwill gesture on that front. It was possible that Zhao Yang could have been part of that. I was at least willing to try."

"So you started meeting with Mae about her father?"

"That's right. Given her role as a would-be Mata Hari, such meetings would only be allowed by the Chinese if they believed that she was making progress in seducing me. We knew her apartment was under embassy surveillance, so we had to put on a bit of a show. At first, I will admit that I saw it as a pleasurable reward for trying to do the right thing.

"As time went on, I began to develop feelings for Mae. That's when I decided to put a stop to it.

"Now, in retrospect I should have reported all of this to CSIS, but I believed that I could handle the situation. I was working on getting Mae refugee status and a Canadian passport. Did you know the foreign minister can issue a passport to anyone on his sole authority?"

"I did not."

"The problem remained the situation of her father. I could get her out, but probably only at the cost of his life. That was a bargain she was not prepared to make."

"So you had done all you could?"

"That was the situation at my final meeting with Mae."

"And now both Mae and her father are dead. Do you know what happened?"

"I do not, in either case. I wish I did. When I learned of her death, I asked the RCMP to investigate as a priority."

"Did you? Would it surprise you to know that my sources say the Mounties are doing nothing at all? In fact, they are preventing the city police from doing their job."

"I am disappointed to hear that. I was informed that her death was a tragic suicide."

"Not according to the coroner."

"You are giving me new information here. I can press for more detail."

"Thanks, but I've got that base covered."

I leaned back and give Luc Champagne an appraising look. He returned it with a smile and the sort of look of eagerness a school kid would have when he was convinced he was about to get an A+ on his report. I decided to let him sweat for a minute, but I had to admit his story seemed plausible, if convenient.

Finally, I said, "So you're the hero?"

"I'm sure you will agree that the term hero would be an over-statement. I let my heart get in the way of my head. I hoped to help Mae, but I failed completely. I can't tell you how bad all of that makes me feel."

"All right. Let's assume that everything you have told me is true." It certainly wasn't an assumption I was making, not yet. "What do you expect me to do?"

Champagne opened his arms in an expansive gesture. "My fate is in your hands. I have told you what I did and why I did it. I had no bad intentions, but I made a grave misjudgment when I decided that I could finesse this for Mae. I accept responsibility for that, but even if I deny everything I have said, and you have no proof of any of it, you know as well as I that any story that suggests the Canadian foreign minister was sleeping with a woman who was, indeed, a Chinese spy, will destroy me, strike a fatal blow to the government and weaken the trust our allies have in Canada. You have to ask yourself if bringing me down is worth the broader repercussions."

I hadn't expected what Champagne would have me believe was a full confession. Was it true? And how would I ever really know?

"I appreciate you being so forthcoming," I said. "It's certainly a complex situation, as you say. Not quite what I expected. I will have to discuss this with my editor."

"As I told you when we first met, I am not the man that people might take me for at first glance."

I had to give him credit for a confounding performance. He had not denied a single accusation, but he had put it all in a context that was a mix of self-deprecation and noble motivation. He told the story naturally, too, not like something he had rehearsed. Really, to whom would he have confessed all of this? It astounded me that he had told me as much as he did.

It was all either an artful lie or a pre-emptive masterstroke. Right now, I wasn't sure which, and I didn't know how I was going to find out.

Champagne looked at his watch. "I have a briefing coming up shortly. Is there anything else I can do to help?"

I took my cue and stood to leave. I turned at the door to ask one final question. My experience was that subjects let down their guard once they thought the formal interview was over.

"Just one loose end we didn't touch on. I was braced yesterday by a couple of guys from the American embassy. Claimed to be attachés for trade and culture. They have taken a real interest in this Mae Wang situation, and they suggested that I shouldn't. Know anything about that?"

Champagne appeared genuinely nonplussed. "The bloody Americans are always sticking their noses in our affairs. Think they run the world. Nothing they do surprises me, but this is the first I have heard of their interest in this situation."

Now he looked worried. Despite all his efforts at containment, maybe that damage with the allies had already been done.

"OK. If you hear anything, will you let me know?"

"Of course, of course," he said, smiling as if I had asked him to undertake some easy and pleasant task. It was the first false note he had struck all morning.

FORTY-TWO

When I got back to the hotel, I was surprised to see Colin in the room. His grey suit coat was draped across the back of a chair and he sat at the desk, pounding on the keys of his laptop. He wore a white dress shirt, but no tie. When I closed the door, he turned and smiled. In the midst of all the stress and chaos, a happy man, I realized. Maybe I was doing something right.

"I thought you'd be out at Baxter," I said.

"Too many interruptions in the newsroom." Then he stood and hugged me, followed by a light kiss on the cheek. He was right about the distractions in the newsroom, but I was sure that he was staying close to protect me. After what happened to Suzy, I wasn't going to argue.

"Where is everyone else?" I asked.

"Suzy is in the other suite. Sleeping, I believe. Mike and that Farrell chap have gone out to, as they put it, 'interview' those two fellows from the embassy."

"Well, good luck with that. I don't think they will get anything out of them."

"I didn't get the impression that it was going to be our kind of an interview. Farrell was carrying that heavy kit bag when they left."

"I hope we're not getting them into some kind of serious trouble. Those guys are CIA."

"Farrell and Reilly seem like the kind of chaps who can take care of themselves."

"They do, but I'm worried that I've drawn Mike into something that will ruin his police career."

"At his age, I doubt he cares about that. One does reach a certain point, you know, where doing the right thing is more important than protecting your place on the ladder."

"You're probably right. It's just that I've already hurt too many people by drawing them into my crusades."

"Nothing that happened in the Adirondacks was your fault."

I disagreed. I thought that everything that happened was my fault. If I had stayed home and minded my business, several people would still be alive today. But then, that had never been my style, and some of them deserved to be dead.

"So what did our friend the minister have to say? Deny, deny, deny?"

I collapsed into the big, soft couch and shook my head. "Actually, just the opposite."

I recounted for Colin the story that Champagne had spun for me. Then I said, "I had better get all of that down. He wouldn't let me record or take any notes."

"Smart move on his part. So what do you think? Is what he said true?"

"I'm sure at least part of it is, but the best lies always contain a generous helping of truth. I don't see how we are going to sift one from the other."

"Neither do I, but I think our choice is simpler than that. If we don't buy the story, we publish. If we think the story is true, then we have a difficult editorial decision. He's right about the repercussions."

"The repercussions aren't really our problem are they? This is the biggest story to come out of this town in years. We know Champagne was having it off with Mae on a regular basis. The PI's pictures and tapes prove that. In itself, that's a huge story. Add in his explanation and all the cloak-and-dagger lead-room stuff and we've got a story that's going to run front page and top of the newscasts around the world."

"Yes, but we can't prove any of what he told you this morning. Didn't he say he would deny it?"

"He did. Why don't we let the readers decide?"

"There's certainly a case for going with what we've got, let the chips fall where they may. I'm going to have to pass this one in front of our lawyers and corporate, though."

"Corporate? Who's corporate these days? We don't even have a publisher."

"No, but there's a senior vice-president in Toronto. He's the one who will fire me if this whole thing blows up."

"You worried about that?"

"Not really. Like I said, our job is to do the right thing, but we also have to do the thing right. We have to get as close to the truth as we can. We're probably just about there. Write what you have, but I want you to take one more run at this Gail Rakic. She has been playing a cat-and-mouse game with us. I think she knows more than she's letting on."

"Agreed, but what's our leverage to get more out of her?"

"You'll think of something. I also want to see what Reilly and Farrell learn from those two embassy types. Their involvement is a disturbing unexplained element here."

"I hope we're going to burn them for what was done to Suzy."

"We will. It's just a case of being judicious in applying the flame."

I wasn't totally satisfied with Colin's caution, but I wasn't surprised either. This was the kind of story that caused lawsuits to pop up like mushrooms in a damp forest. We needed to get it right.

I put in a call to Gail, got her voice mail and started to put together the story of Luc Champagne's bizarre confession. For this draft, I decided to attribute Champagne's version of events to "a highly-placed source in the minister's office."

I looked at my watch. If I hurried, I should be able to rough out this draft in time to get over to court and try to grab Gail on the break. I wasn't sure yet how I would squeeze her, but I knew I'd squeeze her hard.

FORTY-THREE

Reilly and Farrell sat in the blue panel van, watching the wipers slap across the windshield. The day had started out sunny, but a spring storm had blown in just after 11:30. They were parked illegally in front of a four-storey condo on Clarence Street in the ByWard Market, facing the U.S. Embassy.

"Shitty weather," Reilly said.

"Yeah, but just right for what I've got in mind. The worse the visibility, the better for us."

"I hope so. What's your plan exactly?"

"In about 10 minutes we're going to see a black Suburban pull out of the embassy parking garage and hang a left onto Sussex. Those will be our boys, Leggett and Platt. They are going to drive a few blocks down Sussex to Boteler, turn right and then pull into an underground parking garage below a high rise."

"You a psychic now?"

"No, I just know some useful people at the embassy. Usually, we're on the same side. Turns out Leggett isn't too popular, bit of an asshole. Wasn't that hard to find out that he has been boning one of the interns, grabbing a nooner every Tuesday. Girl's name is Joni Brooks. Her dad is a senator from Iowa, Leggett's home state."

"Where does Platt fit into all of this? Please tell me that it's not a three-way."

Farrell laughed. "No, Platt is just the cover. He wanders back to the Market and grabs a sandwich while the boss gets his wick wet. About 1:30, Platt returns to the building and drives them both back to the embassy."

"The girl's going to be a complication isn't she?"

"Not if we time it right. We grab our boys in the parking building, take them for a little ride. Joni's not going to phone back to the embassy wondering where Leggett is, since he was never supposed to be there in the first place."

"What if they don't want to come along?"

"I always find that a gun barrel in the ear is pretty persuasive."

"We need to set some limits on this thing, Farrell. You know I want to beat the shit out of these guys, but our goal is to get some information out of them."

"We can try. These are probably not the two smartest or toughest agents the CIA has, but they are trained to resist interrogation. I'm not optimistic that they are going to roll over unless they think the other choice is seeing their brains splattered on the wall."

"You're probably right, but let's agree that we are not going to go that far. If I can tell Suzy they paid a price, I'll be happy. Anything they tell us is a bonus."

"All right, you're the boss, but at least let me see if I can make them wet themselves."

"I'm in for that."

Reilly and Farrell saw the Suburban surge from the embassy parking garage at the same moment, the rain beading on its shiny black paint.

"OK," Farrell said. "Let's have some fun."

They accelerated quickly around the corner, then fell in behind a beige Camry that was almost on the bumper of the Suburban. The Camry had Quebec plates and was in a hurry. It was a useful distraction on the off chance that the guys in the Suburban were paying attention to the rear-view mirror, Reilly thought.

It was a short drive to Boteler, no more than three minutes. When the Suburban turned right, the Quebecer gave it the horn and finger combo, then roared past. Farrell slowed and pulled up on the street in front of a 12-storey apartment building, distinguishable from the many similar buildings in the city only because it was brown brick, not poured concrete. The United Arab Emirates Embassy was just down the street, a squat, fortress-like structure with an RCMP car parked outside.

"Let's give them about 30 seconds," Farrell said. Then he pulled away from the curve and down into the parking garage. The layout was simple, with one-way traffic and only two floors of parking. Reilly could just see the tail lights of the big Suburban as it turned and descended to the second level.

"OK, now's the tricky part," Farrell said. "We need to get them into the van quickly and quietly and hope that no one comes down to get their car."

"What if they do?"

"You badge them and say there has been a report of a stolen Suburban with embassy plates. Then we figure out it's all just a mixup and drive on."

Reilly pulled on a pair of Oakley tactical gloves he kept in the pocket of his windbreaker, and flexed the hardened knuckles. There was some hand work coming up.

The Suburban had just pulled into a parking spot. Farrell drew the van in tight across its tail, locking the Suburban in place but leaving his own door clear.

Chip Leggett got quickly out of the vehicle, raised both arms in outrage, and shouted, "Hey you assholes. You can't park there."

Farrell jumped out of the van and covered the distance between himself and Leggett in two long strides. Reilly went up the passenger side of the vehicle, just a step behind him. As he got there, Don Platt swung the passenger door open hard. Reilly jumped back, then drove all of his weight forward, shattering Platt's nose with a solid right. Platt was stunned, half in and half out of the vehicle. Reilly grabbed him by the collar, dragged him out of the car and slammed him face first into the side of the vehicle.

"Back off, we're U.S. diplomats" Leggett shouted, like that was a get-out-of-shit-free card. Leggett reached into his suit coat, going for a gun, but he was too slow. Farrell already had the barrel of his Beretta in Leggett's ear.

"Let's just calm down now, Chip," Farrell said. "My friend and I just want to take you and your colleague for a little drive, get to know you better."

Leggett swung back with an elbow, trying to knock the gun from the much-larger man's hand. He might as well have driven his elbow into a tree. Farrell didn't even flinch. Instead, he drilled the gun harder into Leggett's ear and reached up to grab the CIA man by the balls.

"Have I got your attention now, Chip?"

Leggett nodded, wild-eyed. The guy had probably been looking forward to someone laying hands on his equipment, but life didn't always work out the way you hoped, Reilly thought.

"Here's the way it's going to play, Chip. You're going to come along like a good boy and I'm going to make you and your buddy comfortable in the back of my van. You're going to keep nice and quiet while we do that. Play your cards right, and you might even live to pop your girlfriend next week."

Farrell pulled the gun from Leggett's shoulder holster, then man-handled him to the back of the van. Reilly did the same with Platt, who was stunned and wiping at the steady stream of blood coming from his nose and staining his white shirt and grey suit coat.

When they got to the back of the van, Farrell pulled the door open, picked up a piece of duct tape he already had stuck to the interior wall, then wrapped it over Leggett's mouth. Reilly saw that there were two rings welded to the floor of the van, each one with a set of handcuffs attached. Farrell lifted Leggett up into the van like he was a child and hooked him up. Leggett was bug-eyed and, when Reilly looked at the spy's light grey pants, he saw a dark stain spreading down the right leg.

"Well look at that," Farrell said. "Didn't I tell you this would be fun?"

The two of them shoved the wobbly Platt up into the van, taped his mouth and clicked the other set of handcuffs firmly on his wrists.

"I don't know if you boys believe in Jesus," Farrell said, "but you might want to use the next few minutes to get straight with him."

Then they slammed the back doors of the van and were off. Less than two minutes had elapsed.

FORTY-FOUR

It was turning into the kind of day that Derek Hall sometimes experienced in his nightmares, except that waking up screaming wasn't going to get him off the hook. Question Period was at 2:15, less than two hours away, and he still hadn't put together a plausible response for the PM.

Derek had briefed him on the situation quickly that morning, but it hadn't gone well. The PM's main question was, "Why the fuck am I only hearing about this now?" He had a good point. Derek had broken his own no-surprises rule, and he was going to own that, no matter who else had screwed up. That much was clear when the PM had sent a laptop flying at his head. Derek had ducked just in time and backed out of range of the man's fists. Everyone knew the boss thought he had a lot of punching prowess, but Derek didn't intend to become his speed bag. There were limits to the shit he would take to keep his job, although he realized as soon as he thought it that those limits were pretty elastic.

He had Elise Joly on his back, too. The media calls were coming in, but so far the intensity hadn't been as bad as he had feared. It helped that the story was broken by two local crime writers, not one of the distinguished members of the Press Gallery itself. Gallery members could be a bit sniffy about people who weren't part of their club, and that had helped when Elise tried to put them off by pointing to the source and raising a skeptical eyebrow. She was making good use of the fact that the words "love nest" were in the headline, suggesting that it was the kind of lurid tabloid trash that would be beneath the dignity of the worthy thinkers who covered the federal government.

That was only going to last so long, though. The real problem was the opposition. All parties would be on their feet expressing outrage and demanding answers. For their purposes, it didn't matter whether the story was true or false. It was in the media and it put the government in a bad light.

Derek stared at his computer screen, then looked out the window of his Langevin Block office at Parliament Hill across the street. It was a great view. He wondered how much longer he would have it.

He had called in every favour on this, but no one was coming to his rescue. Robertson, that withered old prick of an RCMP commissioner, professed to have nothing to add beyond the fact that an investigation was under way. Robertson had been appointed by the previous government and knew he wouldn't be renewed by the current one. Derek figured this was his way of saying "fuck you."

Agbaje, the national security adviser, was predictably useless. He had a bunch of geopolitical points about relations with China that had nothing to do with the current mess whatsoever. Derek was considering putting him in front of the media in hopes that he would bore them to death.

The biggest disappointment had been Sharpe. After all that spy shit about phoning back on a secure line, he hadn't given him anything that would have been controversial on Twitter. The old bugger was holding back on him. Every instinct Derek had told him that. Even after Derek had said that he would be extremely grateful for any help Sharpe could give him and went even further to say that it would be very worth his while, he got nothing more than a promise to look into it.

Fat lot of good that did, because Derek's world could come to an end in two hours. If there was one thing the PM hated, it was being sandbagged by the opposition. He wasn't good if he got off script, and right now, Derek didn't have a script.

He had even swallowed his pride and called Vanessa, who had been shipped off to be a flack in Agriculture. He apologized profusely for not taking her more seriously when she had told him that a Chinese spy had been murdered. Was there any chance at all that she could connect with this Suzy Morin, see if she could find out where the story was going next? She had told him to fuck himself, which seemed redundant given the way the day was going.

It was Redner and Morin he really had to worry about. They had fired only one barrel. The chances of them having nothing juicy for a second-day follow were nil. If they were using standard media operating procedure, they would wait until they saw what the PM said in the House, then prove him a liar.

Derek pulled open the drawer of his battered oak desk. So many previous chiefs of staff had suffered behind it that he was surprised there weren't blood stains. He took out the manila envelope that contained his resignation. He had written it on the day he had gotten the job, hoping that it would never come out of the envelope. He put it in the pocket of his suit coat. Better to leave under your own steam than to be fired.

Right now, that was about as close to a good outcome as he could imagine.

FORTY-FIVE

The gravel in the parking lot crunched as Farrell pulled the van into a National Capital Commission parking lot just off Timm Drive, where Leggett and Platt had taken Suzy. The lot was shaded from the road by a stand of scruffy cedars. Rain still fell, enough to blur the view from the windshield, but Reilly knew the spot. They were surrounded on three sides by a stunted evergreen forest full of rocky outcroppings and little ponds of water. It was the kind of place where a couple of guys who got lost could stay lost for quite a while.

Reilly listened to the ping of the cooling engine for a minute and then either Leggett or Platt started to kick at the side of the van. "Forget it boys," Reilly said. "No one can hear you out here."

Reilly then motioned for Farrell to get out the van, so they could discuss what to do next without sharing it with their prisoners.

Pulling up the hood on his waterproof jacket, Farrell said, "This is your show. How do you want to play it?"

Reilly sensed that it was one of those moments where his future hung in the balance. His instinct was to give the two CIA assholes everything Suzy had got, with interest. The problem was that, unlike Leggett and Platt when they had manhandled Suzy, he and Farrell were not wearing ski masks. They could be identified. He needed to figure a way to make that unrewarding.

"We've got two goals," he said. "First, we try to find out what they know about this Chinese girl's death. Why were they warning Kris off? Second, we square up what they did to Suzy."

"I'm not optimistic that they are going to tell us anything, not unless we do them serious harm."

"I can't go that far."

"Right, but they don't know that."

"OK, let's work with that."

Farrell opened the back door of the van. Despite his smashed face, Platt looked defiant and ready to fight. Leggett had already clued them to how tough he was when he pissed himself. They would start with Leggett. Reilly pointed at him and Farrell released him from his cuffs and dragged him out of the back of the van. Leggett landed in a puddle, then struggled to his feet. The rain quickly started to soak whatever he hadn't already soaked himself.

Back on his feet and uncuffed, Leggett began to get back a bit of his edge. "You two fools are in way over your heads here. Platt and I are with a branch of the government that you just don't want to fuck with. You're going to end up in body bags, you hear me?"

"Look Chip, we know you're with the CIA," Farrell said. "You can imagine how impressed I am. My friend and I just wanted to ask you a few questions about that dead Chinese girl, Mae Wang."

Now Leggett appeared confused, wiping the water from his face and looking quickly from Farrell to Reilly, struggling to understand. "I don't get it. What does she have to do with you?"

"We have a professional interest," Reilly said. "I think you know why Mae Wang died. We'd love to find out. Think of it as inter-agency sharing."

"Inter-agency? Who the hell are you guys with?"

"That doesn't matter," Farrell said. "Let's just say it's a group that you don't want to fuck with."

"What you're asking for is classified information," Leggett said. "I'm not going to betray my country. You want to find out more, go through the proper channels."

Leggett had a little more sand than Reilly had figured. He lashed a heavy boot into the spy's kneecap. Leggett screamed in pain and went down on one knee in the mud, then struggled awkwardly back to his feet.

"Hey, let's be reasonable," Leggett said.

"Do I look fucking reasonable to you?" Reilly said.

"And remember Chip," Farrell said. "He's the good guy. If it were up to me, I'd just start taking pieces off your body until you start to talk. Everyone does, eventually." Turning to Reilly, he said, "You want me to get the toolkit out of the van?"

"I think we're going to need it. Now that Chip has gotten over pissing himself, he thinks he's tough."

Farrell smiled and said, "I love this kind of shit." Then he started for the side door of the van.

"No, wait," Leggett said. He weighed his options. He might be able to take the older guy, but not the giant. He was a dedicated agent, but not to the point of giving up body parts. What would be the harm if he told them a little bit? The girl was dead and there was no way they had a clue as to the real story.

"The girl was a Chinese agent. I doubled her," he said, making himself sound like a player. "Strictly a low-level asset. In the end, she had no valuable intel. I have no idea how she died. Ask the Chinese, that's my advice. That's all I know."

Reilly and Farrell looked at each other, then Farrell nodded. What Leggett had told them was likely true. If there was more, it *would* require the actual removal of body parts. At least it was something he could take back to Suzy, Reilly thought.

He smiled at Leggett and said, "Now that wasn't so hard, was it Chip? I knew you would be the kind of guy who would co-operate."

Leggett brushed water off his suit jacket, in a vain attempt to restore a fraction of his dignity. "All right then. Now what?"

"Now we move to part two of our agenda," Reilly said.

"Part two? Look, I've told you everything I know."

"I seriously doubt that Chip, but we're going to take you at your word. Now, part two, that's where we've got a problem."

"A really big problem," Farrell said.

"Come on guys, I don't even know what you're talking about. Just let us go, that's the last you'll hear from us."

"See, what I'd like to do," Farrell said, "is to take you two ass-holes for a little walk in the woods. We all walk in, you don't walk out. That's the only way we never hear from you again. Somebody ends up in body bags. Just not us."

Chip looked to Reilly, then said, "No, you don't want to do that. Eventually they will find our bodies. The U.S. government will never let up until the thing is solved."

"That's not really a worry," Reilly said. "Where I am thinking of putting you, years could go by before they find your decomposed remains. They find your vehicle in that parking garage, then the trail goes cold."

"Chip wants to play hard ball," Farrell said. "Maybe we need to get Don out here, see what he has to say."

"Good idea," Reilly said, nodding. "It's not really fair for Chip to sign Don's death warrant."

"Agent Platt is a veteran, tough as nails. You won't break him."

"You could be right Chip, but are you sure he would be willing to give up his life for you?"

Leggett didn't respond to that, but in his own mind, he knew Platt would sell him out in a New York minute.

"Let's see what Platt has to say," Reilly said.

Farrell opened the back of the van, unhooked Platt, then pulled his hands up behind his back and reattached the cuffs.

"Don," Reilly said, like they were old pals. "Sorry about the nose. Chip here was just telling us that Mae Wang was a CIA double agent. Very interesting. Anything you can add there?"

Platt looked at Leggett with loathing. He knew that frat boy would fold as soon as someone said boo. The guy had pissed himself, for God's sake. Whoever these two were, they were going to get nothing from him. To make the point, Platt directed a stream of spit and blood that landed on the big one's shoes.

"Ah, now you've gone and pissed off my friend," Reilly said. "I've seen him pissed off before, Don. I think you'd better lick that mess off his shoes before this turns ugly."

"Fuck you."

Reilly pulled a collapsible baton from his rear pocket, extended it and hit Don a stinging blow. It drove him down face forward into the mud in front of Farrell's feet.

"Let me help you Don," Farrell said, and drove his boot into Don's mouth.

Reilly came up behind Don and dragged him back to his feet. "I hope we've got your attention now, tough guy. See, the other thing we wanted to bring up with Chip here was about some damage one or both of you did to a female reporter from the *Ottawa Citizen*, woman called Suzy Morin. This lady has a lot of friends and some of them asked us to take it up with you."

Platt spit two teeth on the ground and said nothing, but Leggett spoke up in a high, agitated voice. "Look, we know nothing about any reporter. You've got that wrong."

"Really? I noticed that your hands were all bruised and cut,

Chip. What happened there?"

"I told you to leave her alone, you stupid fuck," Platt said. "This is why we're here. It's got nothing to do with the dead Chinese girl. You two are cops, aren't you?"

"If we were cops, we'd be arresting you," Reilly said.

"Oh no, wait," Farrell said. "These two are diplomats. They have immunity."

"You're right. Fellows like Chip and Don deserve special treatment. As it turns out, I've got an idea for that."

In fact, it was an idea that had just come to Reilly, but he liked it. "Originally, I was thinking that maybe I'd beat you two as badly as you did the reporter, but the weakness of that plan is that you'd get over it in time. I'm thinking now we need something more permanent."

Farrell looked at Reilly curiously. This was a twist they hadn't discussed.

"Take your clothes off, Chip."

"My clothes? What are you talking about?"

"You know what I'm talking about. How do you think that reporter felt, being left naked like that? Hard to imagine, isn't it? Good news is, you won't have to imagine it, because it's going to happen to you."

"No, I won't do it."

Reilly took the tactical gloves from his jacket pocket and pulled them on. "Oh you will, Chip. It's just a question of how much encouragement you're going to need. Personally, I would be happy to persuade you."

Leggett looked at Platt, as if there might be some help there. His colleague turned his bruised and battered face the other way.

Leggett shrugged, having identified the path of least resistance. He began to take off his soggy clothes and was quickly down to his boxers, his belly hanging over them, his skin turning pink from the cold rain.

"Keep going Chip, almost there," Reilly said.

Reluctantly, Leggett peeled down the sodden white boxers.

"Whoa, I don't know if I've seen one that small before," Farrell said. "I thought you CIA boys were big swinging dicks. That's barely a cocktail sausage, man. What do you think, buddy? Is it shrinkage or is Chip just unlucky?"

"Definitely unlucky. This really isn't his day. But here's the good news, Chip. We're going to let you live. I just need to get a few pictures so we can all remember this moment, down the line."

Reilly pulled his phone from one of the pockets in his cargo pants, then snapped a few shots of the naked and demoralized Chip, including a couple that included Platt.

"If this showed up online, I don't suppose it would do much for your career, would it Chip?"

Chip hung his head and didn't reply.

"All right, then. We've got better things to do, so we're going to have to leave you boys now." Gesturing to Farrell, Reilly said, "Get their phones, would you? Oh, and Chip's clothes, too."

Farrell gathered up the phones and clothes, then released Platt from the handcuffs. The agent clenched his fists, then relaxed them, wisely deciding that trying to take on Farrell was a losing play.

"Now, it's going to be a bit of a hike for you boys to get back to the embassy. Maybe you can hitchhike, although Chip, I think that's going to be a challenge. Maybe Don can lend you some pants. Just hang a right at the end of this little lane here, it will take you to a main road."

Reilly fixed them both with his fiercest stare. "I hope I've made myself clear here. I don't want to see or hear about either of you again, because if I do, I won't be as friendly next time."

Leggett nodded. Platt just stared at the mud in front of him.

As they pulled out of the parking lot, Reilly flexed his hands and breathed deeply, trying to get his heart rate down. He had really wanted to spend a little more quality time with Chip, square up what he had done with Suzy, but he knew what happened once the red rage took over. Chip didn't know it, but it actually was his lucky day.

"You worried about the van being identified?" he asked Farrell.

"No. The plates aren't mine. The truck itself is going to be burned out down a deserted road within the hour."

"Excellent."

FORTY-SIX

Finishing the draft of the Champagne story had taken a bit longer than I thought. By the time I got to court, the afternoon session had already begun. I took off my shoes to empty the water out of them, then shook off my umbrella before opening the door at the rear of the court as quietly as I could and slipping into a seat in the back row. With my luck, Bernstein had momentarily paused and was shuffling the pages of a yellow legal pad. Without a show at the front, everyone turned to look at what was happening at the back, including Justice Roderick Macpherson. The judge turned his baggy red face towards me and gave me a withering look. He didn't like it when anyone distracted from the proceedings in his court. Just a couple of weeks ago this would have been a real concern for me.

On the plus side, Gail Rakic was among those who turned around. She wore a black suit, white blouse, single strand of pearls. I would have advised her to save black for the verdict. I caught her eye and twisted my head back toward the door. I hoped it was a look that conveyed how urgently I needed to speak to her.

Gail had already ignored the voice mail and text message I had sent her, and now she turned her attention back to the front again. Bernstein was questioning a witness I didn't recognize, a man who looked to be about 75, balding and stooped forward in the witness stand. The too-big checked sports coat that he was wearing and the oversized glasses that people had worn in the '70s made it look like the witness was a shrunken version of his former self. Conservative Party volunteer, I guessed, probably up to lie about the money.

I surreptitiously took out my phone and sent Gail another text, improving the quality of the bait. "Have a way to get Sonny off. Meet me outside now."

I was overstating what I had to offer, but I knew Gail wouldn't be able to resist. I left the courtroom and sat in the waiting area outside the door. It was deserted. Within two minutes, Gail came out of the courtroom, too, with an expression that mixed hope, fear and anger.

She walked up to me and said, "This had better be good. I need to be at Sonny's side."

"It is. Take a seat."

She reluctantly perched beside me and I said, "How is the case going?"

"Not that well. Since we lost the Mae Wang angle, Ben has been struggling. The judge's questions tell me that he's skeptical. No one likes politicians. You know that. I think we've got a 50-50 chance."

"I can up those odds, but I need something from you."

"I've given you everything I have. Did you get something on Champagne?"

Her look was so hopeful that I almost felt sorry for her. I was sure that she had been doling out the truth in little chunks, though. Now, I wanted to get everything that was left.

"There is a story coming on Champagne. I can tell you the details, but only if you can tell me more about how Mae Wang died."

Gail got right in my face, trying out her bossy bitchiness. "Look, I've done a lot to help you. If you can save Sonny, you have to do that. He's innocent. What kind of person are you?"

"Right now I'm the kind of person who is trying to get the truth about Mae Wang. That PI stuff was great, but I know there is more. When are you going to be straight with me?"

Gail looked away, visibly trying to calm herself, then reached into her purse. She pulled out her cigarettes, then put the package back. "God, I need a smoke."

"It's still pissing down rain."

She sighed and said, "Let's say, hypothetically, I did have some additional information about Mae Wang. How is that going to help Sonny? You already have a story on Champagne."

"I do, but we don't have him dead to rights. He could still wriggle off the hook. For you to win, you need Champagne's credibility to be destroyed. I need to know if he had a direct involvement in Mae Wang's death. If he did, think what Ben could do with that. Once it's proven that Champagne is a lying shit, anything Ben wants to imply about what he did to Sonny becomes believable. This is the get-out-of-jail free card, Gail."

She didn't like that, and leaned back in her chair and gave me an appraising look. "How do I know that I can trust you?"

"You don't have to trust me. Give me the truth about Mae Wang, and I'll give you the details of the Champagne story before it hits the paper, let you and Ben prepare your next move."

"What if I tell you something and it doesn't help your story."

"If it's true, it will help my story."

"And how do I know you will follow through?"

I reached into my purse and pulled out a printout of the rough draft I had just finished. Colin would freak out if he knew what I was doing, but he would forgive me if it paid off.

"This is the story, as it stands. It's yours when I'm satisfied that you've finally told me all you know."

Gail looked at the pages like she wanted to grab them out of my hand, but instead she said, "If I tell you what really happened the day Mae died, it has to be for your knowledge only, not for the paper. I need you to swear to that."

"Done."

Gail squeezed my hand, then said, "I'm going to trust you." She looked up at the ceiling, then wiped away a couple of uncharacteristic tears. "When the PI first approached Mae to ask for her co-operation in testifying against Champagne, she flatly refused because the regime had her father in prison. I understood that, although it was very disappointing. Ben said we could still call her as a witness anyway, use it as an opportunity to put questions to her, but he wasn't sure it would seem convincing.

"Then we got word that Mae's father had died. I thought it was worth one more chance to persuade her to help. I was trying to save Sonny's life, our future. She agreed to meet me, but said it had to be on the roof of your building. We weren't recording in her apartment at that point, but she said others were.

"I pleaded with her to help, but she said there was nothing she could do. Yes, her father had died, but she still had a mother and a brother back in China. If she helped me, one or both of them would be put in prison. Mae said she had only met with me to get me to stop pressuring her. She said that she was trapped, that her life was already ruined, that she had no way out.

"Then she surprised me. She turned and began running for the edge of the roof. I could see that she was going to jump. I ran after and tackled her. We both went down on the gravel, me on top. Then she turned and kneed me, knocked the wind out of me. I rolled off.

"Mae staggered to her feet. Her head and knees were bleeding. She gave me a desperate look, then leaped off the roof."

Gail paused, as if considering whether to end her story there.

"This next part is the thing I am ashamed of. I should have done something. Called 911 or told the police what happened, but if I did, I would have to explain why I was on that roof with her. Adrenalin took over. I knew she wanted to die, and she had achieved her goal.

"So I did nothing. I took a Valium, then caught a cab to court."

I didn't know what to say. I had not seen that coming. I knew what it was like to be willing to do anything to protect someone you loved.

Gail stared off into the distance, as if I were not there. Despite that, I knew she was waiting to hear what I had to say. Even when we know we have done something awful, we still want someone to say it's all right. I decided to oblige.

"She wanted to die. It wasn't your fault."

"Maybe, but it doesn't stop the nightmares. What if I hadn't pressured her? She never would have been on that roof. It was as if I had left her with no other way to escape."

Gail shook her head, as if trying to dismiss the memory from her mind. I knew from experience that it wasn't that easy.

"All right," she said. "I've given you what you want. Now, can I please have that story?"

I handed Gail the story and said, "Good luck."

As I headed back into the rain for the walk to the Chateau Laurier, I was already thinking about the rewrite. After chasing Mae Wang's killer for so long, I had just found out I had been wrong the whole time.

Or had I? The Chinese, Champagne, maybe even the CIA, had all played a role in the drama that put Gail and Mae on that roof on that cool spring morning. They hadn't pushed her, but they forced her to the edge. Mae was a victim of those who stole her life, no matter how she left that roof. My job was still to get as much justice as I could for her.

FORTY-SEVEN

I always made a point of avoiding the *Citizen* offices on Baxter Road, partly because my life was downtown and I hated the suburbs, but also because I couldn't stand to get tangled up in the whole corporate, chain of command, cubicle world. When I was starting out, I had loved newsrooms. People could smoke at their desks, cuss to their heart's content and talk back to the bosses, all of whom they addressed by their first names. The newsroom was still full of scribblers and newshounds, relics from the days of typewriters and hip flasks. They understood news and they understood people because they had come from the bottom up. Now, my average colleague was 25 years old, held at least one master's degree and understood Snapchat.

Sometimes, I had no choice, though, and my meeting with Colin about the Champagne story was one of those times. It wasn't Colin's fault. "Corporate," as he called the evil presence of head office, was in the building and had demanded a briefing on the story.

As I walked into the newsroom, I saw that it was even more depressing than the last time I had been there. The room was vastly smaller than what I had been used to at the *Star*, which was about the size of a football field. The *Citizen* newsroom was more like a small-town arena, but without the ice. It wasn't the size that bothered me, but the lifelessness. The last time I had been out at Baxter had been an election night, all hands on deck. With every journalist in the room, there was at least some semblance of liveliness and purposeful activity. This afternoon, the place was a morgue, the few people present staring intently at their computer screens.

I saw Colin in the glass-walled cubicle he warranted due to his high position. His suit jacket was off and his sleeves were rolled up. I thought he looked worried, suddenly older. He had a red pen in hand and was slashing at a document on his desk, then scrawling in additions. My story, I was sure. Colin was awfully old school when it came to some things. Most things, really.

I walked into his office without knocking and said, "So, are you cutting the shit out of my story?"

He looked up as if surprised to see me, then glanced at his watch. Maybe my being right on time had taken him by surprise. He put his pen down and focused on me.

"No, not at all, just rewording a few points to satisfy the concerns of the bloody lawyers."

"Good, because this is still *my* column, right?"

"It will have your style, of course, but we need to consider that we are giving this news play."

It was a bit odd discussing fine points of journalism with Colin in his office, given the changed nature of our relationship, but I could act professionally if I really had to.

"No problem. I'd like the see the final draft, though."

"I wouldn't have it any other way."

In the end, I had told him everything Gail had told me. I had too many secrets already in my life. I didn't want to add another. After relating the whole story of what happened to Mae on the roof, I said, "What are your thoughts on the Gail Rakic situation?"

"Intriguing information, but she is not the focus of our article. Nor did she commit any crime. Obviously we have to acknowledge that the death was a suicide brought about by the actions of others, but we don't need to bring her into it."

I nodded. It seemed fair. Even if Gail had called 911, it wouldn't have made any difference. If she felt guilt, then that was her punishment.

"Our focus here has to be on Mae," Colin said. "I like the way you have cast her as a victim of geopolitics."

"Sounds awfully dull when you put it that way. I didn't actually use the word geopolitics, did I?"

"No, and if you had I would have taken it out."

He leaned forward then and looked at me intently, as if he were trying to get inside my head. It was a habit I didn't really care for.

"The main thing I want to ask you is just how certain you are that Champagne is dirty? How strong is your gut instinct? We're burning this guy here. After this story, he will be done and he won't be the only casualty."

It was the question that had occupied me on the drive out to the

newsroom. Some journalists could nuke a target without blinking
an eye. I wasn't one of them. Not anymore. A devastating story
like the one I had written would have real, lifelong consequences
for Champagne. Part of me said that Champagne had decided his
own fate when he got tangled up with Mae. I didn't entirely discount what he had told me, though. I had known enough guys
who wanted to play the white knight for an attractive woman. Still,
what was he thinking?

The story would most likely blow up the prime minister and his
government, although I can't say I really gave a shit about them. If
they were driven from office, they would quickly be replaced by
another gang of equal value.

No, my main concern was Mae. People needed to know what her
life had meant and how she had died. To me, she was a courageous
woman who would have done anything to help her father. I only
hoped that I would have done the same, in her position.

"To be honest, I'm not 100-per-cent sure, but even if we take
what Champagne said at face value, he has to go as foreign minister. And we have to tell Mae's story. There is no way he doesn't bear
some responsibility for her death, even if he wasn't on that roof. I
think this is one of those times when we have to put in everything
we have and let the readers decide."

I knew that last was a bit of a dodge, but I wasn't going to argue
against my own story.

"Agreed, and this CIA angle that Reilly and Farrell have brought
in is intriguing. Who knows how that will play out in the end, but
it gives another whole dimension to the story."

I didn't know how Reilly and Farrell had managed it, but the
picture of Chip Leggett naked in the mud was a collector's item.
I wished we could put it up on Twitter, but it was our protection.

Colin and I had avoided talking about the fact that this was a
career-making story for both of us. It would generate international
headlines. It wasn't why I had written it, I told myself. I had no idea
where the story would go when I first started to look into Mae's
death. Somewhere in the depths of my black little heart, I took
joy in knowing that this was going to be my moment and that it
was going to come at the expense of some pretty bad guys. It was
everything that I had failed to achieve in the Adirondacks, and at

far less personal cost.

"Other media still lagging?" I asked.

"Yes," Colin smiled. "No one has done more than match our story. We will be miles ahead when this new piece hits."

"What do you figure corporate wants?"

"Christ knows. The chap's a bit of a bed wetter. Probably just wants us to hold his hand, assure him that it's all good and true. I know he also enjoys the concept of my 'reporting' to him. Seems to get his trouser snake to uncoil."

As I tried to shake that image from my mind, Colin's desk phone rang. He picked it up, listened briefly, then said, "Right. We're on our way."

"We have been summoned," he said to me. "Best behaviour."

I vowed to try.

FORTY-EIGHT

Derek Hall cracked open another Red Bull, his sixth of the day. He took a sip while drumming nervously on his desk with a pen. What had he forgotten? He'd called in favours with every news organization on the Hill, promising unspecified future scoops in exchange for laying off the Mae Wang story, which he assured them, 100 per cent, was a crock of shit that would end up embarrassing the *Citizen* and them, too, if they followed it.

So far, the wall was holding. Most had gone with a bare bones Canadian Press version of the story and played it down. Derek refreshed the *Citizen* website again. Still nothing. Maybe that was a good sign. According to Elise, the paper was getting close to its deadline for the next day. If they got past 4 p.m., six at the outside, he might be in the clear for now.

Maybe Redner and Morin didn't have a second barrel to fire. It would be surprising, but sometimes things broke his way.

Then there was the matter of the American embassy employees who had been roughed up by two guys they thought were Canadian cops, then left in some parking lot, the one guy without clothes. The embassy had made an informal inquiry and Derek had been trying to get Luc Champagne to smooth things over, but the minister was conveniently incommunicado. Ever since Derek had tried to find out more about any possible connection between Champagne and the Chinese girl, the minister had clammed up. That couldn't be good. With any other minister, all Derek had to do was keep mentioning the PMO and they folded. Not Champagne. He acted like he didn't give a shit.

The American thing didn't seem to have anything to do with the Chinese problem, but it was still part of the shit storm he was facing.

At least the PM had managed to keep the opposition at bay during Question Period, expressing serious concern about the girl's death while not promising to do anything about it beyond demanding answers from the appropriate authorities. It had been going pretty well until he got into partisan territory, reminding the Conservatives that one of their own members had gotten into trouble over amorous emails exchanged with a Chinese journalist. The boss could be such a jackass when he got off script. The idea had been to lead the questioners away from the notion that there was any connection between the dead girl and anyone on the Liberal side. Instead, he'd pointed them right at it.

Sharpe had been no help, either. It was no mystery why. The new regime had shown the old warhorse the door within weeks of taking office. Clearly, he was still bitter and in no mood to come to their rescue now. The bigger worry was that Sharpe knew something and would use it.

Derek thought about another Red Bull, then decided against it. There was still a long day ahead. He needed to ration his caffeine, and pray.

* * *

Sharpe scanned the *Citizen*'s page-one story again. Once one got past the trashy headline about spies and love nests, there wasn't a lot of substance to it. In his considered view, the PM could withstand the story if the two journalists couldn't put more flesh on its bones. And there was so much more flesh to be had.

As a patriot, he knew that his duty was to keep his knowledge to himself, as he had for decades. It was what the job demanded, but then, he didn't have the job any more. One could argue that the duty persisted all the same, but he found himself in a tricky spot. The PM was mercurial in most respects, but one could consistently rely on him to act in his own self-interest. If a substantial portion of the whole story came out, the PM and his minions would be looking for someone to hang it on. The logical fall guy was Sharpe himself. He had been national security adviser at the time that some of the worst offences had taken place, although it wasn't really his job to prevent that. Clearly, CSIS and the RCMP had dropped the ball. But who better to blame than an old has-been who was already off the team?

When threatened, make a pre-emptive strike. That had always been his advice. It was an appealing option in some ways, but the challenge would be to avoid being sucked down by the vortex he was creating. That would not be easy.

He scanned the major news sources to see if anyone was developing the story, but uncovered only copycat coverage. It was still possible that all this would blow over. Was that what he really wanted? Uncharacteristically, he found himself uncertain.

Then he plugged the thumb drive he had received into his computer and began to peruse the now-familiar file again. It really was quite a story. It would be a shame if it was never told.

FORTY-NINE

Colin and I walked down the corridor to the publisher's office in silence. I knew that I was thinking that some little shit from head office wasn't going to spike my story. I hoped that Colin was thinking the same.

"Who is this bird we're seeing?" I asked.

"Thomas Putnam, senior vice-president of content production."

I would have been surprised if Putnam had ever produced anything more valuable than a memo, but he was near the top and I was just a slug on the bottom.

As we entered the publisher's office, there was no sign of life. The outer office felt abandoned, like an empty house. The blue carpet was starting to look a bit threadbare and I noticed a large light-coloured area on the oak wall panelling. When I had first started at the paper, that spot had been covered with a large "artwork" that was nothing more than a white board with hundreds of nails driven into it. I wondered if someone had taken it down because it was a brutal reminder of the bed of nails the business had become, or if it had been sold off for scrap metal to help keep the creditors at bay. The publisher's secretary was long gone, her oak desk dusty and abandoned. For that matter, the paper no longer had a publisher either, the thinkers at head office having determined that a local paper was best run by an executive in another city.

"Let me do the talking," Colin said.

"Yes, boss."

Colin gave me a sidelong glance, but didn't rise to the bait. He straightened his suit jacket and marched quickly down the short hall to the publisher's inner office. I followed.

As we entered, Thomas Putnam held up a single finger to warn us not to break his concentration. He was staring intently at his phone, fingers flying. Angry Birds, I wondered?

Putnam couldn't have been a day over 35, but he had thinning red hair that was spiked up in a vain attempt to disguise its scarcity. Everything about him was slight. His black suit, two buttons done up, couldn't have been more than a 36 regular. He had a square little head set on a skinny little body and an expression that said, "Don't fuck with me." Or what, I wondered. Would he bite me on the ankle?

When Putnam finally put down his phone, Colin said, "Thomas, this is Kris Redner."

Putnam looked me up and down, not seeming too pleased with what he saw. He was clearly mulling something. I wondered if he was going to tell us to call him Mr. Putnam.

"Sit," Putnam said. I feared that his next command was going to be roll over.

"Let me cut right to it," he said. "I've reviewed this piece in detail and I have consulted with my colleagues at corporate. I'm afraid we are not going to be able to run it in its present form."

Colin touched my knee just in time to prevent me from offering a frank point of view.

"This is, of course, a story of major national and international significance," he said. "The biggest this paper has had in some years. Are you able to give us some guidance as to what we need to enhance to get it in the paper?"

"Well, I think that's your job. What I see here is a lot of supposition and innuendo that is going to do the government and Minister Champagne a great deal of harm. I don't see the rock-solid named sources and clearly displayed, indisputable fact that I would expect to find in such a piece."

"Is Minister Champagne's reputation our problem?" I asked.

"The well-being and the future of this newspaper is our problem."

"I think that can only be enhanced by outstanding journalism like this that will force all the other media to follow," Colin said.

"And how many are following today's story?"

"I'm sure they are working on it. If we delay we could lose our competitive advantage."

I had been surprised by the weak response from our competitors. Was it a holiday on the Hill? Something was wrong there.

"Nevertheless, I think we need to take the time to get it right.

That was a lesson I learned when I was with MuchMusic. We rushed a show to air without proper market research and it tanked rather badly. Cost us a lot of credibility."

I vaguely remembered reading Putnam's appointment announcement. It had spoken glowingly of his experience in digital media. It didn't say he was some kind of hopped-up DJ who had never spent a minute in the news business. Had he ever even read a newspaper?

"Notwithstanding your music industry experience, more than 30 years in the news business tells me we need to get this story out today," Colin said. "Think of it this way. Today's piece is like a chapter in a much longer saga. We advance the story bit by bit, stay ahead of the competition and keep going until we've got it all."

"Yes, well, I'm afraid those days are gone. There is a strong consensus at corporate that publication would be premature. We need to be mindful of the bigger picture. I don't think I need to tell you that discussions with the government on enhanced tax credits for digital advertising are at a delicate stage."

Colin was starting to get a bit red in the face now. I wondered if it would be at all feasible to throttle the little prick. By the time anyone found his body in this lonely office, the Champagne story would already be online.

Putnam's phone pinged. He glanced at it and said, "We're done here. I have a conference call in two. Get me more."

"So just to be clear," I said, "you're spiking my story to protect corporate financial interests."

"Spiking it? I'm afraid I don't follow."

"It's a journalism term," Colin said. "Back in the days of stories being typed on paper, the ones that weren't going to get into print were impaled on a sharp metal spike."

"Fascinating," Putnam said as he fiddled with his phone. "Did they deliver the paper by horse and buggy back then as well? Now get moving, and think digital as well. I don't see any video aspect here at all. That's unacceptable."

Putnam made a little sweeping motion with his delicate pink hand, as if to brush us out of his office. I got up quickly out of my chair and perhaps Colin thought I was going to go right over the desk and break those annoying little fingers. He put a restraining hand on my arm and gave me the look, then turned me around and marched me out of the office before I could commit any crimes.

Once we were safely out of earshot, Colin said, "What a bloody little piece of work he is. Wouldn't know a news story from his knob and I daresay I know which he has spent more time handling."

"Can you imagine him at MuchMusic? He has to be related to someone there. He's about the least funky white boy I've ever seen. How the hell did he end up here?"

"Corporate, as he calls it, believes that anyone young who has ever so much as played a video game has special expertise that will help them out of their nasty financial problems."

"Sounds like sucking up to the government is a bigger priority than good journalism."

"I expect it is, for the moment. To be fair, they *are* in a fight for their lives."

"Not to mention their annual retention bonuses. You don't think he has a point do you?"

"Hardly. He's a nasty little canker. If this company is going down, it should go with all guns blazing."

"So now what?"

"We get more. You need to get me something. I don't care what it is or how you get it. Then we rework the story, keep it 95 per cent the same and call it brand new. That generally works with his sort. I expect his real goal was to show me he's boss. Once he sees that we are happily licking his boots, he will come around."

Great. I had pulled together every fact and plausible rumour already. I had held nothing back. I needed a new strategy and I needed it fast.

✿ FIFTY

I was awakened by the ring of the land line in the hotel suite. I looked at the bedside clock. It was 6 a.m. Colin was still snoring beside me. I shook my head in a futile attempt to wake up and clear my mind. Colin and I had drowned our sorrows in a bottle of Glenfiddich last night. It seemed a good idea at the time and I had resolved to wake up with a fresh plan of attack, but not this early.

I picked up and heard an unfamiliar voice, older, the tone curt and commanding. "What happened to your story? There's nothing in the paper."

I was used to crank calls from angry readers, but not at this hour or in this location.

"Who are you, and how did you get this number?"

"That's immaterial. I think you might need some help."

That caught my attention, although I didn't think there were strong odds that the mystery caller was going to provide the salvation I needed. It was more likely he was a conspiracy theorist who wore a tinfoil hat to protect himself from the voices in his head. "I suppose you're going to tell me that you have some kind of inside information," I said.

"In fact, I do. Information that I think will astonish you."

"OK. I like to be astonished. What's your information?"

"It's not something to be shared over the phone."

Now I was thinking the caller might be a creepy stalker rather than a tinfoil hat guy, although there was nothing saying that he couldn't be both. Or maybe he was a pal of my friends Chip and Don.

"Look. I don't know you or anything about you. You apparently know that I am at the Chateau. Courier the information to the front desk and I will take a look at it."

Colin was awake now, sweeping his grey hair back and giving me a quizzical look. I shrugged, pointed at the phone, then tapped my forehead. Colin nodded, recognizing that I was probably talking to a nut.

"My name is Sharpe," the man said with a brusque tone. "Google my name and national security. If you want the story of your life, meet me at the Rockcliffe Park Pavilion at 7 o'clock. Don't bring any of your beefy friends. I am no threat to you."

I didn't know exactly where the Rockcliffe Park Pavilion was. Rockcliffe was the swankiest neighbourhood in Ottawa and I hadn't spent a lot of time hanging out there. I guess I would be Googling that, too. The idea that this guy Sharpe had something that was actually useful was a desperate long shot, but I *was* desperate and I didn't have any other shots. Besides, he sounded pretty sure of himself. But then, the crazy ones usually did.

"All right," I said. "See you then."

"What was that all about?" Colin asked.

"Some guy called Sharpe. Says he has info about my story. Something that will astonish me, as he put it. Wants to meet me at the Rockcliffe Park Pavilion in an hour. I'm to come alone."

"Sharpe? What did he sound like?"

"Old and very sure of himself."

"There is a former national security adviser named Sharpe. I can't remember his first name off the top of my head. The guy has been around the secret world forever. Maybe we just got lucky."

"OK. You know where this pavilion is?"

"Of course."

"Let's go then. Drop me close but don't hang around. He said I shouldn't bring any of my beefy friends."

Colin smiled, not sure whether I was giving beefy a positive or a negative twist.

"You sure?"

"Yes. I don't want to scare the guy off. I'm sure I can handle one old man."

It was just before 7 when I reached the park. It was shrouded in fog. It was going to be an unseasonably warm day and was already 20 degrees. I supposed the fog must be rising up from the still-cold Ottawa River. Whatever its cause, I didn't like it. I could see barely

30 feet in front of me. I looked back and saw the tail lights of Colin's car disappear into the gloom.

I had told Colin that I could handle one old man, but how did I know that he hadn't brought any of his own beefy friends with him? I felt sweat start to trickle down my back. Maybe this wasn't a smart play.

Colin had said that we were very close to the pavilion, but all I could see were huge old oaks and maples standing like eerie sentinels in the fog. I was sure the park must be a magnificent place, on a sunny day. I started to walk tentatively in the direction where I hoped I might find the pavilion. The dewy grass soaked my shoes after just a few steps. Now I couldn't even see the road. I knew enough to keep going in a straight line. Eventually that would take me somewhere.

There was a sudden gust of wind and I saw the outline of what must be the pavilion no more than 100 feet ahead. It was a substantial stone structure, open at the sides, with a verandah-style railing all around. It reminded me of the kind of whimsical lakeside thing rich people had back in the Adirondacks, when I was growing up.

Just as promised, there was a grey-haired man sitting on a bench in the pavilion. He wore a blue sports coat over a grey button-down shirt, no tie. His black horn-rimmed glasses made him look like a professor or an accountant, certainly not a spy. Or maybe that was what spies looked like in real life.

We made eye contact as I walked up the steps. I could tell he was assessing me, but his neutral expression didn't tell me whether I had passed. Then he gestured for me to sit beside him. I did, but not too close. This was clearly the guy I had Googled but that didn't mean I could trust him.

'I'm Sharpe, as I'm sure you have assumed."

"I have, and I did Google you."

"I hope it was reassuring."

"That depends on what you've got for me."

"Luc Champagne. He is the real focus of your inquiry, yes?"

"I started out to tell Mae Wang's story, but it seems that Champagne is closely entwined with it."

"Indeed."

"Is this the part where you are going to tell me how closely?"

"That depends. The documents I am going to give you are authentic. You can ask your friend Farrell to verify them if you like. My one condition is that my name never enters into this."

It freaked me out that he knew about Farrell. How many different spooks had been watching me?

"You seem to know a lot about me."

"I still work as an independent contractor in my old line. I have a lifetime of contacts. That's how I was able to obtain what I have for you. Is my condition acceptable to you? I am giving you a story that is pure gold and I want nothing in exchange."

"Come on. You must want something."

Sharpe scanned what little he could see around the pavilion, then he said, "I was the senior guardian of this nation's secrets for many years. Then I was rudely cast aside. That in itself is not sufficient motivation for what I am about to do but, as you will see, Champagne has to be stopped."

"I'm all for that. What's the story?"

"I will give you the short version. The details are all in his file. Luc Champagne is not who people think he is."

"In my couple of discussions with him, it was clear that he likes to be mysterious."

"He does. It's one of the things that draws people to my game. Champagne's life of mystery began when he was in grad school at Harvard. He had dabbled in separatist politics while at McGill, before continuing his education in the U.S., as so many of his type do. At that time, American security agencies had quite a concern about Quebec separation and its ability to destabilize their safe northern border. Naturally, they were looking for people with connections to the movement, people who might be able to feed them information for a price."

"You're telling me that Luc Champagne was some kind of American agent back in university?"

"He was. That's documented. It was harmless enough at the time. He was just another student with generic information to sell. It did cover his Harvard tuition, however. As the threat of separation faded, so did the CIA's interest in Luc Champagne. He went dormant for years. He doesn't come back on the radar until his first successful run for Parliament. Then the CIA approached him again, wondering if he could offer some insight into the thinking of the Canadian government, even though at that time he was only a parliamentary secretary. Champagne wasn't interested. His star was on the rise. He was young and good-looking, and more important, one of the few Conservative members from Quebec. His CIA friends explained that it would all be rather embarrassing if his past were leaked to the media and all they were asking for was the scuttlebutt in the halls of Parliament, not state secrets.

"Faced with the end of his political career, Champagne agreed to work with them again. He was quickly promoted to minister of industry and now the CIA was far more interested. Trade is really the only thing about Canada that's important to the Americans and now they had a direct pipeline into Canada's strategies, and even better, the minister himself in their pocket.

"Champagne was trapped at this point, as so many others around the world have been before him. It's classic tradecraft. A clever operation, I have to admit."

"So you're telling me Champagne is a victim?"

"Not quite. Champagne played along and, as time went on, he started to like his double life. Like so many Quebecers, he feels a weak attachment to the rest of Canada. It's not as if he was betraying his real homeland. When he decided to start positioning himself for the Conservative leadership, his handlers were thrilled. What began as a modest investment in a graduate student had the potential to turn into owning the Canadian prime minister. It would be the next best thing to annexing the country."

I found myself gripped by the story that this old man was telling, even though he was delivering it in a matter-of-fact way. It *was* the story of my career, without a doubt.

"There was only one problem in the way of the plan."

"Sonny Sandhu," I said.

"Indeed. Internal polling was showing that Sandhu had a solid lead on Champagne. He was just as charming and good-looking and was a huge hit with ethnic voters. It seemed an obstacle Champagne could not overcome, so he turned to his CIA friends for some help. It was simple to plant some money in one of Sandhu's accounts, then find a couple of dodgy characters who would sell him out in exchange for a bag of CIA cash under the table. Whatever the ultimate outcome of the case, it would take Sandhu off the board."

"Then the whole game changed when the PM decided to fight one more election."

"Yes. That's when Champagne and his handlers got really creative. They are fortunate that, in Quebec, switching from one party to another is commonplace. Champagne jumped to the Liberals, they won the election and suddenly he was foreign minister. Not as good as owning the PM, but a close second."

"If everything you tell me is backed up, it sounds like Champagne will be the one going to jail."

"It's treason, without a doubt. How that will play out remains to be seen."

"But what about Mae Wang? Where does she fit into this?"

"She was coerced to approach Champagne in Beijing. He met with the CIA station chief there and they discussed how it would be played. The thinking was that Champagne should pretend to fall for the Chinese ploy and the Americans would use him to feed misleading information back. Too clever by half, in my opinion. They ended up burning a major asset for minor gains.

"Then that poor girl jumped off the roof. One can hardly blame her. There was simply no way out of her situation."

Sharpe reached into his inside jacket pocket and pulled out a thumb drive.

"Everything is here," he said. "One additional condition. You need to use it within the next 24 hours or I will have to take the story elsewhere."

"That's not a problem. This will be online within hours."

"Excellent. I will watch with interest to see how all of this unfolds."

"I expect we won't speak again."

"We have never spoken at all," he said. Then he stood up, pulled a pipe from his pocket, lit it, then stepped into the mist. Within seconds it was as if he had never been there.

I put the thumb drive into my jeans pocket and started out through the still-thick fog in what I hoped would be the general direction of the road. I hadn't gone more than 30 feet when a limping man suddenly appeared in front of me.

"Hello Kris," he said. "Remember me?"

Fuck, it was Chip Leggett. I pulled out my cell phone to call Colin, but Leggett lunged for me. I turned and ran, only to slam into Don Platt. He grabbed my arm and twisted it. The cell phone fell on the wet grass and Platt stomped it with his foot, shattering the glass.

"We understand you are in possession of some very sensitive state secrets," Leggett said. "Our friends in Homeland Security would like to take that up with you. It's time for a little ride across the border."

Sharpe looked on, a murky figure in the fog. A secret was like a gun with one bullet. Once it was fired, it became useless. It had taken him a while to work out the optimum strategy, but in the end, he had come up with a plan that gave him an extremely significant marker with the Americans while retaining leverage over the PM, leverage he could use as often as he liked. It was too bad about the reporter. She was well-intentioned, but really, everything had worked out rather well from his perspective.

FIFTY-ONE

Reilly had thought Suzy's idea of going out to the newsroom to help put together the final story was premature, given the state she was in. He wasn't going to argue with her, though, not when he thought there was some kind of chance of reconnecting.

As they pulled out of the Chateau Laurier parking lot, he could tell by the awkward way she was sitting that she was still in physical pain, and that was probably nothing compared to the lingering mental effects of what she had been through. The bruises would fade, but the horror of being sexually abused was like a stain that would never go away.

Still, she had tried to pull herself together. Reilly had helped her with her hair and she had put on a lot of makeup, then sunglasses to hide her black eye. She had even put on a red dress, loose-fitting, and a pair of black shoes with a modest heel. From a distance, she looked something like herself.

"Are you sure you are up for this?" he asked.

"Not really, but I'm going to do it anyway. This is my story as much as Kris's. I want to be there when it all comes together and I want to read it before it hits the paper. Also, I want to look that twit Putnam in the eye. If he tries to block this story again, he's going to feel my claws."

Suzy had been furious when Colin and Kris had told them that this corporate toady was afraid to run the story, and why.

"You heard anything from her about that lead this morning?"

"Not yet," Reilly said. Kris had texted him first thing, saying that she had a source that was going to deliver the documents she needed to lock the story down. She was meeting him at seven. He thought he would have heard something back by now, but maybe she had gone straight out to the newspaper building to start putting it together.

He had been taken aback when Kris had related Gail Rakic's version of what happened to Mae on the roof. So maybe there was no homicide, if what Rakic said was true. It was a pretty self-serving story, but that doesn't mean it wasn't how it happened.

Even if Mae had jumped, it was Champagne and her Chinese masters who had taken her to the edge. Someone had to pay for that, even if it wasn't in a court of law.

Suzy picked up Reilly's phone off the console. He knew she wanted another look at the pictures of Chip Leggett naked in the mud.

As she flicked through them, she said, "He's got quite a set of man boobs, that Leggett."

"He does. His best feature, really."

They both laughed at that. Reilly was encouraged that she could find some way to laugh after all she had been through. It was a start.

"It's early," he said. "We probably don't need to be in a huge rush. You want to stop at Gino's, get some breakfast?"

Gino's was a diner on Elgin, only two blocks from the central police station. It was a place they used to go to most weekends, back when they were together.

"Maybe not there," she said. "I don't want to run into people I know, not any more than I have to. How about Sonny's?"

It was a second-rate roadhouse in a shabby strip mall near the newspaper, but Reilly didn't care where they went, as long as they were together.

FIFTY-TWO

Leggett grabbed my face in his meaty right hand, and twisted my head so that I would have no choice but to look at him. His face was so close to mine that I had a hard time focusing. I could see angry eyes and flaring nostrils. When he spoke, I could feel his spittle on my face.

"You really are fucked now," he said. "The information on that thumb drive is going to put you away for a long time. And we have a witness who saw you meeting with the Chinese ambassador. I think you've been working for them the whole time. You are going to have a hard time proving that you weren't."

I opened my mouth to respond, but no words came out. What was the point in arguing with him? He was right. Leggett had set up an elaborate trap and I had walked right into it. How could I have been that stupid? Then I realized it wasn't Leggett who had done the thinking, it was Sharpe.

Platt twisted my arm up behind my back until it felt like it was going to pop out of my shoulder. "Nothing to say now, smart ass?" he said.

I tried to slow my breathing, to think. What were my options? Platt had me pinned and Leggett had moved too far back for me to even attempt a kick.

There were a couple of positives. I knew they weren't going to kill me and we were in a public place. It was early in the morning and foggy as hell, but surely there must be some dog walkers out. And what about Colin? How far off had he driven? If only I hadn't told him to stay out of sight.

I remembered telling Reilly that I wasn't the kind of girl who'd scream like a B-movie actress, but I figured the time had come. "Rape! Help, help me," I yelled.

Those four words were all I could get out before Leggett hit me with a resounding slap that felt like it loosened my teeth. Then Platt clamped a hand over my mouth. I could feel the metallic taste of blood. My lip was split, I thought.

"Rape, huh? Pity we're in a hurry," Leggett said. "You're not as hot as that friend of yours, but I like it when they scream."

At that moment, I hoped there was a hell.

"Come on," Platt said. "We haven't got time for this. Let's get her in the vehicle."

He began to push me forward. I tried to dig in my heels, but he twisted my arm even higher. I was sure their car wouldn't be far away. I couldn't believe this was really happening, but it was.

In a parking lot at the edge of the park, Colin looked at his watch. This meeting was taking longer than he had anticipated. It was supposed to be a simple passing over of documents. He pulled out his phone and called Kris, only to get voice mail. What the hell? There was no way she'd turn off her phone. Something had gone wrong. He knew it.

Colin felt reasonably confident that he could make his way back to the pavilion in the fog, but it was bloody difficult to see. He popped the trunk of his Audi and saw the tire iron he had failed to put back in its holder after that flat he'd had in April. He pulled it out and hefted it. Not much of a weapon, but something.

Then he thought he heard a scream. A shot of adrenaline set his heart pounding and he raced off through the fog, tire iron in hand.

FIFTY-THREE

Reilly accepted a second cup of coffee from the waitress, a tired bottle blond who looked as if she might have worked the night shift at another joint. Sonny's was kind of a 1970s rec room gone wrong and most of the other diners were old folks from the neighbourhood dragging out breakfast to help fill an empty day. Reilly didn't care about that because Suzy had reached across the table and she was touching his hand. He felt like electricity was running through him.

"I just want you to know, Mike, that I really appreciate everything you've done for me," she said. "You saved me from those guys. If it wasn't for you, I'd probably be dead."

It was a generous appraisal of his performance, Reilly knew. In reality, he'd been stunned by a whack on the back of the head from a heavy branch and he'd allowed Leggett to get away. He did feel that he'd more than redeemed himself during round two, though.

"I'd do anything for you. You know that," he said.

"I do," Suzy said, then she squeezed his hand and looked down. "I haven't been very good to you. *I* know that."

"It's all right," he said. "I can be difficult to get along with. And our work situation, that complicated things."

"Yes, it will always complicate things."

"I'm not going to be a cop forever, you know."

She smiled at that, then winced at the pain it caused her. "You're always going to think like a cop Mike, whether you have a badge or not."

"I guess so. It's what I've spent my life doing. You think that's a problem?"

"No, you are who you are. I can't change that. I don't want to."

OK, so that was good. Reilly hoped this conversation was going somewhere positive.

"I never really told you why I left," she said.

Reilly felt his optimism begin to evaporate.

"The thing is, Mike, I'm at an age where I need to decide what to do with my life. Do I want to get married, have kids? Do I want to devote myself to my career? I've been thinking lately that it's not either, or. I can do both, and after all that's just happened to me, I'm wondering how much I'm prepared to sacrifice for work."

Reilly was starting to get confused now.

"If I'm going to do that, though, I should be doing it with someone close to my own age, someone who's going to be around to be a father for those kids."

"Jesus Suzy, I'm not that ancient."

"No," she said gently, "but you're 20 years older than me Mike. It's just math. My life, the way I see it now, you're not the guy I need."

She paused, then tried again. "I mean, I do need you, right now, but I don't think it's the right thing for me, long term," she said, then nodded as if reassuring herself.

"You've got a concussion, Suzy. You've just been through a terrible trauma. Maybe now's not the time to be thinking about all of this. Besides, right now is all any of us ever have."

"That's true, but I always like to have a plan for the future. You know that, Mike."

Reilly did know that, and it was becoming apparent that he wasn't part of the plan. That didn't leave him any worse off than he had been a few days ago, but why did he feel so bad?

Hope was a bitch.

FIFTY-FOUR

Platt quickly became fed up with my attempts to slow him down and picked me up and carried me like I was a bride crossing a threshold. I tried to get leverage to elbow him, but my attempt was feeble. I might as well have been elbowing an oak.

Leggett pressed a key fob and I saw the lights flash on a big black SUV. It was no more than 20 feet away. I was sure they would bind me and gag me and, once I was in that vehicle, my fate was sealed. If I was going to make a move, it had to be when they tried to wrestle me into the back. I frantically tried to make a plan, but if they knew what they were doing, I wouldn't have a hope.

I had known mortal fear before, but this had all happened so quickly and was such a surprise that I was having a hard time processing it. One minute, I had been in charge, about to reveal a story that would bring down a government and create an international scandal. The next, I was looking at being whisked across the border and locked up. Or maybe they would just kill me and dump my body in the deep Adirondack woods. Maybe I had been fated to die there all along.

I told myself I couldn't think like that. I had to fight. I would wait for my opening. Surely there would be some chance, some point of vulnerability.

Leggett was at the driver's door now, while Platt held me in a bear hug close to the SUV's rear hatch. Leggett pressed another button on the key fob and the hatch began to swing open. I could see rope, tape and a big hockey kit bag inside. The plan was obvious.

I wasn't going to end my life like that. I began to frantically kick Platt in the shins, hammering him with both heels. He grunted, but held firm. I screamed again, a wordless, bloodcurdling screech.

"Tape her up," Platt said, "before someone comes along and complicates this."

Leggett reached into the back and pulled out a roll of silver duct tape and turned to me with a gloating, evil smile. I kicked at him, but he was out of range.

Then he turned back to the vehicle, reaching for a utility knife. That was when I heard a whack like a club hitting a watermelon and Platt went slack, dropping to the ground with me under him. I felt like I had been rolled on by a horse. My face was pressed into the wet grass and my arms were pinned under me.

I saw feet rushing by, then twisted my head to see who it was. Colin was charging toward Leggett, a tire iron raised above his head. Leggett had just turned, the utility knife open in his hand. He dodged away from Colin's blow, which rang off the rear hatch of the SUV.

The two men squared off against each other, Colin wielding the tire iron and Leggett the utility knife. Leggett slashed forward and Colin dodged back, then turned to land a weak blow on Leggett's shoulder. The CIA man grunted, then backed up, tossed the knife to the ground and reached inside his jacket to draw a gun. Seeing that, Colin put his head down and charged at Leggett, slamming him into the side of the SUV.

I struggled to get out from under Platt, who was either dead or unconscious.

Colin had got hold of Leggett's right arm and managed to force the gun up over his head. Leggett responded by seizing Colin's throat with his left hand, then he started to push the gun down. Another foot and he'd be able to shoot.

I had to do something or this was all going to end right here. Digging in with my knees and scrunching my arms up under me, I pushed up as hard as I could. It was enough to roll the felled agent off of me.

Colin must have caught it out of the corner of his eye. "Run Kris," he shouted. "Get help."

I knew there was no time for that. This was down to me.

I struggled to my feet and saw my opportunity when the fight between Colin and Leggett turned the spy so that his back was to me. My mother was a woman who spent a lot of time with bad men in rough bars. She had taught me to fight dirty. "Go for the eyes or the nuts" had been her maxim.

I leaped on Leggett's broad back, got my arms around his head and drove my thumbs back with full force, aiming for his eyes. My left thumb bounced painfully off his skull, but the right hit home.

Leggett screamed in pain, dropped his gun and began turning furiously in circles, trying to get me off his back. I clung on like a rodeo rider and kept working my thumb into the eye. I was probably blinding him, but too fucking bad.

Then Colin finished it with a hard shot from the tire iron to Leggett's skull. Leggett dropped to his knees and I jumped off before he collapsed face forward onto the ground.

Colin bent over, hands on his knees, panting. "You OK?" he managed.

I got shakily to my feet. My ears were still ringing from Platt's slap and I thought I might need some dental work, but I could move my arms and legs. Compared to where I thought I would be by this time, I was better than OK.

"Yes, I'm all right. Thank God you got here when you did. They were about to spirit me off to the clutches of Homeland Security."

"Jesus. What a pair of bastards."

Colin looked down at the two fallen agents, seeming stunned by what he had done. "When I heard your scream, I just went mad," he said.

"Good thing you did."

He picked up Leggett's gun and threw it into the bushes. Then he rolled Platt over and did the same with his weapon. Finally, he found the vehicle's keys on the ground and fired them away into the mist in another direction.

"All right, let's get the hell out of here," he said.

FIFTY-FIVE

The drive back to the newspaper office on Baxter Road was surreal. We drove through placid, leafy Ottawa neighborhoods that seemed light years from the drama we had just experienced. Colin was constantly checking the rear-view mirror, to see if Leggett and Platt had any friends who were coming after us, but we saw nothing out of the ordinary. It looked like our troubles were behind us. The two CIA men wouldn't be chasing anyone any time soon.

I related to him the amazing story that Sharpe had told me, and my assumption that the old spy had set the trap that I had fallen into. He wondered if the information Sharpe had given me might have been false. I momentarily considered that, then realized it had to be real for Sharpe's plan to work.

I had to ask myself why I had trusted someone who had spent a lifetime in a world where lies and deception were the norm. Perhaps I had been blinded by the value of the prize he offered me.

The fog had cleared once we got away from the river, only to be quickly replaced by rain that was now heavy. The wipers beat loudly against the windshield. As we pulled into the newspaper parking lot Colin said, "You sure you are going to be OK to write this, after all you've been through?"

"Damn straight," I said. "Wouldn't miss it." In truth, my heart was still jackhammering and I felt like I had consumed a case of Red Bull.

"All right. I'm going to drop you at the door so you don't get wet, then park around back. See you in a few minutes."

I appreciated the gesture. Colin had his own parking space, but it wasn't close to any of the doors. As the industry had declined, even the perks had deteriorated.

I opened the car door, then quickly jogged toward the side entrance used by employees. I was running head down, using an old copy of the newspaper to keep the heaviest water off my head.

I ran headlong into a large man, then bounced off, stumbling backwards. Shit, I thought, one of the goddamned smokers who liked to hang out by the door.

I was about to give the guy what for, but then I looked up and my jaw dropped. I was speechless. Standing in front of me was Luc Champagne, his tan overcoat drenched, his hair plastered to his head and a look of angry desperation in his eyes. Then I saw the large black gun in his hand.

"So, you escaped," he said. "I'm not surprised."

"What the hell are you doing here?" I asked.

"I am Plan B. I was told that if you showed up, Plan A had failed. Now, give me that information."

"What information?"

He raised the gun. "Don't fool with me. I know that you have a thumb drive full of classified information, and you know how I know. If it comes out, I might as well be dead. I have nothing to lose."

I quickly assessed my situation. The remaining employees would be inside the building by now, but surely some latecomer would arrive or someone would come out for a smoke, despite the rain. The security guard who sat at the front desk was supposed to be monitoring this area on CCTV, but I knew I couldn't place all of my hopes on that. Then there was Colin. If I didn't show up in a couple of minutes, he'd come looking for me. I had to keep Champagne talking.

"Look, you're not going to get away with this, whether you have the information or not. Why not surrender before it gets any worse?"

Champagne responded with a bitter laugh. "Oh, this is about as bad as it gets, but don't worry, there is a plan in place to get out of the country quickly. Once you give me that information, Luc Champagne will simply cease to exist."

"Are you going to kill me? Because if you aren't, I'm going to write this story with or without that proof."

"Perhaps you will, but it will just be your say so. The people I work for want that thumb drive, badly. I have to have it. It's my ticket out."

He raised the gun and pointed it at me, rain dripping from the shiny metal. "I've been very reasonable, even though you've lied to me. Now you have a choice. Hand over that information or I will kill you to get it. It makes no difference to me. Either way, I get what I want."

I took a deep breath and thought about the little drive tucked in my jeans pocket. It contained a hell of a story, but not one that was worth my life. My best chance was to hand it over, but there was no guarantee that Champagne wouldn't kill me anyway.

Then I heard the sound of a car in the parking lot behind me and saw headlights sweep the brick wall of the building. Champagne saw it too and his attention flickered away from me. My first thought was salvation, my second was that now he would have to shoot me and run. I hit the ground and rolled away. It was all I could think of.

Then I heard a familiar, deep baritone voice. "Police. Drop that gun."

I looked up to see Mike Reilly standing in a crouch beside the door of his old Crown Vic, his gun aimed at Champagne. Inside the car, I could see Suzy, a look of horror on her face.

Champagne looked at Reilly, then at me. He was finally cornered.

He glared at me, his angry face streaming with water. "This is all your fault," he said.

Then he raised his gun to his temple and pulled the trigger.

FIFTY-SIX

I hammered away at my keyboard, trying to ignore the fact that half the newsroom was gathered around expectantly and Colin was leaning over my shoulder as I worked. A cigarette and a couple of fingers of Scotch were what I needed, right now, but the newsroom was dry and smoke-free.

The story of Luc Champagne and Mae Wang was sprawling and complicated, and yet I could see it all in my mind. It was the kind of story best written in a single blast under deadline pressure. There was no time to second guess or agonize over the best approach. I was leading with the CIA bombshell, of course, grafting that on to what I had already written. Several sidebars covered every possible angle, but Colin and I had agreed that our struggle with the two CIA operatives was a story best left untold.

I tried to write about Champagne's last few minutes of life as if I were a detached observer, not a participant. Still, the image of his exploding skull filled my mind. That and the bastard saying it was all my fault. A narcissist to the end.

Clearing Mae Wang's name made me feel good, but I felt no triumph or satisfaction in writing about the death of Champagne. He wasn't evil. Luc Champagne was simply a guy who had gotten caught in the updraft of ambition. Were it not for a judgment he had made as a grad student, that updraft could have taken him a long way.

"Hey, there's a TV remote truck setting up in the parking lot," I heard someone shout in the background. I wasn't surprised. Mike had said he would try to keep a lid on what happened as long as he could, but with a dead cabinet minister, that wouldn't be long.

"Just about there?" Colin asked.

"Wrapping now."

"Good. We need to get this thing online."

"Not a problem. I'm sending the final version to you now."

"Splendid," Colin said, then turned to Lew Macdougall, one of the last remaining copy editors. Lew was a balding little Scotsman with a pot belly and nicotine-stained fingers who now held the ludicrous title of chief producer. "Lew, give me 10 with this, then it's yours. Get it online, then I want all of this in a special edition, one section only, 12 clear pages."

"Just like we're a newspaper again," Macdougall said.

"Exactly."

I leaned back in my chair and started to decompress as Colin scanned my story. My mind was still racing. Then I saw my colleagues turn away from me and look at a small, angry man in a brown suit surging toward us like a rat terrier with a stick up its butt. It was Thomas Putnam, the senior vice-president of whatever the fuck it was.

"Wendover!" he shouted. "What the hell is going on here?"

Colin turned toward Putnam with an expression that suggested the man was nothing more than a mildly annoying fly. "We got the detail on that Champagne story, just as you asked."

"What? Why was I not apprised of this? I gave explicit instructions that not a word was to be published on this subject without my direct approval."

"I was told by your secretary that you were in important meetings downtown all day. Not to be disturbed. I'm afraid we still need to cover the news."

"Don't patronize me," Putnam said, his little hands curled into fists and his face twisted in an angry scowl.

Colin rose slowly from the chair beside me and stood about six inches from Putnam. He towered at least a foot over the little boss. "Is there a problem?" he asked.

"You're goddamn right there's a problem. Your office, now."

The rest of the newsroom looked on with the combination of horror and glee that a public fight between bosses always created. I would have liked to have thought our colleagues were all behind us, but some looked uncertainly from one man to the other. That was what being a survivor of buyouts and layoffs did to you.

"Of course," Colin said, showing the way to the office with a gesture of his hand, as if the whole thing was his idea. No one had asked me, but I followed them anyway. If this prick was going to try to take down my guy and my story, he was going to have to go through me first.

The two men entered Colin's office and I squeezed in quickly behind them.

"No one invited you, Redner," Putnam said.

Before Colin could interject, I said, "No, but I forgive your oversight. This is my story."

Putnam scowled, then decided to save his ammunition for the main battle, not a skirmish with me.

"Did you want to see the story?" Colin said. "There have been some startling developments."

Putnam twitched his head sideways, as if shaking off this awkward piece of information. "I don't care what it says. It's not going in my paper."

Colin began to redden in that way he did on those rare occasions when he lost his temper. I expected it was the phrase "my paper" that did it. Myself, I felt an icy calm.

"I've just come from a meeting with the prime minister himself. Senior corporate and ownership were all in attendance. An undertaking was given to grant the industry rather generous tax credits for online advertising. This could be the thing that saves this company."

"Glad to hear it," I said, "but so what?"

"So you don't get something for nothing in this town. We gave an undertaking ourselves, not to publish a word about Luc Champagne and this Chinese girl."

"You what?" I said. "Are you telling me you sold us out?"

"No, I'm telling you that I might have saved your jobs."

"So now we're what, a PR arm for the government? Don't you realize this story can bring the government down?"

"Of course I realize it. That's the problem. We have a PM and a government that is very sympathetic to the industry's situation. Were the government to fall, there is no guarantee that situation would persist. This story is spiked, or whatever the hell you call it. Have I made myself clear?"

"Perfectly," Colin said. Suddenly, he seemed remarkably calm. I wondered what he had up his sleeve. Something, I hoped.

"Just so you aren't surprised later on, you should realize that we have exclusive, top-secret documents from the CIA detailing Champagne's career as an American spy. Oh, and Champagne threatened to kill Kris in our parking lot, then committed suicide when the police intervened. His body is still out there. TV news trucks have just arrived."

Putnam plopped down in Colin's chair and said, "Fuck. Now what are we going to do?"

"I don't know what you're going to do, but I am going to do one of two things. Either I'm going to publish this story or I'm going to go out front and describe the whole thing to the TV reporters live, including the conversation we just had."

Putnam turned a sickly shade of grey. "You wouldn't."

"I beat two CIA agents with a tire iron already this morning, so yes, I would."

Putnam ran a finger around the collar of his blue dress shirt, as if it had suddenly become too tight, and contemplated the end of his career. He looked as frozen and indecisive as a man on a window ledge, clinging to a tall building.

Colin didn't wait for an answer, just stuck his head out of the office door and shouted, "Lew, print it."

ABOUT THE AUTHOR

RANDALL DENLEY is the author of five novels, including *One Dead Sister*, the first in the Kris Redner series. He lives in Ottawa and is a political columnist for the *Ottawa Citizen* and the *National Post*. Denley also got a look inside the world of politics as a two-time provincial election candidate.